# DAWN CHORUS

Elizabeth Newman

MINERVA PRESS
LONDON
MIAMI   RIO DE JANEIRO   DELHI

ISBN  0  75411  514  3



First Published 2001 by
MINERVA PRESS
315–317 Regent Street
London W1R 7YB




Printed in Great Britain for Minerva Press

# DAWN CHORUS

*For Maggie… who tried so hard to understand me, perhaps this will help a little.*

With grateful thanks to International Music Publications for permission to include the words of 'Every Time we Say Goodbye' by Cole Porter.

# Chapter One

'I'm sorry, Chris, this is just not working.'

The words drifted through the opening door as it was propelled forward, the doorknob putting another dent in the dressing room wall. The two men walked in and each wearily planted himself in one of the two chairs that occupied the room.

It was a mere cliché of a dressing room, a small dingy box with a low ceiling from which was suspended a single naked light bulb. A bare mirror leaned against the wall over a rectangular dressing table. Around the edge was a halo of cracked white plastic light sockets, less than half of which were in working order, with a few grimy well-thumbed cards tucked into the frame bearing corny sentiments concerning performances of a more successful bygone era. A collection of empty and half-empty bottles lay strewn across the dressing table, where a dirty green glass ashtray full to capacity spewed its contents. Three rusty metal coat-hangers dangled aimlessly from an old wooden rail, hastily erected by some previous tenant trying to compensate for the lack of wardrobe space. A tired ceramic hand-basin, chipped and cracked, was suspended from one bracket on the wall, its dripping tap leaving the telltale green stain in the basin trailing to the outlet beneath. Above, an old nicotine-stained sign read, 'No Smoking'.

Both men were lost in their own thoughts, and it took much effort from Chris to break the silence.

'Brinn, I'll be perfectly blunt with you. I know it's been hard on you with Carol walking out like that, but to bury yourself in this new play, well, frankly, I think it's a big mistake. I'm not altogether confident that you are suited to this part.'

Brinn began to shuffle uncomfortably in his seat, but he had known Chris for more years than either cared to remember and was prepared to give him a little leeway, just a little. Chris continued.

'You are not a great one for method acting and I'm afraid the part just cries out for it. We are going to have to rethink this one.'

'Look, Chris, I just need a little more time. I know I can nail down this character.'

'I'm sorry, Brinn, but time is the one thing we don't have in abundance.'

Brinn, at the end of his first week in rehearsals after two mind-numbing weeks of blocking, walk-throughs and script changes, was too tired to argue further and besides, it was only a bloody tramp, for crying out loud. What was so difficult about that?

He rose from his chair, crossed to Chris and rested his left hand on his shoulder. Then, making for the open door and purposely not turning to look at Chris for fear he might see the growing despondency registered so clearly on his face, Brinn remarked, 'I'll sleep on it tonight and ring you in the morning.'

Chris shook his head slowly as Brinn stepped through the door. He rose to his feet in order to follow, but paused briefly as his eyes caught an advance theatre poster, pinned to the back of the door. It announced in large letters:

Brinndle Peters
appearing at the Apollo Theatre
in Chris Robbins's brilliant new play
*Life on the Streets*

Chris moved to follow Brinn before his eyes had a chance to read the names of the rest of the cast, who had been waiting all this time somewhat impatiently in the rehearsal rooms outside. He now had to face them with the prospect of more delays.

Brinn walked down the few steps of the rehearsal hall into the cold damp night air. The hall had been hot and rank and he was glad to be outside, even though he had forgotten to pick up his coat.

'I can't go back in there tonight; I will pick it up tomorrow,' he told himself unconvincingly.

His mind raced, and the prospect of a cab home to the empty flat filled him with no satisfaction. He thrust his already cold hands into his trouser pockets and set off on the ten-minute walk across the river to his flat. Brinn, an average build, six-foot-two American, was approaching fifty. He had an oval face, which looked younger than the five decades it had seen. His hair was short, almost cropped, and light brown in colour with a few natural silver-grey highlights. With his vivid blue eyes, he was not an unattractive man, but tonight, because of the rehearsal, he had dressed in old well-worn comfortable clothes and was weary from the night's fruitless efforts. The damp air began to chill him, making him regret the decision to walk home. His flat keys were the only items he had on him and he realised that leaving his coat behind had been his second mistake, as his wallet was in the inside breast pocket. He grew colder by the minute and peered ahead in the hope that there might be a place for him to stop and warm himself. After five minutes' futile searching, he resigned himself to completing the journey unfulfilled.

Brinn quickened his pace and his short heavy breaths, synchronised with each step, condensed in the chill night air in small, quickly dissipating clouds. Just over the bridge, a little ahead of him, he noticed a large white van, lights blazing, with a group of people standing around. Thinking it to be a possible option, he headed for it and in a few moments was alongside the van amongst the group. Much to his surprise, a welcome hot cup of tea and a sandwich were thrust into his near frozen hands. He accepted the tea but refused the sandwich, and after a few sips of the hot liquid, curiosity drove him to the rear of the van to see what he had half suspected. The Salvation Army were out in force tonight. He began to study the faces of his fellow beneficiaries, and then ironically realised that he was among the very people he had spent the last three weeks trying to emulate. To top it off, he had been mistaken for one of them by the provider of the tea.

Though he never would have admitted it, Brinn had always had difficulty coming to terms with people who lived on the streets, which was probably why he had had so much difficulty in portraying the part successfully. His difficulty arose as a direct outcome of a chance meeting back in the States, a meeting that had resulted in him fleeing a beggar whom he had believed was about to draw a knife on him. In reality, he had only been reaching inside his coat for his whisky bottle. The embarrassing event had been observed by a colleague, who had no qualms about using the story when there was a chance of a drink in it, but despite the innocuous event, it had left an unnatural aversion to any subsequent contact.

Brinn had found that in London he could not walk more than twenty yards without being accosted by some form of beggar, or a would-be vaudeville act or someone involved in marketing. Everyone wanted his attention. He had little sympathy with them, these professional beggars, as he saw them. Sometimes, if he was feeling benevolent, he would slip a few coins into a receptacle, but only if he believed the cause to be genuine or the act exceptionally good. Mostly he would just lower his eyes and with determined stride plough a road through, trying to ignore them. The types he objected to most were those who sat with a shivering, half-starved dog at their feet, the animal seemingly a willing participant in the pretence, as though to purposely attract any unsuspecting animal lover. None of them was a real person to him, just an obstacle to be overcome in the rush downtown. He was not alone in his belief that these people were faceless. They were invisible people, on empty streets, to undiscerning eyes.

He was startled from his thoughts by the concerned tones of an elderly gentleman, a Salvation Army officer.

'You poor man, out on this bitter night with no coat, here, take this one. We have a few which are donated and you look as though you need it more than most.'

Brinn was stunned into silence and extended his empty hand to accept the gift, reluctantly putting down the tea in order to allow the officer to help him put the coat on. Inwardly, he considered that it was a shame the officer was not the producer of the wretched play rather than Chris, if, without so much as a word, he had managed to convince him at least.

Ugh! Mothballs. He never could stand the smell. Still, he was grateful as he began to warm up again and hastily reunited himself with the plastic cup of tea. Brinn nodded to the man as a sign of appreciation, noticing that his benefactor would probably have been more at home during the India of the Raj, with his bearing, commanding tones and white moustache.

'Have you somewhere to spend the night, my good man,' the officer continued.

'Oh, yes,' he replied as the group began to disperse, 'and thank you,' he continued, 'thank you for the cup of tea, that is, and the coat, of course.'

As Brinn followed their lead, the officer turned to a younger colleague and remarked, 'I think he's a newcomer to the streets. It's a shame. I don't think he will last very long.'

As Brinn regained his sense of direction, he looked back over his shoulder, tea still in his hand and raised to his lips, checking to see if he was being followed. Reassured, he continued his journey home unimpeded.

On reaching the steps of his flat, he fumbled for the keys in his trouser pocket, carelessly discarding the plastic cup over the railing outside as he did so. He opened the front door, reached in and switched on the hall light. Then, stepping through, he closed it again behind him, his relief evident in a long sigh. A moment or two passed before the door reopened and the coat came flying through the air in the direction of the plastic cup. The door closed again and the hall light was extinguished.

Usually a late sleeper, Brinn was in no special hurry to get up on this particular Sunday morning. His uneasy night was now compounded by the thought of a decision to be taken and a phone call to be made. Predictably his first call was not to Chris regarding the play. As Brinn's hand groped from beneath the safety and warmth of the bedclothes, he punched the automatic dial for Carol. He shaded his eyes from the diffused daylight with his right hand, tucked the receiver under his chin with the left, and quickly tried to formulate a decisive line of approach. He hoped against hope that this time he might find the right words and she would give him another chance, though deep down he wasn't really sure if he wanted one. All he could manage however, were the few sad sentences he had used so many times before.

'Hi.'

'Oh, hello, Brinn, it's you,' she replied, annoyed that he had rung again.

'Of course it is. Who else were you expecting,' he snapped back.

'Don't start that again, Brinn. This is all so pointless.'

'Please, Carol, wait. Give me another…'

There was an audible click and she had hung up before he could finish. Brinn remained on the bed, wondering why he continued to ring her. It was as though he was stuck in a loop, he knew she was with someone else. Just habit, he surmised. In the beginning he had thought himself lucky to have Carol. Many of his friends had tried and failed to date her at one time or another, but she seemed drawn to him.

Perhaps, in retrospect, it had been because of his success and equally, maybe, it was a sign of his decline that she had left him. She was tall, slim and auburn-haired, with hazel eyes that never really told you what she was thinking. He had been fascinated by her from the first moment he had seen her at one of his opening nights, though he could not remember which now. She had hung back after everyone else had gone and he had found himself inviting her out for supper, then back to his flat and the rest was, as they say, history. There was no doubt about it, she was great in bed, but it always seemed that he had let her down. Not that she said anything specific, quite the contrary, but he never felt completely in control.

It had been her decision that he should lease this flat. It was very comfortable, but not entirely to his taste. The living room was too big and the bedroom was too small. He could never find any of his things and the place was always in a bit of a mess, much to her consternation. Carol had often taken great pains to point this out to Brinn, but being so preoccupied with his work, he had never taken much notice.

Naked, and dragging the bedclothes with him, he half crawled, half walked to the window and opened the curtains. Glancing down into the street, he noticed it had been raining and the road and pavement were shiny with the dampness that reflected the silhouette of the buildings and cars below. It was a grey, cold day and as he looked down again to see if the milk had arrived, he spotted the discarded coat. His mind wandered back to the night before, his meeting with the Salvation Army and his mistaken ID. A half smile curled his lips, and then he hesitated as a thought crossed his mind.

Tripping over the bedclothes in an effort to reach the phone quickly, he was sent sprawling headlong, banging his shin on the edge of the bed. It had a knock-on effect, the momentum of the bed jarred the bedside cabinet, which was displaying a gilt-framed photo of Carol. The resulting collision sent the once-cherished photo crashing to the floor, splintering the glass in the frame. Brinn lay there cursing himself and rubbing his shin. His hand stretched out for the phone a second time, but this time he hit the automatic dial for Chris, who picked up his receiver a few moments later.

'Chris, it's Brinn. Look, about yesterday, I've got an idea. Do you think you could cut me some slack, say about two to three weeks?'

'This is not another one of your half-baked ideas...'

Brinn did not allow Chris to finish.

'No, no, of course not! Now listen! You know what you said last night about method acting? Well, I know it sounds like sheer lunacy, but I have decided that I stand a better chance of grasping the depth of this character if I go out on the streets and live like he would.'

'You're right, it does sound like sheer lunacy,' Chris cut in. 'It's dangerous out there. You've no idea what drives those people in your own country, let alone in this one. You must be stark raving mad! Certifiable! You might be killed!'

'Are you going to cut me that slack or not?' Brinn replied quickly, as though caution might cost him the decision.

There was a pause. Then Chris came back, 'God, how did I ever get tied up with you, Brinn? You should be sectioned. You stretch friendship too far.'

'Far enough to get me those three weeks?' Brinn pressed.

There was a long pause, the unmistakable sound of a hand being placed over the receiver and a few choice mumbled words.

'Two, tops. That's all I'll give you, and, for crying out loud, carry a gun or something. I hope your insurance is all paid up.'

'Thanks, Chris, I knew I could count on you. Look, I need one last thing. If anyone gets hold of you and wants to know where I am or whether you know me, for God's sake say nothing. If the press get hold of this, my cover will be shot. You know what they are like. You understand, Chris, absolutely no one, okay.'

'Are you sure about this, Brinn?'

'That's the way I want it.'

'Okay, Brinn, it's your funeral. Anything else?'

'Yeah, I thought guns were illegal in this country.'

'Get out of here! Keep in touch by mobile. Don't get involved with junkies or...'

Brinn cut in again, 'Yeah, yeah. Bye, Chris,' and hung up, too soon to hear Chris quietly wish him good luck.

Chris replaced the receiver and sighed. Having known Brinn for so many years did not make his often spontaneous madness any easier to bear. Now, at forty-nine, Chris had survived the tough early days of Brinn's career as an actor and was tired of being used as his glorified agent. He had had to support Brinn financially as well as mentally, and now he felt a little resentful that he was being used again to prop up his antics.

Brinn's career had started slowly to begin with, bit parts

here and there – until Chris had intervened and helped land him a role in a serial that lasted some years. That had established Brinn as an actor of sorts, although Chris never got a word of thanks for it. When the part came to an end, Brinn had been worried that he would find it difficult to get another role, possibly being typecast as so many serial regulars were. The contrary, however, proved true. He landed a few notable Broadway parts and a semi-successful film, but it seemed that from there on, at just about the time he had met Carol, things had started to slide. Chris had always told him he had a big head and one day he would have to join the real world again.

Now, he thought, is hardly the time to be proven right.

Chris, a little overweight perhaps, round-shouldered maybe, had always been made out to be unyielding by Brinn, something he harboured resentment about. Possibly he had been hard on Brinn in the past, but not many producers had to go through what he had with someone who despite his faults, Chris still considered to be a friend. He had hoped to distance himself a little from Brinn after his own marriage had gone pear-shaped two years before, due in some measure to Brinn's erratic behaviour. Brinn, however, had that 'bad penny' syndrome, and when he turned up, he somehow always managed to beat the resolve out of him. Chris lifted the receiver to his ear again and slowly began the long process of putting on hold the rest of the cast for what, he hoped, would be only two weeks.

Brinn's sudden rush of activity had left him in something of a dilemma; what should he wear and what should he take? He had strewn the bedroom floor with endless combinations of shirts, trousers, and jumpers but still he remained naked on the edge of the bed. While he was giving the matter some serious thought, he stooped down to pick up some of the broken glass that was spread over the carpet and, with his mind not fully on the task, he managed to slice through his forefinger and thumb with one of the shards. A short blasphemous phrase accompanied him to the bathroom, where he hoped to find a few plasters. Then, as he stood before the bathroom cabinet applying overly large dressings to his wounded fingers, it dawned on him the choice was simple; he would wear the rehearsal outfit that had fooled the Salvation Army officer.

'The coat, the coat,' he muttered to himself and rushed back into the bedroom, where he pulled on a pair of tracksuit bottoms from the heap on the floor. He ran and stumbled down the stairs, along the hallway and opened the door.

The milkman, who had just arrived, was a little startled to see his customer up so early and half-naked at the door. Rather coyly, Brinn began to imitate the actions of a jogger, but realising he was bare-chested and unshod, he grabbed the bottles of semi-skimmed milk from the milkman and retreated inside again. As he stood with his back to the door, panting slightly from his exertions and waiting for the sound of the milk-float's departure, he wondered how he had managed to get the only milkman in the area who still delivered the milk on a Sunday. Brinn acknowledged his latest portrayal had been a dismal failure and hadn't fooled the milkman for a moment; he also wondered whether he was cut out for this kind of thing at all. Timidly, he opened the door and peered around it again to see if the milkman had gone. His hopes realised, he stretched over the railing, grabbed the coat and shook it a couple of times to get the rain off it. Hastily, he retreated back into the warmth of his hallway.

In front of his bedroom mirror, he stood proudly viewing himself, first on the right then on the left, congratulating himself on the masterstroke of retrieving his old squash shoes from the garage. They had lain there since the time he had worn them home following an all-nighter at the local with Chris.

When was that now? he wondered. Oh yes, just after he split up with his wife. We staggered back across the park so blind drunk that we ploughed through the lake gathering some dog excrement as we emerged on the other side.

'There, perfect,' he said aloud.

He picked up an old backpack and crammed in a few 'essentials' like the mobile phone, a change of clothes, electric razor and Mastercard. Patting his right wrist, he decided to keep his Rolex on. He did not have a gun, sadly, but he really thought he would not need one. Then he pulled on the still damp overcoat and headed towards the front door. He grabbed a hunk of bread from the kitchen, took one last look at the hallway and let himself out of the flat.

## Chapter Two

He had no real plan of action, but he was determined to last out the three weeks.

Or was it two, he thought as he looked up at the unpromising weather. Yes, two, he mused, I'm sure Chris said only two.

He chewed on the bread as he headed towards the underground station where he thought it likely he would find some down-and-outs. Or possibly it was more politically correct to call them street people these days. He checked his breast pocket for the one hundred and fifty pounds emergency spending money he had allowed himself for the two weeks. Not a great deal of money to him, but enough to help out if he absolutely had to get a room somewhere should the weather deteriorate any more.

Brinn at first did not notice the quizzical and slightly contorted expressions on the faces of the people whom he passed in the street, nor as he descended the stairs into the ticket hall of the underground station. He joined a queue of people waiting to be served at the ticket office, and a moment later the coloured man from behind the glass addressed him.

'Yes, sir,' he asked Brinn in a rich Caribbean accent.

'An all-day explorer, please, zones one to six,' and he handed the man a twenty-pound note.

The man's eyebrows rose in amazement as he eyed the note suspiciously. He held it up to the light and turned it over to assess its authenticity.

'Do you mean a Travelcard, sir?' the man said, still unsure of the stranger who stood in front of him.

'Sure, if that's what you call it,' Brinn replied.

Only partially satisfied, he passed Brinn the ticket and the change, then ignored any further contact with him and began to address the next customer. Brinn did not bother to check the change – just thrust it into his coat pocket and went through the barrier towards the platform. He continued to mull over just how he was going to proceed. He boarded the first train that arrived and sat in a corner seat staring straight ahead. Knowing that eye contact was not recommended at such close proximity, he tried hard to stare up at the advertisement boards instead. The train was warm, as usual; in fact, warmer than usual and after a few stations he began to nod off.

He had no idea how long he had been dozing when he awoke to the sensation of someone shaking his arm.

'Oi, mate, your coat is steaming,' announced a spotty adolescent who was very audibly amused. 'And it's givin' off an 'orrible pong.'

Brinn roused himself and after a brief check around, realised that he was positioned directly over the heating system, and his coat was beginning to dry out. Combined with the dog excrement smell from his squash shoes, the vaporising mothball aroma from his coat was causing the other passengers some distress.

Brinn got to his feet and stood at the door as the train pulled into the next station. When the automatic doors slid open the incoming blast of warm air intensified the obnoxious odour already filling the compartment and produced convulsive coughing from the other passengers, which brought many handkerchiefs out of confinement to be held to noses. He stepped off the train, much to the relief of the other passengers. Now even he could no longer ignore the almost choking aroma of his clothes, so he proceeded as fast as he could to the exit. He kept as much distance between himself and other travellers as he could as he navigated his way through the tunnels and up the escalators. As he reached the outside, the fresh air seemed to dull the redolence that clung to him and, turning his mind to his more immediate need of somewhere to stay for the night, he put the incident behind him.

He walked the pavements for some time in his search through the alleyways and back streets for any signs of tramps or vagrants. After an hour or two, he was totally exhausted and he decided to stop for a coffee and a bite to eat. He chose a well-known bistro to refresh himself, but he was completely unaware of how incongruous he appeared or how many other customers left the premises because of his presence. He placed his order with a concerned waiter, who returned to his counter and put a call through to the manager upstairs. Still a little anxious, the waiter was unwilling to pursue the order. However, in the absence of the manager, and with the continued gesturing from Brinn, he reluctantly complied.

Once he had refreshed himself and regained his strength, he decided to give it another try before calling it a day. As he stood up to walk over to the counter to pay his bill, he accidentally kicked over his backpack, which had been sitting at his feet. The mobile phone, razor and credit card that he had placed so casually inside were sent spinning across the floor until they came to rest just in front of the manager, who had at last arrived from the office upstairs. He bent down to pick up the items, inspecting them thoroughly one by one.

Brinn, all apologies, walked over to him in order to re-trieve them. There had been several credit card thefts reported in the area by the police and the manager felt he had grounds for suspicion in this case, as no tramp he had ever seen wore a Rolex, had a mobile or carried a credit card. So while the waiter took Brinn's money, the manager slipped out the back to make a phone call. Brinn picked up his change and left the Bistro leaving the waiter to spray the immediate area behind him with a can of rose-scented air freshener.

As Brinn stood on the pavement outside, he took a long look in both directions and tried to make up his mind which way to go next. He decided to cross the road and try his luck to the west. He began to negotiate his way through the traffic, completely unaware of the police car, blue lights flashing, that had pulled up outside the bistro. The manager rushed out, frantically waving his hands in Brinn's direction and the two officers jumped out of their car, held up the traffic, and chased after him. As they drew level with him, each took hold of one of his arms and then simultaneously pushed him up against a nearby shop front. Human nature being what it is, the startled customers stared out of the window and tried to get a glimpse of the wanted man.

'Hey, what's going on?' Brinn squeaked in protest. 'What have I done?'

'Just keep calm, sir,' one of them replied. 'Purely routine, sir.'

'Now look here, officer, I'm an American citizen. You can't do this to me.'

'We just want to have a look in that bag if we may, sir,' the other officer joined in.

'What right have you got to accost me on the streets like this? I haven't done anything wrong.'

The officer, assessing his tone to be one of defiance, took the opportunity to spin Brinn round so his face was squashed up to the window. Horror-stricken, the shoppers inside took a step back in unison, and Brinn called out to them, as best he could with his mouth distorted against the glass.

'Don't you people have something better to do?'

One of the constables then pressed him, 'Are you going

to let us have a look at that bag, sir?'

'No!' Brinn replied emphatically.

That was, of course, his first mistake, as he found out when they proceeded to caution him, arrest him on a charge of obstruction and cart him unceremoniously off to the local station. The delighted shoppers all broke out into rapturous applause, believing justice to have been done while completely ignoring Brinn's protestations of innocence.

When they arrived at the station, Brinn was frogmarched up the front steps, through the hallway and straight through the door of the interrogation room. One of the arresting constables remained at attention in the room, while the sergeant on duty made preparations to take a statement.

'Well then, sir,' the sergeant began as he pulled out a chair from the table where Brinn was already sitting. 'Are we going to be any more co-operative now?'

Brinn, perched on an old wooden chair opposite the sergeant, clutched his pack to his chest like a comfort blanket and sheepishly replied, 'Yes, sergeant, of course. I am sorry.'

He offered the bag to the policeman, who upended it and tipped the contents onto the table between them.

'Well, well,' he said. 'And what do we have here?'

Brinn was having a hard time with reality and barely able to believe his ears. The whole event was beginning to sound just like an extract from an old nineteen-thirties B-movie. He wanted to reply, 'A change of clothes, my mobile, razor and credit card,' but was still reeling from the shock of being arrested and thought caution might be the best policy, so he remained silent.

'Are these items yours, sir,' the sergeant continued.

'Look, they are mine all right! That's my mobile and my razor and here is my credit card with my name on it, see, Brinndle Peters. Now, please, what have I done wrong.'

The desperate words all came out in a flood as Brinn fought to make sense of the ludicrous scenario.

'You have been arrested on suspicion of possessing stolen goods and obstructing my officers in the line of their duty.'

'What?' Brinn shouted. 'That's ridiculous! These things are mine.'

'Can you prove that, sir?'

'Yes, I can. Bring me a pen and paper and I will duplicate my signature. You can check it out with the one on the card.'

The sergeant thought for a moment and then signalled to the officer who, without a word, left the room to collect the objects requested.

A few nervous moments passed until the officer returned bearing the items of stationery. Brinn picked up the ballpoint rather awkwardly, because of the pain in his fingers and the large plasters covering the injuries; then, trembling a little, he began to scrawl his name, which, to his horror, in no way resembled his usual signature. Frustrated, he angrily crossed through it and tried again, still with little success.

'Bit of a problem, have we, sir?' the sergeant asked sarcastically.

'No,' Brinn snapped back. 'It's just these plasters; I cut my fingers earlier and now I can't grip the pen properly.'

The sergeant gave the other officer a knowing look.

'Of course, sir. Please, by all means, have another go. There is no hurry. We have all the time in the world, don't we, Constable.'

The constable pursed his lips and nodded enthusiastically. Ten minutes passed and Brinn's fingers were raw and bloodied and his fifteenth attempt at signing his name looked less like his signature than the first.

'Okay, I give up! I can't do it, but I am Brinndle Peters

and these are my things.'

'Perhaps, sir, there is someone who could identify you.'

'Oh God! Yes, of course! Where's the phone.'

He was refused access to the mobile phone, as it was considered 'potential evidence', but he was escorted to the front desk where he furnished the sergeant with Carol's home number.

Please, please be in, Brinn wished to himself.

The line connected and the phone at the other end rang four times before Carol picked it up.

Yes! Brinn thought, there is a God in heaven.

'Seven three nine four two one,' the voice at the other end read off automatically.

'Good afternoon, madam,' the sergeant began, 'this is Walter Street police station here, Sergeant Carter speaking. We have a man in custody who says you know him. I wonder if you would be so kind as to identify him for us.'

'What is his name?' she asked curiously.

'He claims to be a Mr Peters, Brinndle Peters. Do you know of such a man, madam?'

The line went quiet for a moment, and then, exasperated at yet another call concerning him, she replied, 'No, I don't know him and I don't want to either.'

The line went dead and the sergeant turned to Brinn.

'No luck there, then, sir. She says she doesn't know you. Another number, perhaps?'

'This is ridiculous! Of course she knows me. We're, we're good friends, or we were. I can't believe that she said that.' Brinn thought quickly and then added, 'Chris Robbins, five nine five five four, he can sort this mess out.'

The sergeant dialled the number, his patience almost gone, and had to wait a little longer for the phone to be answered.

'Hello, Chris Robbins speaking.'

Again the sergeant repeated his little speech.

'Brinn who?' Chris replied, playing the part, he thought, beautifully. 'No, sorry, never heard of him. Can't help you out, sergeant.'

'He has never heard of you either, sir.'

Brinn made a grab for the phone, but was held back by the sergeant.

'Give me that,' Brinn demanded, 'Look, you don't understand. I told him not to tell anyone he knows me. This is silly. Let me speak to him.'

'Really, sir.'

'Yes, you see I'm incognito. No one is meant to know that I am here.'

'Well, at least you have succeeded in that, sir. No one seems to know you at all.'

The sergeant thanked Chris for his co-operation and replaced the receiver.

'I think, sir, a spell in the cells, while we try to sort out this little mess.'

Brinn protested his innocence wildly, quoting sections of habeas corpus, as the sergeant indicated to the officer to take him down to the cells.

'Oh, and Constable?'

'Yes sir?'

'Make sure the ventilation system is turned on to maximum.'

After phoning the credit card company, who gave the address, and the mobile phone company, who confirmed it, an officer was sent round to Mr Peters's home to see if anyone was there. Naturally, he obtained no reply to his repeated knocking at the door, so the officer tried the flat above and made contact with a Miss Henshaw.

'Yeth, I know him a little, and yeth, I would be prepared to accompany you to the stathion to identify him, as long as I can sthit in the front stheat of your lovely patrol car.'

A very frail, short-sighted spinster, whose speech was impaired by loosely fitting false teeth, Miss Henshaw did not get out much and was thrilled to be going on such an exciting trip.

'What hath he done, murdered thomeone?' she enquired. 'He alwayth did look a bit thifty to me,' she volunteered, pushing her loosely fitting pebble lens glasses farther up her nose. It was a regular occurrence with Miss Henshaw that when she became excited, they had a tendency to slip.

Intrigued by the various knobs and gadgets inside the car, Miss Henshaw began to explore her new environment.

'Oooo, what doeth this do?'

'Please, Miss Henshaw, don't touch any of the switches on the dashboard,' the nervous constable emphasised as he tried to maintain the vehicle safely on the highway. Miss Henshaw, who could be selectively deaf at times, ignored his pleas and continued with her inspection of the latest technology, about which she quite obviously knew nothing.

'Thith one looks interething. How doeth it work?'

An audible click and the patrol cars siren blasted into action.

'Miss Henshaw, please.'

The constable grabbed Miss Henshaw's hand and tried frantically to pry her fingers from his control panel while simultaneously wrestling with the steering wheel with his other hand. It proved too difficult a task even for his skills, and he was resigned to continue the last half mile to the station with sirens blasting, lights flashing and a gleeful Miss Henshaw waving her arms out of the window to startle pedestrians.

The young officer, dazed and exhausted, took a firm hold on her elbow and escorted her into the station. After a brief pause at the desk to collect the duty sergeant, Miss Henshaw was led off to the cells to try to identify the waiting Mr Peters.

'Are you going to put him in a line-up?' she asked optimistically.

'No, madam, this is not *The Bill*.'

Miss Henshaw's disappointment was almost tangible as she followed the sergeant to the cell where Brinn was being kept. Brinn, who had been sitting on a hard bench with his head in his hands, got to his feet at the sound of the approaching footsteps.

'Is this the man you know as Mr Peters, madam?' the sergeant asked her.

Unfortunately, Miss Henshaw, only ever five foot nothing on a good day, was not tall enough to see into the cell, so she proceeded to jump up and down in order to get a glimpse of him through the peephole. After a couple of attempts, the sergeant nodded to the officer, who then picked her up and held her close to the small window in the door. As he did so, Miss Henshaw's blood pressure went through the roof, her glasses slipped over her nose again, and she screamed at the top of her voice,

'Yeth, that'th him, that'th the beast. Hanging ith way too good for him.'

'Thank you, Miss Henshaw, that will be quite enough. Are you absolutely sure that this is Mr Peters?'

'Oh, of courth I am. What do you think I am, blind or thomething? I would know him anywhere.'

The sergeant indicated to the officer to remove Miss Henshaw to the comfort of the hallway and to give her a cup of tea. Then, unlocking the cell, he released Brinn.

'All right, Mr Peters, it seems we have a positive identification by one of your neighbours, a Miss Henshaw.'

That batty old woman from upstairs, Brinn thought to himself; but I hardly know her.

He refrained from informing the sergeant of this fact as he saw his freedom looming into sight. The officer brought the backpack to Brinn, who now stood in the hallway a few feet from Miss Henshaw.

'You are free to go, sir, and we have dropped the charge of obstruction against you.' The sergeant turned away from Brinn and towards the officer as he began to talk to him. Brinn, who wanted to make some sort of protest at his treatment, was prevented from doing so by Miss Henshaw, who was tugging at his arm.

'Do you know, thonny, I've just been inthrumental in bringing a vilinouth criminal to book. What do you think about that then?'

Brinn realised that Miss Henshaw had not made a positive identification. He wished she would keep her voice down, as he saw his more urgent need was to get the hell out of there before the police smelt a rat and put him through the whole thing again. As tactfully as he could, he excused himself and made a controlled dash for the door.

'Well, how rude,' she called after him. Then, turning to face the officers who were talking together, Miss Henshaw said aloud, 'Thergeant, it's as I have alwayth thaid. You can't trust anyone theth dayth. During the war we hardly thaw a coloured perthon in our neighbourhood at all.'

At this point, Miss Henshaw had the sergeant's undivided attention as she continued, 'Now they are all over the thity. Oh, I know you might consthider me to be a teeny weeny bit prejudithed, but when that Mr Peterth moved in, I thought to mythelf, there ith a prime candidate for the electric chair.'

The sergeant, beginning to sense a possible hiccup in the procedures, asked her, 'Miss Henshaw, are you suggesting that the Mr Peters you know is a coloured gentleman?'

'Why yeth, naturally thergeant, but I thought you were aware of that.'

Outside Brinn had picked up speed and dodged his way

through the early evening commuters and last minute shoppers in a panic, trying to escape his imagined pursuers. After about ten minutes, he felt reasonably safe, enough to slow down and check to see if he had managed to evade them. He was relieved as he realised that either he had lost them in the crowd, or they had not yet made the connection with Miss Henshaw's error.

At a more leisurely pace, and after he had regained his bearings, he continued to walk in the direction of the river. The thought reassured him that crossing it would put more valuable distance between him and the Metropolitan Police. He steered a course for the bridge he saw just ahead, and was about to cross over when he noticed a plume of smoke spiralling up from behind one of the shoreside parapets. He hesitated, caught between wanting to give the whole idea up and the need to prove himself to Chris. Brinn put his hand into his pocket and withdrew a coin. He tossed it into the air and caught it on the back of his hand.

'Right.'

The 'tails' result partially made his mind up for him and he began to walk towards the smoke. His idea was that he would just take a quick look at this, and if it proved un-fruitful, it was off home for him followed by a hot tub, a brandy and an early night. He descended the steps down to the embankment and turned the corner, expecting to find an archetypal representative of some BBC2 documentary programme that he seemed to remember watching some time ago depicting typical people and scenes from street life. Instead, he was confronted by the sight of a group of three men, far from typical in appearance. All of the men were big, two of them were black and the remaining one, an Asian, was busy adorning the underside of the bridge with a colourful design using spray paints. None of the men seemed to Brinn to be quite the type he was looking for. The one nearest him turned to look over his shoulder, eyeing him up and down contemptuously.

'What do you want, man?' he said, turning his back again as he did so.

The artist paused in his endeavour and put his paints down on the ground.

Brinn astonished himself as he heard a weak reedy voice, which he barely recognised as his own, saying, 'Can I join you?'

The three men, equally astonished, looked at each other and smiled a strange knowing smile. Brinn realised a little too late his mistake, and began to back away.

'Sorry, guys, my mistake. Sorry to bother you; I'll be going now.'

The last thing Brinn remembered before he passed out was the biggest of them kneeling on his chest. As he rifled through Brinn's pockets, a brief glimpse of a large boot flashed past the corner of his eye, it was followed by a sharp thud to the side of his head, and the hiss of a spray can that faded with unconsciousness.

At about eight o'clock, Brinn began to come round, though he would never have known the time as his Rolex watch had been one of the items removed during the fracas along with his phone, razor, credit card and money. Brinn did not think it kindness on their part to have left him his change of clothes. His head felt as though it would explode and his chest hurt, but most of all his pride was damaged. He lay there feeling very sorry for himself.

Day one, he thought. Board a train, alienate the entire compartment, get arrested for something I did not do and flee custody, meet some street guys and get blown away. If I go home now, Chris will never let me hear the last of it.

He had begun to move gingerly in order to get back on his feet when, surprisingly, he felt someone else's arm slipped under his, to help him up.

An unemotional female voice asked, 'Need somewhere

for the night?'

Brinn, all at once glad of the offer and of the hand up, brushed his coat down as he turned to view this good Samaritan. He saw a woman, maybe mid-to-late thirties, nice enough looking, but dressed down even more than he was. She had brown shoulder- length hair and expression-less grey eyes, which stared from a pretty but unimpassioned face. She wore faded blue jeans that were torn in several places and a zip-up waist length corduroy coat that covered a maroon-coloured jumper. All of five feet six inches, she appeared slim, but it was difficult to tell beneath the baggy clothes, encumbered as she was by a bulky backpack. She continued to support his arm and he was grateful for this, as his legs had all the stability of jelly.

'That would be real fine, thanks,' he said at last.

'Can you walk okay?' she asked.

'Yeah, yeah, I can manage.'

She started slowly at first, allowing him to get his breath back.

'This is a bad place to stay,' she said.

'You don't have to tell me,' he replied.

'Did they take much?' she continued.

'Everything,' he answered, wanting to say mostly his pride, but thought it might blow his cover.

They walked on in silence for ten minutes or so, then Brinn, eager to get a feel for his current situation, spoke into the silence, 'What's your name?'

She did not reply. A few seconds went by and he tried again.

'Sorry, I did not get your name.'

With irritation clearly growing in her voice she said at last, 'How long have you been on the road?'

Trying to think fast on his feet he replied, shrugging his shoulders, 'Oh, about five years.'

'Then you should know better than to ask.'

Realising his mistake he tried to retrieve the situation by adding, 'I've only been in England for three months.'

'How the hell have you survived then?' she replied incredulously.

'Well, as you can see for yourself, I haven't,' he said, as he tried to make light of the situation.

After ten minutes of slow progress across town, they began to descend some dark concrete steps that led beneath a car park. The woman seemed at ease, but after his last encounter, Brinn was a little apprehensive, so he closed on the arm supporting him, bringing her closer to him.

She called out ahead to as yet unseen faces, 'Hi guys, I'm back.'

A barely audible voice, sounding slightly slurred, returned, 'That you, Sarah?'

The 'guys' now loomed into view in the gloom, and Sarah continued. 'Yeah, who else? Look, I brought someone with me. He's looking for a place for the night.'

'Is he clean?'

Brinn observed that this enquiry emanated from a six-foot, forty-year-old ruffian, not unlike those he had already come into contact with. He halted abruptly. Sarah reassured him and then turned to answer the question.

'Yes, Josh, he's clean, no tracks,' she replied.

The first voice chipped in again. 'He's not a cop, is he?'

'No, Pete, I'm sure of it. He's too stupid for one. I've just picked him up, literally, from under the bridge. You know, "Carlos territory". They cleaned him out. I don't think he's who he's pretending to be, but he's harmless to us.'

Brinn was trying hard not to register any signs of irritation on his face when the third man said, 'Then, welcome, sir, welcome. We gladly offer you our meagre hospitality. Please avail yourself of all our facilities, few though they are. We are always eager to welcome new members to our little enclave.'

'Oh, College,' she replied wearily to the elderly gentle-man, who seemed to Brinn rather smartly dressed for a tramp. With a full head of silver-grey hair and a small goatee to match, the tall, elegant, rather grandfatherly-looking gentleman appeared slightly out of place.

Sarah turned to Brinn and in a hushed voice said, 'College used to be on the stage. Shakespeare, I believe.'

The phrase, 'Oh how the mighty have fallen', flashed through Brinn's hazy consciousness.

'Yes, my dear boy, Sarah is quite right. All the great companies, all the great theatres, but forgive me. Where are my manners? You're not from these parts, are you? One of our American cousins, I perceive.'

'Yes,' replied Brinn, his head now beginning to throb wildly again. 'I'm sorry, I've just got to sit down.'

Sarah eased him onto an old mattress, one end of which was up against one of the walls of the lower floor of the car park.

'He has had a bad crack on the head,' she told the others. 'I'll just leave him till the morning. He should be okay then, I hope.'

The group nodded in agreement and turned back, each to his own preoccupation and left Sarah to take care of Brinn. His body began to tremble uncontrollably, perhaps due to the concussion or the cold. She gently eased off the foul-smelling coat and lowered him onto the mattress. Brinn turned immediately onto his side, while Sarah took a bright orange, well-worn sleeping bag from her backpack and prepared to unzip it for use. He recoiled a little at the sight of it, believing it would smell as bad as the mattress he was now lying on, but he was pleasantly surprised and very grateful when a floral aroma greeted his nostrils. He pulled it over him and the warmth partially pacified the shuddering of his body.

She bent over him, her voice only a little less flat than before, 'Move over a bit, I've only the one sleeping bag.'

Reluctantly he complied and Sarah slipped in behind him as she pulled the sleeping bag up and heaped cardboard over the two of them, sealing out the cold. In a mutual effort to keep warm, he allowed her to slip her arms around him and close the gap between them just as he drifted off into unconsciousness.

## Chapter Three

The first thing Brinn heard the next day was birdsong. His first thought was that his bed seemed uncharacteristically uncomfortable; his second, that he must have left the window open last night. Then came a moment's realisation, crashing recollection followed by an involuntary shudder. He was reluctant to open his eyes yet, as to do so would render all the events of the previous day more than just the dream that he hoped they had been. That was, until his next breath revealed mothballs! Still reluctant to lift his eyelids and visually confirm his worst nightmare, his next sensation was Sarah's voice as she called to him. 'American! American! Wake up! I have a mug of tea for you.'

Confused at first by the method of address, he did not respond immediately, but then lured by the possibility of some other scent filling his nostrils, he foolishly sat bolt upright. His head started to swim again, but having made it into the vertical position, he fought to prevent the loss of such hard-won ground. After a few moments disorientation, his head began to settle and he held out his hands to receive the tea. Sarah dumped the mug unceremoniously into his hands, but what Brinn thought she meant by mug of tea, and what he actually held in his hands, were two different things. This strangely brown liquid in its old, chipped and badly stained enamel mug was hot, but was it tea? There was only one way to find out; he lifted it to his lips, swallowed, and instantaneously regretted having done so, but he was desperate for something to drink, so he braced himself for another try. After the fourth sip, his tongue was growing accustomed to the taste, though he wasn't sure if his stomach ever would.

Brinn's other senses settled themselves into some sort of order and he looked around at his new surroundings. In the low firelight of the previous night, it had been difficult to see where he had been taken. But if his estimation was correct, he seemed to be on the lower floor of a multi-storey car park. Only one car occupied the area, as a mound of builders' rubble, aided by cement waste, had set solid across the entry ramp, preventing any further arrivals descending to this level. The lone car would never again venture onto the roads, as it had been completely burned out. It stood with the front passenger door ajar and the boot lid raised, resting on nothing more than its wheel hubs. The fire had completely ravaged the interior and left nothing but skeletal remains. Brinn supposed local youths had been responsible for the demise of the car, as that was so often the case back in the States.

The next thing that caught his eye was an old Sainsbury's shopping trolley, useless, with one wheel missing and the wire mesh frame kicked in on one side. Over against one wall, away to the right of him, was a blackened patch of ground that had been used to light numerous fires. Sooty deposits extended way up the wall and across the ceiling that constituted the floor above. A small feeble fire burned there now, framed by the debris used to kindle it. Three separate heaps of indistinguishable belongings, no doubt treasured possessions, were set equidistant from the fire. The only other one was the pile close to him by the mattress, which he supposed belonged to the woman he now knew as Sarah.

He turned his attention to the others in the group, all like him beginning to rouse, and wondered if he looked as pathetic as they all did.

'You look pretty pathetic this morning, American,' Sarah began, confirming his worst fears.

'Thanks, I feel much better already, and the name's Brinn, not American.'

'Sorry, I have grown used to the idea of it now. It will be sort of a nickname for you; you're stuck with it. How is the tea?'

'I'm sorry,' he spluttered, 'This can in no way be described as tea.'

'Used to something better, my boy, are you?' College now joined in. 'Perhaps a little Earl Grey or Lapsang more to your liking?'

Brinn realised his stupidity and bit his tongue.

'Oh, leave him alone, College,' Sarah replied. 'By the look of him he still has a thick head.'

College grunted and returned to his tea. Josh, the six-foot ruffian, stirred now, cleared his throat several times with a hoarse rasping hack and spat the resulting yellow phlegm on the ground beside him. Brinn shuddered at the sight and turned his head to look away. For some reason known only to himself, Pete began to sob softly. He rocked back and forth on his haunches with his arms clasped tightly around his body, a tortured wild expression deep in his eyes. Sarah moved toward him and rested an arm over his shoulder, to which he quickly clung.

'It's all right, Pete,' she said softly, 'there is no one to harm you now.'

The sobs died away and she put a refill of the brown liquid into his cup from the kettle taken from the fire.

College stood and took a random sample of broken wooden boxes, which he broke up roughly and threw onto the fire. He picked up a stick and prodded the ashes, sending a shower of sparks into the air. After a few attempts, the fire revived and small flames licked around the pieces of wood accompanied by a satisfying crackling noise.

He looked up from the fire, but not at anything in particular, and announced in broken sentences, 'Off to the Adelphi today; they have got a job for me. Found out yesterday. Big part, lead or supporting lead. Can't remember now. Be back late, so don't wait up.'

With that he threw the stick back on the ground and strolled off, clutching an old battered black umbrella that he had pulled from his belongings. The others said nothing, used as they were to playing out this little charade so many times. Brinn felt a shudder creep down his back, but put it down to the damp morning air.

'What are you up to today, Sarah?' Josh asked.

'Just the usual,' she began, 'oh, and trying to sort out this American here.'

'I don't need sorting out,' Brinn replied from behind his mug.

'Okay,' she said, 'I'll leave you to it then.'

Brinn wished he had more control over his temper, but that had always been one of his problems. It was partially the reason Carol had left him and partially the reason Chris's wife had left also.

Brinn had often resented Chris's wife, she had seemed to him pompous and distant. There was no doubt that she was good for Chris, a more faithful supporter of his work he did not think it possible to find. She had found it hard to mix with the type of people that Chris had to socialise with because of his standing as a producer, and whenever there was a cast party or an award dinner, she was seldom to be seen. That made Chris miserable and quite often he would return home very drunk; but those were the good nights, Brinn remembered with a wry smile. He felt only a little guilty when he remembered how he had given her such a hard time during the cast party following his last success. It had been her own fault; even though the party was held in her house, she had no right to suggest that Chris was the only reason Brinn had had such rave reviews in the past. Brinn, who by his own admission had been the worse for drink, just would not believe the success had all been due to Chris and his brilliant production. The thing that really clinched it however, was when Chris had taken his side in the ensuing argument and not hers, as he had so often done in the past. It was the final straw; they had a blazing row and she upped and packed her bags there and then in the middle of the party and left Chris for good. Chris drowned his regrets during a long drinking bout that night, something he could have avoided if he had tried a little harder. Perhaps he hadn't wanted to dissuade her from leaving.

Brinn realised that with no visible means of support, he would be sunk for the next two weeks. He capitulated.

'Look, I'm sorry,' he began. 'It's this wretched head of mine. You're right; of course, I do need some help.'

He was verging on sincerity and quite proud of his attempt at penitence, nonetheless effective for his throbbing head.

'Well, you had better get a move on then, you poor thing. I'm just about to leave.'

Sarah managed to sound equally magnanimous, which unnerved Brinn a little.

'Josh, will you stay with Pete for a while?' she asked.

'Yeah, okay, just for a while, but I have to go off for a bit later,' he replied.

Nodding to him, Sarah grabbed her backpack and walked off towards the city.

Looking back over her shoulder she called, 'You coming then, American?'

Without a word and with no regret, he put the mug down, picked up his still rank coat and followed her.

'The first thing we must do is burn that coat,' she said.

'It's not that bad, is it?'

'Well, I guess you could live with the mothball smell, but the words "motherfucker" in green paint on the back might give you a bit of a hard time.'

'Where are we going?' Brinn asked after they had crossed the river onto the south bank.

'First, we are off to collect some cash from our only benefactor,' she replied,

'And who is that?' he ventured in all innocence.

'Why, Her Majesty's Government, of course. Do you think we live on fresh air? Well, actually, I suppose it might as well be fresh air considering the amount they give us.' They walked on a little, then she added, 'I suppose as you are from America you will not qualify for any of our benefits, so how exactly have you been managing all the time you've been here?'

Grappling with some sort of believable answer he finally said, 'Er, I had a little money left over after I had worked my passage and I had been eking it out until yesterday. Now I have nothing.'

'Hmm. Bit of a problem, that,' she said. 'Still, if you want to survive, there's always an alternative.'

'Such as?' he asked.

'Well, do you play an instrument?'

'No.'

'Sing?'

'No.'

'Tap dance?'

'No.'

'Juggle?'

'No.'

'Don't hesitate to help me out a little here, American, will you?'

'I would if I could.'

'Can you whistle then?'

'Give me a break.'

'For God sake, what can you do?'

'Ahhh, when I was a boy I could rope a steer from the back of a horse and hogtie it in one minute forty-eight seconds flat,' he offered helpfully.

'When you were a boy,' she repeated slowly. 'You're winding me up, right?'

'No,' he emphasised, 'and I was one of the best of my age group in the whole of the state of Texas,' he finished proudly, 'though it was only a very young steer.'

'And what do you think your chances are of re-establishing this fascinating hobby of yours as a source of income here in the city?'

'Slim,' he said.

'Yeah, too right,' she replied, throwing up her hands in mock despair. Brinn changed the subject, embarrassed as he was at his own inability.

'How does the system work over here anyway?'

'I suppose it starts with the Job Seekers Allowance, which is a benefit available for anyone out of work but "actively seeking work". The amount you can claim depends on your age and circumstances, but if they find out that for any reason you are not looking for work, you lose the allowance straight away.'

'How can they find out?'

'It's a bit hit-and-miss, but they suggest job interviews for you and you have to give proof that you've attended, unless you have some real good reason not to go. Those who want to dodge the system claim that they are better qualified than they actually are. Then when they go to the interviews, well, naturally, they fall at the first post because it is obvious to the employer they are just not up to it. Then there are dozens of ways to simply mess up the interview.'

'I suppose any system can never be perfect, there are bound to be some loopholes,' he interjected.

'There are other benefits, of course; Income Support, Family Credit, Housing Benefit; in fact, some people can make a living out of not making a living, if you see what I mean. The whole thing falls flat on its face when you don't have an address. Without an address, you can't receive post or take phone calls about job offers, and employers just insist on you having an address. With no address, who would give you a job? No job, no money; no money, no address.'

'One hell of a vicious circle.'

'Exactly, and I am one of the lucky ones – I can use a friend's address. If I could ever find anyone who is willing to give me a job, well, who knows, I might even get a place of my own one day,' she said unconvincingly. 'If I really pushed, I could get into a bed-and-breakfast place.'

'Why don't you then?'

'Simple. Everything I have and know is out here. I understand how it operates. As long as I keep to what I know, I feel safe. I'd be a fish out of water in a place like that, and besides, most of these places make you abide by their rules. "Be in by this time; we lock the doors at such and such a time; you can't bring anyone in." I swear the system is designed to suffocate you.'

'What about the others? How do they manage?'

Shaking her head she replied, 'Not everyone can make the adjustment, especially as the system forces us back into responsibilities that we have fled for so long. Our roots and friends are on the street. Living from day to day alongside those whose fortunes are no better and no worse than our own builds bridges between us that the outside does not understand. Uprooting us from what we consider to be our home rarely works, we are usually drawn back to the familiar, the safe, the thing we have known for most of our lives.'

Seeing a mounting disbelief begin to register in his eyes,

she added, 'We don't judge each other, American; there is no need. The rest of society sits in judgement on us already and that is enough for any lifetime. Society is too quick to condemn us for faults they too would have had if their lives had begun like ours.'

Brinn was beginning to recognise when he had gone too far, so he kept quiet. As they continued along their present route to the DHSS, they passed a large building with colonnades and porticoes, elaborately ornate in style. Feeling the need to talk about something else, he asked, 'What is this place? I've not seen it before.'

'Oh, it's the central library,' she replied.

'The system seems to take better care of its books than it does its people,' he observed, in a hopeless attempt to regain a little deference, if indeed he had had any in the first place.

'I don't suppose it's any different in the US, is it now?' she commented.

A short distance farther and they had arrived at their destination. They joined several other people all going into the building, an old single-storey block squeezed in between an estate agents on one side and a sex shop on the other. A narrow dark alley ran down both sides, a haven for muggers, Brinn thought.

Inside the entrance there was a machine with a notice requesting you to 'take a ticket and sit down', the ticket supposedly to establish your place in the queue. Sarah took one from the machine and led Brinn into the long room. They found a spot to sit along the side wall a little ahead of them on their left, facing inwards and overlooking the central block of seats. Fortunately for all concerned, they sat just under an open window, as the walk in the fresh air had done little to sweeten the aura that clung to Brinn. The resulting through draught prevented the odour from the coat distracting too many of the customers, although one or two did turn and take a second look to see who was responsible for it.

Sarah looked at her ticket. It bore the number twenty-nine, and Brinn noticed the electronic sign on the opposite wall entitled 'next customer' displayed the number twelve.

'We're in for a long wait, then,' he said to Sarah, who nodded.

'It's usually like this.'

It was only nine forty-five, and already the room was just over half full. As it was obvious that they would not be going anywhere for a while, Brinn took the opportunity to make some mental notes for future reference.

To begin with, the room they were in resembled an old school classroom, with a colour scheme to match. The lower half of the walls had been painted chocolate brown, while the upper half was beige in colour, a wooden rail separating them at the midpoint. The windows were long and thin and set high in the wall with sash cords to operate the opening mechanism. Despite their size, little light actually penetrated from the alley and, as a consequence, all the strip lights in the room were on, all those that weren't broken, that is. Under their feet, dull parquet flooring gave off a distinctly disinfectant smell. The chairs that they sat on were wooden, slatted and most definitely ex-school issue, though fortunately not the very small ones that accommodate primary school children. In each of the two corners opposite the entrance stood a single desk, both of which had holes for inkwells and a groove cut horizontally in the top that, he presumed, used to be where a pen would have rested. Jammed up in one of the rear corners, a little farther along from the door, was a very unsanitary-looking coffee machine. It seemed for all the world as though it might have served during the last war, as it appeared to have sustained a great deal of localised damage.

The three booths that formed the hub of the operation

were all but minor fortifications, encapsulating the clerk against the applicant. With nothing between the customer and the rest of the world, it didn't strike Brinn as being a very private arrangement, especially if you needed to discuss something personal. A glass panel in front of a wire screen was the only obstacle separating the official from the enquirer; even so, it was a fortification worthy of the President himself.

It was easy from where they were sitting to see the rest of the hopefuls, an amazing mix of young, old and middle-aged, all with the same intention that Sarah had – to survive. A young mother grappled hopelessly with a runny-nosed child who, it was plain to see, was out of control. Another little boy beat a second over the head with a well-worn teletubby as he tried to get him to release his grip on a car that he obviously wanted very much. At the front of the room stood a little girl who simultaneously picked her nose, called to her mother, and pointed to the boys who fought on the floor. The child's mother – well, Brinn thought, it must be the mother – tried against mounting odds to ignore the situation. Her attention and effort being wholly directed towards the runny-nosed child, she hardly noticed the growing annoyance of several of the other people in the room. They had obviously grown tired of the noise and shifted about in their seats grumbling audibly, hoping to gain her attention. One elderly gentleman, unbelievably, managed to sleep through it all, despite the commotion. A group of three teenage boys, who had turned their chairs around into a small circle, busily discussed teenage things. Their occasional roars of laughter brought a distasteful tut-tut from an elderly woman who sat in close proximity, and who added a disgusted scowl to her repertoire when they retaliated with a few objectionable gestures.

Being in such close proximity to the booths, Brinn

picked up snippets of conversation coming from them. Hard as he might try to ignore them, it was almost impossible given the way they had been designed. In the right-hand booth sat a well-dressed woman with a small dog in her lap. Brinn could not work out why someone who appeared so prosperous would need to avail herself of the system, but as he overheard some of the conversation, all became clear.

'Good morning, George, how are you today?' she said to the spotty-faced youth behind the glass.

'Oh, good morning, Mrs Braithwaite,' he said warily, 'and what may we do for you today?'

'Well, first of all, I would like to thank you for arranging that mobility allowance for me. It has made all the difference to Fred and myself. Fred, that is my husband, you know.'

'Yes, I do know.'

'Now we don't have to walk down to the Derby and Joan club on a Thursday any more, we drive all the way instead.'

'That must be nice for you,' the young man replied, barely managing to conceal his exasperation.

'Oh yes, we have such a wonderful time there dancing to all the old favourites. In fact, we won a prize for our spirited rendition of the lambada last week.'

Brinn gave the young man his due; he was doing his best to maintain a professional attitude towards her. In the next booth, as one man left, a young girl took his place. Brinn thought she could not have been more than fourteen or fifteen at most. Surely girls like this should be in school? Then, as she turned slightly to lower herself into the chair, Brinn noticed that she was heavily pregnant and with his question answered he shifted his gaze.

'Do you want a coffee?' Sarah suddenly asked, jolting him out of his observations.

'Do you really think it's safe?' he replied, looking in the

direction of the machine.

'Yes or no?'

'Okay then, black, and hold the sugar, thanks.'

Sarah stood, walked over to the machine, and returned a few moments later with two plastic cups that were rapidly distorting because of the overly hot liquid. Handing one of them to Brinn, she resumed her seat. He spent the remaining time shifting his cup from hand to hand, blowing on it and trying not to mind too much that the contents tasted as though they, too were a relic of the war.

Sarah's number finally appeared on the display and she went over to the booth that had just been vacated, while Brinn remained in his seat. On this occasion, he strained hard to hear the conversation taking place between Sarah and the clerk, still desperate for any snippet that would give him more insight. Unfortunately, the small dog was now adding its own voice to the hubbub, and Sarah and the young woman on the other side of the glass partition could hardly be heard.

At first, the small dog was nowhere to be seen. It had slipped its collar and its shrill yapping was lost somewhere beneath the chairs, his owner too lost in her own conversation to notice its disappearance. Then, as if operated by radio control, an upturned shopping bag shot across the floor. On its side was depicted a scene from *Star Trek, the Next Generation*, the bridge of the *Enterprise*, no less. Its directional guidance system had obviously malfunctioned, as it came to rest up against the wall; Captain Picard had apparently been abducted by aliens. They had done their worst, as he now resembled a small, dazed Yorkshire terrier wearing a blue ribbon and sporting hair, for the first time in a long time.

It was becoming clear that, having grown tired of their war, the two boys had emptied mum's shopping all over the floor and put the bag to a far better use, as they saw it. This joint mission into the far reaches of the galaxy had been instrumental in making them the best of pals, and they had combined forces against the Federation. The owner of the dog at last realised the frantic muffled yaps were indeed coming from her precious pup, and leapt to her feet to rescue it, leaving the greatly relieved official to select a different customer, and the woman to another unsuspecting colleague.

Meanwhile Sarah was being asked, 'Have you been actively seeking employment, paid or unpaid, over the last fortnight?'

She answered, 'Yes, I have a list here of the ones I went to.'

She handed him the piece of paper she had just removed from her coat pocket.

'Ah, yes, thank you. And you say none of these were any good?'

'Oh no, the jobs were fine; they just didn't want me.'

'Yeeeees, I see. Well, have you had any employment, paid or unpaid, over the last fortnight.'

'Obviously not.'

'Are you still living at the same address?'

'Yes.'

'There you are then, Miss Miller, your Giro will be with you as usual. Thank you.'

Sarah dutifully stood up and gestured to Brinn to follow her out of the building. As he was passing through the door, Brinn looked back to see if Captain Picard had been rescued by the Klingon who had been chasing him so frantically round the room.

Their next port of call was Al's Cafe some ten minutes' walk away. One thing was for sure, if Brinn could not get the material that he needed for the play, at least he would get fit. His stomach started to rumble as he recollected that he had not had anything to eat since yesterday's hunk of bread. Then it hit him – the overwhelming aroma of cooking bacon, and his mouth began to water uncontrollably. Sarah took him round to the back door that was already ajar, and the sound of Pavarotti on the radio being accompanied, badly, by what Brinn supposed was Al drifted out to meet them.

'Al,' Sarah called out over the din.

'Ahhh, Sarah,' he replied, 'how have you been, my dear, and who is this with you? Your new boyfriend, perhaps?' he said teasing her.

'Al, you know I only have eyes for you,' she replied.

'Naturally,' he replied, patting his large stomach. 'Where else, in the whole of this beautiful country, could you possibly find another Italian half so handsome as me?' They laughed, and then he added, 'Would you and your friend like something to eat?'

The uncomplicated generosity of this man took Brinn a bit by surprise. After all, he had never met him before and Al had nothing to gain from the gesture. Al had a natural Italian accent, but his speech was heavily laced with West End phrases. He was short and stocky in build, looking, Brinn thought, a typical Italian right down to the grease-stained apron. Gifted with gentleness, he gave the impression of being a favourite uncle who turned up at Christmas loaded with gifts. Al ushered them through from the kitchen to the cafe while Sarah did the introductions, and explained that her companion's name was American, and not 'motherfucker' as was indicated by the green lettering on the back of his coat.

The room was about twenty-five square feet, vaguely reminiscent of the nineteen sixties in decoration, with grey formica tables and red plastic chairs placed in lines down both side walls. Adorning the tables were round squeezy tomato ketchup bottles, glass sugar dispensers and a selection of cutlery, little of which matched, but despite the old-fashioned appearance of the place, it was spotlessly clean. The walls were lined with many old photos, which Brinn supposed to be of family and friends with maybe the odd celebrity from the nineteen fifties thrown in for luck. The crowning glory, and for Brinn the most exciting discovery of all, was an old nineteen fifties American jukebox.

Forgetting his ravenous state, Brinn asked, 'Where in the world did you find this, Al?'

'Oh, I have had it for years, since it was new, I think. I have had it mended so many times now it's a miracle it still goes.'

'Can I give it a try?'

'But of course.'

Brinn approached the icon with the kind of reverence and awe that most people reserve for church. He ran his hands over the chrome ornamentation and fingered the red rectangular buttons, his eyes twinkling with long forgotten memories.

'It still has some of the old numbers on it,' Brinn shouted to Al from the other end of the room.

'Yes,' came the reply. 'I never saw the need to change them; some are a bit scratchy, but the old ones are the best ones.'

Brinn fished around in his pockets for some change, and then remembered he was penniless.

'Sarah,' he called, 'have you any change?'

'I'm not putting money into a jukebox,' she replied, but before Brinn could protest on aesthetic grounds, Al came up behind him.

Accompanied by a graphic demonstration, he said, 'You don't need money, American. Just clout it, here.'

The turntable jerked into action and Al indicated that Brinn should make a selection. With so many choices and only a fraction of time to make them, Brinn hit two keys without properly identifying them. Elvis Presley's 'Blue Suede Shoes' was as much of a surprise to him as it was to Al and Sarah, who smiled broadly at each other across the room.

'Sorry,' Brinn said, 'I hit the wrong buttons.'

Al joined Sarah at one of the tables, where he cleared all the things away and laid it with a clean cloth and cutlery. He pulled out a chair for Sarah, much as if he had been in a high-class establishment up town. When Sarah was seated, he did the same for Brinn, who reluctantly joined them a moment later.

With a tea towel decoratively laid over one arm, he took out a stubby pencil and a note pad from his apron pocket. Then, licking the lead, he stood ready to take down their order.

'Two of your usual, my good man,' Sarah announced, joining in with the game.

'Two… of… the… usual,' Al repeated and penned simultaneously.

'With tea?' he continued.

'Yes, please, that would be very nice,' she said.

At this point, Al leant forward and half whispered into Brinn's ear, 'Would sir mind terribly removing his overcoat as it is creating an atmosphere that is bad for business.'

They all began to laugh and Al disappeared into the kitchen at the back with the coat over his arm and humming 'Blue Suede Shoes' in time to the jukebox. Warmed by the laughter, Brinn began to relax a little. Genuinely interested, he asked Sarah casually, 'Why do nice people like you continue to live like this?'

She paused for a moment, undecided whether to tell him or not, then answered, 'You're very nosy, American. Look, we each have our own reasons and I warned you yesterday about asking too many questions. Are you sure you were on the road in America? It can't be that much different over there.'

Brinn checked himself and thought this time before he spoke.

'Please don't misunderstand me. I'm not prying. I just do not understand why. You seem very bright and intelligent. Why don't you go for another option? You could easily get a job, even accommodation. The others I understand, but not you.'

She took in a breath and was about to shout him down when Al returned with the tea and the moment was lost.

'Here you are, sir, madam,' he said, and as he placed the mugs on the table in front of them 'Blue Suede Shoes' faded out.

'Thank you, Al,' Sarah replied, followed by Brinn.

Al, already halfway back to the kitchen, simply waved the tea towel in recognition as he left the two of them to their thoughts. They sat in silence, occasionally sipping the tea, until Al returned five minutes later with two enormous plates of 'the usual'. It consisted of bacon, two eggs, mushrooms, tomatoes, beans and fried bread.

'Al,' Brinn said in surprise, 'you're a magician.'

Al, pleased with his guest's remarks, grinned broadly and then, remembering something, turned to Sarah.

'Thank you, my dear, for the gesture. Lovely flowers on Carmen's grave. I saw them this morning when I went to pay my respects. It was a nice thought.'

'You're welcome,' she said. 'Carmen was a real lady, Al. Everybody in the neighbourhood loved her.'

Al's soft warm face began to tighten and he turned slowly to prevent his tears from spoiling his guests' meal. He nodded in agreement as he walked back to the kitchen, leaving them to their food in peace. Brinn was dying to ask the obvious question, but after his last attempt, he decided against it. Sarah noticed the question in his eyes and thought, on this occasion, she would risk an explanation.

'Two years ago yesterday, Al's wife, Carmen, died. A long painful illness. Cancer. Never any hope from the first day it was diagnosed. I helped where I could, sat with her while Al had to work in the cafe, and ran errands for them. He could not bear to be parted from her, insisted to the hospital that he would take care of her himself, and he did, right up to the end. They were a great couple. Treated me like their own. I was on my way back from the cemetery yesterday when I bumped into you.'

Brinn was not sure how to respond, so he kept his own counsel. He was afraid he might put his foot in it again and she would clam up completely on him this time.

After they had finished their meal, they chatted with Al as they did the dishes together. Al then produced an envelope for Sarah, which contained this week's offering from HM Government. She took it gratefully and they tendered their goodbyes, promising to return again soon. Just as they stepped through the front door, Al produced an old coat of his along with a few sandwiches in a paper bag. Then, without a word, he gave them to Brinn and closed the door behind him. Sarah and Brinn walked down the street past the alley where Al was, unknown to them, finally putting Brinn's odorous overcoat to rest in the dustbin.

The weather had turned colder, even in the short time that they had been in Al's, so Sarah decided to take refuge in the Underground.

'It's much warmer down there,' she said to Brinn.

'We would have to pay money, wouldn't we?' he replied, trying to emulate her earlier frugality.

'Who needs money? It's all in the timing,' and she began to explain how to beat the system as they approached the station.

'Joe Public puts his ticket into the machine and the barrier swings open. If you time it just right and the guard is looking in the other direction, you can just squeeze through before the barrier shuts again.'

She took Brinn by the hand and led him to a corner of the ticket office where he could see clearly the operation of the barriers. After her sixth attempt to explain the process, Brinn thought he had mastered the theory and was confident enough to give it a go in practice. Sarah went first, performing like a professional, raising her arms in triumph on the other side as she gave a little twirl.

'Come on, American,' she urged in a forced whisper and giving a beckoning hand gesture. Brinn stepped forward and, as he did so, a suspicious guard noticed him. Brinn's first attempt was a total failure and the guard now began to move forward in an attempt to apprehend him.

'Over, over.' Sarah was almost shouting.

The guard was now at full tilt. Brinn saw him fast approaching and managed to produce an adrenaline surge that, after a brief run up, sent him over the barrier.

Sarah grabbed his arm and dragged him off at speed down the escalator towards the Circle line, as he called out with elation, 'Did you see that? It must have been three-foot-six at least, and I did it in one shot. Not bad for a forty-nine year old, eh?'

'Never mind that now,' she said, breathing hard. 'We have the guard on our tail. We can't hang about. Come on! Run.'

With the guard now close in pursuit, they rounded a corner onto the platform. Running down one side, through the dividing arch and back down the opposite side, they finally boarded a waiting train whose doors were already beginning to close. The guard staggered round the corner, hands resting heavily on his thighs and bent over double with the effort of running. He watched helplessly as the train pulled out, barely able to draw each breath, let alone stop the departure.

The train was crowded and bemused passengers looked on in some disdain as Brinn and Sarah collapsed in laughter at one end of the coach. Brinn could hardly speak. It had been a long time since he had run or jumped like that.

'It feels,' he said between gasps, 'like I'm having a heart attack.'

'Rubbish!' she replied. 'You're just unfit; you're as red as a beetroot.'

'How can you say that, when I leapt over that barrier?'

'Yes, it's amazing what fear can make you do,' she said, 'and besides American, it was only two-foot-six.'

They sat in silence for a while and although he didn't like to admit it, Brinn was glad of the chance to get his breath back. They did not talk much, but occasionally one would catch the other's eye across the carriage and a broad smile would break out on their faces. Brinn was intrigued with his new companion. He wanted to find out more about her, but every time he tried, he met with a barrier. He desperately wanted to know her better. As for Sarah, well, she was still unsure if this new companion was quite what he pretended to be, or if she could trust him yet.

Switching trains, if a ticket inspector appeared, allowed them time to warm up and for Brinn's blood pressure to return to normal. Mission accomplished, they alighted at a station where Sarah knew there were no barriers and they could pass through unchallenged. The early afternoon traffic was heavy and they had quite a way to go back before reaching the car park, but neither of them was in too much of a hurry.

When they did arrive, Josh was nowhere to be seen, but Pete was still in his sleeping bag. He was hunched up with his arms wrapped around his knees, rocking back and forth, occasionally sobbing to himself.

Sarah went straight to him and asked gently, 'Have you

been like this all day, Pete?'

He nodded to her, and she put her arms around him, cradled his still rocking body and synchronised her movement to his own. Brinn was touched by her tenderness toward Pete, an unfamiliar emotion to him.

'Why are you so unhappy today, Pete?' Sarah asked, though she knew the answer to the question already.

'You go away, you leave me,' was his pathetic reply.

'That's not true,' she said, lifting his tear-streaked face to look at her. 'I will always be here for you; you are special to me.'

Uncontrollable sobbing gripped the boy, who Brinn guessed, could only have been eighteen or nineteen years old. He could see that there was nothing he could do to help and he was too embarrassed to ask, so he retreated to the mattress and tried to make himself comfortable. Sarah continued to rock Pete for some time until, at last, he fell into an exhausted sleep. She laid the thin body down, covered him with his sleeping bag and a threadbare blanket, and rejoined Brinn on the mattress. Brinn reached out his arm to put around her shoulder, but withdrew it at the last moment, unsure of the gesture's reception. He checked in his pocket for the paper bag given to him by Al. Locating it, he brought it out and offered it to Sarah. She took one of the sandwiches and, indicating that it was sufficient, she returned the bag to Brinn. He took the second sandwich, and bit into it. As he chewed on it, he stood and carried the bag over to where Pete was asleep. He placed it on the ground beside the sleeping boy and then returned to the mattress.

Neither Sarah nor Brinn derived much pleasure from the meal and both spent the next few hours collecting a few bits of wood and making up a fire for a brew-up. With nothing much else to do, they lingered over the tea until the early evening darkness and the increasing cold compelled them to retreat to the relative warmth of Sarah's sleeping bag. Sarah collected some cardboard and Brinn unfurled the sleeping bag that he had pulled from Sarah's pack. Despite the cold, Sarah chose not to adopt the position of the night before, and though a little offended, Brinn knew better now than to ask why.

## Chapter Four

The following morning, both Josh and College were back at the car park, having returned sometime during the night.

College was in his bed and making indefinable noises. He was unconscious, reeking of alcohol, and there was a pool of acidic vomit just behind his head and, it would seem, over his coat as well.

Josh appeared to have been sitting up the entire night beside the now cold fire and was surrounded by the trappings of drug abuse. He was shaking visibly and Sarah rose and lit a fire from the few bits of wood and old newspapers still lying around in an attempt to warm him and the others. Every so often, Josh spoke a few, incoherent words and gesticulated wildly as though holding a conversation with an imaginary friend. For him the long cycle of abuse, regret, rehabilitation, and abuse again, had left him only with a legacy of badly ulcerated arms and collapsed veins. His last visit to the doctor had revealed a new problem; now he was HIV positive as well, yet another reason to lose himself in the almost daily trip into forgetfulness.

Sarah loathed these mornings most of all. She began the brew-up for the tea and was startled by Brinn who came up behind her.

'How can you go on like this?' he said softly, trying not to alarm her.

She turned, anger overtaking the loathing she felt. 'Are you thick or something? If you had ever really been on the streets, you would already know the answer to that.'

Taken aback by this uncharacteristic attack, he automatically snapped back, 'Okay. So I'm stupid. Why the hell don't you tell me, Sarah, tell me?'

It was her turn to be surprised by the reply.

'They are family, American,' she answered, her voice steadying. 'I have known them for more of my life then I have my own family. We have grown together. When I first came onto the streets, I found it hard to cope. Each time I was ready to give up on life, they were there for me. So what are you telling me? That now our positions are reversed, I should give up on them?'

'I cannot believe that you have ever been as bad as this,' he said, exasperated.

'Believe it, American. We are all as bad or as good as each other out here. Even you must have your problems. After all, you're here, aren't you, or is it just some elaborate hoax?'

She paused and then added, 'You know, from day one I have had my doubts about you.'

'I am nothing more or less than you see,' he said, trying to comfort and reassure her. 'We Americans just have a different way of handling situations. We are not so reserved as you British. Why don't you tell me about them, so I can understand their situation? Maybe even help in some way.'

His words had the desired effect and she slowly nodded her assent. They went back to the mattress and he put the sleeping bag around her to prevent her from getting cold. Then, returning to the fire, he poured her a mug of tea. He was more cautious now in his approach, for he thought this might be a difficult transition for her. He had no direct experience to draw on, but he had been told that you messed around with other peoples' emotions at your own risk. Brinn recalled the few times he had meddled in Chris's life, and had met with disastrous consequences, and they, after all, were people he considered stable. He knew nothing about Sarah. Returning to her, he put the mug into her hands and she began to calm down as she slowly sipped the liquid. Brinn sat beside her as she started to speak.

'Josh was not always like you see him now. About thirty years ago, he was, as the world saw it, successful, normal. He was young and ambitious and had a responsible job as a manager of an up-and-coming electronics company. With a house, fast car and money in his pocket, he had loads of fair weather friends, as many as you could shake a stick at. His working hard to secure his position in the company meant he had little time for a social life. Then one Christmas, when the office threw its customary party, he met a girl from the accounts department. He'd seen her around the place lots of times before. She was younger then he was and completely irresponsible. Perhaps that was what attracted him to her, I don't know, but she lived a far more exciting life than the one he had, or so he thought. Apparently, to begin with, he had no idea that her life style included the drug scene. He was so in love with her he could not see what she was pulling him into. They went to some dodgy parties and he became involved in a culture that he knew nothing about. He admitted it himself – he was totally naive – and before he was fully aware, he was in too deep to get out. It sucked him in, used up all of his money, and sucked the very life out of him. He lost his car, his house and his job. The so-called friends vanished. The girl left him when the money ran out and he was devastated. Josh started his life on the streets then. He had nowhere else to go, but he just could not get her out of his head. He continued to try to contact her, pestering her at work and at home. Finally, the police cautioned him, and then she took out an injunction against him because of the nuisance calls. That was when I first met him. I had been on the streets for only three weeks. I was green and terrified of everyone and everything. Josh took me under his wing and was like a brother to me, protecting me from situations that could very well have cost me my life.'

As Brinn listened in silence, he grew more and more uncomfortable. His recognition that parts of Josh's life were not unlike his own alarmed him, and he began to wonder if opening this can of worms had been misdirected. It was incredible how just a very little information about a person could so completely alter his conception of him. No more was Josh the 'idler', the 'ruffian', or the 'hopeless junkie' with no aim in life except where to go for the next fix. He was no longer invisible, for he had a face, a heart, a soul. Brinn knew if he was any kind of a man, he would at least feel pity, but just as when he had heard of Carmen's death, he was totally unmoved. He lifted his hand and pushed his fingers over his head, his eyes closed, while he tried to dispel the thought that he might after all be totally heartless.

Sarah had finished her tea and, leaving Brinn deep in thought, went to pour a second one. Before she returned, she stopped a moment to check on Josh and College. Satisfied, she started to talk again as she resumed her place next to Brinn.

'You probably remember the nineteen forties.'

Brinn looked over to her.

'Have a heart, honey! Bit far back, even for me,' he replied.

'Sorry! Only joking. Anyway, that's when College was in his prime. He was tipped to be one of our finest actors, up there with Olivier and Gielgud. Unfortunately, the strain of being at the top took its toll on him and he began to drink, only a little at first, you understand, just to steady his nerves and help him with his lines. Then he would occasionally turn up late for rehearsals and was irritable with the cast and crew when he did eventually arrive. Thousands of pounds in wasted time and resources were flushed down the drain and this increasing pressure just made him drink the more. His brain was so addled after six years of virtually continual drinking, that he could hardly remember his words and he spent most of his time in his dressing room. His friends, who had now dwindled to a handful, tried to tell him he had a problem, but he just couldn't see it. His long-suffering wife saw no hope of change and finally left him, taking their son, who College absolutely adored, away to her mother's in Scotland. The final insult was when he was denied access by the courts because of his unreasonable behaviour. The offers of work dried up until all he could get were occasional parts for the voice-overs in commercials. The money from this was insufficient to maintain his colossal drinking bouts, and so he sold the only thing left that he prized. It was a collection of memorabilia from the old days. It meant everything to him. In the end, he was left with nothing but dreams of the past and imaginary offers by long-gone producers. Maybe it was because he missed his own son so much, or partly because I never got on with my own father, but College and I hit it off from the start. He calls me "his little girl", and I don't mind, because it's nice to feel I have a father sometimes.'

'His name's not really College, is it?'

'You get to choose your own name out here. Most do it because they don't want to be found; others because remembering who they were is just too painful. We chose College for him because he speaks so beautifully, just like a college professor. You're bloody lucky you didn't get stuck with the one on the back of your coat.'

Brinn ignored the remark, which was intended to be humorous. He was turning over the things he had just been told, trying to assimilate them.

'What's the matter, American?' Sarah asked when she saw the expression on his face. 'You asked to hear this. Can't you take it now?'

'It's not what you think,' he replied,

'A bit too close to home, perhaps?'

Brinn drew in a sharp silent breath as her words stung

him.

'Perhaps you're not so different from us after all.'

He looked round at all four of them again, confused about how he should, if he should, proceed. It was like looking at his own image in a carnival mirror – four distorted reflections of himself all equally him and all equally wounded and wounding. The sound of a continual stream of cars rolling over the concrete tiers above as they wound their way up to an unoccupied space in the car park distracted him for a moment.

'Do try to keep the noise down, my dear boy,' College slurred slightly as he sat up cautiously.

Brinn was unsure what motivated him at that moment, but College's words were all the catalyst he needed. He stood, went over to the fire and poured three further mugs of tea. Sarah looked on in amazement as he took the first mug over to College and set it on the ground. Brinn helped him to remove his acrid- smelling coat, which, unintentionally, triggered another bout of violent vomiting. He waited for the involuntary convulsions to subside and then replaced the coat with his own, the one that Al had given him the previous day.

He offered the mug to College, but he declined with a polite, 'Thank you, my boy, but I believe it would just have a detrimental effect on me at present. Thank you all the same.'

He then took a mug to Josh, first clearing the area carefully of the used needle, discarded foil and empty amphetamine bottle. This time he had to help Josh raise the mug to his lips and drink, as Josh's own hands still shook from the effects of the drugs. Sarah could hear him gently coaxing Josh.

'Try to take some, Josh. You might dehydrate. That's it! Come on, just one more sip.'

Next she saw him take a mug to the still sleeping Pete

and place it by his side quietly, trying not to disturb him.

For over an hour, he returned periodically to each of them, seeing to each of their immediate needs. Finally, he helped Josh to lie down, and, covering him with a blanket, he pulled himself upright to ease the muscles in his aching back. Worse than his back was the realisation that he had just released half a lifetime's compassion that had been previously locked away inside of him. Sarah could see the strain on his face and that he was emotionally shot, so she went over to him and began to rub his back, easing her thumbs just between his shoulder blades.

'Mmmmm, that feels good! Ah, just a bit lower! Yes, there. That's it, honey. Oh, marvellous!'

'It was a kind thing you did, American. You have the ability to surprise even me. Let's take it easy today. I have my giro to cash and we could pretend to be normal like ordinary people.'

Brinn just nodded as his muscles relaxed under the effective massage. 'Do we have to go right this minute? I'm rather enjoying this,' he said.

Sarah stopped immediately and went to collect her pack.

A dejected Brinn continued, 'Hey! What do I have to do to get a little attention around here.'

'Grow up,' she offered helpfully.

'Will they be all right?' he asked as he watched her pick up her pack and begin to walk away.

'American, they have been like this for most of their lives. It is, you could say, normal for them. Your intervention was a welcome break in an otherwise difficult existence, but they will survive.'

There was still one question pressing his mind, but right now, he did not think he wanted to hear the answer.

There was a post office quite close by, but Sarah preferred the one a bit farther away as it had the tendency not to become so crowded on giro day. Brinn enjoyed the walk. It gave him a chance to clear his head and sort out his feelings. They stopped off at a newsagent where Sarah spent the last of her cash on two rolls, a bar of chocolate and a carton of orange juice. The orange juice was consigned to her pack, in case of emergencies, while she shared the other items equally with Brinn as they proceeded on their way.

By the time they were two streets farther on, they had finished their food and Sarah, without breaking her stride, picked up a bottle of milk from the doorway of a terraced house. Brinn tried to suppress his views on the removal of the item, even though he had been the victim on several occasions of such a theft. His face, however, was more than a little slow to display a similar disinterest. Sarah, seeing his incredulity, said, 'And you've never done this before, right?'

Brinn shrugged and lied, 'Well, yes, I've done it, but usually from the steps of a bank or office. You know, someone with money.'

'According to the Oxford dictionary, theft is "dishonest appropriation of someone's property". I don't remember anything about having to distinguish between rich and poor.'

She offered him a drink from the bottle, which at first he rejected on moral grounds. However, the roll he had eaten had been ham, and very salty, so when she offered it a second time, he overcame his morals about the subject, feigned reluctance and accepted.

As they approached the Embankment, they could smell the distinctive odour of the river at low tide. It was not quite so bad at this time of year as it was during the summer. The heat made it worse. The river that was at the heart of the city had been there before it when its banks had been only marshy ground. Hundreds of years of history washed in and out with the tides, together with a little untreated sewage, the occasional chemical discharge and any rubbish the public deemed fit to throw in. All of history lay recorded and locked up in the silted blackness. The river was eternal, though changing itself in the face of endless change. It would be here tomorrow and the next day, and the day after that. The city would alter around it, people would come and go, but the river would remain.

The tall city buildings were partially obscured by the chill morning mist and a watery sun could be seen trying to break through the haze. There had been a little light rain overnight and, as the sun became stronger, the dampness was vaporising, adding to the overall ambience. An occasional lone jogger pounded past them, unaware of their existence, transfixed by the sound of some musical impetus emanating from a walkman. Many commuters, already on their way to work, carried undisclosed documents in nondescript briefcases, all looking and acting very much alike. Heads down with an even stride, they were determined to close the distance between station and office as quickly as possible.

The traffic was relatively light as yet, but they still needed to be vigilant when crossing the roads; city drivers were notorious for their selective vision. They passed several people sleeping in shop doorways, huddled close to the gap between ground and door where any remnant of illicit heat could be caught as it escaped to warm their sleeping bodies.

Builders were beginning to arrive for work at sites all over the city, different parts of it, requiring repair and refurbishment at different times. The men sat awaiting their instructions for the day from yet absent foremen, exchanging friendly banter and general conversation and dressed in already muddied overalls, some wearing, some carrying the customary hard plastic hats, each a different colour depicting a different status. One or two were engrossed in daily tabloids or smoking cigarettes. The volume of conversation rose to compensate for the increased traffic flow.

A full load of foreign school children disembarked from a coach parked in a side street. Expectant, and excited to begin a whole day's visit to the city, each carried a packed lunch and a satchel. Their eager chatter added to the growing noise. A teacher struggled to maintain order, calling, as she must now, at the top of her voice. A little ahead, at one of the buildings undergoing a metamorphosis, a skip sat, its contents overflowing onto the pavement. An elderly woman was sifting through the unexpected windfall, gleaning any item deemed worthwhile. She appeared abnormally bulky, wearing many different layers of clothing, topped off by a long coat, its buttons strained to almost breaking point. The strap on one of her shoes was broken and flapping free, and the heels of both were worn down almost to the sole. Several bags, no doubt containing her entire wealth and life, were strewn around and a backpack, possibly foraged from an earlier scavenging trip, hung from one arm. Her face seemed set in a permanent scowl, and her labours were accompanied by her low mumbling voice.

The city was swelling with buses, taxies and lorries, pulsating traffic coursing through the streets like blood through the veins. It was coming to life all around them, a thousand separate events adding vital stimulation to bring the city to consciousness. The beast was waking from its sleep.

Brinn and Sarah arrived outside the post office just as it opened. Only a few people had entered ahead of them, making the process a quick and simple one. They emerged into the growing sunshine and Sarah was pleased with her sudden, if temporary, wealth.

'We will have to be extra careful, now there are two of us,' she remarked to Brinn.

He wished that he still had the cash that he had set out with, so at least he would not be totally dependent on her now. There was little point in wishing now. They walked back slowly in the direction of the Embankment and decided to sit a while to try to plan the rest of the day. The Embankment was still fairly deserted, the first rush of commuters over and the hard-bitten tourists not due to flood the area until around ten thirty. Brinn felt more relaxed now, but he still had that one question left to ask.

He exhaled deeply and then, looking across to Sarah, he asked, 'What about you, Sarah? You didn't tell me about yourself.'

'Neither did you.'

'That's different, and besides, I asked you first.'

'You don't play fair, American.'

Brinn let the subject go for a few moments and then the compulsion grew too strong and he asked, 'Would you really mind telling me?'

'It does not make very interesting listening,' she added.

'I can be a very patient person, despite all evidence to the contrary,' he ventured.

She smiled at this and pushed her hair back out of her face, then turned her head to look for somewhere to sit. She grabbed Brinn's arm and yanked him off towards a vacant bench. They both sat down. Then, leaning forward with her arms resting on her legs, she took a couple of deep breaths and with some effort began.

'My father was a very hard man. He and my mother did not get on very well. In fact, they fought constantly and sometimes he would become violent. I remember a time, when I was very small, seeing her with an occasional black eye or bruised arm, but she never complained. She always had an excuse for him: "He does not mean it", or "It was an accident" or "He had a little too much to drink last night". The funny thing was you'd think she would have left him, but she never did. I read somewhere once that if it happens often enough, you get so used to abuse that it becomes part of your life. You grow to accept it and you become conditioned. I guess that was what happened to Mum. We knew all along, of course, my brother and me, but we were powerless to do anything. He was too strong for us. Me and my brother David – he is ten years older than me – often wondered why the doctor did not guess what was going on. My mother often had to visit him, but he never saw through her excuses. Even the neighbours, who must have been able to hear the commotion, did nothing.

'For me, it started on my twelfth birthday. Up until then, I had only been beaten a few times, but something changed between him and my mother and things got worse.'

Sarah shifted her position and sat back on the bench with her arms wrapped around her body. She had moved, not because she was uncomfortable with her seat, but because she was uncomfortable within herself.

'Mum had bought me this lovely pink party dress with daisies around the collar and hem and a big bow on the back. I just loved it and wore it to the party that afternoon. I was sitting at the table with my friends, eating and laughing, but mum made me go upstairs to their room to retrieve the crackers and balloons that she had forgotten to bring down earlier. I opened the cupboard and bent down to get them, but did not hear my father come in and shut the door behind him. I was surprised to see him, as he was not expected home from work until later. He told me to put the things on the bed and go over to hug him. I was only a bit afraid; he seemed all right, but his moods could change so quickly, you see. He said how pretty I looked in my new dress and I remember being pleased, until, that is, he started to touch me.'

Her voice faded out and she stared straight ahead as if

watching the whole thing on a video replay. Tears, a few at first, started to run down her face, as she continued slowly.

'Every time he would say "it's all right, I won't hurt you".' Turning to Brinn, her eyes were wild as she said, 'But he always did. And you want to know the really funny part? It's silly, I know, but it's such a vivid memory – the box of crackers on the bed got crushed when he raped me. That's all I could think about you see, the bloody crackers getting crushed. When I took them downstairs, my mother thought my crying with pain was hysteria due to the crackers being busted and as she couldn't shut me up, she sent my friends home as a punishment.'

The memory, so obviously painful, triggered tears, and as she spoke, her voice broke up, so that Brinn had some difficulty in understanding her.

'Two years, he raped and beat me. Tried to tell mum that I did not understand what he was doing. Mum would not believe me; David could do nothing, I tried to explain, I tried!'

'It was not your fault,' Brinn cut across the sobbing, desperate to put an arm around her. But worried she might react the wrong way, he held back. The crying subsided and Sarah was still when she continued.

'He got me pregnant, but it did not show till I was almost four months gone. I still did not realise what had happened to me, and when Mum found out, she accused me of screwing with one of the boys from school. I am sure she knew it was Dad, but she just could not face up to it. Then together, they arranged an abortion for me, on the quiet, with some old friend who had been a doctor once, but was struck off for something or other. I was so scared when he arrived at the house, I did not want to go through with it, but Mum said if the neighbours found out, they could never hold their heads up in public again. They would not be allowed to live it down. He did it in the same room where my father had raped me so often before. The bed had been covered in plastic sheeting. I remember a galvanised bucket and some instruments laid out on a bedside table. I pleaded with Mum not to let him do it to me, but they made me breathe something awful from an old cloth. It made me feel sick at first, then everything went swimmy and I guess I just fell asleep.'

After a short pause, she continued, the words coming slowly and more painfully now.

'When I woke up, I could hear voices in the next room. The three of them had left me, thinking I was still out. I remember feeling something wet and sticky with my hand, and when I looked at it, it was red with blood. I was terrified. I had had only one period before and it was nothing like this. My head felt fuzzy but I managed to look around the room to see if I could find something to wipe myself on. Then I saw it lying on the bed next to me, half-protruding from a plastic bag. It looked like a tiny rag doll. I hurt so much, but I was still able to roll over on my side to take a closer look.'

Her voice was now measured and almost whispering.

'It was a baby girl, I think, so tiny that she would fit in the palm of your hand.'

She lifted her left hand as if recalling the event, then looking up, she closed her fingers slowly into a fist.

'Every finger, every toe perfect. Her eyes were shut tight and when I touched her she still seemed warm. I was just about to pick her up when the doctor rushed into the room and snatched her away. I couldn't even say goodbye.'

Her fist was now so tightly clenched her nails were digging into her palm. Brinn took hold of her hand and gently prised her fist open. She shuddered as she continued, unstoppable and angry now.

'My mother came into the room to clean up the mess and my father stood at the door watching me with such an expression I knew then that I could not stay in that house. I had to get out as soon as I could. When I had recovered sufficiently, I slipped out one day when they were both at work.'

She looked away again and pulled her hand free from Brinn's as she added, 'I have never trusted or been with another man since.'

Brinn felt a little sick and completely helpless. In a way, he wished he hadn't pressed the issue in the first place, because now he was too impotent even to offer compassion to this tortured girl.

'I found out a few years ago,' Sarah added calmly, 'that they don't think I can ever have children of my own. I'm too messed up inside.'

Brinn stood and paced around the bench; he was unfamiliar with having to deal with such raw emotion, choosing rather to distance himself from it instead, but he couldn't ignore it; it was here, next to him, demanding his immediate attention.

A small group of pigeons had settled in front of the absorbed couple, their gentle cooing the only sound on the air. Brinn, who could not find the right words to sufficiently describe his present mood, or to express to Sarah his regret for her situation, welcomed the distraction. A nearby car sounded its horn, startling the birds.

Taking his cue from their departure, Brinn turned to Sarah and extended his hand towards her, saying, 'What do I have to do to get a shower around here?'

Harry's did not really belong to Harry, but everyone knew it as that. It was an old dilapidated Victorian bathhouse that had been condemned several years before, but somehow the local council had not quite got round to pulling it down. Fortunately, neither had they arranged for the water or gas supply for the heating to be cut off. Ah, bureaucracy!

This was to the advantage of the local community who were, at the moment, able to use it free of charge, courtesy of Harry. Harry used to be the janitor when the baths were still open to the public. Now he remained on the council payroll more in the capacity of a security guard in order to prevent vandals from gutting the place. An elderly man, and not quite your everyday security guard, Harry was tall, thin and bent over at the shoulders, giving the almost comical appearance of an animated walking stick. Able only to proceed by a succession of shuffling movements, he was nonetheless an amiable man.

The baths that he so dutifully tended had been built in the eighteen hundreds. The construction was mainly of red brick supported by a cast-iron framework, and topped with a slate-and-glass roof. The entrance hallway, as well as most of the interior, was clad in a mosaic of pale green and white tiles. They had all seen better days and many were chipped or broken. The words 'Public Baths' appeared majestically in black tiles at one end of the hallway, though the 'L' in public had been removed by vandals, leaving the words 'Pubic Baths'. A foundation stone beneath proudly proclaimed, 'Opened in 1872, by the Mayor and Councillors of this fair city.' Tall, heavily frosted windows with bars over them graced the walls at intervals of about fifteen feet, and large wooden doors marked 'Entrance' and 'Exit' stood at the far end. On either side of the pool was a line of changing cubicles, one side for men and the other for women, but by now, most of the wooden doors had rotted away.

The ceiling was very high and consisted of glass panels held together with ornate ironwork, which allowed streams of light to illuminate the expanse below. Over the years, the heat and condensation had taken their toll on the ironwork, and rusty-coloured stains and residue ran down the walls in several places. Some of the ironwork had been eaten through by rust, and a large quantity of glass was missing because of the now defective structure. Pigeons had taken up residence in the rafters, taking advantage of the accessible shelter and, typically, had left their usual calling cards, as excrement adorned much of the superstructure. Now empty of water, the pool occupied the greater part of the floor space. A few steps at either end led down to an area some three feet deep at one end and eight feet at the other. Many dry leaves, blown in through the broken glass above, moved restlessly in the bottom of the pool like stranded fish after the tide had gone out. In its day, it had been considered one of the finest municipal baths in the area. Now, like so many things and people, it was just considered down and out.

As they entered the hallway Sarah called out, 'Harry, it's Sarah; are you there?'

A moment passed and they heard footsteps coming towards them down the passage.

'Sure I am. Where else do you think I would be? I suppose you want to use the facilities?' Harry said as he approached them.

'Yes, we would, and you wouldn't happen to have a couple of towels and some soap, would you?'

'Ha, nothing changes! Still the same old Sarah. How come you don't ever carry these things with you?'

'You know me Harry, always travelling light.'

Harry pulled his index finger across his upper lip and sniffed.

'Well, okay. You know where things are, but you will both have to use the ladies' showers – the water doesn't work any longer in the gents.'

Sarah blew Harry a kiss as she skipped off down the corridor with Brinn close behind. En route to the ladies, they stopped briefly at a long cupboard to pick up the towels and soap that Harry kept especially for Sarah. As they passed through the pool area in order to get to the showers, the empty baths caused their footsteps to reverberate around the cavernous space, and the flock of startled pigeons took to their wings. Brinn thought he could hear faint voices; laughter; splashing; faint echoes from a distant, happier past when the baths were in use and the clientele were paying customers. He halted at the door to listen, but no, it was his imagination, or the wind, or the leaves, or maybe ghosts.

The ladies was not so different from the rest of the building. It was still decorated entirely with the tile mosaic, but very much smaller than the baths themselves. A long wooden bench lined one wall and coat hooks were positioned at equal distances above. At one end of the room, there was a white-tiled shower area with a lowered floor and two water nozzles on the wall above.

Sarah began to undress first, with a somewhat bemused Brinn looking on.

'We have little choice but to share,' she began nervously. 'You don't mind, do you, American?'

The tension eased in her voice a little and she laughed as she noticed a similar nervousness in Brinn's eyes.

'Er, no, if it's the only way to get a shower,' he added.

Sarah stepped into the shower first and, facing into one corner, blindly stretched out her hand behind her to turn on the water. The initial stream was icy cold, and her body broke out in goose bumps. As it slowly warmed, the goose bumps subsided and the water ran down over her body soothingly. She stood with her hands pressed to the tiled wall and her head turned up into the torrent.

Brinn stood beside her moments later, a little embarrassed, but too preoccupied with his need to wash to dwell on it. He turned on the shower and after three days since his last encounter with water, it felt good, almost sensual to him. He would have dearly loved to have some shampoo, but in the absence of it, he began to lather his hair with the hand soap. Then he thought he could smell the faint aroma of conditioner, and he turned to see Sarah rinsing some out of her hair. Irresistibly, his eyes, like the water ran down over her body exploring every curve, and the need for shampoo gave way to other desires.

He felt guilty, but in that moment he wanted her. Sarah turned to allow the water to run over her back and as she did, she met his eyes. A shudder went through her body as she saw the way he looked at her. Harry was too far away to call, and too old to be of any real help, and all her previous experiences had conditioned her to think that it would be pointless to struggle or protest as it only hurt the more. In an instant, her expression changed to one of total impassivity and her eyes glazed, the only defence she knew and the one she had practised most often before.

'Just don't hurt me, American,' she whispered.

Any thought of making love to her left him at that moment. Awkwardly he stepped forward and, after a moment's indecision, loosely embraced her, trying not to frighten her any more. He held her in the water's stream for several moments, before she pulled back a little and looked up into his eyes questioningly. Slowly, he shook his head once, and lifted his hand and swept the wet hair from her face. She stretched up in a quick movement and kissed him childishly on the cheek. He let her go and they resumed their shower and towelled off, neither one uttering one word of reproach nor explanation. After they had dressed, they picked up their things and walked out of the door.

Briefly thanking Harry, they left the baths behind them and headed off back towards the Embankment. The early afternoon sun was bright enough, but produced little heat to warm them, and they soon grew cold.

Above the traffic noise, they hardly noticed a screeching of brakes and a car door opening and slamming shut again, but when a man's voice, one that Brinn was not altogether unfamiliar with, called, 'Excuse me, sir,' he turned to see the face of the constable from Walter Street police station. Brinn froze for a second, then, without a word, grabbed Sarah's hand and made a run for it.

'There's no time to explain,' he shouted at her, 'just keep running.'

Always travelling in pairs, the second policeman, who had seen the flight from his position in the police car, revved up the engine and flung open the passenger door to receive the other constable. With tyres squealing they sped off down the road in hot pursuit of the supposed 'fleeing suspect', and his accomplice.

Brinn led Sarah down a side road and into a department store. They slowed as they hit the upward-bound escalator to appear more like ordinary shoppers, but still checking wildly about them to see if they had been followed.

'What is this all about?' Sarah whispered breathlessly.

'Not now,' he panted, 'I'll explain later.'

They continued their flight to the top by way of the lift, which they picked up on the first floor. Then, heading for the emergency staircase, they cut through the furniture department and, believing themselves to be out of danger, slowed a little and descended the stairs at a more even pace. One flight from the ground they halted and sat on the top step to get their breath back.

'Come on American, what is all this about?'

'Well,' he began, 'I think they want to arrest me for theft and obstruction, but it would be more accurate to say they should arrest me for impersonating myself.'

Sarah tried to follow his reasoning, but just then she spotted the two constables through a glass partition speaking to the shop manager who was pointing in the direction of the lift.

'Down!' she shouted to Brinn. 'They're just in there.'

They both ducked and began to slither down the remaining stairs to the ground floor. A quick check in each direction, and they stepped through the door into the cosmetic department. Wearing a deceptive air of disregard, they slowly walked towards the exit, then sprinted the last few steps through the exit and into the open air.

Just as Brinn was about to dash off across the road, Sarah put out her arm to stop him.

'Hang on a minute,' she said, grabbing an apple from an unsuspecting street vendor's stall.

'This is no time to stop for lunch,' Brinn said to her in exasperation.

'No, wait,' she said, biting from the apple as she ran over to where the police car stood.

She momentarily disappeared around the back of the stationary vehicle and then reappeared sporting a mischievous grin. She glanced both ways, then picked up speed, and as she passed Brinn she grabbed his arm and dragged him off just as the constables emerged from the store.

Checking first the direction in which the criminals were now fleeing, the policemen ran over to their car and jumped in. The driver quickly switched the ignition on. The engine turned over, but, mysteriously, did not fire.

'Come on, come on! They're getting away!' the constable urged.

The driver repeated the process, but still the engine refused to start. The frustrated constable pounded on the dashboard as if the vibration would aid the endeavours of the driver, but to no avail. The car refused to co-operate.

Now, a greater distance away, Brinn and Sarah slowed to a jog and then to a walk, still occasionally checking behind them.

'What were you doing behind the car?' Brinn asked her breathlessly.

'Oh, it's an old trick,' she replied. 'If you wedge something in the exhaust pipe, the engine won't turn over. They are probably still there now, trying to figure it out.'

Brinn began to chuckle and then laughed out loud, partly from relief and partly because he could see in his mind the baffled expression on the constables' faces.

'You really are something,' he said,

'Why, thank you, American. I'll take that as a compliment.'

They carried on walking for a while, and then Sarah turned to Brinn and stopped him.

'Up until now,' she began, 'I have had my suspicions about you, American. You've asked too many questions and behaved as though you don't really belong with us. However, it appears you have a criminal record so you have just gone up in my estimation at least seventy-five per cent.'

'I'll take that as a compliment, shall I?' he replied.

She looked deep into his eyes and smiled, and for a moment he thought he saw her begin to thaw a little.

The evening was drawing in and the streetlights began to flicker in long strings, illuminating the city. The tallest of the buildings stood out against the sky with their own individual patterns of light extending up into the night air, regally crowned with the obligatory red warning light, deterring any aircraft foolish enough to fly so low. Coloured neon hoardings flickered, advertising their wares to uninterested onlookers, and shop windows stood out against the grey buildings containing dummies depicting tableaux from some unknown Greek tragedy. Lines of exhausted shoppers queued patiently waiting for brightly lit red buses that always seemed to arrive in threes. Like long red snakes they gorged and disgorged themselves of their unsuspecting prey as they pulled up at each stop. Impatient drivers honked horns and gesticulated wildly, falsely believing their actions would hasten their departure from the congested thoroughfares.

Then, as the roads began to empty and the pavements cleared, a hush fell on the city; a slower, more gentle rhythm beat in the heart of the beast. Laughing companions entered street cafes and restaurants, intent on culinary delectation and recreation. Theatregoers eagerly sought intellectual diversion, whilst lovers walked the quiet Embankment, arm in arm, lost in the ambience that the seductive city emitted in its drowsy state. The beast was preparing to sleep again.

Along the Embankment, Brinn and Sarah walked side by side. The sky was clear, the evening chilly, and Brinn shivered. The absence of a coat was now most keenly felt.

'You cold?' Sarah asked, quietly turning to him.

'A bit,' he replied.

Then, taking him completely by surprise, she slipped her arm around his waist and pulled him close to her. Brinn reciprocated gladly by putting his arm around her shoulder and began to derive warmth from the contact.

'Tomorrow, we must get you another coat. You won't survive long out here without one,' she told him.

The aroma of a fast food vendor stopped them in their tracks. A look, a smile, and they altered direction towards the evocative smell. Sarah purchased two beef burgers and coffees, handing one of each to Brinn, and they went to find a bench to sit on overlooking the river. As they ate, small pleasure craft drifted slowly by, bringing music, laughter and the sound of faintly clinking glasses.

'The city sure is beautiful at night,' Brinn observed, sipping the steaming liquid.

'Beautiful, yes, but dangerous, too,' Sarah replied, licking the relish from her fingers.

Brinn wanted to ask, 'Why dangerous?' but thought the question would undermine his new status as a fully paid-up street person, so yet again he remained silent. He wrapped his hands around the polystyrene cup and the transferred heat made him feel warmer. Sarah gathered up the redundant wrappings from the burgers and took them over to a nearby bin, depositing them there. She did not return to Brinn, but rather walked over and stood by the wall overlooking the river. Brinn rose and went over to join her.

'Penny for them,' he said.

'They are not worth that much,' she replied. Then not quite able to look at him she added, 'What you did earlier – I mean what you didn't do – well, I, I appreciate it. It's my own fault really. If I had realised the gents was out of action…'

'It's nobody's fault,' Brinn interrupted.

He put his now empty cup down on the wall and placed his hands on her shoulders, turning her gently to face him.

Then, with a big smile on his face he said, 'But, believe me, it wasn't easy.'

She smiled warmly back at him and they turned and headed back towards the car park.

## Chapter Five

The dawn chorus was again the catalyst that roused Brinn
from sleep, though it did not seem to have any effect on the
others. For the hundredth time, he rolled onto his other
side, in a pointless attempt to get comfortable. There had
been a frost overnight, and the cardboard was stiff and bore
a white crystalline coat that cracked as he moved. Somewhere deep beneath it lay Sarah, who, like Brinn, was
wearing every item of clothing she possessed. At about two
in the morning, when it became so cold neither of them
could sleep, all their remaining clothes had been put on as a
barrier against the weather.

Sarah woke up, disturbed by Brinn shuffling about. She
tried to remain motionless. Experience had taught her that
any movement in these harsh conditions would bring an
unwelcome draught of cold air. Stretching to relieve his
discomfort, Brinn undid all her good intentions.

'You're impossible! Can't you keep still?' she shouted at
him.

'What?' he said restlessly.

'You're moving about too much. Keep still.'

But her warning came too late. All the warm air dissipated and cold air replaced it. Sarah shuddered and, with a
deep sigh, resigned herself to getting up. She left Brinn to
fidget on and went over to set the fire, not so much for the
heat it gave, for that was little enough, but more for the
secure feeling it engendered. It was the focal point of their
existence.

Josh was already awake and he reached out and took her
hand as she passed him.

'You all right, Sarah?'

'Yes, Josh, I think so,' she replied.

'Be careful with him,' he said, jerking his thumb in the direction of Brinn. 'I'll break his neck if he lays a finger on you.'

Sarah remembered how Josh had protected her in the past and did not doubt his intentions for a moment. She patted the hand now resting on hers and then continued to set the fire. A single flame rose, barely warming the air, and Brinn, hobbling badly and wearing the sleeping bag around his shoulders, joined them.

'Morning, Josh,' he said yawning.

Josh, staring into the fire, mumbled his greeting in return.

Then he looked up at Sarah and asked, 'Any of that tea going?'

'It will be ready in a moment,' she replied. 'What's the matter with your leg, American?'

'I think I must have pulled something when we were running away from the police yesterday.'

Josh turned his head to look at Brinn with growing interest.

'It was not too bad at first, but it seems to have stiffened up overnight,' he continued, as he rubbed the aching muscle.

'The wages of sin, eh?' Sarah laughed.

Then Josh, who chose his words carefully, asked, 'Why were they chasing you?'

Brinn, with feigned contempt and a wry smile replied, 'Josh, how long have you been on the streets? You should know better than to ask a question like that.'

At that moment, Sarah saw something she had not seen for a long time. A smile crept across Josh's lips and he extended a hand to Brinn. 'I'm not sure I trust you yet, American. You're way too slick, but if the pigs are after you, then maybe you're all right, man.'

Brinn took Josh's hand and shook it. 'You too, Josh,' he replied. 'You too.'

Pete slowly emerged from his protective pile and walked over to the fire and stood at Sarah's side. He put his arms around her. She responded, raising her arm and lowering it gently on his shoulder.

'Tea, Pete?' she asked.

Pete nodded, and Sarah released her hold momentarily to retrieve a mug of tea from the pot.

'Please take your medication today,' she said quietly to him as she handed him the mug.

He nodded and, taking the tea, returned to his bed. Sarah squatted down next to the fire. In a hushed voice she said to Josh, 'I have got to take the American here out to get a coat this morning, but I'm a bit worried about Pete. Do you think you and College could take turns to keep an eye on him?' Josh nodded and Sarah continued, 'Try not to leave him on his own for too long, please, Josh. You know what he gets like.'

Josh nodded again. Sarah stood up, returned to the mattress and started to pack the cardboard away neatly. Brinn joined her and rolled up the sleeping bag and stowed it under the mattress.

'No, I want to take it with me,' she said to him.

Brinn shrugged his shoulders and tucked it into his pack instead. As she picked up her own pack and turned to leave, Sarah spoke to Josh once more.

'You won't forget, will you, Josh? Ask College when he wakes up to help you. Keep an eye on Pete, okay?'

Dismissing them with a gesture, Josh turned back to the fire. Brinn and Sarah departed, with Sarah for once more than a little apprehensive.

They were heading for the newsagents where they had picked up their breakfast the day before, and Brinn assumed that they would do so again today. Sarah however, walked straight past and continued to walk through unfamiliar streets for a further ten minutes, coming to a halt outside a Salvation Army hall.

'Breakfast,' she said, eyebrows raised and an impish grin on her face.

Entering the building was like stepping through a time warp. The hall was long and completely clad in wood. It had a raised platform at one end, with a large coloured banner reading 'Jesus is Lord' hanging on the wall above. A light oak-coloured altar table stood immediately beneath, with a matching lectern two feet in front of it at the edge of the stage. At intervals along the opposite wall were small stacks of wooden chairs with book carriers on the back. Piles of dusty well-worn hymnbooks crowded for space on the window ledges, while the windows above looked as though once, long ago, they had been the proud bearers of beautiful stained glass. Now, only a few fragments of coloured panes remained, the missing spaces having been substituted with plain or frosted oddments, creating a crazy patchwork effect.

A legacy of inner city vandalism, Brinn thought to himself.

The floor of the hall had been temporarily transformed with odd sets of tables and chairs haphazardly arranged with cutlery and condiments. A few diners were already in place, making short work of the food in front of them. Brinn followed Sarah to the line of expectant diners yet unserved, and they waited patiently to receive their offering.

Minus the traditional hat, a female army officer, clad in uniform and wearing a long white apron, was busy cooking and serving for the line of down-and-outs. She was not so ably assisted by a younger, more nervous girl recruit who was also clad in the traditional garb. It appeared to be the first time that the recruit had tendered her services in this line of work. The fear of contact with unwashed humanity was visibly etched in her face. One by one, she gingerly handed plates through the hatchway that separated the kitchen from the hall to those queueing patiently. In turn, Brinn and Sarah took the plates handed to them and retired to one of the empty tables to examine their meal.

'It's good, but not quite as good as Al's,' Brinn remarked, knife and fork in hand, resting them in an upright position on the table.

'Any port in a storm,' she replied, the remark's significance eluding Brinn.

Quite a crowd had built up in the hall now and several uniformed officers passed from table to table talking to their occupants. Sarah had finished her meal quickly, and she stood up and looked around as if searching for someone.

'I won't be a moment. Hang on here a moment,' she said to Brinn, leaving him to finish on his own.

One or two of his fellow diners were beginning to look him up and down warily and he began to feel a little uncomfortable. Relief arrived, Brinn thought, in the shape of an elderly male army officer who asked if he might join him. Brinn welcomed the distraction gladly. The officer smiled broadly at Brinn, but said nothing.

A few embarrassing moments passed, until Brinn broke the uneasy silence and asked, 'Pardon me, but do I know you? You seem a little familiar.'

'Why, yes, son, in a manner of speaking you might say that. As soon as I heard your accent, I said to my commander, that is the nice young American gentleman we met a few nights ago when we were out in the van. He remembered you, too, as the one we have all been praying for.'

Recognition registered across Brinn's face as he remembered the incident.

'Saved my life that night,' Brinn said as he recalled how cold he had been.

'That's what we are in the business for, son. Excuse me just a minute while I fetch you some leaflets to read.'

Sarah, who had returned clutching some items of men's clothing, waited for the officer to leave Brinn's table. Then she swooped in and urgently suggested that he might like to follow her immediately. Brinn protested, telling her that it was impolite as the officer was returning at any moment, and after all, had they not just provided them with a meal?

'Have it your own way. Don't say I didn't try to warn you. I'll wait for you outside,' she said and she exited the hall.

Sarah waited the twenty minutes it took Brinn to extricate himself, sitting in the sunshine on the adjacent wall swinging her legs. Eventually, an embattled and bemused Brinn emerged, clutching a wad of leaflets in his hand. Bold lettering at the top proclaimed such titles as 'What is it like to be a real Christian?', 'Salvation, your only hope', and 'Jesus, yesterday, today and for ever'. With her arms folded defiantly and an 'I told you so' expression on her face, she waited for him to speak.

'What hit me?' he asked, as he looked back over his shoulder in the direction of the hall.

'Old-time religion,' she said triumphantly with a broad smile. 'You will learn by your mistakes, American. Anyway, I managed to get you these things from their store out back, so it was not a total waste of time.'

She held each item aloft, and then up against him, to see if the size was about right. The two shirts were fine, the trousers a little too long, but not bad, and the real prize in the collection, the much-needed overcoat, had only one button missing. Folding the things, she put them in her pack. Then, together with the still dazed Brinn, she set off for the laundrette.

An odd building jammed in between a butcher and a florist, the laundrette seemed like a haven after a storm. Along one of the interior walls stood a bank of top-loading washing machines, elderly, but serviceable. Half the length of the opposite wall was taken up with industrial-sized tumble dryers set two feet up from the floor. Beneath was a long wooden bench which at present held an old tramp and two young women. The other half of the wall contained a soap and conditioner dispenser, a pay phone and a change machine with no interior working parts, or change either.

Perhaps it had worked once years ago, Brinn thought, but it must have proved too great a temptation for the district's light finger brigade.

On the floor in front of the washing machines were two oval, red plastic washing baskets. Both were completely unserviceable as one had had the bottom kicked out of it and the other contained an ugly child who was playing 'boats'. Brinn did not think it worth anyone's effort to try to evict the child, as he would probably have bitten them.

Sarah began to remove the items designated for the wash from the backpacks. The sleeping bag was one, the few items acquired from the Salvation Army store were the second, and some underwear of hers and Brinn's constituted the remainder.

Then, turning to Brinn she said, 'Come on, hand them over.'

'Pardon me?' he replied.

'Your clothes! The extra ones you put on last night.'

'No way,' he protested. 'I'm not undressing in here.'

'No, you idiot! Just the dirty ones on top.' Then, to deliberately add to his confusion and embarrassment, she turned to the young women and said, 'You don't mind if my American friend takes his clothes off to put them in the wash, do you?'

Their faces lit up and one replied, 'What! Like that advert on the telly where he is left in only his underpants?'

'Well, not quite that far,' Sarah said, looking at Brinn to reassure him.

'Oh, shame!' the other woman shouted back, retreating behind her hand to exchange a few coarsely humorous remarks concerning Brinn's physique with her friend.

'There you are,' she said to Brinn again. 'You are in the clear.'

Brinn, trying to half conceal himself beside the last tumble dryer, began to peel off his external layers, throwing them over to Sarah, who put them in the machine. The ugly kid had now disembarked from his vessel and was standing directly in front of Brinn watching intently. Brinn was in the last throes of trying to remove his trousers, without first having removed his shoes. He knew this was a mistake even before he started, but the presence of the ugly kid had distracted and unnerved him slightly. He had managed to get one leg out, but was hopping about the floor madly as his right shoe had stuck fast in the leg of the trousers. The ugly kid was in hysterics, as were the two women, and Sarah had to come to his rescue, providing something to hold on to and an extra pair of hands.

'You really should be in street entertainment, American. You're very funny,' she said, kneeling on the floor laughing.

'This whole thing is ridiculous,' he said angrily and then to the ugly kid, who was still helpless with laughter, he snapped, 'What's the name of your boat, sonny, *Titanic*?'

'No,' the ugly kid said, 'It's the *QE2*.'

'Pity!' Brinn replied, glowering at the boy who then went scooting back to one of the two women and buried his head in her lap. A little sheepishly, he occasionally peered up, to observe his protagonist.

'Calm down, American, he's only a kid.'

'Not for much longer if I can get hold of him,' Brinn replied.

The shoe came free and Brinn was able to stand on his own two feet again. Sarah finished loading and setting the machine before the two of them took their place on the bench. The ugly kid grew a little bolder and let go of his mother and on hands and knees tried to salvage his boat unobserved. Sarah settled with an old magazine, while Brinn tried to doze. Images of the ugly kid imprisoned in one of the tumble dryers and rotating like items of washing drifted through his mind. He was woken by a sharp pain in his shins, and when he opened his eyes he saw that the brat had slammed the boat into his legs. He stood only two feet in front of him, a broad triumphant grin on his face. Brinn picked up the basket and was about to hurl it when he felt Sarah's arm across his.

'Yeah, okay. He's only a kid, I know,' he said, and with a frustrated sigh, tucked the basket under the bench he was sitting on, wedging it in with his legs. Reduced to a cease-fire, Brinn folded his arms across his chest and stared the boy down with a 'touch the basket and you die' expression on his face. The brat studied Brinn for a moment, then decided that perhaps this time it would be too risky. He coyly backed away to the safety of his mother's side. Brinn sighed, satisfied that it was now safe to close his eyes again.

About three quarters of an hour later, Brinn woke up to find the women and the ugly kid had gone. Only he, Sarah and the old tramp remained. Brinn had not really taken much notice of the old man with all the commotion earlier. Now, in the absence of any distraction, apart from watching the washing rotating in the tumble dryer, the old man drew Brinn's attention. Sitting at an oblique angle in the corner, the old tramp seemed oblivious to everything going on around him. His eyes were the only part of his face visible through hair and beard, both of long coarse strands, some matted with filth. He wore boots on his feet; no socks, just boots, open and without laces and the tongue draped forward. With an old brown mackintosh tied at the waist with string covering a pair of shabby green corduroy trousers, he made a sad and yet, at the same time, slightly comic figure. The hardest thing for Brinn to grasp, however, was that the old gent seemed to be holding an in-depth conversation with no one in particular. It was like watching an excerpt from the old James Stuart movie, *Harvey*; all the gestures, the inflections and responses were there, but most definitely without a visible Harvey. Sarah's voice cut across Brinn's thoughts.

'DTs,' she said. Seeing him shake his head, mystified, she added, 'Hallucinations, from alcohol.'

Brinn nodded his understanding.

'Can we do anything,' he asked.

She shook her head.

'Just leave him alone. He's safe and warm here until the police move him on.'

The tumble dryer had stopped and Sarah busied herself with putting the clothes into the packs, while Brinn made himself useful rolling up the sleeping bag.

'Armani,' she said, impressed, as she noticed the label on the now freshly laundered shirt Brinn had brought from home.

'Yes,' he replied. 'I, er, picked it up at a charity shop.'

'Lucky you,' she added, satisfied with his answer.

They left the tramp behind in the laundrette and decided to return, with the heavy packs, to check on Pete.

Sarah could not quite put her finger on it. Everything seemed the same as when they had left earlier, but there was something not quite right. They were turning the corner at the bottom of the steps leading to the car park's lower floor. Their eyes grew accustomed to the gloom; College and Josh were nowhere to be seen.

Pete was all right, though, Sarah thought. She could still see him curled up in his bed exactly where they had left him. She went to put her pack down on the mattress, and it was Brinn who first spotted something wrong. Something dark and damp was oozing from Pete's sleeping bag, turning the ground gradually red.

'Pete!' he called out, as he began to walk over to the figure on the ground. Pete gave no reply, but Sarah turned as she heard the anxiety in Brinn's voice.

'No, stay there, Sarah,' Brinn said firmly, with his hand extended in her direction.

She stood staring at the small bundle on the ground that she knew as Pete, unable to move even if Brinn had given her a direct order to do so. Brinn slowly lifted the corner of the sleeping bag, and saw that, as he had feared, Pete had slashed his wrists. An old broken vodka bottle lay at his side, blood highlighting the jagged edge. Pete was still alive, just, but his breathing was shallow and laboured, and his skin very pale.

'Sarah,' Brinn called urgently, 'go for an ambulance now!'

She was still too shocked to move and remained rigidly bolted to the spot.

'Now, Sarah! Go!'

Suddenly snapping out of her trance, she ran out into the street to find a phone box. Brinn pulled off his sweater and tossed it to one side. Next his shirt came off, which he began frantically to tear into long strips. Brinn wrapped them tightly round Pete's wrists and the pressure caused him to groan, but he made little movement. Blood was still seeping from the wounds through the makeshift bandages, and Brinn had to repeat the process several times before he could stem the flow completely. It seemed like an age, but finally the ambulance pulled up outside. Sarah ran in ahead of the paramedics, having remained on the street, partly in order to show them the way, but mostly because she was afraid to look at Pete.

The two men worked quickly and professionally on Pete, simultaneously asking all the standard questions about name, age and address. Brinn had to prompt Sarah continually for the information, dazed as she still was. Having stabilised Pete as best they could, the crew began to load him into the ambulance. Brinn made use of this opportunity to grab another shirt from his pack and put it on. Then, looking around, he managed to attract the attention of one of the paramedics. He took him aside and spoke a few words to him, to which the young man nodded.

Both Sarah and Brinn were allowed to accompany Pete in the ambulance on the journey to hospital. As they raced through the streets of the city, the siren blaring, Brinn kept a wary eye on Sarah. She seemed calm enough, but the blank expression on her face worried him. He wished she would cry or scream or something; anything.

They pulled up outside the casualty department and rapidly became superfluous as the team of trained doctors and nurses rushed Pete on a trolley through double swing doors. Sarah seemed uneasy as a very young nurse ushered them into a small sad little room just down the corridor from where Pete was being attended to. It was just like hundreds of waiting rooms all over the country.

The walls were lined with plastic chairs, and a small coffee table in the centre of the room bore magazines from millennia ago. A box of children's toys that had a beaten-up old teddy bear on the top stood in one corner, while discarded toys lay strewn across the floor. A few tired posters adorned the walls, calling the viewers' attention to 'holiday vaccines', the 'danger of unprotected sex' and the 'family planning clinic'. The one point of contact with the outside world was a small window with horizontal bars, a relic, no doubt, left over from a less compassionate age. Brinn sat down opposite the door, and Sarah picked up one of the old magazines and flipped through the pages. She had hardly had it in her hand for thirty seconds when she threw it down on the table again, and began to pace up and down the floor, desperately ill at ease.

'What's the matter, Sarah?' Brinn asked her.

'I can't stand these places. They give me the creeps.'

A voice could be heard in the distance over the tannoy.

'Would Doctor Matthews report to triage in the casualty unit please. Would Doctor Matthews report to triage in the casualty unit please. Thank you.'

Then silence, with just the quiet humming of the overworked Victorian heating system in the background for company. Through the frosted glass in the door they could see people in white coats rushing past. One nurse pushed a small trolley by the window, and a doctor held on to his stethoscope to prevent it swinging about wildly as he ran. Then silence again. Brinn and Sarah looked at each other. Their eyes exchanged the feeling of total helplessness. Sarah sat down heavily, and all that was left for Brinn to do was to comfort her, though there seemed little point, as most of his previous attempts had ended in disaster. He gave it a try anyway, managing to put an arm around her, but it was Sarah who drew him closer to her.

The time passed slowly, but then it never passed any other way in a hospital. The thirty minutes they had to wait for news could easily have been thirty hours, and when finally a nurse came in, Brinn jumped to his feet.

'Any news yet?' he asked.

'I'm sorry Mr, Mr... I did not get your last name,' the nurse replied unemotionally.

'Bernard, Mr and Mrs Bernard,' he replied.

'Well, Mr Bernard,' she continued, 'it's going to be a

while yet, I'm afraid. Would you and your, er, wife like a cup of tea while you wait?'

Brinn was irritated with the way she looked down her nose at them and seemed to be aware that Bernard might not be their real name. Still, he kept up the pretence.

'Yes, that would be nice, thank you.'

The nurse left the room, giving Brinn one last quizzical look as she closed the door behind her. The event had not registered with Sarah; her mind was elsewhere, her ears straining at every sound, trying to glean some information from the activity beyond the confines of the waiting room.

The tea arrived five minutes later and, without a word, was set on the table. The nurse left with only a curt 'thank you' from Brinn for her trouble. He poured Sarah a cup, which she did not pick up, so he took it and placed it in her hands.

'Here, this might help a bit,' he said.

She looked up at him blankly, as if she was unable to recognise him. In an effort to try to communicate with her, he added, 'It's a bit of a mess, isn't it?'

Still looking at him, her expression began to change to one of anger.

'What the hell do you know about it anyway? You've been here five minutes and all of a sudden you're an authority.'

She slammed the cup onto the table, sending much of the contents spilling over the surface. Then she stood up, her hands and her voice shaking as a confused torrent of words poured out. At that moment, the distinction between Brinn and her father had become rather blurred for Sarah, and it took Brinn a few moments to realise what had happened.

'You were never any good to us from the beginning. You set mum against me and you made her make all those arrangements, didn't you? Didn't you? Have you any idea just what that butcher did to me, you bastard? He did not even bring sterile instruments. I was four months pregnant when you let him loose.'

Brinn took hold of her arm to try to calm her, but she shook him free, and looked straight into his eyes, her voice at breaking point.

'She was so small, tiny like a doll. Helpless, and you killed her.'

Sarah broke off and stepped back, the anger very apparent in her face now. Suddenly, she swung her arm wildly and slapped Brinn across the side of his mouth. He put his hand to his stinging face, stunned for a moment. Then, knowing he had to do something to snap her out of this, but unsure of exactly what that something was, he took her in his arms and kissed her full on the mouth. She struggled to get free, and succeeded in pushing him away.

'Who the hell do you think you are?' she screamed at him. 'You're not my bloody father.'

'That's right, Sarah,' he said, his voice softening as he spoke. 'That's right,' he said again stretching out his arms, 'I'm not your father.'

Sarah stared at him as she grappled with reality, then her anger melted into realisation, and from realisation into tears, and Brinn took her in his arms again, not this time to kiss her, but to comfort her. The same curt nurse threw open the waiting room door.

'Mr and Mrs Bernard, we appreciate that you are distressed at the moment, but please could you keep the noise down? There are other sick people out here, you know.'

Her words went unheeded, as they were, by now, unnecessary. Brinn continued to hold a sobbing Sarah in his arms, and the first grains of genuine warmth were exchanged between them. The irate nurse, with no further means to vent her frustration, left the room in a huff.

Two hours went by, and the tea had gone cold in the pot on the table. Brinn was up at the window staring out at the traffic below making its way home in the rush hour. His thoughts were in that other world, that other world that seemed so far away now. Was it really only three days ago that he had left it, or was it four? All the days just blurred into each other. The door opened quietly and Brinn turned to see a nervous young man in a white coat with a stethoscope around his neck. Brinn assumed, correctly, that this was the doctor.

I wonder if this is his first time, Brinn thought, knowing already what the doctor would say. There had been just too much blood loss for it to be any different, but he had not mentioned his concerns to Sarah, as she just wasn't in any state to hear them. The doctor came in and closed the door behind him. Sarah looked up from where she was sitting by the radiator and Brinn moved over to join her.

'Keep him away from me, American,' she muttered under her breath while clinging to his arm.

'It's all right Sarah. He's not going to hurt you.'

'Well now, Mr and Mrs Bernard,' he started, trying to ignore Sarah's obvious aversion to him.

Sarah glanced at Brinn, the mode of address having caught her attention this time. Brinn shook his head and she let the question drop.

'My name is Doctor Matthews,' he continued, 'and I have been tending your son.'

Brinn found it amazing how young this doctor was, considering the life and death decisions he had to make. How could he possibly train for moments like these?

'I am very sorry; there is no easy way to tell you this. We did everything humanly possible for your son, but he had lost too much blood by the time he arrived here. He passed away a few moments ago.'

Without a flicker of emotion, Sarah stood and calmly

said, 'I want to see him.'

'Do you think that is wise right now? I mean—'

Brinn cut the doctor short and said, 'If she wants to see him, she is going to see him. Understand?'

The doctor, unprepared for the outburst, raised his arms in a gesture of surrender and said, 'Why, yes, of course. If you will just give me a moment, I will make the necessary arrangements.'

He stood and left the room, and Sarah utilised the interval to ask, 'Mr and Mrs Bernard?'

'It was necessary to get them to take us in the ambulance,' he said.

She squeezed his hand and smiled warmly as the doctor rejoined them.

'If you would come this way, please,' he said to them, indicating the direction down the corridor.

He led them into a side room painted all white and containing nothing but a glass-fronted cabinet, a hand basin, and a stainless steel trolley bearing Pete, who was lying beneath a white sheet. His face and upper chest were visible, and they were the colour of the sheet. His arms had been discreetly placed beneath the sheet at his side.

Odd, Sarah thought, it's the first time I've seen him looking so peaceful.

She smoothed his hair and tenderly moved a strand that was caught in his eyelashes. Then, feeling beneath the sheet, she took out one of his limp, bandaged hands and held it up close to her cheek. Brinn left Sarah to say her goodbyes while he went to the front desk to try to straighten out the slight next-of-kin error. Brinn was joined moments later by a tear-stained Sarah, and they departed together, walking in silence, leaving the baffled charge nurse shuffling through his record cards and log sheets.

They stepped out from the warm clinical atmosphere of the hospital into the cold city air. During their ordeal it had begun to rain again, and neither of them could really face the long walk back.

'We'll use the tube.'

Her words surprised Brinn, who thought that surely she did not intend to try that now, not now of all times. He thought better of arguing with her and followed her into the mass of commuters heading for the station. They fitted in well; blank-faced, expressionless automatons in a seething tide of humanity. As they approached the station entrance, Sarah produced some money from her pocket, bringing a silent sigh of relief from Brinn, who could remember only too well his last efforts at 'winging it'. She purchased two tickets and they passed on down the escalators with the throng to the platform that was packed, but fairly subdued.

The first rush of warm air propelled down the tunnel by the oncoming train washed over the sea of faces, ruffling hair and blowing loose rubbish along the track. Then the lights, the roaring and the screeching of brakes, and the train had arrived. As though they had no will of their own, the mass jostled onto the train and wedged into a space already crammed almost to capacity. Brinn turned to face Sarah in order to get a better grip on a handrail over her head. More passengers packed in and it seemed madness to him that they didn't stop. Surely, they could see how full it was already. The train lurched forward and the sudden jolt caused Sarah to lose her balance. Brinn released his hold on the rail and put his arms around her to prevent her from falling any further. She was glad of human contact and responded by putting her arms around him. Then, closing her eyes, she tried to block out everything. She had some vain hope that, if she tried hard enough, the memory of today would just go away. Endless minutes passed, but neither one of them was counting, until the train stopped and they had arrived at the station closest to their destination. Brinn led Sarah off the train and back towards the car park. Each tried to make some sense of their emotions, but both longed more for tomorrow to come.

Josh and College were there, waiting for them as they descended the steps.

'How is he?' Josh asked them before they had any time to think.

Brinn stopped abruptly,

'What do you mean, "How is he?" The hell you care! How did you know there was anything wrong with him?'

He waited for a reply, but none was forthcoming, then continued.

'You weren't here, were you?'

Seeing Brinn's incredulity, Sarah interrupted, 'Calm down, American.' Then she turned to Josh and said, 'I'm sorry, Josh, he died.'

Josh looked away and did not see Brinn advancing towards him, but became alarmed as Brinn grabbed his jacket and screamed at him.

'You knew, you bastard, and you did nothing! You could have prevented this!'

Brinn lifted his clenched fist and was about to hit Josh when Sarah grabbed his arm and hung on. 'American, stop! Not like this! You don't understand.'

Brinn, needing to vent his anger on something, walked over to the shopping trolley and kicked it hard, knocking it over.

'Please, American,' she began more softly, and taking him by the hand, she led him over to the mattress where she encouraged him to sit.

'It's difficult for you to understand, I know, but we live by different rules out here. Josh could no more have phoned for help than I could walk off a cliff. For a start, he is wanted by the police. We all are for one thing or other. Things are more complicated for him because he's a known junkie and scared rigid that if they pick him up, they will put him away for good. Pete knew this, as we all do, and we all have to take our chances out here and play our hand as we see it.'

'Small comfort for Pete, or his family. For God's sake, Sarah, he might have lived!'

Sarah shook her head, trying to find the words that would pacify him, but he found his voice first.

'He could have got help. He could have made a difference. You all could.'

'What are you playing at?' she said. 'You're not one of us, or you would understand what's going on here.'

'It's different in the States.'

'Yeah, right!'

'Look, I'm sorry. This whole thing has got to me.'

'Bullshit!'

'Sarah, please. Just look at me. Do you really think I'm kidding?'

Sarah looked hard at him. There was no doubt that he was shaking, but that proved little. He could just be trying to cover his tracks.

'Please Sarah,' he urged, 'help me out here. Cut me a little slack.'

Sarah knew she would probably end up regretting her decision but she said, 'Okay. Okay, American, but you had better be a fast learner, because I'm just about sick of covering for you. We have lived a lifetime being used, abused, or rejected, or a mixture of all three. We don't need you on our backs as well. If you had struggled to survive as we have against a life that sapped you of the one thing vital to everyone's existence, you might just have an idea of what was going on. It's not the lack of a home, nor the lack of money, not even the absence of a family. It's the desperate need to be valued as a human being, to regain the self-respect that has been torn from us by our circumstances.

Society tells us to get off our backsides: "You can change, you can get help, you can make a proper life for yourself." So desperate are we to fit in, we dutifully try and seek help, we try to change, only to find that we are sent back to the very situations which threw us a curve in the first place, and we are no more near our goal than before we tried. The do-gooders all disappear off to their comfortable warm homes, patting themselves on the back for a job well done, while we try to grapple with a lifestyle that is unfamiliar and frightening. Yes, we are accepted, as long as we conform, as long as we can prove ourselves worthy, but the moment we start to struggle, society turns its back on us again. Our only hope then is to return to what we know and to each other for comfort and support. Then we are labelled pariahs. The only answer, as far as society is concerned, is to shove the responsibility onto someone else. Is it any surprise that few of us can cope? If you lose the plot like Pete, you make the choice and get out. Surely to God, you must know all this already, American. After all, you say you have been on the streets now for what, five years?'

'Yes, but it never got so bad that I needed to take that decision,' he replied.

'You're lucky then, aren't you, American, that you don't have to kill yourself like Pete. There are other ways to get out. College, for example, his way is booze. Josh, drugs. What's yours, American? What's your get out clause?'

This was the second time she had make him think about his situation and he did not feel he would be able to sidestep the issue quite so easily this time. He felt trapped. His whole life had been a sort of escape, just as theirs had been. The continual need, for instance, to ring Carol, even though he knew she had only used him. He had needed that security. There was his inability to face the idea that his career was slowly slipping into obscurity, his past successes merely a thin veneer separating him from reality. That he continually let Chris down was not in dispute, and maybe he had been the instigator in his separation and ultimate divorce. God, what a mess! The only real difference between them was that they retreated from their nightmares here on the streets aided by drink or drugs, and he retreated from his behind the dubious security of money and respectability.

'I'm not sure,' he said at last, trying to convince himself more than her, 'but I know I would never let it get that bad.'

'Bravo, my boy!' the long silent College joined in. 'Perhaps you will succeed where we have failed.'

Brinn felt embarrassed at his stupidity and, turning his back to them, he lay down as though to sleep. At that moment the thought of returning to his other, more safe existence was a great temptation. He hated being forced to take a good hard look at himself, but even more, he hated feeling vulnerable.

Sarah made the usual arrangements with the bedding, and tried to slip in behind him.

'Sometimes you can be wonderful, American, but the rest of the time you can be a complete bastard.'

On this occasion, it was he who was reluctant to make any contact and he shrugged her off as she attempted to comfort him. He preferred to remain with his own thoughts. It was the longest night of his life.

## Chapter Six

Brinn was the first one to surface the following morning. Restlessness had driven him from the mattress. Sarah trembled a little as he rose, so he rearranged the sleeping bag and cardboard around her before he went to make up the fire.

'I think you might have a bit of a temperature,' he said to her. 'You're mighty warm and a little pale. How do you feel?'

'I'll be okay,' she replied.

Brinn's ability to light a fire was tested to the limit, the only combustible material available being slightly damp. Then, finally, with the assistance of a few bits of dry paper that a sheepish Josh handed to him, he managed to get it going. Brinn was unable to express to Josh any regret for the events of the night before, or sorrow for the loss of his friend, as he was still unsure where wrong ended and right began. He settled for resting his hand briefly on Josh's shoulder, but quickly removed it again when Josh flinched. It was obvious to him that it was going to take more than just a gesture, and still not inclined to make a decision, Brinn let the matter drop. The thought of food began to occupy Brinn's mind and he went over to Sarah and sat down beside her.

'You up to a visit to Al's?' he asked.

'Yes, sure. Just give me a few moments to pull myself together.'

Sarah sat herself up wearily and tried to shake the muzzy feeling from her head, hoping the weakness and aching in her arms and legs would dissipate with some tea. Brinn was in quite a hurry to get to Al's, and practically dragged Sarah away from the others, but not before she had managed to have a few words with them alone.

When they arrived, Al was at the front of the cafe seeing to some other customers, so Brinn steered the feverish Sarah through to the kitchen at the back.

Al followed them through seconds later and said, 'Ah Sarah, American, twice in one week? What is the special occasion?'

'Al,' she began, 'I'm afraid I have some rather bad news. Pete, he… he killed himself yesterday.'

Al stood stunned for a moment, then with his hand to his mouth he nodded slowly and said, 'Ah, yes, poor Pete. I think it had to come to this. He was too good for this world.'

Al's heavy sentimentality would have seemed out of place if anyone else had spoken it. From Al, however, it conveyed a genuine respect for the human life that had been taken so young, so tragically. Sarah stepped forward and hugged him.

Then, as she stepped back again he remarked, 'You don't look too well, Sarah. You taking good care of yourself?'

'I'm fine, really, just a bit of a cold, I think,' she said, dismissing the issue with a wave of her hand. 'Do you think you could let the others know and tell them we will meet on Sunday in the usual place, up by the monument.'

'Of course, it will be no problem. Now go and sit yourselves down. I'll get you both something to eat.'

Brinn followed Sarah through and they sat down at the same table they had used before.

'What is all this about?' he asked her.

'Funeral arrangements,' she replied.

'They can't arrange it that quickly and on a Sunday, can they?' he continued as he fiddled with the sugar dispenser.

A moment's pause was followed by a feverish barrage.

'Why don't you tell me who the hell you really are, American?' she began, the sudden outburst interrupted by a fit of coughing. 'Everything you do and almost everything you say make it quite obvious you are not one of us. Everyone knows that next of kin seldom want any of us at the real funeral. It's certainly so in Pete's case. His mum never accepted that he would not live with her and she blames us for the guilt she feels. Having us at the graveside would only remind her of how he chose to live his life. It can be too much for them.'

'Then, what funeral are you talking about?'

Fighting the growing ague, she replied wearily, 'We hold our own kind of service. We get together to remember Pete.'

Fortunately for Brinn, the food arrived just as she finished speaking, so he was able to avoid any further ignorant questions.

'Here you are, my dears,' Al announced as he set the loaded plates before them.

Sarah had insisted on lighting a candle for Pete, though Brinn did not see the need for it. In the doghouse again for opening his mouth before he had thought through what he should say, he tagged along meekly without any protest. The pleasant tree-lined garden around the perimeter of the cathedral provided a welcome respite from the traffic's constant drone. It was hard to believe such a haven existed only a few steps away from the raging madness out on the street. An austere grandeur crowned the building that rose from the flowerbeds and paved terraces below. Decades of fealty and worship had been absorbed into the stones, imparting a slightly arrogant air to the static monument to man's attempt to impress God. A cascade of steps drew the eye up to the entrance where many a great personage had once trod. Now, though, only long queues of inquisitive tourists shuffled their feet, impatient to begin their avocation of trophy-hunting courtesy of Kodak.

A sign at the entrance announced two pounds fifty pence per adult, children under five free, reduction for OAPs and coaches. Discarding his initial thoughts about the morality of charging to enter a church, Brinn asked, 'We can't go in, Sarah. Look how much it is.'

'You don't have to pay if you're going in for private prayer,' she replied, 'but whether they would believe us or not is another thing. They try to dissuade homeless people on the grounds they clutter up the place and make it look untidy. Just keep your mouth shut and do exactly as I do.'

Taking him by the sleeve, Sarah pulled Brinn up the steps and they joined the queue.

Down on the road below, two coaches had drawn up to disgorge their occupants. A swarm of Japanese tourists, whose usual excited chatter could be heard above the traffic, spilt out onto the pavement. They were weighed down with a wealth of photographic devices – Nikon, Canon, Olympus – enough to have opened a small shop with. Sarah kept a wary eye on one of the two groups, studying its progress along the path and up the steps. As the end of the first group drew level with her, she grabbed Brinn's hand and pulled him out of their own line, to merge between the Japanese.

'You are too tall, American. You will have to squat down a bit.'

Brinn did not have a chance to rationalise the absurd instructions before Sarah grabbed the waistband of his trousers and yanked it hard down. Realising that if didn't comply with the request, the chances of him ending up with his trousers around his knees were high, he quickly responded. In his 'Groucho Marx' type position, and half concealing his face behind a hastily gathered information booklet, he struggled after Sarah through the revolving door. A short way into the main cathedral and away from the entrance, they extracted themselves from the Japanese tour group and made their own way in the opposite direction.

Already the nave of the cathedral contained several different groups of eager tourists. The German, French and, of course, the Japanese groups, had language translations provided in heavily whispered tones, while heads tilted back to follow and observe the direction of each guide's pointing finger. A smaller group scurried across the floor, hot on the heels of their interpreter who held high her umbrella with a yellow handkerchief tied to it as a rallying point.

Sarah took Brinn on a detour around the visitors and led him to the area set aside for private worship. Despite her efforts, they were being observed by an overly concerned usher. They had first caught his eye with their odd behaviour at the door, and convinced he was on to something, he continued to watch their movements closely from behind a pillar.

Against a wall to one side of the nave was a long shelf containing many lighted candles all at different stages of combustion. Sarah took a few precious coins from her pocket and deposited them in the offertory box next to the sign, 'new candles for sale'. Then, taking a light from one of the already ignited candles, she placed it on the shelf and stood watching it for a moment. Sarah retired to one of the many nearby pews and knelt forward to pray.

Brinn joined her, but sat back with his arms resting over the back of the pew. He had always been a person of few beliefs, other than those of self-preservation, the need for fame and the acquisition of wealth. As he looked around the cathedral at the marble tombs dedicated to the rich and famous, he decided that these attributes had paid off in their day also, gaining them a place in history. His momentary daydream alarmed him and he removed his arms from the pew as he envisioned his own tomb some years hence. Visions of aggrieved friends pelting his resting place with rotten fruit and vegetables and creditors spray-painting abusive witticisms suddenly haunted him. He shuddered and slipped from his seat onto his knees beside Sarah, but only partly for Pete's sake. It was mostly for his own.

There was a polite and discreet cough behind them that brought both Brinn and Sarah from their thoughts to the attention of the watchful usher.

'Excuse me, sir, are you on your own or are you with a party?'

The guilty pair looked first at each other then back to the usher, and Sarah replied boldly, 'Why, yes, we are with the party of Japanese.'

Brinn, realising just how ridiculous this must have sounded, added as he stood, 'Yes, that's right. We are, er, related by, er, marriage. I'm Mr Wong, and this is Mrs Ling.'

Sarah looked at Brinn, her eyebrows raised and incredulity written all over her face. Then, simultaneously, they started to laugh. The usher looked down his nose at the pair, and sniffed loudly. Most conversations and silent prayers ceased and all eyes turned to look at the near hysterical pair.

'It's all right,' Brinn said, still chuckling, 'we are just leaving.'

He grabbed Sarah's hand, and pulled her towards the exit.

'You really are an idiot, American. Mr Wong and Mrs Ling! What are you like?'

Sarah giggled as they walked down the steps.

'It's your fault for saying we were with the Japanese. What else could I say?'

'Just leave all the explanations to me from now on, all right. It's obvious you'd never win an Oscar for a performance, unless it was a comedy.'

They spent the rest of the day walking around from place to place telling others about the arrangements for Pete's 'funeral'. It was a humbling experience for Brinn, the second of the morning, to see just how and where these people lived. Some of them were better off, but most worse off than Sarah and the others.

They met a group of older men who held court on the north side of the river. A regal throne indeed, were the benches on the north bank of the river, that had highly polished wooden slats spanning elaborate cast iron sphinxes, entirely set on a raised concrete platform. In the early summer the group would solicit help from passing tourists from under the delicate green canopy provided by the newly sprouting birch trees, and at night they would sleep the sleep of inebriety. In the winter, they would decamp to warmer climes, perhaps the shelters, or doorways, anything rather than experience the cruel icy wind that rolled up the river from the sea. Proud men these, with little of this world's riches, but always ready to share their piteous wealth with their own kind. They were harmless, and not aggressive in their soliciting like the new type of beggars just recently on the scene. Sarah spoke to them for several minutes about the 'funeral', and Brinn listened to their concerned response to the death of Pete.

One of the men turned and offered Brinn a drink from a water bottle bearing the label 'Volvic natural mineral water'. Brinn, not wishing to appear ungrateful, received it and wiping the opening first on his sleeve, took a swallow before he saw Sarah frantically signalling to him. The reason for her distraught gesturing became apparent when the liquid ignited his tongue and the accompanying vapour burnt his sinus. Immediately, he spat out what hadn't been already swallowed with the next breath, which triggered jocular mirth in his benefactor, but did little to alleviate his own discomfort.

'What the hell was that?' he asked in a pained, hoarse, high-pitched whisper.

Sarah, coming to his rescue with the emergency orange juice replied, 'I think it was diluted Vodka.'

'Vodka? Vodka diluted with what?' His voice was now reduced to a rasp.

'Methylated spirits, I think. Yes, definitely methylated spirits,' she concluded as the men all nodded their heads in confirmation.

Brinn was only sick the once, but that was enough. The orange juice had not mixed well with the previous cocktail, and the explosive combination retained all of its corrosive qualities on the return journey.

Their next visit was to a place under a railway arch that was blocked off at one end. An old settee stood in the gloom, half illuminated by a shaft of light from an unknown source above, spilling forth an odd spring and a large amount of horsehair filling. A large crate, which served as a table, was placed almost centrally, and held the remnants of a long night of drug and alcohol abuse. Cigarette ends lay like a carpet over the floor and an acrid odour filled the space. The only useable chairs consisted of two seats that had been removed from a car, and three square foam-filled settee cushions. Curious stains and cigarette burns adorned all of them. Every vertical surface that was visible displayed a cornucopia of colourful graffiti announcing individual's street names and gang slogans.

The first person Brinn observed was a painfully thin man with a heavily lined face and short straggly greyish-brown hair. His glazed eyes did nothing to instil confidence in his ability to communicate, and a broken cigarette was hanging from his lower lip. He held a half-empty can of lager in his hand that was tilted at an acute angle so that the contents dribbled out and ran down his coat and over his shoes. He stood amidst a few discarded cans and the only sign of life was the sound of irregular rasping breaths filling his lungs.

Over in one corner, Brinn could just make out a couple, both similarly dressed in leather trousers and jacket. The male was about twenty years of age, as far as he could tell, and had green spiky hair with shaved sides. Many chains criss-crossed his outfit and occasionally caught the light as he moved about in the gloom. His partner, though not unlike him in dress, had some striking facial differences. Her head was completely shaven, except for a black flash which reached from the mid-point of her forehead back to the nape of her neck. Her only chain was attached to a ring through her ear and looped down to another in her nose. The make-up she wore was very heavy and mostly black in colour, especially around the eyes, but it did little to conceal the deep scar on her right cheek. A pair of brightly coloured, red, high-heeled shoes, which sank into the soft earthen floor as she moved, accentuated the whole outfit.

A young man caught Brinn's attention next. He seemed almost normal, wearing a typical baseball cap in the long accepted manner of back to front. He had a sweatshirt tied around his waist by the sleeves, and blue jeans that, although they appeared threadbare, with today's eccentric fashions it was hard to tell if they were old or designer label. A pair of rather well-worn trainers, which once would have been top of the range, had been revamped with spray paint.

Having for so long been uncomfortable around street people, Brinn had hoped that the more contact he had with them, the less of a problem it would become. Although to some degree he was less concerned when he was close to

Sarah, still there was something in their eyes that disturbed him – something of loneliness, something of fear, something haunted. Or perhaps it was something of his own reflection he saw there. He did not find it easy to speak to them, and often, because of their physical state, it was impossible to do so. Just seeing how they lived, and hearing from Sarah a little about their lives, had produced a reaction that a few days before he would have considered foreign to him. It was compassion – not pity, for pity he considered to be a negative emotion, more of an insult to a hurting individual, as cursory as it was empty and soon forgotten. The compassion that was growing in Brinn was a warm living thing that urged him to help, though ignorance at present paralysed his every attempt. Still, at least now inside him was the desire. It was, at last, not his own selfish reason, but his need to reach out to them that now moved him.

Their route back took them through areas Brinn hoped he would never have to travel through at night. Sarah seemed unperturbed by the gangs of youths, some of whom blatantly carried knives, or improvised weapons, made of chain or steel. These weapons would vanish from sight at the first hint of authority, but in the seclusion of the dark alleys and back roads, they were brandished flagrantly. Each gang member took the floor in turn, in some ritual tribal show of superiority. Still, it was better they were engrossed in their own affairs, Brinn thought to himself. Sarah strolled past the display, her only interest was in their foraging expedition. Brinn tried to look equally distracted, but any close inspection would have revealed the occasional bead of sweat rolling down the side of his face.

Every so often Brinn had observed Josh or College returning with combustible material for the fire, it now seemed to be Sarah's turn. They had already found half a broken orange crate and some cardboard, though that was a little damp for immediate use. When Brinn found a discarded pallet behind a wheelie-bin, Sarah went wild with delight.

'You are wonderful,' she said giving him a hug. 'That will keep us going for a couple of days at least. Do you think you can get it back?'

'Yeah, piece of cake,' he replied.

Watching her excitement at the unexpected gift, Brinn had a flashback to last Christmas when he had given Carol a watch. The shop assistant who had originally sold it to him was loath to part with it, hoping, probably in vain, to eventually possess it herself. It was a solid gold lady's Rolex, beautifully crafted, and Brinn had thought Carol would be over the moon with it. On Christmas morning when she opened the box, her reaction had somewhat disappointed him.

'How nice, a watch! Thank you dear,' she said, with what Brinn had grown to recognise as muted sarcasm.

He looked at Sarah again, who was all smiles and realised that for her, as for the others, this was a gift indeed. Their lives revolved around food, heat and shelter, and a bonus like the pallet was far more precious to them than the watch was to Carol.

They arrived back at the car park about four in the afternoon and dropped off their booty beside the already ignited fire where Josh and College were sitting. It was going quite well, and a few new faces Brinn had not seen before were also warming themselves at it.

'Hi, Sarah,' one of them called out to her.

She acknowledged with a wave of her hand, but refrained from conversation.

She was looking very pale as she turned to Brinn and said, 'Josh's friends. Be very careful, American. Try your best not to antagonise them, and don't look at them, or at what they're doing.'

Brinn, intrigued now, found it hard not to glance occasionally in their direction, and he noticed that the two, who had remained silent, were busy slipping things to Josh, who in turn handed them cash. They remained with their backs to him for the main part, looking around nervously at every strange sound or movement. Brinn guessed they might be wary because he was present and a strange face. College had put a brew on, but chose to quench his own thirst with several swigs from a methylated spirit bottle that was already half empty.

'Want some tea?' College asked with difficulty.

No one took him up on the offer. Brinn only then noticed that Sarah had gone over to the mattress and was lying down on it. She was shaking visibly, and completely unable to cover herself with the sleeping bag that she had somehow managed to extract from the backpack. He went over to her and covered her, even taking off his own coat to add to the layers.

'You okay?' he asked, putting his hand to her forehead.

She did not answer but felt very hot to him.

'Any of you guys have any Paracetamol?'

The futility of his words registered only after he had spoken them. Brinn knew Sarah had cash on her, but she was in such a state he did not think it a good time to go searching for it. Besides, it would be much quicker to get it from the others. There were a few negative gestures in response to his question from the visitors, then he said, 'Can you lend me cash to get some? She's burning up here.'

Josh and his friends ignored Brinn completely, but College perked up.

'Here you are, my boy. It's not very much, but you might just get something with this.'

He handed Brinn one pound and seventeen pence, probably everything he had,

'Thanks, College,' he said genuinely, and closing his fist

around the cash, he set off for the chemist just down the road.

He half ran, half walked the quarter mile, but as he crossed the road to the nearest chemist, he saw it was closed. The sign, 'half day closing today', was hanging behind the glass of the front door.

'Primitive backward country,' he muttered under his breath as he started off again to the one farther down the road. Out of breath he arrived at Johnson's chemist and went straight in and up to the counter.

'How much is your Paracetamol?' he enquired breathlessly of the girl partially concealed behind the first aid sundry display.

The young assistant, who appeared not to have been in the pharmaceutical business for all that long, was masticating wildly on minty-flavoured gum.

She gave Brinn a measured look before replying flatly, 'Two pound fifty.'

'Haven't you anything a little cheaper?' he asked with a note of desperation in his voice.

'Only a packet of our own brand of ten tablets for one pound and twenty pence,' she replied holding them aloft.

'Look,' Brinn said, only just holding back the growing irritation that was beginning to manifest itself in his voice, 'I've got only one pound seventeen, if I have worked it out right, and it's an emergency. There is a very sick woman who needs these. Can't you stretch a point?'

'Sorry, it would cost me my job,' she replied almost inaudibly through the gum.

Brinn gave up with reasonable and tried outraged instead.

'Read my lips,' he snarled. 'There is a very sick woman who needs these. I've got one pound and seventeen pence. Look here! See? And you're going to take it and put it in your till, and I am going to take the Paracetamol, okay?'

The girl's eyes grew wide and she stepped back from the display, still clutching the Paracetamol.

'Mr Johnson,' she cried out over her shoulder, 'you'd better come quick. There's one of them old tramps in here trying to steal the stock.'

Brinn slapped the money down on the counter and, using his right hand for support, leant as far over the counter as he could and grabbed the tablets from the girl with his left. He didn't wait for Mr Johnson to put in an appearance, but legged it as fast as he could all the way back to the car park, childishly laughing at the incident between gasps.

Sarah would be proud of me, I must qualify as a hardened criminal by now, he thought.

As he came to the entrance of the car park, the first thing he noticed was College, apparently out cold and lying awkwardly on the ground. Josh was nowhere to be seen. His concern aroused, he saw the three men who had been doing business with Josh now standing over Sarah. One had hold of her shoulders and was pinning her down. The second, a coloured man, had succeeded in pulling her jeans off and was about to rape her. The third just stood by, egging the others on and apparently waiting his turn.

Brinn sprinted forward and grabbed a piece of timber from the fire and rushed over to where Sarah lay. The men, all too preoccupied to notice, did not see him coming and Brinn was able to get a lucky swing in before his presence was discovered. He smashed the wood over the head of the coloured man, who promptly keeled over onto the floor, narrowly missing Sarah. Brinn further immobilised him with a kick in the ribs.

The second man, who had been pinning Sarah, was at first stunned by the rapid turn of events. But then he rose rapidly from his kneeling position and was able to raise his arm in time as protection against the blow now levelled at him by Brinn. His arm took the full force of the blow, and Brinn was sure he heard it crack. In any event, the man was unable to participate any further in the fight.

The third man had gone to the assistance of the first, shortly after he had fallen, and was at present helping him to his feet. Brinn hovered over Sarah with the timber raised in his left hand and beckoned them on with his right.

'You want some more? Come on, there is plenty where that came from. I've got a full head of steam, so if you want to spend the next six months at your orthodontists getting your teeth fixed, then come and get it.'

The would-be attackers looked at each other and then began to back off, and, to save face, hurled profanities and idle promises of future grievous revenge. Brinn waited till they were long out of sight, then threw down the timber and knelt down by Sarah. She lay on the mattress, not having moved an inch, the expression on her face the same one Brinn had seen in the shower. One of total resignation. Very carefully, he pulled her jeans back on, rearranged her clothing and covered her with the sleeping bags. Then sitting on the edge of the mattress, he lifted her up into his arms, and held her rocking her like a child. She shivered in his arms and he reached for his coat that had been discarded on the ground and wrapped her tightly in it. He laid her down and went to fetch a mug of tea from the fire. College was moaning, but Brinn had to see to Sarah first. He returned with the tea and helped her take a couple of the tablets he had so precariously liberated, washing them down with a sip of tea. As he laid her down again, she curled up into a ball and rolled over, turning her back on him.

Brinn went over to College, who was coming round now, 'Sorry my boy,' he said. 'I tried to stop them, but I'm just too old for heroics, you understand. Is she all right?'

'I think so, and don't you worry, old timer, you did all

right.'

Brinn helped him to sit up and gave him a mug of tea, putting his own blanket around his shoulders. A few of Pete's things were still lying around so Brinn picked up the old blanket which had been heavily blood stained and wrapped it round his own shoulders. He went to sit on the edge of the mattress near Sarah, and set himself to the task of watching over her for the night.

## Chapter Seven

It was 9 a.m. and Brinn was just about to give Sarah the last of the Paracetamol, having given them to her at regular intervals through the night. Her temperature seemed to have come down, but she remained incommunicative and listless.

As she finished the tea Brinn had brewed for her, he said softly, 'Are you feeling any better, honey?'

Sarah did not answer immediately and when she did, her response caught Brinn totally off guard as he had expected an emotional outpouring connected with the events of the previous night. Sarah simply lowered the mug from her lips, stretched up and kissed him on the cheek.

'It's okay American,' she said equally softly. 'I'm all right, really I am.'

He was relieved, in a way, not to have to deal with the issue, though he considered that it might be unhealthy to keep something like that locked up inside.

Changing the subject he said, 'You would have been proud of me yesterday. I sort of stole the packet of Paracetamol from the chemist. You should have seen the look on the assistant's face. I think she thought I was going to shoot her or something.'

Sarah gave him a warm but tired smile, then, after a moment, kissed him again, but this time half on the mouth.

'You're crazy! How do you sort of steal something?' she whispered.

Glad of her interest he replied, 'Well, I paid for some of it and stole the rest.'

Sarah smiled, but the smile faded away as a shudder

gripped her body. She steadied herself and continued,

'Did you really hit that man with a plank, or did I just imagine it?'

'No, I really hit him,' Brinn replied cautiously. Then, standing to his feet, he demonstrated the action again with his empty hand. 'And I think I might have broken the other one's arm. There was an awful crack when I made contact with it.'

She managed to force a smile and, responding to her effort, he reached out to hug her, sending the tea she was still holding all over them both. They started to laugh a little as they made an attempt to brush the liquid from their clothes.

'Was College all right? I seem to remember one of them having a go at him.'

'Yes, he's fine, a real hero. Just a bit winded, I think. He left real early this morning, so I guess there was no permanent damage.'

The weather was changing again and the cold, combined with the rain, had produced thin feeble sleet. Brinn looked over the low wall to the street outside.

'I don't really think that you are quite well enough to be up and about today. You should stay in the warm,' he said.

'Sounds great, but it's not very practical,' she replied.

'Well, how about one of those shelters I've heard so much about?'

'Unfortunately they don't let anyone in till after 4 p.m. Rules. And they're not exactly what I would call welcoming.'

'That doesn't matter,' he said. 'It will get you off the streets and into somewhere dry tonight. We will just have to sit it out till then.'

Brinn stood up and with a wildly flamboyant gesture, picked up the end of the mattress nearest to Sarah's feet and dragged it with Sarah still aboard to the wall nearest the fire. Then, breaking up part of the available wood, he banked up the fire.

'Oh, that feels good,' she said as the fire began to warm her.

Brinn joined her on the mattress, placing his back to the cold wall. Then, he gently coaxed her so that she rested against him, with the back of her head on his chest. He heaped up the bedding over her. As she settled, he asked, 'Do you like stories?'

'Oh yes,' she said. 'When I was very small, my father used to read to me at bedtime.' Her voice trailed off into a whisper.

'Perhaps it's not such a good idea, then,' he said tactfully.

'Oh no, please, it's all right really. I would love to hear one of yours.'

'You're sure about this,'

'Yes, American, I'm sure.'

So Brinn began to relate an abridged version of Homer's *Odyssey*, a story that he had known and loved since fourth grade back in Texas. It was all he could think of on the spur of the moment. He enjoyed the telling of it almost as much as reading it. He told of the great king, Odysseus, who, in returning from the war, struggled with fate and the gods in order to get back to his cherished wife, Penelope. She remained faithful, while desperately repelling suitors and waiting hopefully for her husband's return.

Sarah loved it. She loved the sound of Brinn's southern drawl and the way he managed to give each character a slightly different voice.

At one point, she turned her head and remarked, 'You should be on the stage, American; you would make a wonderful actor.'

Clearing his throat and continuing with more care, he

gave a spirited rendition of the last fight followed by a tender recital of the final love scene between Odysseus and Penelope as they were reunited.

'Bravo! Wonderful!' she cried as she clapped her hands excitedly.

Brinn did not think he had made that good a job of it, but was pleased with her response nonetheless.

What with keeping the fire going, nipping down to the newsagents for a couple of rolls for lunch and a brew-up for a mug of tea now and then, the time passed quickly.

'We should get our skates on if we are going to get a place at the shelter,' she said. 'I hope you know what you are letting yourself in for, American.'

With these words, they began the task of collecting everything together. Brinn still had only the one coat from the latest haul at the Salvation Army store, but he insisted that Sarah wear it over the top of her own. Then, just as they were about to depart, Josh appeared. Brinn tensed immediately he saw him and was about to walk over and ask him what the hell he thought he had been playing at the previous night. How could Josh even have thought of leaving Sarah on her own with those thugs? But he was prevented from any action when she held out her arm to stop him.

'Hi, Josh,' she said in a friendly tone.

Josh turned to look at her but without any word of acknowledgement. 'I've got a message from Al. Pete's mum wants to see you. Al has set it up for the day after tomorrow at three o'clock in the park by the Embankment.'

Brinn's irritation with Josh had not subsided and, making eye contact with him, he held his gaze as he said to Sarah, 'What's the matter with him? He's got a real bad attitude problem.'

Sarah was still reeling from the information Josh had brought. When she did not reply to him, he turned to look at her.

'What's the matter, Sarah?'

'What am I going to do? What do you think she wants?'

Her voice was agitated and Brinn put his hand on her arm to calm her.

'Take it easy! It's probably nothing more than she wants a chance to chew the fat. Hey, who knows, she may even have had a change of heart and wants to ask you along to the funeral. You never know.'

'American, on a scale of one to ten, that idea doesn't even register a one, and besides, she doesn't need to see me for that. She could have just left the message with Al.'

'I see what you mean, but you have got nothing to lose,' he said, trying to sound optimistic.

'You're right. There is nothing to lose,' she replied, in a manner unconvincing even to herself.

A queue of people were already filing into the building as Brinn and Sarah arrived. Yet another old Victorian edifice, the shelter was an old wharf warehouse that had been partially rebuilt, possibly following the last war. As for how long it had been used for down-and-outs was hard to tell.

Following the slowly moving queue, they entered the building through a pair of large oak doors. A middle-aged man, with greasy black hair and a permanent scowl, peered out through a hatchway from a small poky room on the left. He acknowledged their arrival with a grunt, dislodging some ash from the end of the cigarette he was smoking that was balanced loosely on his lower lip.

'Do you have two beds for tonight?' Sarah asked him.

The man grunted again and, pushing the register forward, he indicated where they were to sign. He handed them each a token with a number on it.

'Men upstairs, women down; showers at the end of the corridor; use of towels extra. Must be out no later than nine thirty. Next.'

'Are you going to be all right here, on your own I mean?' Brinn asked her as they moved out of the way of the next customer.

'Yes, I'll be fine. It's you I'm worried about,' she replied. 'Just remember, keep everything with you all the time. Don't turn your back on your things or you will lose them.'

'Right,' he replied with growing apprehension.

Brinn began to climb the excessively ornate cast-iron staircase leading to the first floor. He looked back once to see Sarah disappearing into the women's accommodation downstairs.

At last, he thought, one decent night's sleep on a real bed.

Momentarily, he stood on the top stair looking around for the succession of rooms he expected to find, one of which he supposed would correlate to his token. All that he could see, however, was one large room that was crammed with beds, barely eighteen inches separating them. Many of them were already occupied, making it a little difficult to read the numbers on the headboards. Brinn squeezed his way down the narrow aisle in what he hoped was the right direction, uttering the occasional, 'Excuse me,' or 'Pardon me', as he stumbled over protruding arms and legs on the way.

It was with a measure of triumph that he finally arrived at his designated location, having had to make only one course correction. He was notably relieved that no one else was occupying his bed as at that moment he did not feel up to a full-scale dispute concerning the issue. Throwing his bag down first, he then proceeded to run his hand along the length of the bed, giving it a hearty shake to ascertain its stability. The bed proved stable enough, if just a little squeaky, but he noted that the mattress was decidedly unsavoury to say the least. Nothing daunted he lowered himself onto it, comforting himself with the thought that at least it was warm and dry, and Sarah would have a chance to recover.

He wondered if he should undress for bed, but it was a little early still and so he deferred the decision till later. A quick glance around the room to check his fellow inmates did little to boost his flagging confidence. Two of them appeared to be ex-boxer types with flattened noses and misshapen ears. There was a group of six males of different ages sitting on two of the beds at the end of the room. All were obviously the worse for drink and, despite the notice downstairs announcing 'No alcohol on the premises', they had managed to smuggle it in. The resulting rowdy behaviour consisted of the exchange of not very humorous anecdotes at the top of their voices and raucous songs. There was an Irishman with an invisible companion similar to that of the old tramp in the laundrette. Yet another inmate sat on a bed with his knees drawn up to his chest, clutching desperately at his sheets. He seemed a little reminiscent of Pete, and was obviously frightened and possibly mentally unstable. Brinn was relieved to see Sarah appear at the door.

'We can go downstairs for a cup of tea, if you like,' she mouthed to him.

He was only too glad to oblige. It was a chance to escape this insanity, if only for an hour or so, and, grabbing his bag, he followed her down the stairs.

The 'dining room', as it was called, was like most of the rest of the building, in pretty poor shape. The room itself was on the opposite side of the ground floor to the women's dormitory. The door opened into a room with a wooden floor that was warped and uneven. The walls had plaster missing and bad patches of damp showing through, causing the little paper that still remained to peel back and hang in loose strips. Large chunks of paint had flaked off the iron joists above them, falling in unnoticed deposits on the floor. There was a double hatch in the wall opposite and, on the counter below, stood a huge old battered aluminium teapot. Beyond the hatch was the kitchen, containing equipment that could have been installed as little as ten years ago, but probably hadn't had a clean since.

'It's self-service here,' she said to him, approaching the counter and helping herself to two cups.

'This is a goddamned awful place!' he said at last, as they sat together at one of the many tables.

'You may find it hard to believe, American, but this is one of the better ones.'

'You're right,' he said, 'that is hard to believe.'

'Do you have a home in the States?' she asked him.

'You mean in Texas?'

'Yes. That is where you live, isn't it?'

This was going to be a difficult conversation, but he thought with a few omissions, he could make it sound plausible. After all, he was a professional actor. He did this sort of thing for a living, and acting was just a bit like lying with style. The only difference was that there was no script. He would just have to ad lib a bit.

'Kind of,' he replied thoughtfully. 'My mother lives there. She has a house of her own, but I travel around so much I don't get to see her as often as she would like.'

'Doesn't she live with your father?' she asked.

'No, not now. He died when I was a kid. I hardly remember him at all, so I must have been real small when it happened, but my mom always said what a great guy he was.'

'I'm sorry, it was stupid of me to ask.'

'It's not a problem. As I said, I hardly knew him,' he replied.

'What's your mother like?'

'She's wonderful, even with all the travelling about that I

do, she never complains. When I phone her...'

'Phone her?' Sarah interrupted. 'You phone her from England?'

'No, sorry, I meant when I was in the States.'

Brinn thought how quickly this might get out of hand. He would have to try to be more careful.

'Oh, I see. I'm sorry. Go on, please.'

'Where was I? Oh yes! She is always happy to hear from me when I phone her.'

'If it was so good, why did you ever leave home, if you don't mind me asking?'

Brinn had driven himself between a rock and a hard place. He would have to do some quick thinking to get around this one.

'Sorry mom,' he prayed heavenward, hoping that if she ever found out, she would forgive him the big lie he was just about to give birth to.

'She got involved with another man. He was not right for her and I told her so. I said to her one day, how could she think about another man? Pop had only been dead six months. If you don't get rid of him, then I will go.'

'Six months. What happened then?' Sarah asked, sitting up and leaning forward into a more attentive position.

'Well... er... we all had a big fight. Mom said she would never leave him, so I had to go.'

'How awful! What happened about your job?'

'Job? Oh, my job!'

This just got harder the deeper in he got. Now it felt like climbing a glass cliff covered in grease wearing little more than ice skates.

'I was so depressed,' he continued, 'my performance at work dropped. The boss called me in and after several warnings he fired me.'

'What job did you do?' she asked.

'Er... I was a, um...' His ideas were beginning to dry up

now. 'I was a factory worker,' he finished quickly.

'A factory worker? Doing what?'

'Doing what?' he repeated. 'Oh yes. Building cars.'

'Pretty responsible job, then,' she said.

'Yes, I suppose so,' he replied, relieved he had made it.

'So why come to England, then?'

Not quite made it apparently. Just one last hurdle.

'I came because street life is much harder in America. We don't have the benefit system you have here. I just thought I might be better off.'

Not bad, he congratulated himself. Finished with a flourish, and to top it off, Sarah looked reasonably impressed.

'I'm sorry, American,' she said, extending her hand across the table and resting it on top of his.

'I did think sometimes you were a fraud, but after what you have just told me, I would like to apologise. Forgive me, please, for mistrusting you.'

All the sweetness of the earlier victory evaporated, and he felt like a prize heel.

They passed the next hour or so watching the new arrivals and drinking their tea. Then, at about ten o'clock, they wished each other a good night and retired to their beds.

Decision time had arrived. He could put it off no longer. Should he risk removing his clothes? He settled for a compromise. He kicked off his shoes, stripped off his jumper and shirt, but kept his trousers on. Then, remembering the warning advice Sarah had given him, he stowed his pack beneath the bed, and his spare clothes beneath the pillow. He assured himself as he pulled back the covers that the sheets at least would be freshly laundered. He was wrong, however. Although they had been washed, they still retained the ghostly outline of ancient stains that even the most powerful detergent would have been hard pressed to subdue. Gingerly, he climbed in and pulled the covers over his body, shutting his mind to the possible origin of the telltale marks.

Just eighteen inches away from him on the next bed, was a child, maybe seven years old and very scared. His father, or at least Brinn supposed it was his father, was in the next bed after that and was continually trying to comfort the lad.

Brinn chose a moment when the reassurances had subsided, and asked, 'Your first time here?'

'Yes. Yours too?' the man replied,

'Yeah, say, why did you bring the boy? It's the last place on earth I would expect to find a kid.'

'No choice. I lost my job three weeks ago, was already well behind on the mortgage repayments, so lost my home too, everything.'

The man fought back his emotions for the sake of the boy and then continued, 'My wife and baby are downstairs. I hope they are all right.'

Brinn tried to reassure him.

'Don't you worry none. I have an English friend down there. I'm sure she will keep an eye on them. She's an old hand at this sort of thing. My name's Peters, by the way, Brinndle Peters. My friends call me Brinn.'

'Mine's Colin, and thanks mate.'

His son began to whine again and Colin turned to console him.

Brinn tried to relax, but found it relatively difficult. The fear of imminent assault or worse played on his mind. The odour in the room was oppressive – stale sweat and testosterone never made good companions. Brinn tried to stifle it by plunging his nose deep into the pillow, but that too, emitted a musty smell that was almost as bad. Someone threw the light switch and the room was plunged into darkness, apart from a shaft of light penetrating the room from the landing. The boy began to cry again and in the darkness all the sounds in the room became amplified. He admitted to himself for the first time that he was afraid. It seemed odd to him, but out on the streets it had not seemed so bad, but then he did have Sarah. She did not appear fazed by anything, and this had instilled confidence in him in turn. Here it was different, she was downstairs and he was out on a limb.

All through the night, men were either coughing or snoring or mumbling in their sleep, and Brinn thought he heard, at one point, someone vomiting violently in the corridor. Every now and then the group of illicit drinkers would break out into an unrecognisable chorus, only to be silenced by angry protests from the other residents. A commotion began a little away from him near the door. Against the faint light from the hallway, Brinn could make out a group of men, two of whom were pinning another to his bed, while the others were in differing stages of undress. As a violent struggle ensued, accompanied by plaintive cries of fear and pain, it became clear what was happening. Colin called softly to his son to join him in his own bed, offering protection against the profanity in progress. Brinn's mind raced, as he hovered between the desire to intercede, and the fear of doing so. Then he thought of Sarah.

God, I hope she is all right down there!

He gave in to his fear and turned his back on the violation that was taking place a short distance from him. Feelings of shame filled him, as the memories of his words to Josh echoed in the dark.

'You did nothing, you could have prevented this!'

Now he was gripped by the same immobilising fear and did nothing. He felt such a hypocrite. As the frenzy subsided, the only sound was a miserable sobbing. Brinn pulled the covers over his ears and tried to shut it out of his mind. The smug, self-righteous attitude he had adopted when upbraiding Josh had now evaporated and he was left feeling remorseful at his complicity.

He dozed fitfully, waking at intervals when spasmodic coughing or the incoherent choruses grew too loud. In his estimation a couple of hours had passed when he became aware of a scrabbling noise beneath him. Startled, he opened his eyes and turned over to see someone dragging his pack from beneath the bed. Quickly he thrust out his hand and caught hold of the protagonist, who then fought to free himself from Brinn's grip. Still maintaining his hold, Brinn managed to sit himself up and then separate the thief from his plunder.

'I think you will find that these things belong to me,' he said firmly.

'Sorry, mate, no 'arm meant. I didn't think they belonged to anyone,' the man replied.

'Well, as you can see, they do.'

With profuse apologies, the man backed away and retired to his own bed. Brinn prayed that he would never have to live through another night like this.

Morning dawned. He had not slept a wink since his things were almost stolen during the night and his relief was almost tangible. Practically the first to his feet, he was unrealistically eager to take a shower just to be doing something to take his mind off the events of the night before. He picked up all his things and headed for the showers, looking back once to make sure he was not being followed.

The facilities consisted of three heavily stained wash basins, green with lime scale and age, a solitary toilet, that was full almost to capacity with excrement and urine and did not appear to be in working order. Each shower cubicle was clad in white tiles, or Brinn supposed them to have been white once, as now they were yellow, heavily smeared with body grease and unspeakable grime. Only three showerheads out of the eight available were in use for the entire floor, but he did not think there would be a rush for them at this time in the morning or at any time of the morning if it came to that. Combined with the urgent need for a shower, he desperately wanted a shave. Brinn hated the stubble that had been growing daily more dense on his chin, and it was at that itchy stage. He rubbed his cheeks with his forefinger and thumb, while he studied the problem looking at his reflection in a cracked mirror above the middle basin. A flash of inspiration sent him back into the dormitory and he bent over the bed next to his and gently woke the man.

'Sorry to disturb you, but do you have a razor? Mine has been stolen.'

The man nodded, reached over the side of his bed and fumbled in his holdall for the item.

'I'm sorry, it's only an old style open razor and not very sharp at that.'

'Oh, that's fine. I'm so desperate to stop the itching, I'd even considered using broken glass.'

'That bad.'

'You bet ya!'

Brinn returned to the toilet block and forced himself to use one of the showers. He was in and out and towelled down in a matter of minutes. After last night, he did not want to remain naked and vulnerable for any longer than was absolutely necessary. Brinn had not wished to impose further on Colin's kindness by asking for the use of his shaving foam as well, and in the absence of any, he began to lather up with toilet soap instead. Colin had been right, the razor had practically no edge. By the time Brinn had finished using it, there were several nicks on either side of his face and a patch of stubborn bristle still remained clinging defiantly along the left side of his jaw.

After changing into a fresh set of clothes and returning

the razor, he headed down hoping to find Sarah. As luck would have it, she had beaten him to the dining room and was already sitting at a table with a cup of tea.

'You look much better today,' he said by way of greeting.

'I can't think why,' she replied, 'though I wish I could say the same about you. You look terrible. What have you done to your face? You look as though you had a run in with a lawn mower.'

'Thanks!' he said, ignoring her remarks about his face. 'It was an interesting night.'

Sarah turned her head away and tried to conceal a smile.

'You can get used to it in time,' she said yawning.

'No, thanks, I don't think I want to. I'll stick with the streets, if it's all the same to you.'

'You catch on fast, American!' A note of sarcasm had crept into her voice.

Then Brinn, remembering the young man and his son, asked, 'Did you see a mother and baby down here last night?'

'You heard them, too?' she replied.

'No. It's just that I bunked next to her husband and boy last night. He told me about her and the kid.'

'Yeah, what a shame! Poor woman couldn't get the child off to sleep. Had a dreadful time, scared to death because the others kept shouting at her to shut the brat up, or there would be trouble.'

'What happened?'

'Well, I wasn't getting much sleep anyway with the noise, so I took it in turns with the mother to walk it up and down the corridor in the pushchair. It did the trick eventually; it kept it quiet. That's why I'm up so early, I've just finished the last shift.'

She stretched and yawned again wearily. Brinn reached over the table with the intention of kissing her, but she saw what was coming and pulled away instantly.

'You had better get something to eat,' she said to him, in the same flat tones he remembered from their first meeting.

Brinn dutifully rose and walked over to get a cup of tea and a bacon sandwich, the only breakfast on offer, from the serving hatch. He gestured to Sarah to see if she wanted one. She declined, with a shake of her head, so he rejoined her at the table.

'I've got a surprise for you, American,' she said unexpectedly as he sat down,

'Oh?'

'We're going to the opera tonight,' she added triumphantly.

Brinn could not imagine what she had in mind. He knew from experience that the tickets were not cheap. Even in the States, he would have been lucky to see much change from a hundred-dollar bill. Besides, they would not let you in unless you were dressed for the occasion. He did not want to burst her bubble, but the few clothes they had hardly qualified them for a trip to the morgue, let alone the opera. So, as he replied, he did so with caution.

'Yeah, sounds great,' he said, while wondering if he should slip back home and get his American Express. His American Express! He had completely forgotten about it. The damn thing had been stolen on Sunday and he had not phoned the company to cancel it. He must get to a phone, though he suspected it was already too late.

'I'm sorry to be a pain,' he added, 'but I have to get to a phone this morning. It's about, er… it's about a job.'

His last words did not sound too convincing, but it was all he could think of on the spur of the moment.

'A job? What job?' she replied in mild derision.

'Colin, upstairs, he told me about it. It's nothing special, but we need the money right now so I thought I would give it a go.'

'Okay. So things are a bit tight, but what is this mysterious job?'

'It's er… a toilet attendant at King's Cross Station.'

'Well, we can't have you miss an opportunity like that, can we? There's a phone box just down the road a bit. We can call in there on the way out.'

'Fine, shall we go then?' he urged, standing and pulling her chair out abruptly.

'Where's the fire?' she spluttered as she almost choked on a mouthful of tea. 'It's not as if you'll have much competition.'

'We all have to start somewhere,' he replied indignantly. 'I'm only trying to help.'

'Yes, you're right. I'm sorry, American. I didn't mean to be such an ungrateful cow.'

She stood up and, downing the last swig of her tea, she accompanied him to the door, dropping off their tokens at the hatch as they left.

Brinn was relieved to find that the phone box was empty as they arrived, and turned to Sarah for the cash needed for the call.

'It's just one thing after another with you, American,' she said.

'I'm sorry, I would not ask if it were not important.'

'I'm only joking,' she replied, 'don't take me so literally.'

He took the money from her and entered the box.

'I don't think there is room for the two of us in here,' he said, closing the door behind him.

Sarah wandered off a little way and left him to his 'important phone call'.

Brinn's undue haste caused him to fumble with the money and the phone. He dropped the receiver first, then, after retrieving it, the fifty pence fell from his impatient hands. From outside the box Sarah watched him with growing incredulity. The conversation Brinn was having with the person on the other end of the line was obviously an animated one. First he began to wave his arm around, then his voice rose to almost audible tones. She wondered how any potential employer would want this maniac Yank to work for them. Brinn's gyrations had spun him round, and he noticed he was now facing Sarah. He turned back quickly and lowered his voice again, putting his hand close to the mouthpiece to help deaden the sound. When finally he emerged, he looked inconsolable.

'You did not get the job, then?' she said.

'The job? Oh the job. No I did not.'

'I'm not surprised.'

His mind a million miles away, he added, 'Look, I've just lost three thousand five hundred pounds.'

Trying hard to contain her mirth she said, 'Is that a month or a year?'

'I'm sorry, I don't get you.'

'Well, if that three thousand five hundred was for a year's work, the job isn't worth having in the first place. If it was for a month, well, you more than likely would be expected to provide some extra little service and, if that's the case, unless you really want to give the "personal touch", then you might want to consider giving it a miss altogether. Mind you, you have the looks for it, and, I think the expression is, a great pair of buns.'

The weather had cheered up a bit and the sun was making a bold attempt to put in an appearance as they set off again. They did not head directly for the car park, as Sarah's calculations from the night before had revealed a deficit in their financial affairs.

'I don't think we are going to make it through this week, American. It's just not possible for both of us to live on just the money they give me. We will have to switch to plan B, and go into the centre for a couple of hours on the streets.'

Brinn thought this might mean one of two things.

Either she was thinking of forcing him into prostitution, or they were going begging. He admitted to himself that although the first option had no appeal for him and the second scared the hell out of him, he still preferred the second choice.

'What do you mean, plan B?' he said with reserve.

'We are going begging,' she replied. 'You do know how to do that, surely?'

'Well, yes, but a person has to have some standards, and I like to draw the line somewhere, so if I have a choice I would rather get it some other way.'

'Beneath you, is it? Well, it doesn't matter anyhow, you don't have a choice. No money no food, no food and you, my principled American, go hungry.'

He thought for a moment, juggling with the idea of a long fast and then said, 'You are sure there is no other way round this?'

'Not unless you want to become a male prostitute. Perhaps you should have tried harder for the job at King's Cross.'

'No, it's okay. I'll give plan B a try. What do I have to do? I mean, where is the best place to go?'

The words came easily enough with the options on offer, but the thought of it still left him cold.

'Where there are the most people usually works best, I find,' she replied somewhat sarcastically, 'but first, do you know what you are going to say? Judging by your efforts so far, you're going to need a little practice. I'll pretend to be a passer-by, and you ask me for the money.'

Sarah backed up a little and then proceeded to walk past Brinn. On her first pass, nothing happened. Brinn just stood there, hand extended and mouth wide open, but no sound.

'Well, American?' she said.

'Sorry, I was a bit undecided. I couldn't think what to

say,' he offered pathetically.

'Well, make a decision, for God's sake. Try it again.'

She backed up for the second time, and as she was about to begin her walk past, Brinn said, 'It's no good, I just don't know what to say.'

Even in his student days at acting college, spontaneity had never been one of his strong points; he worked better from a script.

'Oh, for goodness sake, it's not hard really. A child could do it. Ask if I have any spare change.'

'Okay, I've got it now,' he replied.

Sarah began to walk forward again and just as she drew level with him he said, 'Have you any spare change, please?'

Sarah turned to look at him, incredulity etched on her face and, trying hard not to sound too disparaging, said, 'Couple of things wrong there. Firstly, you will have to speak up. With all the traffic noise, no one will hear you. Secondly, you don't sound desperate enough, as though you really need it. It's more like you are asking someone to pass the milk, and it's a real shame you tried to shave this morning. The stubble would have lent some authenticity to you.'

Sarah paused for a moment and then, taking his chin in her hand and turning his head to see both sides she added, 'Mind you, the all-over, pathetically lacerated, semi-hairy look is quite effective in its own way.'

'Is there anything else?' he asked, removing her hand from his face.

'No, I don't think so. If you can get that right, that will just about cover it.'

This had not been unlike the barracking he would have expected from Chris, and he was a little annoyed. Sarah made her last pass from the other side this time.

'Right, get it right this time, okay?'

Brinn performed beautifully and completely satisfied

Sarah's critical observations.

'Okay,' she said, 'you'll do.'

She picked up her things and with Brinn in tow and muttering to himself, she set off for the city centre.

They took up position in an underpass linking a tube station with the street.

'I'm only going to stay with you till you get the feel of it, then I'll leave you on your own.'

'If you think that's best,' he replied, hoping she would change her mind.

'Yes, two adults together don't stand much of a chance, so I'll go to the other end of the station and catch the ones you miss.'

Sarah withdrew from her pack a plastic cup.

'You'll find this helpful,' she said, putting it into his hands. 'Only ever keep a little loose change in the bottom, remove any big coins or notes if you are lucky, and put them in your pocket.'

'Why?' Brinn asked.

'The sight of a full cup makes the next person think you don't need any more. It's a psychological thing, trust me.'

She stood back a little from him and observed his first attempt. The words he had practised earlier dried on his lips. He saw the look on Sarah's face, but before she could speak, he managed to force the words out, albeit a little disjointedly. Each successive attempt made the sentence easier. Sarah shook her head and turned to leave, but after a few steps she halted, returned to him and kissed him on the cheek.

'Good luck,' she whispered.

'I'm going to need it,' he replied under his breath.

On his own, with the plastic cup held out and repeating words he found it hard to put any feeling into, he braced himself. Suddenly, prostitution seemed to be a better idea. A ten pence piece was dropped into his cup by a child whose mother had prompted him. Brinn was so surprised, he stood open-mouthed in mid-sentence. The mother smiled at Brinn and retrieved her child, who was by now regretting the donation of what had been his pocket money. He tried to snatch the coin back from the cup, but Brinn was too quick for him and held the cup up high out of reach. The child put his tongue out at Brinn as his mother dragged him off along the passageway, and Brinn, not to be outdone by a child, waved the coin in the air to torment him.

After about the tenth repetition of his lines, Brinn began to relax a little. After all, he comforted himself, it was just like acting before a live audience, only here they were very much closer. He still had only ten pence to show for his efforts, but he did not feel quite so uncomfortable going through the motions.

Then another few coins were dropped into his cup and he was equally surprised, but did not forget to say 'thank you' although he left it until the woman was almost out of earshot. He looked into the cup that now held a fifty pence piece and two ten pence pieces. His elation at having succeeded, was somewhat out of proportion to the event, but this early on it was still a novelty to him.

The triumph spurred him on and after an hour had elapsed, he had acquired a further three pounds and seventy pence in odd change. Then things started to slow up a little, and Brinn relaxed again and started to observe the faces of the people who passed him. He had been so preoccupied with the effort of collecting money, he hadn't really paid much attention to the people giving it to him.

There were those who were obviously irritated by his soliciting and walked straight past as they glowered in his direction. Some were clearly embarrassed as they tried to manoeuvre round the other people, looking in every direction but his. Then there were the overtly curious, who stared and smirked at the sight that greeted their eyes.

Only three categories of benefactor seemed to exist. The first was the lavish giver, who only seemed interested in the effect his gift had on the people with him, rare but welcome nonetheless. Secondly, was the reluctant benefactor who was halfway past before he grudgingly found a small donation and turned back to toss it into the receptacle. The third type were a little scarier; they offered their donation, with helpful advice and words of consolation, as though the donation gave them the right to dictate its use. Looking down into his cup again, he remembered the advice Sarah had given him earlier. He removed everything except eighteen pence in small change and it brought an almost immediate response of sixty pence in total from three passers-by.

He was just wondering how Sarah was doing when he noticed what he thought was a familiar figure coming down the passage towards him. He spun round to face away as he recognised Chris's distinctive outline approaching him. Brinn was torn in two directions, undecided whether to remain anonymous and conceal himself, or bluff it out.

Then, with a deep breath, he turned again just as Chris stopped a few steps from him, and with an unrehearsed Cockney accent, he said, 'Got any spare change, mister?'

Chris halted for a moment, and with an expression that clearly displayed puzzlement, put his hand into his rear pocket and fished out some change that he dutifully deposited into the cup.

'Thank you, sir,' Brinn added with a whimsical tug of the fetlocks for effect.

Chris turned and was about to continue on his way when he paused again, hunched his shoulders and turned back.

'Brinn?' he asked. 'Is that you? Good God, man, you look like shit.'

Brinn smiled and said, 'Had you fooled though, didn't I?'

'Damn right, you did,' Chris replied, clapping Brinn on the back. 'How's it going?' he added.

'Sorry, Chris, can't really talk now,' he said, checking to see if Sarah might have spotted them together. 'I'm meant to be earning my living, but look, do me just one favour, will you? At the other end of the station is a woman who is begging too. Blue jeans, brown corduroy jacket. Help me out here and put a large sum in her cup, will you.'

'Sure, what do you suggest?'

'Oh, say about forty to fifty pounds should do it.'

'You're crazy! You'll get me arrested, Brinn. She'll think I want a bloody good time for fifty quid.'

'I shouldn't worry too much on that score, but if it is a real problem, just make it fifteen to twenty then.'

'Okay, will do. When you heading back anyway?'

'Don't know yet, but I will be in touch. Now hop it, you're interfering with trade.'

Chris set off in the direction that Brinn had given him for Sarah and, by way of an afterthought, Brinn shouted to him, 'Don't tell her you know me, Chris.'

'As if I would… And Brinn?'

'Yeah.'

'Do something about that accent of yours, it stinks,' he shouted back as he disappeared around the corner.

About three quarters of an hour later, Sarah rejoined him, beaming.

'How did you do?' she asked him.

'Not bad, I think. How does twelve pounds nineteen sound to you?'

'Mmm, not bad at all, but how does thirty-four pounds and fifty pence sound to you?' she said, trying not to sound too superior.

'Pretty impressive,' he replied.

'I can't take all the credit for it, though. There was this really weird guy who must have put in at least twenty quid in rolled up notes, but then he hung around a few yards away. It was a bit scary. I thought he was after something.'

Brinn feigned horror as he asked, 'You don't think he wanted, well, you know?'

'For twenty quid, he'll be lucky. I might have stretched a point and given him a blow job, but it would take a hell of a lot more to get me into bed, and I don't mean money.'

Brinn struggled hard to keep a straight face.

'Ah well,' she added, 'at least it will keep us going till next week.'

## Chapter Eight

Sarah took Brinn via the market on the way back to the car park. It was open every Saturday and she knew a few of the stallholders, who kept damaged fruit and vegetables back for her.

'Market people are a friendly lot,' she remarked. 'They are the salt of the earth. I've known some of them since the time I first hit the streets.'

Along with the produce, they managed to pick up a few broken crates and paper waste to carry back and use on the fire. Sarah was never one to overlook a gift horse, and there was always something for free available on market day. Laden with their booty, they struggled back to the car park.

Sarah started the process of lighting the fire and making something edible from the vegetables they had brought back with them. With the aid of a pocketknife and a saucepan with no handle, she prepared vegetable soup and to Brinn's surprise, although it was a bit thin, it still tasted quite good.

It was about six thirty as they sat down to eat, and they had hardly taken a mouthful, when two men joined them from the direction of the stairs, two men whom Brinn had not seen before. Every step was a struggle for them, the sheer effort of movement registering clearly on their faces. It was hard to tell just how old they were, their faces were so pale and gaunt. Their clothes hung loosely over their bodies, concealing their painfully thin torsos and limbs beneath. Dark, sunken questioning eyes peered out from hollow sockets, while a smile of recognition revealed yellowed and missing teeth. A woolly hat worn by one was pulled down unnaturally in order to conceal a large lesion on his temple. The other had smaller, more numerous blemishes around his eyes and on the backs of his hands. The warmth of the fire seemed to revive them a little, restoring, if only temporarily, colour to their gaunt faces. Sarah welcomed them and asked Brinn to give them some of the soup. Obligingly, Brinn stirred the broth and poured a little into two spare cups. Then looking up at Sarah first as if for conformation, he gave them each one. They took them gratefully but with difficulty, and acknowledged the gift with a nod. The man in the hat was unable to maintain his grip on the mug, and it started to slip from his hands. Brinn stepped forward in an effort to help him keep hold of it, wrapping the man's hands once again around the vessel. There was a silent acknowledgement between them and then, looking up at the man, Brinn was shocked as he saw his face for the first time in more detail. Papery thin skin was stretched taught over a fragile bone structure, the few remaining wisps of hair, thin and brittle, protruded from beneath the woolly hat. He gave Brinn a weak smile by way of thanks, then resumed his attempts to drink the liquid nourishment. No words; no conversation; no emotion; and as they had arrived, without a word, so they left.

Brinn looked to Sarah for an explanation, and she remarked quietly over her mug, 'Aids.'

A shudder went through him. Yes, he had heard of it, seen reports on the television, read articles in the paper, but despite its prevalence, he had not known one single person who had contracted it. He struggled with his reason; he knew all the arguments about it not being passed on by ordinary contact, and felt ashamed that he was still repelled by the event.

He collected himself, and cleared his throat before asking, 'How old are they?'

'Brian's twenty-one and John is twenty-five,' she

replied.

'Jesus, practically still kids. Are they together, a couple? I mean are they…'

'Homosexual? Yes,' she said completing his sentence. 'You have a problem with that, American?'

'No.'

'You don't sound too sure about it.'

'I'm sure. I just don't understand what makes them tick,' he replied.

'You mean you don't understand why they choose to screw each other and not a member of the opposite sex.'

'No, that's not what I mean.'

'It's okay, American. Lots of heterosexual people think that way. Why should you feel bad about it?'

'Look, you've got me all wrong—'

'Have I? You're not perhaps a bigot by any chance, are you?'

'I don't think so,' he replied.

'You still don't sound sure of yourself.'

'Hey, what is this? The third degree. As far as I am aware, this still is a free country. I can think what I want.'

'So, come on, then. What do you think?' she said, turning to him.

'Okay, you asked, so I will tell you. The whole thing just can't be right.'

'What can't?'

'The way they behave. The way they act on the streets. Flaunting themselves.'

'Anything else?'

'Yes, it's just not natural.'

'God, you are a bigot, American.'

'Just for once I would like to hear you call me by my name.'

Brinn was irritated. He did not consider himself a bigot as she suggested, and he did not think he was going to win this argument either.

'Don't change the subject! Just because a few are camp, a little eccentric, you condemn them. I can think of half a dozen heterosexuals who are equally as eccentric maybe, but I wouldn't ostracise them for it.'

'It is not quite the same, is it?'

'Isn't it?'

'Well, what about their sexual activity?'

'Now we're getting closer to it! So you do mind that they screw each other, then.'

'No, not really.'

'So, what then? You tell me.'

'You know very well what I'm trying to say, Sarah,' he replied as he felt increasingly more flustered.

'Yes, but I would like to hear it from you all the same.'

Brinn was noticeably uncomfortable with these things, but he hoped Sarah could not see it.

'All right then, you win,' he replied as evenly as he could. 'It's disgusting, the very thought of it; anal sex between two men. There you are! Happy now?'

'So you're saying sex between homosexuals is okay, as long as it's not anal.'

Every sentence was difficult for Brinn. His embarrassment was plain now to anyone and Sarah was making the most of it.

'Well, no, but—'

'Heterosexual couples never have anal sex, then,' Sarah interrupted, taking advantage of his awkwardness.

'No, I mean, yes.'

'You don't sound too sure again.'

'All right! It's just sex between two people of the same gender that makes me feel uncomfortable.'

'And my father, what he did to me, that was all right, I suppose, because we're not the same gender?'

'You're twisting what I say, Sarah and besides, it's different. He raped you. You were little more than a child.'

'It seems to me that your criteria are in danger of becoming a little blurry, American. I will tell you something for free. Were you aware that one in ten people are gay, but, because of prejudice, maybe only one in a hundred are in a secure enough position to come out. The rest live, for the most part, a miserable existence, pretending to be "normal" to their friends and family and even to their bosses, whom they fear would sack them if they found out. That means there is a strong possibility two people you know are gay, but they are just too bloody frightened to tell you. People you may have known all your life, but you just can't see it. It all boils down to the fact that what they do in bed is no more your business than what you do is theirs. They are people, pure and simple, just like you and me.'

Sarah left him with no more excuses, and little more to say. She had not convinced him, but it had left him thinking again, something he had done rather a lot of recently.

'We will have to make a move soon, if we are not going to miss the opera,' Sarah said, jolting him out of his sulk. 'Unless,' she added, 'you've changed your mind now.'

Brinn thought for a moment. He was irritated about the incident, mainly because he was having a hard time convincing himself that Sarah was probably right. He finally settled the conflict in his mind by telling himself it might take a while, but he would eventually come round to her point of view. After all, he wasn't a hard man. He could rationalise any reasonable argument that was presented to him. He could console himself that at least he had helped one feed himself, and given time, even Sarah would see him as a caring individual. The slow job complete, he returned to the question in hand.

'No, that's all right. What do you think I should wear?' he replied automatically, without any thought of the impact of the words.

'Just how many choices do you have?' she replied tentatively.

Together they made their way towards the opera house. The evening air was pleasant but cool. The rain had finally let up and the sky was clearing. They walked beneath a vast inky blackness, the night sky dotted with numerous pinpricks of light, making the city seem very small in comparison.

Brinn still had no idea what was going to happen, but he had learned to realise that if Sarah said they would do something, even if he did find it a bit odd, usually something happened. He could see a group of well-dressed people milling around outside the entrance of the opera house, and hoped that no one he knew would be there tonight. Expensive chauffeur-driven cars pulled up on the road and discharged their occupants to swell the crowd. More joined the throng from the direction of the Underground station, but Sarah took no notice of any of them. In fact she seemed completely unaware of that other world, much as they were of hers. Unnoticed, they slipped down the side of the building and around to the rear, where there was quite a large tarmacked area for lorries to unload and the performers to park. Over in one corner, there were two people who stood either side of a large oil drum that was punctured with holes and through which the glow of embers could be seen.

Sarah took Brinn's hand and led him towards the figures, neatly sidestepping a few parked cars and a skip. She acknowledged the two men, who had utilised some rubbish from the skip and were now sitting on reproduction eighteenth century furniture and warming their hands over the brazier. The serviceable seats were all in use as Sarah and Brinn joined them. Improvising, they sat on a low retaining wall behind, first padding the damp brickwork with folded remnants of material also gleaned from the skip.

Turning to Brinn Sarah remarked, 'All mod cons.'

Brinn just nodded as the observation, like many English colloquialisms, mystified him. There was some friendly banter from the small audience, just as though they had all been a party in the dress circle. Even the intermission drink had been taken care of, as one of them had thoughtfully brought a bottle of something that on this occasion, Brinn declined gracefully. It seemed surreal to Brinn that these people would even want to listen to this type of music, let alone derive any pleasure from doing so.

A moment later it started, as through the air drifted the beginnings of the overture. Brinn thought he recognised it as Bizet's *Pearl Fishers*, but was not really sure. They all settled and a hush fell over them. As the evening continued, wave after wave of rich melodies and counter harmonies filled the night air. Brinn was quite enjoying this illicit visit and he turned to share the moment with Sarah.

Her face was one of total peace. Her eyes were closed and her head moved very slightly in time to the fluctuations in the music. The crackle of the fire and the occasional flare of flame only helped to enhance the atmosphere with a diffused flickering light that illuminated her face. Halfway through the first act and in the glow of the fire Brinn thought he could see tears on Sarah's face. She turned unashamedly to him and said, 'I've always loved this piece; it's one of my favourites.'

He nodded to her, lifting his hand to smooth away the wetness from around her eyes.

'I'd love to be able to see all the costumes and to applaud with everyone else at the end. I've made a pact with myself. One day, one day I will be able to go.'

Brinn made a mental note to treat her to a trip there

when his two weeks were up.

Walking home later along the Embankment, they stopped again to watch the boats drifting silently by in the night. The moon's eerie light was lost in the reflective glow from all the other sources of illumination along the bank. Still, it held an amorous enchantment for the many lovers enjoying the welcome, if all too temporary, dry spell.

'Mrs Bernard, tomorrow,' Brinn remarked.

'You do have a way of spoiling the mood, American,' she replied.

It was hard to get used to the night noises. They came in many guises, sounds that he would not normally worry over or associate with any danger, locked up safely in the confines of his own home. He could never be sure if the sound he thought he heard was gunfire from a robbery taking place, or only a car backfiring. The breaking glass could have easily been a cat, scattering milk bottles in its path, but just as easily a burglar breaking and entering. Perhaps the distant howls were those of a drunken youth making his way home after a long night at the pub. Equally, it might be a fox scavenging the city for food and calling to its mate. Could anything be done though, if it should turn out to be a woman in mortal fear, repelling the unwanted advances of an assailant? Were those squealing tyres a rapid escape? And the clatter of dustbins only the stumblings of a drunken man? There was no protection out here. It was, as it seemed, a frightening place. He could become used to the sounds in time, the noises no longer startling him from his slumber, but he could never become used to the fear.

Sarah grew apprehensive as the time grew ever closer. As arranged, at exactly three o'clock, Mrs Bernard arrived at the gardens. She was nothing like the person that Sarah had expected. Mrs Bernard was perhaps in her mid-fifties, very well dressed in a grey suit with a patterned chiffon scarf tied around her neck, the loose ends draped over the lapels of her jacket. Her face was drawn, but that was to be expected in the circumstances after the ordeal of Pete's death only days before.

She walked right up to Sarah, her body tense, her face expressionless, and slapped her sharply across the face. Brinn, alarmed, stepped in and took hold of her wrist to prevent her landing a second blow. The action was, however, unnecessary, as the emotion was spent in the first strike.

Sarah nursed her sore cheek and straightened almost to attention as if expecting more of the same, but she offered no word of obscenity nor any rebuke in her defence. Mrs Bernard broke down and Brinn let go of her wrist, enabling her to reach into her pocket for a handkerchief.

'I'm sorry,' she blurted out after wiping her eyes. 'I'm so sorry. These last few days, I have not been coping very well. Everything I ever valued was lost when Peter died.'

'Look, this is not a good place to talk. Let's go over to the bench under the trees over there.'

Brinn motioned to a spot some fifty yards away. The three of them walked in that direction and Brinn took hold of Sarah's hand, squeezing it as a sign of his unspoken support. They all sat down, Brinn at one end, Sarah in the middle and Mrs Bernard at the other.

A few moments of uncomfortable stillness passed until Mrs Bernard spoke into the uneasy silence.

'I have always felt you took him from me, you know,' she said getting straight to the point as she saw it. 'It has been very hard for me to come to terms with, but I am sorry I slapped you just now.'

Sarah remained silent, still trying to eradicate the vision that was on replay in her mind, triggered by the single stroke, of her father slapping and beating her. Brinn recognised the glazed expression from that day in the showers, so he bridged the gap in the conversation.

'It is all right, Mrs Bernard. We appreciate that you have been under a great deal of strain since Pete died. We would very much like to help you if we can. What is it that you wanted to see us about?'

'Please, would you call me Janice? I would like so much for us to be friends; and you are...?' She trailed off, waiting for an answer.

'I'm Brinndle Peters, ma'am, but my friends call me Brinn.'

'You are very kind, Mr Peters. I know this is going to sound a bit irrational, but I need to have the missing pieces of my son's life in order to make sense of his death. Can you understand?'

'I think so, ma'am. I'm sorry, Janice.'

'I feel like I have been going quietly mad. Everything that has been important to me is gone now, as though it never existed, my complete life a total waste.'

Brinn looked at Sarah, who still seemed unresponsive and continued in the absence of any contribution from her.

'Perhaps if you could start at the beginning, Janice, and we will try to fill in the gaps.'

'The beginning seems so far away and so much has happened since. I think it must have started when Peter was small. He was always a little dysfunctional, but we, that is, his father and I, put it down to youthful exuberance. It didn't become a real problem until he was about fourteen and he seemed to develop selective forgetfulness. He started to let people down and missed appointments, growing steadily worse until his father and I finally arranged for him to see a specialist. After many tests and a lot of heartache, they diagnosed he was suffering from schizophrenia. Drug therapy was started immediately, and it helped for a while, but it hinged on his remembering and wanting to take the medication. Sometimes he forgot and sometimes he just refused to take it, and it was on one of these occasions, when his father was depending on him, that Peter's negligence indirectly caused his father's death. Peter loved his father dearly and could not come to terms with it; he never was able to forgive himself.'

While Janice had been relating the story to Brinn, he had taken hold of Sarah's hand. He interlinked his fingers with hers and gently stroked the back of her hand.

'What happened to his father?' Brinn asked Janice.

She took a long, almost inaudible, breath that she exhaled slowly as she replied.

'Peter's father was diabetic. He had been all his life, and although we had the odd problem, it had never amounted to anything that any one of us could not cope with. Peter had helped his father several times before when he had become hypoglycaemic, bringing him something sweet to eat to bring him out of it. Everyone in the family knew the risks and the procedures to follow if he ever became unconscious. Then one day, one of those days when Peter refused to take the medication, his father had a bad episode that led to unconsciousness. Peter sat the entire time, in his own world, on a chair only three feet away from him. They said at the hospital that my husband might have survived long enough for someone else to find him if only Peter had been able to turn him onto his side. You see, my husband inhaled his own vomit, causing him to choke to death.'

With these words, she lost her hard-fought battle with self-control and broke down again. A few inconsolable moments passed until she was able to continue.

'It was not really Peter's fault, but he just could not come to terms with the thought that he might have been responsible. He partly blamed me, I think, and he tortured himself over it for months before he left home.'

Sarah had partially begun to respond to Brinn's soothing caress. She had heard much of what had been said and although she was unable as yet to express her feelings, she extended her arm gingerly and laid it gently across Janice's left shoulder. Together they wept for Pete.

As if coming round from a bad dream, she said slowly, 'Please, don't feel bad. He never held you responsible. He told me he felt so guilty about his father that he had run away so he would not have to think about it every day. I promise you, Janice, we did not try to keep him from you; he just could not face you knowing what he had done.'

'I believe you,' Janice said, 'but why didn't he phone or write? Just a line, a word. I was so worried about him.'

Calmer now, Sarah turned to look at her and replied.

'When he first came to us, I got him to see a doctor and between us we managed to get him to take his medication again. For a while he was fine. Then he realised that when things got bad, if he didn't take the medication he could retreat back completely into his own world and block out the painful memories. Then it just began to snowball. He took it less and less until it came to the point where he began to feel that everyone was against him or was about to run out on him. It became so desperate we no longer knew what to do for him. The more we urged him to go home, the worse it seemed to be for him. In the end, all we could do was to support him as best we could.'

The three of them sat in silence for what seemed like an age, and then Mrs Bernard turned to Sarah.

'How I have misjudged you, my dear. Please forgive me, and thank you, thank you both.'

Brinn jumped in to take advantage of the positive attitude that Janice was conveying.

'Do you think it would be possible for us to pay our respects at his funeral? It would mean so much to both Sarah and me.'

Both women stared at him, Sarah in anger and Janice with incredulity.

'No! No! I'm sorry, it's far too soon for that.'

Janice stood suddenly. Turning to leave, she said again, 'I'm sorry, really I am, but it just wouldn't work. You understand, don't you my dear?'

Sarah did not reply, but brooded over her anger at Brinn's insensitive request. Janice bit her lower lip, turned and walked away. Sarah waited for Janice to be out of earshot before she turned on Brinn.

'You bloody idiot! What do you think you were doing? I told you the way it is.'

'I only thought…'

Brinn stopped as he saw the look on Sarah's face.

'You only thought,' she interrupted. 'Perhaps that's your problem, you only don't think.'

Feeling totally impotent he stood and moved away.

'It wasn't a lot to ask of her,' he said in his own defence.

'Not a lot, just everything. For God's sake, American, exactly which part of your body does the thinking for you, 'cos it bloody well isn't your brain.'

'I was only trying to help.'

'Well, perhaps in future you should stop trying.'

Several minutes passed before her anger and frustration subsided. Sarah ambled over to his side.

'I am sorry, American, of course you were a great help.'

He moved away from her, peeved at her put-down.

'Petulance, American!' she called after him in a sing song voice.

'I'm not petulant,' he replied, very petulantly.

Sarah smiled, and her smile infected him and she put her arms around his waist and hugged him.

It was early that evening at the car park when Josh's sudden appearance startled them. He was clearly agitated, but Sarah was unsure if this was due to his lack of a fix, or some other compelling event. Josh began to scatter his belongings frantically searching for something.

'What's the matter, Josh?' Sarah asked.

'They are coming for me.'

'Coming for you? Who's coming for you?'

'My dealer, and the pigs,' he replied.

'I don't understand, Josh. What has happened?'

'Look, I don't have the time for this now!' He paused and then continued irritably, 'I didn't have enough cash for the last drop. I got into a fight with the pusher. It all got out of hand and I stabbed him.'

'You killed him?' Sarah said alarmed.

'No, no, I don't think so. Look, he's okay. It's no big deal.'

'Josh, how...' She did not have an opportunity to finish.

'I need to get away for a bit. Can you lend me some cash? I've got to get away.'

'Calm down, Josh,' Brinn interrupted.

'Mind your own fucking business, American,' said Josh. 'Are you going to help me, Sarah, or not?'

'What do you need?' she replied.

'Can you give me fifty quid? Then I can get up to Manchester and I know some people there that owe me a favour.'

'Hey, hold on a minute, Josh.'

'Not now, American!' Sarah shouted at him. 'Won't you be followed, Josh?'

'I can't stay here, understand? I can't,' he said, his desperation beginning to change into aggression.

'All right, all right, but I only have forty-two pounds,' she said, taking it out of her jeans pocket.

'That will do,' he replied, snatching it from her hand.

'Look, I know this doesn't have anything to do with me, but that's all the money she's got,' Brinn yelled.

'How many times do I have to tell you? Keep out of this!' Josh shouted back. 'You're right, it has nothing to do with you!'

'Anything that affects Sarah has to do with me. You want to make an issue out of it?'

The two men stood at arms' length, facing each other down, only seconds from outright conflict. It took Sarah's intervention to calm the situation.

'Josh, wait! Brinn, please, not now,' she said, pushing herself between them. 'If they are coming, we don't want to waste time here arguing. Josh, we will go with you as far as the station, and I will hang onto the money until we get you there.'

'You can come, but I don't want him along,' he replied, pointing his finger inches from Brinn's face.

'Josh, you might need a diversion, and if Brinn doesn't go, than neither do I.'

Josh, faced with no other options, agreed reluctantly and handed the cash back to Sarah.

It was a very difficult journey to the main station. Josh needed his next fix, having missed the last. His inability to remain still for any length of time was causing suspicion among other passengers on the tube as he paced the length of the carriage. Sarah did what she could to calm him, but he was beyond help. Shrugging her attempts away, every approach met with instantaneous recoil. He was becoming more aggressive and withdrawn and Sarah was afraid he would never make it as far as Manchester. At the station, Josh stood next to Sarah at the ticket office with his arms folded tight around him and shifting his weight from foot to foot. Sarah bought the ticket for Josh and as they headed off to the platform, Brinn noticed two familiar faces over by a news-stand.

He halted Sarah and said, 'Don't say anything and don't turn round, Sarah, but I think the two men behind us by the paper stand are the two who visited Josh at the car park.'

'Are you sure?'

'Pretty well,' he replied.

'How long have we got till Josh's train goes?' she asked.

'Ten minutes, I think. Look, take Josh and make sure he gets on the train. I'll handle things here.'

Sarah turned now to face him, and her worried look conveyed more than just the words could.

'Be careful!'

'Don't worry,' Brinn said to her. 'It's nice to know you care, but I will be okay. Trust me.'

She hugged him and took Josh by the arm and led him in the direction of the platform. She looked over her shoulder once to see if Brinn was all right, then hurried a less than willing Josh over to the waiting train. Brinn kept his eyes on the two men, watching to see who would make the first move.

The two men had been following Josh since they had caught up with him and his friends at the car park. The first man was an Asian of medium build. He had been responsible for pinning Sarah down on the day of the attempted rape. The other was black, taller and more heavily built. It was he who had been first in the queue to rape her. They had been hoping to catch Josh on his own, but now that he was with the other two, they had decided to play it cautiously and hold back. The black man wanted a chance to get even with Brinn for the injury he had sustained to his head. He was, however, under strict orders to 'get Josh at all costs', and his personal vendetta had to wait until later. Aware that they were pressed for time, with the police not too far behind them, they were irritated and nervous as they waited impatiently for an opportunity. Then they spotted Sarah and Josh as they ran along the platform and the two men agreed that now was their best chance to get to Josh. Sarah posed no real threat. They could not see Brinn for the moment, so they made their move.

Brinn crossed the concourse to intercept.

'Well, hello there! It's good to see you two again,' he said as he came up behind and between them, resting a hand on each man's shoulder. The men shrugged him off and glared at him.

'You'll get what's coming to you after we've dealt with him,' the black man muttered under his breath as they continued with their primary mission, leaving him behind. He ran around them and proceeded to walk backwards ahead of them.

'Please, I'm sure we can come to some arrangement. If it is a matter of money…'

'If you don't get out of our way, I'll tear your fucking head off,' the Asian said, clenching his fists, anticipating some resistance.

'I can see friendly persuasion is having no effect, gentlemen,' he said, placing both hands on the shoulders of the black man in a feigned gesture of friendship.

Then, in one movement, he brought his leg up sharply and pulled the man forward until his knee made contact with his groin. The black man buckled immediately, drew in a gasping breath, and collapsed into the foetal position on the ground. Brinn took enormous pleasure in felling the man who had so very nearly raped Sarah. The Asian hesitated only a few seconds while he weighed up whether to help his friend, who was now helpless and moaning, or to lash out at Brinn. His decision made, he grabbed Brinn by the elbow, spun him round, and landed a hastily aimed blow that caught Brinn just below his rib cage. Brinn reeled, and with the wind knocked out of him, went down on one knee and struggled to find his breath. Just as the Asian was about to take a swing at Brinn for the second time, the black man managed to splutter a few words, and pointed in the direction of the platform.

'Never mind him! That bitch is helping him get away!

Quick!'

The Asian responded to the urgent instructions, relaxed his fist and set off at a cracking pace down the concourse. Brinn rose almost immediately, though still impeded by the blow. He pursued the man, who was running in the direction of Josh and Sarah, as best he could.

Sarah was in the process of bundling Josh onto the train.

'Here,' she said, giving him the remainder of the cash and the ticket, 'take this.'

Josh sat down in the compartment and Sarah reached up, kissed him goodbye, and closed the door.

'Good luck, Josh,' she said to him and then, noticing the sound of approaching running footsteps, she turned to see the Asian coming down the platform towards her. She looked first at Josh and then for a means of escape, but ran forward instead, in a feeble attempt to stop him getting to Josh.

The man just pushed her aside with one sweep of his arm saying, 'Out of the way, bitch!'

The train was ready to leave. The guard shut the few open doors and his arm was raised to signal to the driver. Brinn, now fully recovered, was on the platform and running. He passed Sarah and rushed straight at the Asian, just before he could open the carriage door. The momentum sent both of them sprawling across the platform. Brinn picked himself up first, and with the other man only half on his feet, Brinn returned the punch he had received earlier accompanied by several more. Neither man had the upper hand in the ensuing fight, but it lasted just long enough for the train to pull out of the station. Seeing it depart, his antagonist, breathless and backing away, held out his hand in Brinn's direction. Brinn, only too glad for the apparent ceasefire, bent over to catch his breath.

'You've not heard the last of this, man. We will get him and you in the end.'

Brinn straightened and pulled back his fist to strike him again, but the man was already turning to leave. Brinn leant forward again. He had little inclination to follow and besides, Sarah was stood at his side, her hand resting on his back.

'You all right, American?'

'Yeah, just a bit winded.'

'Still out of shape, then. You have a nasty cut here,' she added putting her fingertip to the wound on his forehead.

'It's okay, just a bit of a scratch.'

'Let me have a look at it.'

'It's fine! Don't fuss.'

Neither of them had spotted the advancing security guard, who had been alerted by a member of the public. This community spirited individual had spotted the incident on the concourse, aided the 'poor coloured man' to his feet, and called an ambulance as he seemed unable to walk. Then, indicating to the guard the direction that the 'assailant' had taken, she helped the guard to locate Brinn.

'Is that the man over there, madam?' the constable asked, pointing in the direction of Brinn.

'Yeth, thath the man, conthable. Do you think there will be a reward?'

'Well, madam, if you let me have your name, I will make the enquiry for you, but I would not be too optimistic.'

'The nameth Henthaw, thonny, Miss Henthaw, and thith ith the thecond time I have athithted the police. Perthonally, I think I have earned thom thort of reward.'

The guard took little notice of her, his attention on the incident taking place on the platform. He abandoned Miss Henshaw and proceeded down the platform towards Brinn, closely followed by Miss Henshaw who had far from finished with him.

Breathing a little more easily now, Brinn noticed the guard at the other end of the platform. Could it be? No surely not again! That mad woman Miss Henshaw from the flat above his was on the platform. He looked around frantically for a route to escape. He saw an overhead walkway.

'Come on,' he said to Sarah. 'We have to get out of here now.'

He took her hand and ran towards the steps. At the same time the guard, fearful of losing his quarry, began to run from the far end of the platform. It was going to be a race to see who got to the walkway first. The guard had the edge for all of two seconds until he fell headlong over the crooked end of Miss Henshaw's umbrella.

'Not tho fatht, thonny! You can't go yet. You will need my name and addreth if you are to potht me that reward.'

It had been, in Brinn's words, a hell of a day, and he felt like he needed a couple of hours with his head down. Unfortunately for him, they still had the 'funeral' to do, not that he minded really.

They walked hand in hand up the hill towards the monument and joined the group of other people who had already gathered. Everyone seemed at ease and, Brinn thought, why not? They were among friends after all. Al was there; College, who was sober for once but possibly not for long, and the other faces were a few of those Brinn had seen around the city while he had been out with Sarah. Someone had lit a fire, and all those gathered stood around talking quietly, exchanging news and warming themselves against the chilly night. Brinn and Sarah eased themselves into the group, and she immediately joined in conversation with one of the old men from the Embankment. She slipped some cash – Brinn could not see how much – into the old gent's pocket. For a moment, Brinn wondered if the man's motive for being here was purely one of sentiment. He turned to observe the others and began to catch snippets of conversations and anecdotes about Pete and the things he had once said or done – times when they had laughed together and times when they had cried. It seemed to Brinn that they were talking about a different Pete to the one he had briefly known. All he had seen of Pete was the timid, confused boy totally out of touch with reality. Here, among his friends, he was portrayed as funny, clever, streetwise and several other attributes, that in his short acquaintance Brinn had not had the time to experience for himself.

Perhaps a man is more than the sum of all his parts, much more certainly than appears on the surface. Perhaps he is the sum of all the people's lives he has touched. Be it for good or bad, a man is the result of a lifetime's interaction with his fellow man.

Brinn turned to Sarah to see her face lit from the reflected glow of the fire. Her every breath etched in the cold night air. Just like a child, she lifted her hands to her mouth to blow some warm air into them and stamped her feet to drive away the cold. Brinn took hold of her collar and lifted it up around her neck. She momentarily dropped her hands and he zipped up her coat the last few inches. He felt he would have liked to kiss her as she smiled back at him. She looked so trusting, so needing. A few people started to drift away, and some stayed just for the fire, while Sarah passed among them chatting to some, reassuring others. But after twenty minutes, only Sarah and Brinn remained.

'Let's not go back to the car park tonight,' she said. 'I want to do something memorable to mark the day.'

He nodded and allowed her to lead him back down the hill, and towards the city again.

Sarah stopped outside the rear of a building, one of the many undergoing massive repairs in the city. Ladders, walkways and scaffolding covered almost the entire back of the building, leading upward ultimately to the third floor.

Sarah beckoned for Brinn to follow her, but he became alarmed as she began to climb up onto the scaffolding.

'You cannot be serious,' he said.

'Oh yes, I am,' she said in a hoarse whisper, 'and do you know you sound just like that prat of an American tennis player, what was his name...?'

'You don't mean John MacEnroe?'

'Yes, that's the one,' she said.

'No, I don't,' he replied emphatically, knowing all the time it would be useless to argue with her. He gave up the argument and began to climb after her instead. It was not as difficult as he had imagined it would be. Access to the first walkway was via a ladder that one of the work crew had inadvertently left in place. Someone would be for the bullet in the morning, Brinn thought to himself. His biggest problem with this was that he couldn't bear to look down. Heights were not his thing. He would get nervous just a few feet off the ground unless he was sure there was no danger, and here he was not sure.

Sarah got to the top long before Brinn did, and as his head appeared over the edge of the flat roof, she extended her hand to help him up the last few inches.

'Ta rah!' Sarah exclaimed, whilst Brinn struggled against his dread and with legs that were weak with fear.

'That was the easy bit,' she said to him. 'The next bit is a little more tricky.'

'What do you mean, a little more tricky?' he said.

'Well, come over here and I'll show you.'

Sarah took Brinn, who was by now clinging to her hand for dear life, over to the edge of the building. There was a gap of about two feet six inches over to the adjacent building, just a little too much to step over comfortably. It would require a jump.

'We have to get over there,' she said, pointing across the gap.

'Oh, no!' Brinn replied backing away. 'Here's where I draw the line. There is no way you are getting me over there. Absolutely no way.'

'That's a pity,' she replied. 'The only other way is to climb back down the scaffolding, but in this light, well, it could be very dangerous. After all, it's harder to find your footing in the dark on the way down.'

Brinn eyed her suspiciously, and peered over the edge of the building that he had just scaled.

'You're telling me that it is possible to jump that distance safely,' he said pointing to the gap.

'Sure it is! I tried it two weeks ago,' she said reassuringly.

Brinn approached the gap again with caution, while weighing up the probability of his imminent death.

Then, after a long and protracted decision making process, he said, 'Okay, but you go first, and for goodness sake be careful.'

Laughing at him, she backed up to give herself a good run up, waited a moment and then ran as fast as she could at the precipice. Landing safely on the other side, she turned to see Brinn shaking his head with his hand over his eyes.

'Come on, American, your turn now.'

Still shaking his head, he turned to pace out the run up to the edge.

'Oh God, I'm going to die!'

'Don't be silly! It is only a couple of feet,' she replied.

Brinn, not a religious man, crossed himself anyway, then rocking backward and forward as he had seen long-jumpers do, he sprang into action. It all went deathly quiet as he sailed through the air, coming to land at last, a few feet from where Sarah stood.

'Well done!' she congratulated him. 'See, it was not that bad after all.'

Brinn's face was white, and it took him several minutes

to recover before Sarah could lead him to a skylight in the roof that was partially open.

'We're going in here,' she said, now more in a whisper. 'Help me lift it up. Oh, and by the way, I lied. I guess I had better come clean. I didn't try it two weeks ago. I was going to, but I didn't get the chance.'

'Why do I find that not surprising?' Brinn replied grimacing as together they pulled at the framework of the skylight until it was fully open.

'It's a bit of a jump down, American, but after that last one it should be a piece of cake.'

Brinn muttered some mildly profane statement, while he waited for Sarah to drop through the opening. Then, responding to her encouragement, he dropped through and found himself sprawled on top of a large pile of empty cardboard boxes.

'Any more surprises?' he asked as he struggled to find his feet.

'These weren't here two weeks ago when I checked it out,' she said in her defence.

'Oh, so you did check it out, then? I was beginning to wonder. Where the hell are we anyway?'

'We are on the third floor in a store cupboard of a departmental store, but we are headed for the second.'

'Are there no guards in these places?'

'Of course there are, silly, but the one who works here is on the ground floor. He hardly ever comes up to this level. He prefers to watch the television in the control room.'

'Hardly ever?'

'Yes, hardly ever, and besides, that's half the fun, not really knowing if or when he might show up.'

Sarah crept quietly, followed by Brinn, round to the emergency stairway, and quickly descended the flight of stairs to the floor below. She opened the door that led onto the second floor and peered around to see if the area was clear. Satisfied, she entered, pulling a reluctant Brinn in behind her by his coat lapel. The entire floor was in total darkness, the only light provided by the glow from the street-lights outside shining through small windows set high in the wall opposite. He tripped over something, stumbled, and then the domino effect took over and several other indefinable things fell to the floor.

'Shhhhh!' she said as she helped him to his feet. 'Try to be more careful.'

'It would help if I could see where I was meant to be going,' he replied.

'Your eyes will get accustomed to the dark in a moment,' she said as she felt her way farther into the room. Brinn heard her scrabbling around.

'What's all this stuff around here, and what are you looking for?' he asked.

'We're in the electrical department, I hope, and I'm looking for a… Ahh, here it is!'

There was an audible click and a startled Brinn heard music.

'Shut it off,' he urged her. 'The guard will hear it.'

Sarah ignored his request.

'Dance with me, American,' she said.

'Are you nuts? Turn that music off.'

'Dance with me, please.'

Brinn prayed that the guard was stone deaf or at least had the television turned up loud as he groped in the darkness in the direction of her voice. Finally he made contact with her hand.

Over the radio, Ella Fitzgerald sang the words,

'Every time we say goodbye, I die a little; every time we say goodbye, I wonder why a little.'

Brinn pulled Sarah close to him and began to move and turn to the music. 'You are totally crazy,' he told her.

'I know that. I'm just surprised it's taken you all this

time to work it out.'

The voice cut in again, 'When you're near, there's such an air of spring about it; I can hear a lark somewhere begin to sing about it.'

Emboldened by her relaxed mood and the slow rhythm of the music, he pressed his body closer to hers and put both arms around her. Sarah pulled away from him, and switched off the music.

'What's the matter? Did I tread on your foot or something?' he asked.

'It's not that. Come on, there is something else I want to show you.'

She dragged him halfway across the department, causing him to collide with several other objects that he fought hard with to prevent them crashing to the floor. When she came to a standstill, the space they occupied was a little less dark than the surrounding room. Brinn could just make out the faint outline of an enormous reproduction Elizabethan four-poster bed. It appeared that the whole of this part of the department had been given over to a display of Elizabethan artefacts, the centrepiece being the huge bed. It was bedecked in lavish tapestries, satinised curtains and silk sheets, and around it were arranged several shop dummies that had been dressed in typical clothing of the era. Her notorious father, King Henry the Eighth took pride of place, standing head and shoulders above the others, legs astride and hands firmly on hips.

'Pete and I saw it advertised in the local paper three weeks ago,' she said, 'and we just had to come to see it. Apparently, it's been a big tourist attraction. Pete wanted to jump on the bed. He had never seen anything like it, but the manager caught us trying it out and had us removed by the security guard.'

Brinn had almost forgotten about the guard, and checked for the sound of any possible approaching footsteps.

'On our way back to the car park, he bet me I wouldn't have the nerve to get back in after dark and sleep in the bed for a night. I accepted the bet; even cased the joint to find out the best way in, but Pete got sick again and I was just too worried to leave him alone at night. Up until he died, he kept telling me he was going to hold me to the bet and I was only using him as an excuse not to go through with it.'

'Sleep here tonight! You want to sleep here? What about the guard?' he interrupted.

'I'm staying,' she said firmly. 'I need to do it for Pete. If you want to go, then go.'

Sarah began to remove her clothes and stripped down to just her T-shirt, determined to see it through. Brinn wavered for a moment, then deciding he probably could not get back out of the building without help, resigned himself to stay. He joined her between the sheets after stripping down to his boxer shorts. Then, grudgingly, he pulled up the covers over his body. It took a few moments for his body to warm against the coolness of the silk sheets and for him to relax enough to turn to face her.

'I am glad you decided to stay, American,' she said as he pulled the cover up over her ear.

She smiled, wide-eyed with that childlike look he had seen in her face before. Brinn watched as she closed her eyes and felt her relax down into the bed beside him. He was longing to reach out and touch her, but he feared she would pull away and this rare tender moment would be lost. He tried to imagine some way he might be able to hold her at least, so that he would not alarm her and possibly reignite the painful memories that plagued her. His left hand was free, so he moved it towards her, rested it on the side of her face, and began to caress her cheek with his thumb. Sarah opened her eyes wide and enquiring, startled at the unexpected contact.

'Easy,' he whispered to her. 'It's okay.'

She drew reassurance from his words, partially relaxed again and closed her eyes. When he felt she was comfortable, he extended his thumb across her mouth, her eyes opened again, but this time they glowed warm with pleasure. He eased himself forward, and brushed his mouth against hers, then waiting a few moments, repeated the action again, applying a little more pressure this time. Her body tensed and became rigid beside him and he cursed himself for rushing.

'I'm sorry,' he began, and then checked himself from saying, 'I'm not going to hurt you.'

He continued stroking her mouth and cheek, hoping he could regain her confidence. Slowly, she unclenched the taut muscles in her body and was easy again beside him. A single tear rolled down from the corner of her right eye, and he brushed it away tenderly with his thumb, unsure of its meaning. Hesitantly he tried again, gently applying his mouth to hers. She remained still, but this time she did not freeze. Gradually her response to him increased, and the next time they kissed, her mouth parted a little to receive him. He felt her breath against his cheek deepening, and with the next kiss he slipped his tongue into her mouth. Her reaction was swift and she drew back immediately, turning her head away to one side.

When she had first mentioned that she had not been with another man since her father had raped her, he had found the idea a little ridiculous. Surely, after all this time had elapsed, she would have sought solace in someone's arms. Her every reaction to him now, however, only reinforced just how inexperienced she really was. He calmed her again, stroking her hair and her neck and reassuring her in low whispers, 'Only if you want to, honey. If you want me to stop, you only have to say so.'

His right elbow, on which he had been resting all this

time, was now retaliating with a vicious attack of pins and needles. He desperately wanted to shift his position, but was aware any movement might frighten her further. In the end he just had to say, 'Look, I'm sorry, but my arm has gone to sleep. Do you mind if I move it?'

It was enough. It broke the ice and she laughed gently, enabling him to ease her closer to him. Her taut, frightened expression gave way to soft wrinkles around her eyes and mouth and for the first time he thought he saw the traces of desire in her eyes. As her soft laughter subsided, he resumed kissing her, trying again to reach her tongue. This time he met no resistance and he explored her mouth tenderly. Responding to him, she slipped one arm around him, cautiously feeling his back with her hand. Brinn moved from her mouth down to her neck, just brushing her skin with his lips at first, then kissing it warmly. Using only his fingertips he moved his hand down over her T-shirt, then over her stomach, finally resting on her upper thigh. Her laboured breathing was audible now. She trembled a little, but did not resist him.

Brinn reversed the direction of his hand, and slipped it beneath her T-shirt allowing his fingers to trace the outline of her breast, while he watched her face for the slightest sign of reluctance. He resumed kissing her more fervently now, and, withdrawing his hand, laid it on the bed beside her. Brinn shifted his weight onto his hand and eased himself carefully over her. Then transferring most of his weight to his forearms, he held his body motionless, allowing time for her to adjust to this new sensation, time for her to object or reject him. To his surprise, she put her hands on his shoulders and pressed her fingers deep into his flesh. He found the slightly painful sensation stimulating and he closed his eyes against the growing excitement that surged through his body.

Sarah released her grip and put one hand at the base of

his neck, and the other in the middle of his lower back. The moment had arrived that he had been both longing for and dreading. If he got it wrong now, there would be little chance of retrieving the situation. He pressed into her a little, and then a little more, each time aware that he might have to stop at any moment, until finally with a sigh tinged with pain, she gave way beneath him. The ache inside him was greater than he had known for a long time, but he held back waiting for her to respond again. He was as patient with her as he was tender. By now, all thought for his surroundings or the possible intrusion of the security guard, had evaporated. Sarah arched her back slightly, pressing her hips up towards his and slowly, rhythmically, he began to penetrate her. Warm in her arms and lost in each other, time passed unnoticed until Brinn felt Sarah's body tremble beneath him as she came. The expression of surprise and exhilaration in her eyes triggered a powerful response from him and though he had fought to suppress any vocalisation as he made love to her, as he came, an involuntary low moan escaped his lips. In the darkness, the only witnesses to the lovers were the ghostly Elizabethan figures that seemed strangely animated by the flickering lights of passing vehicles penetrating from the streets below.

Brinn didn't want to move, but concerned that his bodyweight might be causing her discomfort, he eased himself over to her side and then turned to face her again. Sarah had her eyes closed, but her face seemed to be glowing and she looked beautiful to him. He kissed her on the mouth and she opened her eyes, smiling, a little embarrassed at her own pleasure. A dozen confused thoughts flooded his mind. He wanted it to be this good again, and he did not want to lose Sarah after he returned to his own world. I'll tell her in the morning, he thought. He would ask her to come back with him. The combination of lack of sleep for Brinn and the exertions of the day for them both, caused them to linger, when departure would have been more prudent. The bed was warm and comfortable and their release had been so complete, sleep was inevitable.

The next morning, the first thing they were aware of was laughter. They awoke to find the early morning cleaning staff had arrived for work, and Brinn and Sarah the object of their mirth.

'You've made our day, mate,' the eldest male employee said, grinning from ear to ear. 'The manager here is a real bastard to work for, pardon my French, miss, and we have been hoping someone would rub his nose in it. He'll get in the shit for this for sure. Go on, hop it, quick, 'fore he catches you! You can use the staff entrance on the ground floor.'

It appeared the female staff were in for a treat, too, as Brinn, the first to leap to his feet, had forgotten his present nakedness. Looking down, he noticed his condition and hastily grabbed a sheet to cover himself while simultaneously trying to dress.

'Go on! Back to work, you lot! Give 'em a break,' the male supervisor said, ushering them away.

His statement was greeted with moans of derision and disappointment from the gathered ladies as they reluctantly filed back out the way they had come. On their own again, the couple hastily dressed and, without delay, fled.

By the time Brinn and Sarah were outside on the pavement, they were both helpless with laughter and had to sit for a moment to catch their breath. Brinn was just about to lean over and kiss Sarah, when he heard his name called out from somewhere behind him.

'Brinndle Peters, as I live and breathe, how have you been? Or, more to the point, where have you been?'

Taken aback at the sudden mention of his real name,

Brinn stood up automatically to confront the oncomer. It took several moments to realise the balding fifty-five year old, whose name was Chaz Walters, was an old acting colleague from way back. Chaz spoke again before Brinn had a chance to make the connection.

'Your producer friend, what's his name? You know who I mean,' Chaz began as Sarah stood and began to back off slightly. 'You know,' Chas continued, 'Chris, yes, that's it, Chris. Well, he has put the word out everywhere trying to track you down, something about the play's opening date having to be brought forward, and that you should come back from your latest escapade asap, whatever that means.'

Sarah looked over to Brinn in disbelief and growing realisation, as he tried a damage limitation exercise.

'Look, not now, okay? I'm a bit busy. I'll call you, all right?' he said, moving off in the direction that Sarah had already started to run. Chaz called after him.

'We'll do lunch, okay? Phone me, Brinn.'

Sarah was well ahead now and steering a course for the underground. She skipped easily through the barrier and ran down the escalator with no conscious thought for her ultimate destination. Much to his surprise, Brinn got the timing right and slipped through just as easily. He tried to run down the escalator but was unable to dodge the other passengers quite so successfully. He arrived on the platform just as Sarah jumped gratefully onto a waiting train, the doors of which were already closing. He stood pleading with her through the glass of the closed door.

'Wait, Sarah, please let me explain. Don't do this, honey.'

The train started to pull out and the last thing he saw as it left were the tears in her eyes and her fist pounding on the glass, as she mouthed the words, 'You used me, you bastard.'

## Chapter Nine

With not enough cash for the tube fare, Brinn had to walk some of the way back to his flat. His feet were sore and he was tired and disconsolate. He let himself into the flat with the spare key that he kept concealed in a flowerpot on the step and walked into the hallway. It smelt, as all places do that have been locked up for a while, stale and uninviting. He made the decision to have a bath and a few hours sleep. Then, perhaps, he could go and try to find Sarah and explain everything. She would have had time to cool off by then. Quite where he would start with his explanation, he was not sure yet, but he hoped to hell it would come to him. Last night the loose ends of his life had started to come together and gel for the first time. He had known what he wanted and where he was going. Now, it was all just a big mess again.

Brinn had his bath. The hot water soothed him, and he drifted off into a light sleep.

He had been dozing only for twenty minutes when the sound of the phone roused him. His first irrational thought was that it might be Sarah. Half dazed, he leapt out of the bath, grabbed a towel and stumbled along the passage. Turning into the bedroom, he threw himself across the bed and grabbed the receiver. Breathlessly he said, 'Brinndle Peters.'

'Brinn, thank God. I've been trying to get hold of you since the day before yesterday. It's Chris. Have you heard? The play has been brought forward.'

'Yes,' Brinn replied flatly.

'Good! Now look, I've got all the crew together and we

start again tomorrow. Did you get some useful stuff on the road? We're all looking forward to seeing the new material. Sorry, but I must fly. Just had to make sure you will be back on line tomorrow. You sound like death. Try to get some sleep. See you there. Ten thirty, yes?'

Then, without waiting for any reply Chris hung up.

Brinn put the receiver back and sat up on the edge of the bed. Reaching over to the answering machine, he awkwardly turned it on. He could not face any more calls right now and the one call he did want was not likely to come. After all, he rationalised, there was no way Sarah could know his number. The need for a cup of coffee drove him to the kitchen. It would have to be a black one, as the only bottles of milk in the house were the two he had left on the side on the day of his departure. Unfortunately, time had addled them, and they were more cottage cheese now than they were milk. He emptied them down the sink, rinsing the congealed lumps down the waste pipe, then swilled out the bottles while he waited for the kettle to boil.

The coffee revived him. He had gone without coffee for the last eight days and the sudden rush of caffeine was a pleasant sensation. Sipping it as he walked, he took the coffee upstairs with him, and prepared to get ready to go out again.

Thirty minutes brought Brinn back to the car park, but there was nothing there – no people, no belongings and no trace of inhabitants at all. Brinn checked to see if he had come to the right one. Yes, this was it. The old burnt-out car, the trolley he had kicked over, the cement heap, but nothing else. He had not thought the task was going to be easy, but he was hoping at least to find some trace, someone who could help him. Brinn systematically covered all the places he thought she might be. He tried the post office; DHSS; the laundry; Harry's place, and even, very cautiously, the Salvation Army hall. Fortunately, dressed as he was, he was mistaken on this occasion only as a volunteer, but there was no sign of Sarah anywhere.

Al, Brinn thought, go see Al.

A further five minutes on the tube brought him to Al's. Al was at the back in the kitchen as Brinn arrived at the open door.

'Al, you must help me. Please. Help me. I can't find Sarah anywhere.'

'I'm sorry, American,' Al replied heavily. 'She does not want to see you. There is very little I can do.'

'But she has been here, Al, please.'

'What you have done, it is unforgivable. You knew how it was with her, and you took advantage. Back in my country, we know how to deal with people like you. You're worse than a dog. Even if there was anything I could do, I would not help you. Now, please go.'

Al closed the door on Brinn, and Brinn knew it would be futile to pursue the issue any further.

Brinn was grateful that he had the play to concentrate his mind on and necessity propelled him back into the old routine. As the opening night drew near, he became more optimistic about the play again. His new material was helping to enhance his previously flat performance. Rehearsals had been going exceptionally well. Chris was very pleased and word had gone round that this could very well be Brinndle Peters's comeback performance. Brinn had been uncharacteristically helpful with the direction and production, assisting less seasoned performers to shape their characters. The tension that had existed between himself and the rest of the cast and crew had dissipated as the rehearsals had progressed. Brinn's new lease on life had a profound effect on their attitude to him, and his perform-ance benefited from their support.

During the last few days, Chris had also been amazed at

the difference in Brinn. His attitude, his ability and his personality seemed to have changed totally. Sometimes though, when Brinn was sat on his own, Chris wondered at Brinn's pensive preoccupation.

'Brinn,' Chris called out as he walked up to him during a break, 'I want to talk to you.'

Brinn, who had been re-reading part of the script, looked up.

'I'll cut the crap. This character you are playing, he's spot on. Sympathetic angle, too, it's amazing. It's way beyond anything any of us had hoped for. Everyone has noticed it and they're all asking me. I can't give them any answers because you won't talk to me about it. Come on, Brinn, you can tell me. What happened to you out on the streets? You've been a different guy since you came back.'

'I told you twice already,' Brinn replied, irritated at what must have been the tenth enquiry that he had fobbed off concerning the subject. 'I just met some street people, lived among them and got to know them a bit.'

'I'm sorry, Brinn. You will have to do better than that. You met someone, didn't you? Yes, I can see it in your face, you old dog! You met a woman.'

Brinn put down the script and got up to leave the room.

'Running away won't change it, Brinn,' Chris shouted after him.

'I'm not running anywhere. I'm going for a coffee.'

Chris caught Brinn up out on the pavement and accompanied him to the Bistro in the next street. The two men entered and sat at a side table. Chris ordered.

'Two coffees, please. You still taking yours black, Brinn?'

Brinn nodded.

'One black, please.'

The waiter acknowledged the order, and they had to wait only a few minutes in silence before the coffee was set down in front of them. The waiter looked at Brinn quizzically.

'Excuse me, sir,' he said addressing Brinn, 'but I think I know you from somewhere. You seem very familiar to me.'

Brinn realised that this was the waiter he had encountered on his first day, who, unless he had a second job, was in the wrong place, and, averting his eyes, he declined to reply. Fortunately for Brinn, Chris thought he had the answer.

'This is Brinndle Peters. You have probably seen him in the theatre. He is an actor.'

'An actor? Mmm, yes. That must be it, I suppose.'

The waiter seemed a little unsure, but had other customers to serve and so he left them in peace.

'This woman you met,' Chris began, 'it's the same one I saw you with at the station, wasn't it? Come on, Brinn, tell me about her. You can't let it go by now, I'm on to you.'

'There is nothing to tell,' Brinn replied.

'So it was her, then? I knew it!'

'Look, Chris, can we leave this? I just don't want to talk about it.'

'Okay, I can take a hint, but whoever she is, she was good for you, and Brinndle Peters, if any man needed a good woman, it is you.'

'Thanks, Chris. I had managed to work out that much for myself!'

'You must have realised by now what a total bastard you were becoming.'

'Thanks, Chris! Whenever I need a few words of comfort, you always come up trumps.'

'Glad to be of help, old man.'

The opening night went exceptionally well, despite a glitch when one of the stage lights overheated and had to be turned off to prevent it from igniting a strip of Astroturf that had been placed too close by one of the stage crew. No one but the crew and cast noticed and, being seasoned troopers, they carried on magnificently. The reviews exceeded even Chris's expectations. After all, he had expected some hostile reaction from the critics, not least because of Brinn's previous personality record. However, the floods of congratulations and offers of future work for Brinn proved even Chris wrong, and established Brinn as a re-emerging star once more.

The play was set to run for months, maybe even a year or so, and Brinn found his sometime estranged friends beginning to gravitate back to him. One of these was Carol, who turned up unexpectedly two months after the opening. Cynicism made Chris wonder if she was allowing just enough time to see if the play would be a flop or not, before making her move. He had never liked her very much, and word had it she was only ever attracted to 'well-known' people. Rumours had spread like wildfire before she met Brinn, when she spent six months with several different members of the same pop group who were in the limelight at the time. Chris felt justified in his condemnation of her, but Brinn never seemed to notice or care about it.

It was a full house the night Carol turned up again, and just as the first time she had met Brinn, she waited around until he had showered after the show, using the excuse that she wanted to congratulate him on a fine performance. A little wary of her this time, Brinn did not ask her back for supper, but agreed to meet the following day, as there was no performance scheduled. He saw her on and off for the next three weeks, meeting for dinner, taking in an odd show or two, but despite all her manipulative efforts they slept together only once. Brinn derived little satisfaction from the union and he found a reason to dissuade her when she suggested she move back into the flat with him. For Brinn, the relationship with Carol was something he didn't really think about, certainly not with any view to permanence anyway. As far as Carol was concerned however, Brinn was now eligible once more and definitely a prospective marriage partner.

The cast and crew had arranged a surprise birthday party for Chris. It was to follow that night's performance, and many of Chris's old friends and colleagues had been secretly invited too. Chris was popular with colleagues of his own genre, though popular meant, in some cases, an easy touch. Many that had worked with him, and even a few who had not, found a new respect for the quality of work he produced. Arrangements had been made with a large nearby hotel to take over their conference room on the ground floor. It was a large room with a small stage at one end. The rest was mostly carpeted but for a twelve-foot square of wooden parquet flooring that passed as the dance area. A succession of glass doors lined one of the long walls and beyond lay the patio and the garden. On the opposite wall were two wooden doors, one of which led to the kitchen, and the other to a small cloakroom. The band had been booked, and the food was laid on for the evening. It seemed likely the celebration was set to go on long into the night.

Some while after the performance, Brinn emerged from behind the curtains, crossed the stage and jumped down to where Carol had been waiting for him.

'Sorry it took so long,' he said, offering no excuse for the delay. 'Do you really want to go tonight? If I'm honest, I'm all in, and could do with a quiet night.'

'Brinn! I've just bought this new dress for the party, and I have had my hair done. Please try to make a little effort, just for me.'

He stepped forward, and putting his hand on her shoulder moved to kiss her on the cheek and signal his compliance. At that moment, they heard from somewhere in the auditorium a single slow handclap, and, emerging from the gloom at the back, a figure appeared. They both looked up and Brinn thought he could just make out Sarah walking down the side aisle.

'Amazing performance,' she announced sarcastically, continuing the applause. 'Truly original! Inspiring!'

'Sarah?' Brinn asked, as he began to walk towards her, excusing himself from Carol. 'I spent hours looking for you.'

'I can't think why,' she said. 'I thought you had all the material you needed, plus a little bonus, I seem to remember, and besides, maybe I didn't want to be found.'

Brinn put his hand gently on her back and guided her towards the rear of the room again, where he hoped they could not be so easily overheard. Then he continued, 'I wanted to explain, to try to—'

'Explain?' she interrupted, 'there is nothing to explain, American.'

Brinn could not remember how many times he had longed to hear her call him that again.

'It is quite obvious what your game was. While you needed something, I was useful – for a while anyway. Then, when you had taken all you wanted and I was no longer useful, abracadabra, you'd be gone. Simple.'

'Sarah, it wasn't quite like that.'

'No, and why was that? Let me see, now. Oh yes, I remember, you got caught by dear old Chaz. Hard luck, American! It was my own fault, I guess, you took me in so completely. Basically you're no different to any other bullshitter. Take my father, for instance. He only screwed up my body, and you, you screwed up everything else.'

Brinn wanted to respond, but he let the outburst go, firstly because he knew it was partially true, and secondly because he did not want to get into a full-blown argument here in front of Carol. She was now standing with her arms folded, shifting her weight impatiently, and looking, so obviously, at her watch.

'We need to talk,' Brinn said.

'Do we?' she replied.

'Yes, Sarah, please. I know I don't deserve a chance to explain, but if you did not want to talk, why did you come here?'

She remained silent.

'Let me just sort out my arrangements for this evening, and I will meet you at,' he thought for a moment, 'at Al's, ten o'clock, okay.'

Sarah looked across at Carol and wondered if she was the 'arrangement' he mentioned, then turned back to Brinn.

'Not one minute later,' she said.

'Not one minute later,' he echoed reassuringly.

She turned and left, while Brinn went back to Carol to try to lie his way out of taking her to the party.


Sarah had arrived early at Al's and was in the kitchen with him drinking tea.

'Are you sure you want to do this, Sarah?' Al began. Pausing thoughtfully for a moment, he continued, 'I suppose it might not hurt to see what he has to say, at least, but are you really sure you are up to hearing it?'

'I don't know what I really want,' she replied.

'You sleep with him, yes?' Al asked with a sideways look. 'I can tell you, I know, no need to deny it. You are different now to how you used to be. Not so scared, not so hard.'

'Oh yeah, and living on the street, those were two of the things I really needed to lose.'

The sarcasm that etched her words annoyed Al.

'Don't change the subject. Did you?'

Sarah blushed and bit the inside of her mouth to suppress a sheepish smile.

'I knew it! About time too, Sarah. Love him, do you?'

'It was just the one night,' she said dismissively.

'Yes, but for some, one night is a lifetime and it is not his fault he looks so much like—'

Al was prevented from finishing his sentence by the sound of the bell over the shop door as it opened. It was Brinn, three minutes early for his appointment.

Al went through first to greet him, followed by Sarah, who remained silent. Al showed them to a little table away from the window. Then he locked the front door, turned the 'open' sign around, pulled the shutter down and left them to talk.

After an awkward silence, Brinn started the conversation.

'Did you enjoy it, the play, I mean?'

'I have not seen many,' she said. 'I don't have much to compare it to, but yes, it was quite good.'

Brinn was glad Sarah was not a critic. Good and bad reviews are all publicity. The public either come to see how good a show is, or to see if it is really as bad as the critics say. Indifference kept them away in droves.

'I have missed you,' he said at last and genuinely.

'Seems you managed pretty well without me.'

Her remark was directed towards the absent Carol. Brinn ignored it, but defended himself.

'I looked for you for hours, searched everywhere; even went back to the Salvation Army place, that's how desperate I was.'

'Yes, so you said already, but it's a bit hard to believe after all the lies you have told. That business about your mother, for instance.'

'Not all of that was a lie, only the part about the other man, and you must admit, I had you going there for a minute.'

Sarah did not find the remark as amusing as Brinn had hoped she would.

'This is getting us nowhere.'

She stood to go, but Brinn caught her arm, and pulled her forcibly back down into her seat. She rubbed her arm to repress the mild discomfort.

'Look, I'm sorry, that was stupid of me,' he said, 'but this is difficult for me, too.' He waited for Sarah to settle again before he asked, 'How is College, and have you heard anything from Josh?'

'Does it really matter to you?' she asked.

'Yes,' he said indignantly. 'I would like to think I'm not quite the bastard that you seem to think I am.'

'It's too late for that.'

Brinn bit his tongue as he realised he had walked right into it, and he knew exactly what was heading his way next.

'If you cared so much, why did you use us then?'

He knew he was pleading a hopeless cause, but took a shot at it anyway.

'I meant no harm. I didn't set out to hurt you.'

Brinn just could not get anything right tonight. Even as the words left his lips, Sarah's eyes glazed and she retreated completely from any conscious communication.

Behind her fear, Sarah was beginning to feel angry. It was not the usual emotion that accompanied her withdrawn state, but then many things had changed for her too, since the night in the department store. The pressure from her anger built up until it took physical form and she reached for a discarded cup of cold tea that had been left sitting on the table. Deliberately, she threw it over him, her anger dissipating as she watched the liquid run down his chest. Brinn reeled back, scraping the chair noisily over the floor, and too late, he put his arms up in defence.

'My suit!' he said brushing the liquid from his jacket.

He was not sure whether to be angry or laugh. The suit

had cost him nearly a thousand dollars. He scanned the table and his eyes rested on a plastic tomato ketchup bottle. He grabbed it, stood and squirted the red sauce over her hair and face. The action made him feel ridiculously vindicated, but the feeling soon subsided when he saw the expression on Sarah's face.

Slowly, she lifted her hands to her face, wiped the mess out of her eyes, blinked and began to laugh a little. She rubbed her hands on her jumper and seized the sugar dispenser from the table in front of her. On her feet now, she walked around behind Brinn and ceremoniously pulled out his collar, tipping at least half of the contents down his neck. Brinn stood up, grimaced and, pulling his shirt out, he tried to liberate the sugar before it worked its way into his trousers.

By now he was laughing, too, and seeing nothing else to use as a weapon, he proceeded to the kitchen, followed by Sarah. On one of the work surfaces was a large tub of dripping. Brinn dipped his left hand into it and grabbed the passing Sarah with his right. He lifted her jumper up and smeared the greasy mass onto her stomach rubbing it well in. When he was satisfied at his creation, he let go the jumper and patted it into place.

Sarah looked at the grease oozing through from beneath her jumper. Then, with a feigned scowl, went to the refrigerator where she knew Al kept all sorts of interesting things. Her fumbling fingers fell immediately on a can of spray cream. She closed the refrigerator door with a sinister chuckle and emerged triumphantly, holding the can aloft. Brinn backed away in mock horror as Sarah shook the can, extending her arm and grabbed the waistband of his suit trousers.

'No, really, that's not such a good idea, Sarah!' he protested, as Sarah pressed the nozzle and ejected all the remaining contents of the can into his boxer shorts. Then, imitating his actions with the dripping, she massaged it into his groin, finally patting it into place. They were almost hysterical now and the noise had alerted Al, who was descending the stairs to investigate.

'Mama mia!' he cried, followed by several other sentences in fast Italian that neither of them understood. The laughter halted for a moment as they looked at the shocked Al. Then, looking back at each other, they burst out all over again. They began to skid about in the slimy mess and, desperate to keep upright, they reached out to hang onto each other, only succeeding in slipping helplessly to their knees. The laughing died a little as they looked at each other, then Brinn risked a kiss, which was gently rebuffed because of the lingering taste of tomato ketchup. Brinn pulled back and spat it out, wiping his mouth on the cuff of his ruined suit, and offering the other cuff to Sarah to do the same. She accepted and, when she had removed the worst of it, Brinn took her in his arms and tried a second kiss, to which she responded warmly. Al manoeuvred around the battle zone still muttering in Italian.

Then he halted, looked at the embracing couple, smiled and said, 'You English! In my country, we lock up mad people like you, and don't think you will get away without cleaning up this mess. For goodness sake, you look like a bad pizza. Never would I serve such a thing in my cafe.'

Sat down with a cup of tea that Al had provided, Sarah said, 'Sorry about the suit, American.'

'Oh, never mind about that, it's not important. Look, I want you to come out with me tonight. I know it's short notice, but it's the producer's birthday and the cast and I are throwing him a big party at a hotel. I would like to take you along.'

'Now it's you who are crazy,' she replied. 'Just look at me.'

'You look great to me,' he said leaning over and kissing her again. 'Come with me, please,' he whispered, taking hold of her hands.

'I'd be like an exhibit in a zoo, and I don't just mean because of the ketchup.'

'It won't be like that. Please, come with me,' he urged.

'It's all right, American, she will come with you,' Al called out from the kitchen, where he had been cleaning up the battle zone. 'I have something for you upstairs, Sarah,' he continued. 'You can wear it; I know Carmen would approve.'

Sarah looked back at Al, and then to Brinn. Both were urging her on to go.

'Okay, but you're both stark raving mad.'

'Great,' Brinn added, as he stood and started to head for the door. 'I'm going home to shower and change. I will be back for you in twenty-five minutes. Al, make sure she's ready.'

Sarah went upstairs with Al, who showed her Carmen's wardrobe. She had had some wonderful clothes, none of which Al could bring himself to throw away. He pulled out a towel from a drawer and she took it and went to the bathroom to clean up. Then he left Sarah alone to shower, and to choose which dress she would wear to the party. Fifteen minutes passed and Sarah had still not come down the stairs. Al became worried and returned upstairs to see what the problem was. He found Sarah sobbing on the bed, she had only progressed to the point of putting her hair back in a loose ponytail and was still wrapped in the towel.

'Sarah, what is the matter?' he asked. 'The American will be here soon.'

'Oh, Al, this is hopeless. How can I go to this party? To any party, come to that.'

'You don't like any of the dresses?' Al asked.

'No, no Al! They are all beautiful. It is just me. I am no

one and the people at the party will all be important, important to the American, anyway.'

'Sarah, stop this! You are as good as any one of them, probably better than some, and you're important to Brinn. That's all that matters.'

Sarah hugged Al and, wanting desperately to believe him, tried to pull herself together.

'I think you should wear this one,' Al said, holding aloft a dress he had taken from the wardrobe. 'It was one of Carmen's favourites, and just like her you will look like a million lira in it.'

Brinn pulled up in his car outside the cafe, freshly showered and wearing another suit. The first one, a total write-off, he had consigned to the dustbin. Shortly after, he had contacted Chris by phone to warn him that he was bringing Sarah to the party, and asking him not to mention the incident at the station to her. The blue tie he had chosen matched his eyes perfectly, and studying his reflection in the mirror, he felt good about himself again. From the car, Brinn could see Sarah inside the cafe kissing Al on the cheek and making her goodbyes. He had to look twice as she got into the car beside him to check if it was really her. The transformation stunned him; she had legs!

'Wow! You look great,' he said. 'I love the hair.'

'Thanks, American,' she replied. 'Al said I scrub up real good. You should see the things of Carmen's he still has up there. It's a bit sad; romantic, too. He can't bear to throw anything away.'

Brinn pulled away from the kerb, and joined the traffic heading towards the city centre. Periodically, he looked across to try to see exactly what Sarah was wearing beneath the black coat she had on, but had to give up as he almost hit an oncoming car.

'You're not a very good driver,' she said teasing him.

'I'm usually better than this,' he replied, 'and besides, it's not my fault you British are all on the wrong side of the road.'

The room was full to capacity and the ordered commotion inside conveyed a general mood of excitement and enthusiasm. The band was playing a medley of jazz numbers, mostly from the fifties, Chris's favourite music. Everyone who mattered had turned up and the champagne was flowing freely with the sound of the clink of glasses punctuating individual conversations.

A little after eleven thirty, Brinn and Sarah entered the room. The din died a little as some turned to see who the newcomers were, but the conversations soon resumed as explanations as to the identity of Brinn's escort were sought from any source. Sarah felt a little uncomfortable, unused to being the obvious object of curiosity for so many. She wondered whether any of them would have given her a second thought if they had passed her on the streets.

Unfamiliar with the formality, Sarah struggled against Brinn as he tried to remove her coat. With a little difficulty he succeeded and for the first time he was able to see the dress beneath it. It was the perfect choice, he thought. A plain black sleeveless shift dress that came to just below the knee was offset with a thin red belt and matching heeled shoes. Framed within the round neckline of the dress was a gold chain and locket that had once belonged to Carmen. It had been Al's suggestion that she wear it. He thought that it might give her confidence knowing that he and Carmen were watching over her. With her hair up and wispy strands cascading down over her neck, Brinn's was not the only head that turned to look at her. Brinn took her over to the bar and gave her the first glass of champagne she had ever had.

'Hey, go easy on that stuff,' he said in a loud whisper as

she downed the first one as though it were water.

'Sorry, I am very thirsty,' she replied.

'If you have a thirst, try the Evian. It's less volatile.'

Carol, who had the ability to stand out in any crowd whatever the circumstances, was holding court at one end of the room. Surrounded by latent admirers, she had heard the entrance the couple had made and was now in the process of disentangling herself from her group of followers. Excusing herself, she walked over to where Brinn and Sarah stood, then, completely ignoring Sarah she looped her arm through Brinn's.

'Hello, Brinn, I thought you said ten thirty,' she said.

'Yes, sorry, I was a bit held up.'

'I can see that,' Carol said with a derisory look in Sarah's direction. Chris had also seen Brinn's arrival and had been watching from the other side of the room. It was he who came to Sarah's rescue now.

Tapping her on the shoulder he said, 'You must be Sarah. Brinn has told me all about you. I am Chris Robbins. I know it is hard to believe, but it is my fiftieth birthday today.'

Sarah smiled at Chris and took the hand that was now extended to her by way of introduction and friendship. She had the strangest feeling she had met him somewhere before, but discarded the idea as unlikely, given their opposite social strata. Chris guided her away from the battle zone, on the pretence of getting her a drink, leaving Brinn to face Carol alone.

'Why did you bring her here with you?' Carol enquired.

'Because she was instrumental in keeping me in one piece while I was out there. I felt I owed her that much,' he replied, cautiously removing his arm from hers.

Carol was irritated that he had uncoupled himself, and she replied sarcastically, 'Oh well, if it is simply a debt you have to pay, then I suppose there can't be any harm in that, can there?'

Over at the bar, Chris had given Sarah another glass of champagne and was engaging her in small talk when he noticed Carol turn in their direction. She left Brinn standing in the middle of the room on his own and walked nonchalantly up to the bar next to Sarah.

'Hello, Sarah, isn't it? I have heard so much about you from Brinn. It was very good of you to come tonight, and it was very brave of you, too.'

Sarah could feel the hair on the back of her neck bristle. If she had been on her own territory, the subsequent conversation would have probably resulted in a catfight, but she was not on her own territory. Besides, the warm glow of the champagne was beginning to mellow her responses.

'Brave?' Sarah replied after a little thought, as Chris shuffled his feet and tried to think of a way he could extract her from this.

Fortunately, at that moment, a toast was proposed from the other end of the room, and the subsequent hubbub gave Chris enough cover to drag Sarah out from under Carol's nose. While Sarah nursed a fresh glass of champagne, he led her quickly into the adjoining cloakroom and shut the door. Sarah giggled with the effects of the champagne.

'Chris, we hardly know each other,' she said taking another sip from the glass.

'I'm sorry, Sarah, I'm not altogether sure if it was a good idea for Brinn to bring you here tonight.' Chris said honestly. 'He and Carol, well they go back a long way, and she's, she's just a bit…'

'Belligerent,' Sarah said with a growing difficulty.

'Well, yes, a bit,' Chris said a little surprised. 'Are you all right, Sarah. I think it might be an idea to lay off the champagne for a while and drink the Evian instead.'

'I'm fine Chris, just fine. I don't need Evi… Eviii…'

'Evian,' Chris offered helpfully.

'Yes, that's the stuff, and you don't have to make excuses for what's her face. I appreciate what you are trying to do, but it is unnecessary. I have been looking after myself for years now, and the puerile ravings of that cantankerous man-eater don't worry me in the slightest.'

Chris's mouth dropped open as he wondered if Carol had at last met her match.

Sarah rejoined the party, still musing over where she had met Chris before. She wandered over to the bar, sat down and allowed the bartender to pour her yet another champagne. Brinn joined her moments later, looking more than a little flustered.

'Giving you a hard time, is she?'

The words flowed from Sarah, assisted as they were by the champagne.

'It is probably my fault,' he replied. 'I have not had time to explain things to her properly. I'm rather afraid she still thinks that she and I are…'

He stopped as he watched Sarah down yet another champagne, slamming the glass down on the bar as she finished, licking her lips.

'You really should go easy with that stuff, especially as you are not used to it.'

'Nonsense, I'm fine,' she replied. 'It's just like lemonade, the bubbles go up your nose.'

'Yeah, up your nose and straight to your head. Honey, you're tight.'

'Nooooooo,' she replied, shaking her head slowly.

'Come on, I want to introduce you around, if you can still stand, that is, and preferably before you pass out on me.'

Brinn took her by the hand and led her around from group to group, explaining who she was, and how valuable she had been in forming his latest character. Sarah said little all this time, just answering a few questions and listening politely to the grateful appreciation, some genuine and some obsequious, that streamed in her direction. It was a sobering experience, the growing awareness that she seemed after all as much an abstraction to Brinn as she was a curiosity to his friends.

The attention that Brinn was now paying to Sarah was not amusing Carol in the slightest. She decided it was necessary to 'clear the air', as it were, between her and Sarah. Carol approached one of her admirers and whispered something to him. He nodded his consent and, leaving the group, walked over to Brinn and on some pretext dragged him away from Sarah. Seeing her opportunity, Carol gathered Sarah up, glass of champagne and all, and coaxed her into the garden.

'It would seem, my dear, as though you need to be made aware of a few facts,' Carol began.

It was good to step out onto the patio of the hotel garden, the cool air refreshing after the stuffy atmosphere of the conference room and the intoxicating effect of the champagne. Sarah thought it might soon become equally as uncomfortable out here, if she did not get a grip on the situation. Excusing herself for a moment, Sarah returned to the conference room and retrieved a half empty bottle of champagne from the bar.

'Sorry about that,' she said as she sat down opposite Carol at one of the patio tables. 'I find that tomato ketchup makes me very thirsty. Don't you find that?'

'I'm sorry, but I have never tasted any,' Carol replied in bemused irritation.

'Really! You must try some, it's great on burgers,' she said standing up and looking round. 'I'll see if I can get you some from the bar.'

'No, really, there is no need,' Carol said, grabbing Sarah's arm and pulling her back down on the chair. 'Look, I didn't come here to discuss junk food.'

Sarah sat up in the chair and tried to look interested in what Carol was trying to tell her. Taking Sarah's hand in hers and adopting a more patronising tone, Carol continued.

'Now, Sarah, I can call you Sarah, can't I? I already feel as though I have known you for simply ages. Brinn is continually talking about you, and the fact is, with you being that much older than me, I feel like I can talk to you much as I would, well, to my own mother.'

The age difference between them was actually only a small one, but the significance of the pronouncement did not go unnoticed by Sarah. She allowed Carol to continue voicing her opinions, although it crossed her mind that if Carol called her mum, even once, she would end up wearing the drinks.

'As you have been such a help to Brinn,' Carol continued, 'I felt you should be one of the first to know. I have decided that it is about time Brinn and I made some permanent commitment to each other. I know he has been thinking along those lines himself, and tonight seems the perfect time to announce it. Do you know, Sarah, that in that room are several really big people, who could be so good for Brinn's career? I've been buttering them up all night.'

I'm sure you have, Sarah thought to herself as she eased out of Carol's grasp.

'You see, Sarah,' Carol added, 'Brinn needs a guiding light. He has always been very reluctant when it comes to pushing himself forward. I feel, well, we both feel, that we would make the perfect couple.'

'Well, my dear,' Sarah replied taking up Carol's hands this time and slipping into the role of 'mother' that Carol had so carefully crafted for her. 'I may call you dear, may I? Well, it seems to me that there is no real problem here.'

Sarah manoeuvred herself so as to be eyeball to eyeball

and in an almost comradely huddle.

'There is an old saying,' she whispered, 'when the hands of Big Ben are on one minute to midnight, tomorrow is only sixty seconds away.'

Sarah completed her sentence with as serious an expression as she could manage and a knowing nod, while desperately trying not to laugh out loud. Carol began to nod in unison, frowning heavily, trying to draw the deep meaning out of what she believed to be some ancient adage.

Then, at last, having lost the battle she said, 'Yes, I see what you mean. Absolutely right.'

Carol thanked Sarah profusely and even gave her a friendly hug as she left the garden for the party. Carol closed the door behind her, believing herself to be vindicated in full.

Sarah, with her back to the closed door, convulsed in helpless laughter for several minutes, partly because of Carol, mostly because of the champagne.

'Sixty seconds until tomorrow,' she spluttered and gasped as tears rolled down her face.

She stood unsteadily and tried to walk to the door, but swayed wildly and grabbed the back of the chair instead. Doubled over, and still chuckling, she sat down exhausted. The tears would not stop rolling down her face as the fine line between laughter and sorrow was breached. The tears, just like the laughter, were uncontrollable. All the things she had seen and heard during the evening had only reinforced her own growing concern. There was little future for her with Brinn. She had to face it. She could not exist in this alien world, no matter how much she wanted to do so. It had struck midnight and it was time for Cinderella to go home. A little relief washed over her as she acknowledged her fears and accepted the inevitable, but the pain, it would not go away.

Brinn came into the garden and she quickly reverted to

mendacious laughter.

'Where have you been?' she began. 'I have just had a great time out here with Carol. She is such a hoot and completely daft. I haven't laughed so much in ages.'

'Yes, I have just seen her inside. She's acting most peculiarly.'

Sarah tried to struggle to her feet again.

'Say, I think you've had about enough, don't you? If it is all right with you, I think we should go now.'

'Sure, why not?' she said.

Then with a flourish of her hand, she finished off her glass of champagne and the one that Carol had left behind also. Brinn took her arm and led her back into the conference room. He looked around the room to try to locate Chris and, seeing him over by the bar, he steered Sarah over towards him. Brinn offered their apologies for their early departure, indicating that this was due in part to Sarah's over indulgence. Brinn left Sarah with Chris while he went to retrieve Sarah's coat from the cloakroom. Chris snatched the opportunity to say the few words he had been trying to say to Sarah all night.

'You are good for him, Sarah. I hope you manage to work something out between you.'

Sarah managed a semi-sober reply.

'Thanks, Chris, I will always remember what a nice bloke you are.'

Then she lapsed into confusion again.

'Do you know, you look vaguely familiar to me? Have we met before?'

Brinn returned just in time to hear the tail end of the conversation, and hastily helped her into her coat. He thanked Chris again and guided Sarah away, without alerting Carol to the fact that they were leaving. Not too difficult a task, as she was preoccupied with convincing her gathered admirers that she was to be the future Mrs Peters.

Outside, the rush of fresh air seemed to revive Sarah's memory process. She stood bolt upright and turning to Brinn, said as best she could, 'Do you know, I think that Chris is the same pervert that gave me all that money in the underground station.'

Brinn steered the car into the stream of late night traffic heading out of the city. He looked several times at Sarah, who seemed to be lost in her own thoughts. Not wishing to intrude, he maintained the silence, having some thinking of his own to sort out. Brinn's mind was reliving the interaction he had had with Carol before discovering Sarah in the garden. The contents of the conversation had thrown him completely and he was trying to assimilate the information.

When Carol had returned to the party after her chat with Sarah on the patio, she had made a little announcement to a few people she was with. She knew exactly the effect such news would have on the gathered onlookers. Like wildfire, the news swept around the room, growing in inaccuracy as it did so.

It had begun life as 'Sarah believes that Brinn and I should not waste any time as we are so well suited.'

It grew into 'Sarah told us we should get married, as it is pointless wasting any more time. We are perfect for each other.'

It was the 'should get married' that was giving Brinn the biggest headache. This very fact he had remarked on to Carol, when he managed to isolate her in the cloakroom after fighting off the congratulations from a few of his friends. A brief argument took place and he had stormed out leaving the issue still unresolved. He could not work out why Sarah had felt the need to say it, if indeed she had said it. There was always the possibility it was another of Carol's inventions to manipulate events.

'Drop me off at the car park after Al's, would you,

American? I don't think I can walk from the cafe, it feels like my legs are made of rubber.'

'I don't think you're in any fit state to be out at all tonight. I think you should come back with me to the flat. That all right with you?'

'What about these clothes? I have to get them back to Al sometime,' Sarah replied.

'Sure, but not tonight.'

'Cinderella is going to turn into a pumpkin,' she said.

'As long as Cinderella doesn't chuck up in my car, I don't think it's a problem. Anyway, I don't think it is a pumpkin, is it?'

'Sorry, I'm a bit muddled,'

'You're not muddled, you're just plain drunk. I did warn you about the champagne.'

The car drew up outside the front of Brinn's flat and he helped Sarah from the passenger's side and up the few steps to the front door. He propped her up against the wall with one hand, while he wrestled in his pocket with the other for the flat key. Needing both hands to open the door, he let go of Sarah, and just managed to open it as Sarah's long suffering knees gave way beneath her and she began to slither down the wall. He caught her in time and, picking her up, carried her into the flat.

'Next time, you definitely stay with the Evian,' he said as he kicked the door shut with his foot and took her through to the bedroom.

He laid her down on the bed, and the movement roused her. She reached up and put her arms around his neck, pulling him down for a kiss.

'You sure are drunk,' he said.

'Only a little, and it is rather a nice feeling.'

'You won't think so tomorrow morning,' he replied.

Sarah wriggled out from beneath him and stood un-steadily to her feet, turning to face Brinn, who had rolled over onto his back to watch her.

'Make love to me, American,' she said.

'I don't usually make it a habit of taking advantage of drunken women,' he said reaching up to take her hands in an attempt to steady her swaying body.

'Please, American, it is important to me. I won't be sick if that's what you're worried about.'

'No. Sick or no sick, it's still against my principles,' he said, feigning outrage. Then after a pause, 'but you can make love to me if you like. I take it you have no such principles,' he added pulling her all the way down on top of him, and kissing her extravagantly.

The night was passing too quickly for Sarah as every moment spent with Brinn was precious to her. The effect of the alcohol was beginning to wear off a bit after the exertions of lovemaking. She thought that if she did not make the move now, she would not be able to do it at all.

'Can I ask you something, American,' she said, turning to him.

Brinn, who was lying on his back, nodded, his mind having wandered back to Carol's odd behaviour earlier. 'Did you ever wonder why I stopped to help you the day we first met?'

'No, not really,' he replied. 'Why did you?'

'Well, you know that I was on my way back from the cemetery?'

He nodded again.

'I was sitting on a bench a little way up the Embankment when you wandered down to talk to those men.'

She had his full attention now, though he was still looking up at the ceiling. 'I saw what happened and I did nothing. I was actually glad of it. I enjoyed watching them beat you up.'

Brinn turned to her, meeting her gaze and asked, 'Is this

some sort of joke? Why, for God's sake?'

'Well, you see, American,' she said softly, hoping the impact of the following words would be only slightly less if she did so, 'but for a few inches in height and a little grey hair here and there, you look so very much like my father.'

Brinn's mouth dropped open in disbelief, and Sarah moved forward to kiss him, but he pulled back out of reach.

'So why help me at all? Why not just leave me, walk off?'

'I did walk away, twice. I returned each time because I was unable to stay away. The thought of you kept drawing me back.'

Feeling sure that she could say nothing more to shock him, he asked, 'Do you mean the thought of me or of your father?'

'My father.' Sarah waited for a moment observing the impact her words had on him. 'I wanted to see them hurt you. No, not just hurt you. I hoped they would kill you. It's true what they say about people who have been systematically abused. We always go back to our own. Did you know that a dog can be trained to show affection when it is beaten? It's just conditioning. It's no different with people. The dog doesn't know any better and neither do I.'

'But I didn't treat you like that.'

The words died on his lips. He knew full well he had taken advantage of her, albeit innocently intended. He turned over onto his back again and Sarah tried to nestle up alongside him, but although he did not protest, he did not respond either.

Sarah woke. It was four o'clock in the morning, and Brinn was on his side asleep with his back to her. She quietly slipped out of bed, dressed and tiptoed round to Brinn's side of the bed where she bent down to kiss him. He stirred a little, but did not wake.

Taking one last look at his face she whispered, 'Goodbye

Brinndle Peters.'

Then, checking around to make sure she had left nothing behind, she let herself out of the flat.

At 10 a.m., Brinn began to stir. He stretched out a little. His arm extended into the side of the bed where he expected to find Sarah. He turned over as his hand found the space empty and cold, and as he opened his eyes he saw that her things were missing also. He sat up and exhaled audibly. The conversation of the previous night echoed in his mind. He still found it hard to accept that she felt nothing for him. Why had she told him? It made no sense.

## Chapter Ten

Brinn woke early, thinking he couldn't remember being conscious at this time since he was on the streets, almost five months before. Why couldn't his agent ever get him a flight on a plane going to New York at a reasonable hour of the day? Grudgingly, he crawled out of bed and almost immediately stumbled over one of the bags he had packed the night before. Cursing and then kicking it, he pushed it to one side, as though it were the bag's fault he had to leave. He wondered why he had agreed to transfer with the play to Broadway.

Chris had told him it was a great opportunity and a fresh start for him. They had arranged for another actor to take over his role this end, and half of the original cast were staying too. Chris had sounded so convincing about it, but for a while now Brinn had hated the part of the tramp. He felt his performances were shallow and empty and he wished he could be doing something, anything, else instead.

Carol was finally out of his life, but this time Brinn had finished it. He had wised up at long last that she was not what he wanted and never could be, not now. It was not her that was causing his apathy, though. It was something else, something Brinn could not admit to yet, not even to himself. He took a shower, but as he returned to the bedroom to towel off, he noticed something shiny, half-hidden under the bed.

Normally it would not have aroused his attention, the place usually being in such a mess, but yesterday he had cleaned up a little because of his imminent departure, and he thought he had picked everything up. Still rubbing himself with the towel, he sat on the edge of the bed and pulled the object out. Sitting up, he held it aloft – a gold chain and locket that after a few minutes he recognised as the same one that Sarah had worn the night he had last seen her. Good and bad memories flooded back – the morning in the shower, Pete's death, the opera, the night in the department store, the party. He sat with his head in his hands, the locket trailing from his fingers while he wondered where it had gone wrong, how had he let her slip away. Too late now, with that damn plane to catch. He had to check in at five thirty, only an hour away.

An hour. He could at least return the locket to Al. An hour was long enough for that. He could just pop in and say hello for old time's sake; let Al know he was leaving for the States. Brinn quickly snapped into action, and, pulling on some jeans and a sweatshirt, he grabbed his car keys, tucked the locket and chain into a pocket, and went out to the car.

At this hour, there were few other cars on the roads, so it only took him twelve minutes to drive across town to the cafe. Brinn felt stupid. Surely Al wouldn't be up at this hour of the morning. He drew up outside and was relieved to observe that the lights in the cafe were on already. Towards the rear of the cafe, he could just see a figure that seemed to be giving the place a spring-clean.

Brinn got out of the car and walked hesitantly up to the front door. He tried to push it open, but it was locked, so he banged on the glass with his fists, trying to get Al's attention.

Al peered down the length of the cafe to see what all the noise was about. He dried his hands on the towel that was tucked into his waistband and began to walk slowly towards this early visitor whom he could hardly make out through the misted glass. He slapped his hand to his forehead as he recognised the outline of Brinn, and rushed to open the door.

'It's you, American. I am sorry. I did not realise it was you at first.'

'That's okay, Al. Look, I really am sorry to disturb you so early, but I'm off to the States in less than an hour and I found this in my flat,' he said, holding the chain aloft. 'I thought you might like it back.'

Al took a moment to recognise it.

'Oh my God, yes, thank you! We thought it had been lost for good. But don't stand out there on the street. Come on in for a minute and I will get you a cup of tea.'

'You couldn't make that a coffee, could you, Al?'

'Sure, now come on in.'

Al led him to the kitchen and plugged in the kettle.

'Should not take long,' Al continued. 'I only just made myself one.'

Two minutes later and cup in hand, Brinn, accompanied by Al, went back into the cafe where they sat at a table.

'Have you seen Sarah? How is she?' Brinn asked him.

'She is good, last time I saw her, that is. She is on her own now, did you know that?'

'No, I didn't. I have had no contact with her at all. What happened?'

'College is off the streets now. Apparently his son had been trying to trace him for over a year, and finally, with the help of the Salvation Army, he succeeded. Sarah went with College when they met for the first time. It was good, American. College was overjoyed to see him again. Now he lives with his son and daughter-in-law and grandchildren. Yes, grandchildren! Unbelievable, isn't it? He is, according to Sarah, a brilliant grandpa.'

'That is great, Al, but Sarah?' he asked.

'I don't see her as much as I would like to, but occasionally she drops by. She is never in one place for very long these days. I asked her to come move in with me, but she wouldn't.'

The phone began to ring in the kitchen, and Al excused himself to go and answer it.

Brinn started to walk down to the front of the cafe, sipping his coffee and studying the photos on the walls. He had never paid much attention to them before, but now they acted as a distraction while he waited for Al to finish on the phone. He glanced at one or two and then, about halfway down, he stopped opposite one that looked a little familiar. He could just make out a group of four people, but it wasn't a very good shot. A shaky camera hand had rendered it a bit out of focus, and bad positioning had cut off the tops of their heads. Brinn recognised Al, however, and a round, very Italian looking mama who was smiling broadly. He assumed, correctly, that this was Carmen. The other female looked a little like a younger Sarah, and the last person seemed to vaguely resemble himself. It was ridiculous, he thought. He did not remember having any photo taken and besides Carmen was dead long before he... Sarah's father!

'I'm sorry about that, American,' Al said as he returned. 'I am having the Environmental Health people in later today and a friend was coming to help me go over the place. Unfortunately he has been delayed. I think I will be doing this all by myself.'

Al noticed Brinn staring at the photos, and came alongside to see which one he was looking at.

'Ahhh, you think you see yourself, yes, American?'

'It's not me,' Brinn replied with growing loathing.

'Of course not! I was only joking. Sarah and I often used to talk about how you looked so much like him.'

'Her father,' Brinn said, almost spitting out the words.

'Her father,' Al said a little confused. 'No, no! Not her father, her brother.'

Brinn turned his head slowly, unsure if he had heard Al

209

correctly.

'I'm sorry, Al, did you say her brother?'

'Why, yes, I thought she had told you.'

Brinn must have looked terrible because Al pulled out a chair for him to sit on.

'You okay, American?'

'Al, please, what is going on? I don't understand.'

Al, seeing Brinn's confusion, asked, 'What is it she has told you, American?' and then sat down opposite him.

'I don't know. It's all so muddled now. We came home from the party the night you loaned her the dress and the locket, you remember?' Brinn said, holding the locket up again for Al to see. 'Then we made love, and she told me I looked like her father.'

'How was the party?' Al asked.

'Oh, the usual crowd, you know. My ex-girlfriend made a bit of a scene, but apart from that… Why, what's it got to do with anything?'

'Maybe nothing. Go on, what happened next?'

'She told me that the first day she saw me, the day I was mugged, she was on her way back from putting flowers on your wife's grave. She had stopped to sit for a while and saw the thugs who had attacked me, and after they had finished, she said she had hoped they would kill me because I looked like her father. That was the only reason she helped me afterwards. Is this making any sense to you, Al?'

'You mean, she helped you, because she thought you were her father?'

'Yes, that is about the size of it, and it makes me sick to my stomach even now when I think about it, that it might have been the only reason she stayed with me.'

'Ahh, but you don't look like her father. You look like her brother.'

'Sorry, Al, you have lost me.'

'Did you ask her to live with you?'

'No.'

'Were you going to?'

'Well, yes, before she told me I looked like her father.'

Brinn stared at his coffee, unable to fit the pieces of this jigsaw together.

Al watched him for a while and then said, 'American, I know she loves you. She has told me often, but sometimes that is not enough. The difference between you is so great. You live in totally different worlds. For you it is parties, newspaper headlines and nice cars. For Sarah, it is the dole queue, the charity of others and nowhere to call home. She tried, but perhaps in doing so she realised something you have missed. She could not bridge the gap.'

'But why the lies? Why tell me I looked like her father?'

'Would you have let her go otherwise?'

Brinn thought for a moment.

'No,' he said emphatically, 'I don't think I would. God forgive me, at first I was real glad when I woke up to find she had gone. What can I do, Al? I want her back. I need her in my life.'

'I can see you do, American, but you would have to make a middle road; one you could both survive on.'

'Damn it, help me, Al! I want to give it a shot. I can find some way to work it out.'

'It's not going to be that easy, American. Are you aware that Josh is dead also?'

Brinn shrugged his shoulders and replied, 'No, but I guess it was inevitable sooner or later.'

'He didn't do it. The pushers caught up with him in Manchester. Apparently he had been siphoning money from his deals with them for a long time, and they had just had enough. No action was taken by the police. They thought it was just another junkie who had overdosed, but the coroner found a cocktail of tablets in Josh's stomach, and Josh never touched tablets.'

'They forced him to take them?' Brinn asked amazed.

'Well, I would do anything with a knife at my throat, wouldn't you?'

'Why didn't he try to get his stomach pumped? The hell I wouldn't hang around waiting to die.'

'He probably would have if they had not finished the job with just enough crack to keep him happy till the pills kicked in. Neat, tidy and cheap, and best of all, it makes it look like he OD'd. With Josh's history, I don't expect the authorities would have given it a second thought.'

'Sadistic bastards,' Brinn interrupted.

'That is why she has to keep on the move these days. The men who killed Josh have been looking for the pair of you since you helped him to get to Manchester. I guess they haven't got to you yet because they have been looking in the wrong places.'

'I've got to find her first, Al, before they do,' Brinn said as he stood to go.

He thanked Al for the coffee, left the locket and chain on the table and headed for the door.

'Hey, American,' Al shouted after him, 'try the back of the market. That's the last place I heard she was sleeping.'

'Thanks, Al.'

'And, American! Good luck!'

Brinn stepped out into the morning light, his mind in turmoil. He got into his car, grabbed the car phone and punched in the number for Chris. Brinn drummed his fingers impatiently on the steering wheel as he waited for Chris to pick up at the other end.

'Hi, Chris, it's Brinn here… Yes, I'm sorry, I know it is only five fifteen, but this is an emergency. You remember Sarah… Yes, that's right. Now listen, she has got herself into some serious trouble, and I would like to help her out.'

Brinn pulled the receiver away from his ear and let Chris blow off some steam.

'Okay, okay, I know I'm a bastard, but I know you love me anyway. I need a couple of days. No, make it a week to be on the safe side. Do you think you can okay it with New York, and book another flight for two this time? But Chris, for God's sake, make it at a reasonable time of day.'

Brinn moved the phone again as a barrage of profanities hit the airways.

'Thanks, Chris, I love you too, and I owe you one.'

Brinn hung up before the next verbal onslaught.

Sarah wasn't at the market, and Brinn found himself retracing the steps of his previous search. One or two people had seen her, but did not know where she was now. It seemed as though she kept pretty much on the move in an effort to avoid contact with anyone who might be looking for her. This was good from her point of view, but made it really difficult for Brinn to trace her. A couple of days passed in fruitless searching. Either the people he spoke to genuinely knew nothing, or they thought he was the enemy and were covering for her. Absolutely no amount of reassurance, either verbal or financial, could persuade them otherwise.

On the afternoon of the third day, his intention was to begin a search of the park. The hope he had started out with was beginning to dwindle. There weren't many places left for him to search. He had just locked his car and walked across the road to the park entrance when he spotted something familiar protruding from the shrubbery a hundred feet down the other side of the fence.

'Sarah's sleeping bag,' he said out loud.

He stumbled in the direction of the orange bag, as his feet moved independently of his brain. Then, regaining his equilibrium, he ran the final seventy-five feet. His heart was thumping in his chest as he stooped down to lift the corner of the sleeping bag, but the face that greeted him was that of a stranger.

'Where's Sarah?' he shouted to the startled recumbent figure of an elderly woman.

'Who's Sarah?' the frightened woman replied.

'The owner of this sleeping bag, where is she?' he added, his voice raised in anger and desperation.

The woman cowered away, clutching the bag up around her chin. 'It's mine! The bag is mine! I did not steal it.'

Seeing the situation was deteriorating, and the woman was now so frightened she would be of little use until he calmed her, Brinn checked his emotions.

'Look, I'm sorry. I'm just trying to find someone. It's real urgent. Can you help me?'

'I didn't steal it, if that's what you're thinking! She gave it to me.'

'No one is accusing you of stealing it, and I don't care how you got hold of the bag. However, if you could help me find the person who gave it to you, I would be very grateful.'

He withdrew a ten pound note from his wallet and held it up for her to see. The woman let go of the bag, and made a grab for the note, but Brinn pulled it back out of her reach.

'When we find her, it's yours.'

He tucked it away in his hip pocket and helped the woman out of the bag and onto her feet.

'It's this way,' she said, collecting her things together and leading Brinn in the direction of the underground.

At the entrance of the underpass leading to the station, the woman halted.

'In there, along on the left,' she said, holding her hand out for payment.

Brinn squinted down the passage and tried to compensate for the darkness that was caused by the vandalised strip lights. He could just make out a small figure that lay facing the wall halfway down on the left.

'You can't have the money till I'm sure,' he said.

The woman protested, but was reluctant to follow, thinking her theft would, at last, be discovered. So she waited at the entrance. Brinn descended the few steps and approached the pathetic figure that was moving a little, but made no sound.

'Sarah,' he said quietly, 'is that you?'

There was no response, so Brinn knelt down and rolled the figure over towards him. It was Sarah, but she was in a terrible mess, lying in her own urine, amid a pile of empty cans and rubbish.

Brinn shouted back to the woman, 'How long has she been here?'

But there was no one there to respond. The woman had left, thinking it better to get away with the sleeping bag while the going was good.

Sarah was barely conscious. Her eyes rolled around wildly and as he tried to move her, he noticed an empty syringe and pill bottle lying on the ground next to her. A wave of panic swept through him as he thought that he might have come too late. Passers-by stared contemptuously at Brinn's futile efforts to sit her up, presuming her to be high or drunk or both. Sarah slumped forward as Brinn tried to remove her damp coat and substitute it with his own. He coaxed her gently and tried to rouse her. Then, placing one arm beneath her knees, and the other around her back, he picked her up and took her along the passage and up to the street. He tried several times in vain to hail a taxi, but the two that stopped refused to take the fare when they saw the state Sarah was in. Exasperated, he carried her the entire distance to his car and then, unlocking the door, he laid her down on the back seat.

'It's okay, Sarah,' he reassured her. 'I'll get you to hospital. You will be all right.'

The word 'hospital' revived her for a moment. The thought of hospital was too fearful to contemplate, even in her present state.

'No, please,' she said weakly, 'not hospital.'

'Be reasonable, Sarah, you need medical attention. It is not so bad there, really.'

'No please,' she urged again, 'I'll be all right. Anywhere but there.'

Briefly he made his frustration evident, but controlled himself.

'Okay, don't worry, I'll take you back to Al's. Perhaps we can sort something out from there.'

He covered her with the car blanket and got into the driver's seat. Progress to Al's was slow. The traffic was heavy and his concentration was divided between steering with one hand on the wheel and checking on Sarah in the back every so often.

Al had recognised Brinn's car arriving outside the front of the cafe, and as he saw him lift what he thought must be Sarah from the back seat, he opened the door to receive them.

'My God,' Al said. 'What happened to her?'

'Not now, Al. Where can I take her?'

'Upstairs, second on the right. I'll lock up and be there in a moment.'

Brinn carried Sarah up the awkward staircase and into the small room where he carefully laid her on the bed. She heaved a little from the movement, and Brinn stroked her forehead until the convulsion subsided. Al entered the room, and Brinn turned immediately to him.

'She refuses to go to hospital, Al. What shall I do?'

'What did they give her?' Al asked.

The thought that this might be the work of the drug gang had not fully penetrated Brinn's mind.

'Oh God! I should have brought the empties with me.

Sorry, Al, it was the last thing going through my mind at the time.'

He thought for a moment and then remembered. 'There was a syringe and an empty bottle of some sort of pills. Paracetamol I think it was. Yes, I'm pretty sure, headache pills. Surely they can't do her any real harm, Al?'

'It's important you try to find out for sure, American. Do your best. See what you can get out of Sarah.'

Brinn turned back to Sarah and bent over her. 'Sarah,' he said shaking her shoulders quite hard. 'Come on, honey, wake up! Talk to me! What have they given you?'

Sarah moaned a little and opened her eyes briefly, then closed them again.

Brinn persisted.

'Sarah, wake up, please!'

This time, the shaking roused her a little more, and she opened her eyes again.

'American?'

'Yes, that's right, honey, it's American,' he replied, lifting her up and holding her in his arms. 'Now try to remember. What did they give you?'

'Crack, I think,' she half whispered. 'No, I'm not sure. I can't.'

'Come on, Sarah,' Brinn interrupted shaking her again.

'Crack and a few tablets,' were the last words she could manage before lapsing back into unconsciousness.

'What do you think, Al? Can we help her?'

'It won't be easy. She should be in hospital, but I know what she is like. She would be out like a shot the minute she comes round,' Al said shaking his head. 'I don't know. We might just get lucky. Try to keep her awake. Get her under the shower and talk to her. I'm going to get something from the chemist.'

Al left the room, and Brinn began to undress Sarah. He left her naked on the bed for a moment, while he went to get things ready. Then he ran through to the bedroom, lifted her up and carried her back to the bathroom where the shower was running. There was no way she could manage to stand by herself, so Brinn kicked his shoes off and climbed in fully clothed behind her, standing her up beneath the cold water. She gasped as the cold stream touched her flesh, and roused almost immediately.

'Yes, Sarah,' he reassured her. 'That's it! Come on back to me.'

Brinn wiped her hair from her face and fought to keep her upright.

'Al is coming back in a minute and everything will be all right, I promise. Don't give up on me now, honey. Hold on.'

Brinn turned Sarah around so the water would fall on her face, and she gasped again and spluttered a little as she spat out the water that had filled her mouth. Her knees began to buckle and Brinn struggled against the wetness of her body to keep hold of her. He was relieved to hear the sound of the shop bell and of Al returning from the chemist. A few hurried footsteps on the wooden stairs, and Al arrived in the bathroom.

'Help me, Al, she's out cold again.'

The two men manoeuvred Sarah from the shower along the awkward passage and into the cramped bedroom. There was only room enough for one of them at a time, so Al waited in the hallway while Brinn pulled the covers back and laid her on the bed. He replaced the sheet over her naked body and turned to Al to see what he had brought.

'It's an emetic. It will help her to be sick. I just pray we are in time,' Al told him. 'I'll go make some up. You bring her round, okay?'

Brinn nodded, turning again to Sarah.

Al paused in the doorway and added, 'If all else fails, American, slap her out of it.'

Then he left. Brinn had heard the comment, but deliberately disregarded it, remembering how Sarah had reacted in the past. He tried everything he could think of, but Sarah remained unconscious. Al returned a few minutes later, holding a glass of brown liquid in his hand.

'Any luck?' he asked Brinn.

'No, I just can't get her to respond.'

Al pulled Brinn back out of the way and put the glass down on the bedside cabinet. He reached over the bed and slapped Sarah hard across the face. She responded almost immediately with a low moan.

'For God's sake, slap her, American! You must bring her round. She must be conscious if we are to have any hope of getting her to drink this.'

The urgency in Al's voice had almost convinced him, but he said, 'I can't! You know what she's like.'

'We don't have time for that now. Just do it, American! If you love her, you can do it.'

Al stepped back and let Brinn into the room. He lifted Sarah up and, holding a deep breath slapped her half-heartedly across her cheek. Sarah's head moved in the direction of the blow, but she did not stir. Brinn grimaced as the outline of his hand began to materialise in an angry red mark on her cheek.

'Again, American, harder.'

Brinn shifted uncomfortably and repeated the blow a little harder. This time Sarah responded, so he hit her again. She moaned, opening her eyes and Brinn lifted her up into the sitting position.

'Sarah! Here! Drink this,' he said taking the emetic from the bedside cabinet and lifting it to her lips.

She pulled a face as the liquid touched her tongue and she tried to pull away, but Brinn held her head firmly, almost forcing her to drink. She spluttered and coughed, but he kept trying until she had taken it all. Finally, he let her rest back on the bed.

'Get her on her side,' Al urged him.

Brinn complied, while Al went to fetch a bowl. The moment he returned, Sarah began to retch, and Brinn just managed to snatch the bowl and put it by her as she vomited for the first time.

'Don't let her roll onto her back. Keep her on her side,' Al said as he stood back.

Brinn put his hand on Sarah's shoulder, and kept it there, braced her while she convulsed and coughed. Ten minutes passed, and there was little to show for her efforts. Al was concerned at the lack of volume, but did not pass his worries on to Brinn. Turning to Al, Brinn asked, 'Do you think that is it now?'

'Looks like it. I think it will be okay to let her lie back now.'

Brinn eased Sarah round and she sighed with relief. Her eyes, though still a little glazed, tried to focus on Brinn as she lifted her hand vaguely to his face. He took hold of it, and turning it over, kissed it tenderly.

'You okay,' he asked gently.

'Think so. A bit cold.' Then, with a widening grin, 'You seem to have three heads.'

Brinn bent down to her and kissed her on the forehead.

'You're soaked through,' she said.

'It doesn't matter. Let's get you into this bed.'

Brinn pulled the remaining bedclothes over her shivering body, and she closed her eyes and began to settle as she relaxed with the increased warmth. Al, who had retreated momentarily to the kitchen, now brought Brinn a welcome cup of coffee.

'You will need this, American. It may be a long night.'

'Thanks, Al,' he replied, taking it gratefully.

Sipping it he eased himself back into the chair.

'Will she be all right, Al?' Brinn asked him.

Al did not want to raise Brinn's hopes too high.

'Perhaps, if we can get her through tonight, she has got a better than fifty-fifty chance.'

'God, is that all? Isn't there anything else we can do to increase the odds a bit?'

'You ever pray, American?'

Brinn nodded, so tired now he had a problem keeping his eyes open. Al took the coffee from Brinn's hands.

'Go on. I'll take the first watch. You go use my bed and get some sleep.'

'You sure?' Brinn replied.

Al nodded and added, 'Get dried off first. There is a spare towel in the bathroom.'

Brinn got to his feet and went in search of the towel. He removed his clothes and laid them over the warm radiator, then dried himself on the towel. Wearily he went into Al's bedroom and collapsed gladly onto the bed, pulling the eiderdown over his body. Drifting off into a fitful sleep brought a mixed blessing. He found his unconsciousness was punctuated with visions of the two drug pushers struggling with Sarah, while every effort he made met with failure. At each attempt, the dream prevented him from intervening by the continual regression of the image no matter how fast he tried to approach it. The violence of the images woke him with a start to find that he had been asleep for barely forty minutes. Unwilling to return to the nightmare, he tried to shake it from his mind and wrapping himself in the eiderdown, he went through to Al and Sarah.

'Sorry, I couldn't sleep. Any change?' he whispered to Al.

'No, still the same. She is hanging in there.'

'I'll take over now. Go on, Al, you get a couple of hours.'

They changed places and Brinn sat down in the chair. He watched Sarah as she lay there, her breathing very shallow, and her hair still wet from the shower. The noise of Al closing the door behind him, though almost silent, startled Sarah from her sleep. Brinn extended his hand to calm her and she took hold of it, feebly pulling him towards her. He made it easy for her, wanting to be closer, and, discarding the eiderdown, he slipped into the bed beside her. He put his arm under her back and she responded by resting her head on his chest. After the frenzied events of the day, it felt good to hold her again, and when Al came in for his shift two hours later, he did not disturb the sleeping couple, but closed the door quietly behind him again.

Brinn woke first the next morning, disturbed by the sound of Al downstairs making preparations to open the cafe. He checked his watch on the corner of the bedside table. It was nine fifteen, a little late for Al, Brinn thought. Sarah was still dozing and Brinn was loath to move, enjoying the sensation of her body next to his again. She stirred and stretched a little, and opened her eyes briefly. Brinn stroked her hair and smiled, relieved that she seemed all right.

'Hey, sleeping beauty, any chance I can get my arm back?'

Sarah looked up at him.

'It's really you. I thought I had just dreamed you up.'

'No, I'm real. Look, in the flesh, so to speak.'

He moved toward her a little in order to kiss her, but she said, 'I wouldn't if I were you. My mouth tastes pretty bad, even to me.'

'That must have been the brown stuff Al got for you last night. It did not smell too great, either.' Taking her advice he kissed each cheek instead.

'Why did you come back?' she asked him in a more serious tone, but before he could reply there was a knock at the door and Al came into the room.

He stood there with a tray bearing two mugs of steaming tea. Brinn sat up immediately, took the tray from Al and put it down on the bedside cabinet. Sarah took her time, but only managed to raise herself onto her elbows.

'Ah, my little angel is all right today,' Al said as he ran his hand over her head and down the side of her face.

'Yes, thanks Al,' she smiled weakly back at him.

'You came close, you know that?'

Sarah nodded.

'If it had not been for the American here, you—'

Brinn interrupted, 'Al, what about some breakfast?'

'Yes, of course, how stupid of me.'

'Just a bit of toast for me,' Sarah said.

'Everything for me if you can manage it,' Brinn added.

'Sure, no problem. You just stay there. I won't be long.'

He left them, and Sarah slid down into the bed again.

Brinn turned to her and slipping his arm beneath her he said, 'What happened to you yesterday? How did you get into this state?'

'They caught up with me, American, Josh's pushers. Well, one of them anyway. The other I did not recognise. I was on my way to the shelter. You remember, the one in Lea Road?'

Brinn nodded.

'It was about six o'clock and I was hurrying to get a place when they jumped me just outside the tube station. The black one put his hand over my mouth and they both dragged me into the underpass.'

Recalling the event was causing her to become a little agitated, so Brinn caressed her face to calm her.

'I remember a sharp jab and being made to swallow something, but nothing after that till you last night.'

She put her arms around Brinn and pulled him closer.

'They wanted to know where you were, but I didn't tell them anything.'

Brinn squeezed her tight and asked, 'They didn't hurt you in any other way, did they, honey?'

She understood the implication of his question and replied, 'No, there were too many people about for that.'

'Do you mean to say people were about and did nothing to help you?'

'It does not matter now, American, I'm here with you, safe. Please let's not talk about it anymore.'

'All right,' he said, and as he kissed her forehead, the door opened again and Al stepped through carrying the breakfast.

Sarah only nibbled at her dry toast and the sight and smell of Brinn's breakfast began to turn her stomach. Brinn had been ravenous, but halfway through he left the rest in deference to Sarah's protests. Tucking the tray temporarily under the bed, Brinn ran Sarah a bath. She was a little shaky on her feet, but with his help she managed to get into the water without too much difficulty. Brinn dressed in his now dry clothes, and left Sarah to soak. He went downstairs carrying the empty plates and cups, and seeing Al asked, 'How do you think she is, Al?'

'Not sure,' Al replied, 'it could be a few days yet. Just be real careful with her and wait and see.'

'She will be all right, though, won't she?'

Al did not reply, but handed Brinn a tea-towel and began to wash up the dirty plates. Five minutes passed in silence then Brinn put the tea-towel down.

'Look, I know she will be okay. She's up there now, a little shaky maybe, but having a bath. How can there be any problem?'

Al opened his mouth to speak, but stopped as he heard Sarah coming down the stairs humming to herself.

'You two seem very conspiratorial this morning,' she remarked.

'Yes, we were just discussing what we are going to do with you,' Brinn replied.

'And what have you decided?' she asked.

Brinn checked with Al as he said, 'You're coming home with me. That will be the safest place for you right now.'

Al nodded his agreement, then walked over to Sarah and looked straight into her eyes.

'This American will take good care of you now. Do just what he tells you, no arguments, you understand?'

Then he hugged her, something he had done only once before, when his wife had died. Sarah smiled at Al.

'Why, Al, anyone would think you did not expect to see me again. I'll only be over the other side of town. I'm not going to the moon.'

He forced a laugh to conceal his emotion.

'Oh, you know me, I just miss your company so much,' and waving his hand in the air with a flourish, he went out into the kitchen.

## Chapter Eleven

Sarah was still a little weak, but as she got into the car she surprised Brinn by asking, 'Let's go and do something wild.'

'No way, it's bed for you when we get back to the flat.'

'But, American,' she protested, 'I'm fine, really I am.'

'Remember what Al said. No arguments. You're under my orders now.'

Sarah poked her tongue out at him childishly.

'I saw that, Sarah Miller,' he said. 'Now you're definitely confined to barracks with only bread and water,' he added with a smile.

Brinn opened the door to the flat and pulled the reluctant Sarah through into the hallway and up the stairs to the bedroom. She noticed the cases on the floor, still packed for his trip to America.

'You going somewhere?' she asked.

'I was going to the States, but there has been a change of plan and we are going next week instead.'

It took Sarah a few moments to make sense of the sentence.

'We, as in you and me?'

'Yep, that's right,' he replied.

Sarah laughed. 'You're crazy! I don't even have a passport.'

'You will have after we visit the passport office tomorrow.'

'I doubt it,' she replied. 'I don't have a birth certificate either.'

'Okay, so we have to do a bit of legwork first, but trust me, by five o'clock tomorrow, you will have a passport.'

Sarah shook her head and remarked, 'Five o'clock tomorrow? No chance! Now I know one of us is totally nuts, and I know it's not me.'

'Okay, so I'm nuts,' he said, 'but you are getting into this bed, right now.'

Sarah opened her mouth to speak.

'Uh, uh, uh, remember, no arguments.' Brinn interrupted her in mid-breath.

She was beginning to enjoy being bossed around by him, it made her feel safe, but she would rather not let Brinn know about it. Stamping her foot in mild indignation and tut-tutting, Sarah removed all of her clothing except for her T-shirt.

'Now, I have a few calls to make, so get comfortable and I will pop back later. Anything you want before I go?'

'Yes, just one thing,' she said, grabbing his shirt and pulling him down towards her. 'This.'

Sarah kissed Brinn full on the mouth and he responded by putting his arms around her.

'Thank you,' she said as their lips parted.

'What for?' he replied.

'For coming back for me.'

Brinn kissed her this time, and then, pulling himself away, he left the bedroom, closing the door behind him.

Brinn checked his answering machine first. Of the three calls recorded, two were from his mother and one from Chris. The latter was the more important, so he rang him back first.

'Hi Chris. It's Brinn. I've just picked up your message on my answering machine.'

'About time, too,' Chris replied. 'Have you sorted out your problem yet?'

'Yes, it's all okay now. A bit touch and go there for a moment though.'

'Am I to take it the spare ticket on the plane is for Sarah?'

'Got it in one. I'm taking her with me to the States, and when things have settled a bit, I'm going to ask her to marry me.'

There was a stunned silence at the other end of the line, till Brinn asked, 'Chris, are you still there?'

'Yes, sorry. It was just a bit of a shock, that's all. You sure about this? I've never taken you for the marrying kind.'

'Never been surer.'

'Okay, just as long as you are. The flight goes on Friday and you'll be happy to hear it is at two fifteen in the afternoon. You can pick up the tickets at the airport.'

'Chris, you're bloody marvellous! Was New York okay about the delay?'

'Okay is not the word I would use, but they know you pretty well by now, and were expecting you to pull something like this sooner or later. Look, I have to go now. I have a taxi coming for me in five minutes. I will join you over there in a couple of weeks. Give my regards and condolences to Sarah. Tell her she could have done much better.'

'Cheers, Chris. Bye and thanks.'

Friday, he thought. It would give him four days.

Brinn thought he should put in the call to his mother next before he forgot and she had to make another one to him.

'Hi mom! It's your prodigal son here.'

'Brinn! Oh, it is so good to hear from you. I was beginning to get a little worried.'

'Mom, you should know me by now. Look, I have some good news for you.'

'Oh, please tell me you have broken up with Carol!'

Brinn smiled. His mother had not liked Carol either and often alluded to the fact.

'Yes, mom, I have, but that's not the good news I meant.'

'It's the best news as far as I am concerned.'

'Okay, mom, I get the message, but I'm coming home on Friday and I am bringing someone special with me.'

'She can have two heads and a forked tail, son, so long as her name is not Carol.'

'Well, she doesn't have either of those things, but her name is Sarah.'

'Sounds good to me, son.'

'I want to marry her, mom.' Brinn added a little sheepishly.

'Sounds even better, son.'

The following morning, Sarah woke first. She felt a little better, thought her abdomen was still sore from retching on an empty stomach the day before. Carefully, she got out of bed so as not to disturb Brinn, and went to the bathroom. She looked at herself in the mirror and wondered what he could possibly see in her, she looked so dreadful. Running her hands through her hair, she decided to wash it, so she turned on the taps in the sink to let the water warm up.

On the window ledge was an array of hair products, most of which she thought must have belonged to Carol. Just like a typical man, he had grown used to the bottles being on the ledge and saw no reason to throw them away. While she waited for the basin to fill, Sarah picked a shampoo at random and then began to scoop the water over her hair. Brinn came in behind her.

'Who's the early bird, then?' he said.

'Oh, sorry, hope I didn't wake you up.'

'No,' he replied, putting his arms around her. 'I just missed you.'

'Are you going to let me finish this, or will I have to stand in this position all day?'

'Sorry,' he said, letting her go. 'Mind if I take a shower while you do that?'

'No, go ahead.'

Brinn pulled the shower curtain round the bath, turned on the water and held his hand under the showerhead, waiting for the temperature to increase. He stepped in and turned his face into the hot water. It refreshed him and he rubbed his face with one hand as he reached for the soap with the other.

'We have to get your passport sorted out today,' he said, his voice raised a little because of the noise of the water.

'Fine,' she replied. 'I'm not sure how much walking I can do though.'

'Not a problem. Don't worry about it. The minute you have had enough, just say so, okay?'

'All right,' she said, wrapping her hair in a towel.

She pulled the shower curtain back and stepped in to join Brinn. He took her in his arms and kissed her. Sarah hesitated for a moment and then said, 'I'm sorry, American, I don't think I can do this just yet.'

'It's okay,' he reassured her, 'in your own time. Just hold on to me for now.'

They left the flat around ten o'clock and Brinn drove to a spot where he knew he could park that was quite close to the Records Office. Sarah managed the short walk without too much difficulty, and the form filling was an easy enough task, although one question about 'mother's place of birth', she had to leave blank. As they went to submit the form and pay for the birth certificate copy, they were told that it would have to be posted to them. A greater problem however, was that it might take anything up to a week to process.

'But we need it today for a passport,' Brinn insisted to the clerk.

'I am sorry, sir, that is the way it works here. We just can't do them on demand.'

Frustrated, Brinn turned to Sarah and asked, 'What are the chances of you getting the original from your parents?'

'You want me to go home to get the original?' she repeated in disbelief.

'It will be all right. I will be there with you. I won't let your father near you and it means we could get this thing sorted out today.'

Sarah was still trying to absorb the idea, and she became pensive and silent.

'Please, Sarah, it means we will be able to go on Friday and leave this all behind. What do you say?'

She nodded once slowly.

'Come on then, no time to lose.'

He took her hand and led her out of the building, leaving the irritated clerk to deposit the useless form in the rubbish bin.

'Right, where are we headed?' he asked her.

'M25, then M3 going south.'

Brinn turned the key in the ignition, and as the engine roared into life, he pulled out into the traffic. Sarah remained quiet for most of the journey, only speaking when a route change was necessary. An hour and a half brought them to a small village on the outskirts of Basingstoke. Sarah guided Brinn down the narrow lanes until a group of terraced houses at the end of a cul-de-sac loomed ahead of them. Sarah trembled visibly.

'I can't go in,' she said.

'I understand,' he replied. 'Just wait here and I will go and make some enquiries.'

Brinn got out of the car, went up to the front door of the

house that Sarah had pointed out to him, and knocked. There was no reply, though he thought he caught sight of the upstairs curtain moving. He tried again, and after a while the door opened a few inches, a chain preventing any further progression. A small frail figure peered through the opening.

'Who is it?' she asked.

'Good morning, Mrs Miller. My name is Brinndle Peters, ma'am. I am a friend of your daughter's. She is here with me now.'

The woman's voice had a note of desperation as she said, 'Sarah? You have brought Sarah here? Where is she?'

'In the car, ma'am. She is a little too afraid to come in.'

There was a moment's pause and then Brinn heard the chain being removed before the door opened a little farther. The grey-haired Mrs Miller was hunched over in a permanent stoop. Her hands were riddled with arthritis; her nose was crooked like that of a boxer's and she had an old yellowed bruise on her cheek. She stared past Brinn out to the car and recognised Sarah sitting in the passenger seat. Mrs Miller gave a little gasp and raised her hand to her mouth. Her eyes, wide with concern, began to fill with tears.

Although Sarah had realised her mother must have come to the door, she could not bring herself to look in her direction. Her eyes remained fixed on some point on her lap. Mrs Miller pushed past Brinn and walked with some difficulty over to where the car was parked.

'Sarah,' she said, tapping on the window of the car. 'It is all right. He is not here. He is out doing some shopping. Please, Sarah, will you talk to me?'

Sarah remained impassive, still staring at her lap.

'I've been worried about you,' her mother continued. 'I did not know if you were alive or dead.'

Her voice began to break.

'Please, Sarah, forgive me. I couldn't do anything, believe me. Please, Sarah.'

She broke down completely, sobbing into her hands. Brinn, who had followed her up to the car, laid his arm across her shoulder to comfort her. The woman froze, and Brinn withdrew his arm, recognising his mistake.

'I'm sorry, Mrs Miller,' he said. 'Can you help us? Sarah needs her birth certificate. That is why I have brought her here. We hoped you could help.' She straightened a little and collected herself.

'Why do you want her birth certificate?' she asked unsteadily.

'Sarah has agreed to come to America with me, and we need it in order to get her passport.'

'America!' she replied, surprised. 'But it's such a long way away.'

'It's what we both want, Mrs Miller, and I believe I can make her happy. At least, I would like a shot at it. Please can you help us?'

Sarah's mother looked at him for a long time, then nodded.

'She should have a chance for happiness, and God knows, there's little enough chance of her getting it here. Come with me. I will get it for you.'

Turning to look at Sarah one more time, hoping in vain for some sign of recognition from her, Mrs Miller headed back to the house. Brinn smiled at Sarah through the windscreen of the car, but she could not look at him.

Brinn followed her mother into the house. It was a typical terraced house – small, but neat and tidy. An old-fashioned three-piece suite stood in a semicircle around a tiled fireplace. Inexpensive china ornaments were arranged on the mantelpiece on either side of an old clock which ticked loudly. Several pictures of relatives adorned a sideboard and lacy doilies covered every surface. It was hard for Brinn to imagine that such violent acts had taken place in this typical representation of suburbia.

Mrs Miller began to root around in the drawers of the sideboard, and then, remembering where she had seen the birth certificate last, went to a cupboard in the dining room.

'Here it is,' she said. 'You will take good care of her, won't you.' Before Brinn could answer, he was halted by the sound of a terrified scream. Brinn grabbed the certificate and ran out of the house. As he reached the doorway, he could see a man pulling a struggling Sarah by her hair from the car.

'What the hell do you think you're doing?' Brinn shouted at the man as he ran in his direction.

The man took no notice, but instead struck Sarah hard across her mouth, sending her sprawling onto the ground. Brinn made a flying tackle, catching the man around his thighs and knocking him over onto the ground.

'Please, that's my husband,' Mrs Miller cried from the house.

Brinn got to his feet first, having knocked all the wind out of Sarah's father. He took no notice of Mrs Miller's pleas, but punched him hard in the stomach as he got to his feet, sending him down on his back again. Sarah's mother had come hurrying up the path and she got hold of Brinn's arm to prevent him from striking her husband again.

'Don't, please don't,' she begged him. 'It will only be the worse for us if you do. Please don't do it again.'

Brinn was breathing hard now and totally incensed, but he managed to get control of himself just enough to remove Mrs Miller from his arm. He turned to Sarah who was sitting with her back half against the car, her mouth bleeding at the corner.

'Go, please,' her mother urged them, 'before he gets up again. Take her to America where she will be safe.'

Brinn looked at the man on the ground as he tried to get

up again, wanting desperately to finish him. Instead, he helped Sarah to her feet and sat her in the passenger's seat, then closed the door. As Brinn turned again, Sarah's father lurched forward and head-butted him, causing him to fall against the car. Sarah jumped in her seat as Brinn rolled across the bonnet and onto the ground. Her mother started screaming at her husband to leave Brinn alone, but, annoyed at her interference, he turned instead and slapped her with the back of his hand. It gave Brinn the chance he needed to get on his feet again. Blood was running from the cut on his forehead down into his eye, and he had to wipe it away in order to see Sarah's father coming at him once more. Brinn waited till the last minute, then brought his knee up into her father's groin. He buckled and dropped to his knees, holding himself against the pain as he hit the ground. Brinn bent over him, breathing hard and shouted at him.

'You bastard! Raped and mutilated your own daughter, beat up on your wife, you're the worst kind of filth there is.'

Uncontrollable anger surged through Brinn and he kicked the fallen man hard in his side, knocking him over onto his back. He stood over him, watching for a moment while he wiped more blood from his face and caught his breath.

'You okay?' he said to Sarah's mother.

She nodded, waving him away. Reluctantly, Brinn climbed into the car and shut the door. Then, slamming the gears into reverse, he depressed the accelerator and sent the wheels into a screeching spin. The rapidly moving car missed Sarah's prostrate father by inches, but Brinn couldn't have cared at that moment if he had killed him outright. One hand on the wheel, Brinn wiped the blood from above his eye again, while Sarah gave one passing look back at her father, who was still slumped on the ground.

Brinn drove straight back to the flat, where he decided to postpone the Passport Office visit until the next day, as he could hardly see out of the rapidly closing eye. The bruised inflamed skin around it was so tight his head ached. Sarah went straight to the bathroom to get some cotton wool and TCP, then returned to Brinn, who was in the kitchen trying to make a cup of coffee. They had hardly spoken on the return trip. He had been too worked up to hold a sensible conversation.

Sarah bathed the cut, and the stinging sensation from the TCP just added to his misery. He took a couple of aspirin with his coffee to soothe his headache as Sarah tenderly washed the dried blood from his face with a little warm water.

'You look like Mohammed Ali after ten rounds,' she said.

'I feel like Mohammed Ali after ten rounds,' he replied.

She leant forward and kissed him.

'Ow!' he said as she bumped her head on his cut.

'Sorry, American.'

'No, don't be sorry, not ever again,' he said, holding her tightly by the arms.

'It's gone five o'clock,' she said, teasing him.

'Okay, okay, five o'clock tomorrow. That all right?'

'All right,' she replied, kissing him again.

At three forty-five on the following afternoon, they walked out of the Passport Office hand in hand, clutching Sarah's new passport.

'There, told you so. An hour and a quarter to spare,' Brinn said triumphantly.

'What about the extra day?' she replied, taking a look at her passport and adding, 'I look terrible in this photo.'

'Wait till you see mine,' he replied.

'Where to next, then?'

'Do you like Chinese food?'

'Never had it,' she replied.

'You haven't lived till you've tried it. I'll pick up a take-away on the way back, and we can eat at home tonight.

Brinn was woken at five thirty by Sarah getting out of bed. He followed her into the bathroom and found her vomiting into the toilet. She stood up and flushed it, and washed her face under the tap to revive herself.

'Sorry if I woke you,' she said as she saw him by the door.

He took her in his arms.

'Perhaps it was the Chinese. Maybe it didn't agree with you.'

'I don't think so. I've been like this, on and off, for a while now.'

'I'm sorry,' he said firmly, straightening up and holding her by the shoulders. 'Tomorrow it's the doctor for you.'

'American, I am not going to see any doctor. It's just a stomach bug and let's face it, the other day didn't help much either. I will be all right in a day or so.'

'Sarah,' he began again.

'No,' she replied emphatically.

'You are, without a doubt, the most exasperating, self-opinionated, stubborn woman I have ever met.'

'Yes, I think I am, but that is the reason why you love me so much, isn't it?'

'Well, if you won't see a doctor, then tomorrow you have to stay in bed again.'

They lay awake in each other's arms until light, when Brinn volunteered to go and make some tea. As he re-entered the room, he pulled back the curtains and noticed for the first time, the slightly yellowish pallor in Sarah's face. He sat on the side of the bed nearest to her.

'Sarah, please, just for me. Will you see a doctor?'

'I'm sorry, American, not even for you. Now, do I get this cup of tea or not?'

Reluctantly he handed it to her.

Brinn was as good as his word. He managed to keep Sarah in bed until lunchtime, but she did not make an easy patient. She moaned, threatened and screamed, but it was the begging that wore Brinn down in the end.

'Please, American, I can't bear to be cooped up in here any longer. I'm going mad. It's such a nice day. The sun will do me some good. Please! I promise to behave. I will do everything you tell me. Please, American. It doesn't have to be for long. Half an hour will do.'

'All right, all right,' he gave in at last. 'If it will keep you off my back; but only for thirty minutes, mind.'

She jumped up from the bed and swung her arms around his neck.

'Thank you, thank you,' she said, kissing all over his face.

'Behave yourself,' he said in a stern voice, while really quite enjoying it. 'You had better get dressed and I will go get us some food for a picnic. How does that sound?'

'Wonderful.'

He kissed her and left her to get ready while he went out to the corner shop.

Sarah found her jeans and a sweatshirt of Brinn's and started to dress. She was putting her arm inside the sweat-shirt when a sharp pain gripped her abdomen and she slumped forward and grabbed hold of the chair. She grimaced as the pain worsened and, bent double, she just managed to stagger to the bed before she collapsed. It was excruciating, wave after wave with little let-up. It must have been ten minutes before the pain eased.

Tears rolled down her face as the fear subsided, along with the discomfort. Slowly she sat up and regulated her breathing, taking a few deep breaths. The door slammed along the hall, and Sarah hastily wiped her face on her sleeve as she heard Brinn coming back along the hallway. Standing shakily she pulled on her jeans just as he came through the bedroom door.

'Good grief, you're slow! I thought you were in a hurry to get out of here.'

'Sorry,' she replied. 'I couldn't find my jeans.'

'Ready now, then?'

'Yes. I just need to rinse my face and we can go.'

Brinn drove them to the park. It was a lovely afternoon. The sun was warm and the air was fresh after the stuffy atmosphere of the bedroom. Brinn carried the food in a carrier bag while Sarah clung to his arm for support.

'Oh God, this is good,' she said. 'Can we go and sit by the lake?'

'If you like,' he replied.

Brinn found a quiet spot where the ground was dry where they sat down and stretched themselves out on the grass. Sarah closed her eyes and enjoyed the feeling of warmth on her face and the smell of sunshine on the damp grass.

'What is it like in the States, American?' she asked.

'Much as it is here, I suppose. The grass is green, the trees are tall and some of the people are nice,' he replied, rolling onto his side to look at her.

'Where will we live when we get there?'

'Well, to begin with, we will have to stay in New York, just until I am finished with the play. Then it depends on what comes up next, but I hope we can go visit my mother in Texas for a few months.'

'Is she nice? Your mother, I mean?'

'Yes, she's the best. Did I tell you what she said when I told her I was bringing you with me?'

Sarah shook her head.

'Well, she said you could have three heads and a forked tail so long as your name was not Carol.'

Sarah laughed. 'I like your mother already. It looks like Carol has quite a fan club. I know it's none of my business, but why did you get involved with her in the first place?'

'You're right. It is none of your business, but I will tell you anyway,' he said moving closer to her. 'Before I met you,' he began, punctuating each statement with a kiss, 'I was a selfish, arrogant, unbearable, vain, pompous old bastard.'

Sarah suppressed a smile and said, 'Well, no change there, then.'

Brinn feigned annoyance and began to tickle her ribs.

'I see, so you think I'm still selfish, arrogant, unbearable, vain and pompous, do you?'

'No, no,' she laughed. 'Stop! I can't stand it. You're none of those things, really. Please, stop!'

'That's better then, thank you.'

'No, you're just an old bastard instead,' she added.

Brinn started to tickle her again and she curled up to protect herself, protesting wildly.

'You play unfair. I'm hardly in a fit state to defend myself now, am I?' she said, unravelling herself.

Brinn kissed her and she relaxed and put her arms around him.

'Lunch time,' he announced to her, sitting up and opening the carrier bag. 'What would you like? I have egg, cheese, or ham sandwiches, chips, apples and coke.'

'Chips?' she said. 'Oh, you mean crisps.'

'Chips, crisps. What's the difference?'

'Oh, say about two hundred and fifty degrees centigrade, I think,' she replied.

'No, you are thinking about French fries.'

'I can see I shall have to learn a whole new language

before I get to the States.'

Brinn handed her one of the egg sandwiches, taking the ham for himself. She looked at it, but only played with the sandwich, not having much of an appetite.

'Don't you like egg?' he asked.

'Egg's fine. I'm just not very hungry.'

'You must have something, Sarah. You didn't eat at breakfast either.'

Sarah tasted a corner, but she had to try very hard in order to swallow it.

'May I have a drink?' she asked.

'Sure, here you are,' he replied, handing her a can.

The liquid helped a little, but it was a real struggle to finish. Brinn offered her another, but she declined. So he finished it off and started on an apple. Sarah manoeuvred herself around behind Brinn, then pulling him gently back, she laid his head in her lap.

'That's nice,' he said, as she put her fingers through his hair.

'You deserve it,' she replied, 'all the running around you have done for me.'

But that was not the real reason she was doing it. The pain had returned, not so strong this time, but enough that he might see it in her face if he looked directly at her. In this position, though, he would keep his eyes closed while she caressed him.

Half an hour passed. The pain had subsided again and Brinn was still dozing in Sarah's lap. She bent forward and lightly kissed him. He woke and, putting his hand behind her neck, pulled her closer to extend the kiss.

'It's getting chilly. You want to call it a day?' he asked her.

'Yes, I think so. I am a bit tired now.'

Brinn gathered up the things and, putting his arm

around her, began to walk back to the car. He could feel Sarah was tired, as she leaned heavily on him, and after throwing the remains of the picnic into the back of the car, he helped her into the passenger seat in the front.

He drove carefully back to the flat, watching her intently, and although she tried to walk up the steps, he had to carry her the rest of the way. As he laid her down on the bed, she winced a little.

'I just need to sleep,' she said, in anticipation of his question. 'I will be fine in the morning.'

Brinn was beside himself with worry.

'Okay,' he said as he covered her. 'I'll leave you for a bit. Try to rest.'

He went out, closed the door behind him, and got to the phone as fast as he could.

'Al, it's Brinn here.'

'Ah, American, how are things? And how is Sarah?'

'Not good. I'm really worried. She says she has stomach pain, is sick every so often and her skin looks a little yellow to me.'

Al was silent for a minute.

'Would she go to hospital?'

'Only if I drag her there.'

'The decision must be yours, American. I don't think I can advise you on this one.'

'Okay, Al, I understand. I will keep you informed.'

Brinn hung up and went back to the bedroom. Sarah seemed settled enough, and his concern eased up a little. He sat in the chair across the room from her and tried to fight all the thoughts that invaded his mind that he might still lose her. He dozed fitfully for a couple of hours, but was woken by Sarah, who had begun to moan and had pulled her knees up to her chest in an attempt to ease the returning pain.

Brinn could stand it no longer. He flew to the phone

and dialled 999. He gave the relevant instructions to the emergency services and urged them to hurry, then slamming the receiver down went back to the bedroom.

'I'm sorry Sarah,' he said as he cradled her upper body. 'I just have to get you to hospital. I don't want to lose you again. Forgive me, honey.'

The pain was now so great, Sarah was unable to reply.

The sound of the sirens sent Brinn out into the street to show the paramedics where to come.

'She's in here, and has terrible pain in her stomach. Please help her.'

Carrying their equipment, the green-suited paramedics hurried into the bedroom.

'Can you tell us what happened, sir?' one of them asked as the other knelt over Sarah.

'I don't know where to start,' Brinn said.

'Well, how about the young lady's name?'

'Sarah, her name is Sarah.'

'Sarah,' the man bent over her said. 'Can you hear me? I'm a paramedic and I have come to help you. Now, can you show me where the pain is?'

Brinn turned back to the man in front of him and tried to recollect the events of the last few days.

'Two days ago,' he began, 'she was attacked in the street. Some pushers gave her a shot of crack and some pills, or at least that's what we think it was.'

'Can you be a bit more specific, sir? It is important.'

Brinn became dysfunctional as he tried to remember the events of that day again.

'Headache pills, that's it,' he said. 'That's why I did not think they were important. They were only Paracetamol.'

'Do you know how many she had taken?'

'The bottle was empty so it could have been all of them, but I don't know for sure.'

'Did she vomit, sir?'

'Yes, a little, but I can't understand it. She has been fine these last two days.'

'Can you remember anything else that might be useful?'

'No, I'm sorry. Please can we get her to hospital now?'

The man turned to his colleague.

'Can we move her yet?'

'I think we had better. Her pressure's really low and she's pretty jaundiced. I can't do much more for her here.'

The paramedic who had been talking to Brinn went out to the ambulance to fetch the stretcher, while Brinn bent over Sarah and spoke to her in hushed tones.

'It's all right! You are going to be all right now, honey.'

Sarah was still doubled up and barely able to communicate.

'She is going to be all right, isn't she?' he asked the remaining paramedic.

'We have to get her to hospital. They will be able to tell you more there, sir.'

They were able to bring the stretcher only as far as the hallway; the bedroom was too small to accommodate it. The paramedics were about to move Sarah between them, but Brinn would not allow it, insisting on picking her up and carrying her to the stretcher himself. The paramedics covered her with a blanket and placed safety straps over her body. Satisfied she was secure, they wheeled her the length of the hall and lifted her down the steps into the street.

A few idle onlookers, alerted by the siren, had come onto the street to gawp. Brinn climbed into the ambulance behind Sarah and one of the paramedics shut the door. Brinn sat down on the seat opposite her.

'Can't you give her anything for the pain?' he asked.

'It might be a little dangerous until we know what we are dealing with here, but we can give her some Entanox, if she will use it.'

'What is it?' Brinn asked.

'It's a fancy name for nitrous oxide, laughing gas.'

The name seemed quite inappropriate for the task it had to perform, but the paramedic put the mask over Sarah's face. She struggled against it, the nauseating smell irritating her lungs. The ambulance radio crackled as the driver notified the hospital of their present status, and then pulled away, lights flashing and sirens blaring, to begin its journey.

'Let me,' Brinn said to the man, taking the mask from the paramedic's hand. They changed places and Brinn got down next to Sarah.

'Sarah, don't fight it, just breath it in. It will help you control the pain. That's it, nice and easy, honey.'

Her struggle subsided as the Entanox began to take effect. Her whole body, which had been in spasm because of the pain, started to relax, and her eyes, at first tightly shut, now opened a little. Each time the pain returned, she gasped in breaths of the Entanox, then relaxed again as it washed through her system.

The radio crackled into life.

'Yes, we are on our way, control. Patient, Sarah Miller, is serious but stable. ETA five minutes. Please have the hepatic surgeon on standby, over.'

The usual inaudible chatter crackled back over the radio and then the driver switched it to the standby position.

They reversed into the casualty bay and Sarah was hurried away from the ambulance through the doors and into the Accident and Emergency department.

Brinn stood helplessly, the sequence of events passing him by like those of a bad dream in which he was equally powerless to intervene or alter the outcome. He felt a hand at his elbow and blindly followed its lead, unable to register the reassuring words now being spoken to him. An anxious, nauseous feeling rolled over him in waves as he entered the familiar waiting room, and ghostly images of the last occasion he was there invaded his consciousness. The nurse left him alone. He could not distinguish whether the events that happened around him were real or only ghosts from the past. A tannoy called out for the doctor. There followed the sound of rushing feet and a rattling trolley. Brinn sat with his head buried in his hands, dreading the moment when the doctor would come in to tell him bad news. At least he could wake up from a bad dream. The doctor arrived just as Brinn had begun to pace the floor.

'Mr Peters?' he enquired.

'Yes,' Brinn replied.

'We have managed to stabilise Miss Miller's condition.'

'She is all right?' Brinn interrupted.

'She's stable. We have to run some further tests to try to isolate the problem. Have you managed to remember anything else that might be helpful to us?'

'No, sorry. I can't think straight.'

'It's quite all right, Mr Peters, I understand. Miss Miller is conscious, if you would like to see her.'

The unexpected reply, threw Brinn for a moment until he answered with relief, 'Yes, please. I would like that very much.'

The doctor led the way to an area in the casualty department that was cordoned off by a curtain.

Before he ushered Brinn into one of the cubicles, the doctor said, 'Please don't be alarmed by all the gadgetry. There are a lot of tubes and things, but every one is necessary.'

He pulled back the curtain and Brinn walked inside the cubicle. Despite the warning, he found it unnerving to see her supine with so many tubes and wires connected to her body. Sarah had her eyes closed. She wore a hospital gown and was covered in a cellulose blanket. She had a drip going into her arm, and her heart and blood pressure were being constantly monitored. There was a tube feeding her oxygen that was attached to a mask which covered her nose and mouth. Another tube, which gave access to her stomach, came from her nose and was taped down at the side of her head. Brinn pulled up a chair and sat close beside her. He took her hand, kissed it, and was careful not to disturb the intravenous line.

'Sarah,' he whispered softly.

She opened her eyes slowly but did not speak.

'Sarah,' he said again.

She turned her head a little.

'American?' she said weakly.

'Yes, it is me, honey. How do you feel?'

'Woozy,' she replied grimacing a little.

'You still in pain?'

'A bit, but it is not as bad as it was earlier. I think they gave me something for it.'

'I'm real sorry I had to bring you here. I was so afraid of losing you,' Brinn said, kissing her hand again.

'Don't worry, American,' she replied, 'it's not important now. I'm so drugged up, you could run a steamroller over me and I don't think I'd notice.'

A nurse came in and began to check the readings on the monitors. She removed the chart from the bottom of the bed, entered the readings on it and then took Sarah's pulse. Brinn smiled at her.

'How's the patient doing, nurse?'

'Oh, just fine,' she replied reassuringly. 'It shouldn't be too long now and the results of the tests will be back. Then we will have a better idea of how things are going.'

She bustled out of the cubicle, replacing the clipboard at the foot of the bed.

'You scared the hell out of me,' he said, putting his hand to Sarah's face.

'Ha, got you back for tickling me,' she replied quietly.

Sarah drifted off to sleep again, so Brinn sat back and listened to the low drone of the monitors and the voices from beyond the curtain.

A few young nurses were giggling at the far end of the ward and another patient could be heard coughing and wheezing uncontrollably. A child's pitiful cry pierced the uneasy atmosphere and the distant wail of an approaching ambulance announced its imminent arrival.

Brinn checked to see if Sarah was still asleep and then left the cubicle in search of a phone. He paused at the nurse's station and asked directions of the young nurse who had attended to Sarah previously. She pointed down the corridor and to the right, and, thanking her, he continued his search for it.

Of the two phones, one was out of order and the other was being used by a patient clad in his pyjamas. It was an odd sight among all the people milling along the corridor, one lone figure in pyjamas and slippers. By the time Brinn had checked his pockets for change, the patient had finished his call and was returning to his ward.

Brinn phoned Al.

'Hi, Al, it's Brinn. I'm at the hospital. I had to bring her in. Al, she was in an awful state.'

His voice broke, and Al said, 'It's all right, American. I'm sure she understands. Which hospital are you at?'

Clearing his throat Brinn replied, 'St Thomas's, the same one Pete was…'

'Yes, okay, American,' Al interrupted. 'I know the one. Look, I will just finish up here and I will come along. You manage all right till then.'

'Thanks, Al. I appreciate it. I might know a bit more by the time you get here.'

'Okay, American, I'll see you soon.'

Al hung up, and Brinn, still clutching the receiver, leant forward till his head touched the box. He could not make up his mind whether to phone Chris yet or wait until he knew for sure. After all, there still was a chance. He put the receiver back on the hook and, retracing his steps down the corridor, returned to Sarah.

As he pulled back the curtain, the doctor was there taking a further blood sample. Brinn's nerves, already on edge, now snapped completely.

'Haven't you people put enough needles in her yet? Can't you leave her alone?'

The startled doctor turned and tried to reassure Brinn of the necessity of the task, but Brinn, who had been bottling up every emotion, just exploded.

'Look at her! Look what you have done to her, you damn vampires!'

'American.'

Brinn turned as he heard the faint voice.

'Sarah,' he said, the anger in his voice evaporating.

'You will be thrown out of here if you don't keep the noise down,' she warned.

The doctor slipped out as Brinn sat in the chair once more and took her hand.

'Sorry,' he said. 'I never could control my temper.'

'You had better go and apologise to that doctor, or the next time he might use a blunt needle on me.'

Brinn thought the possibility unlikely, but to humour her he went to find the doctor.

'Look, I'm sorry I blew up in there,' he said, tapping the doctor on the shoulder.

'That is all right, Mr Peters. Under the circumstances, I think I would have reacted the same.'

'Do you know what the problem is yet?'

'Well, not all of the tests are back yet, but from the results so far, it would seem she has toxic poisoning.'

'But you can do something for that, right? It's curable?'

'As I have already said, Mr Peters, we don't have all the

results back yet so I can't make a full diagnosis. We will only have to wait a little longer. Please bear with me.'

The doctor turned back to resume his conversation with the nurse and Brinn returned to the cubicle.

'Well,' she said, 'did you apologise?'

'Yes, ma'am,' he replied flatly, while trying to make some sense of the doctor's reply.

'Al's on his way. I phoned him while you were asleep.'

'That's kind of him,' she said, shifting uncomfortably.

'You in pain again?'

'No, it's just this gown. The tapes at the back are digging into me. If I sit up, do you think you could sort them out for me?'

'You sure it is all right for you to sit up right now?'

'If I don't, these tapes will drive me crazy.'

Brinn put his arm around her back, pushing to one side the wires and tubes, and eased her into a sitting position. He could see the problem immediately. The open back of the garment was held closed by several knotted tapes that lined up perfectly with her spine. As she lay on her back, they had dug into her flesh. Brinn undid two of the tapes, but the third had formed a knot and he could not free it.

'Hold still a minute,' he said as he yanked the tape from the garment. 'There, that should do it. Stupid design anyway.'

'Thanks, American.'

He eased her back down again and rearranged the blanket over her. Sarah spotted the still knotted tape in Brinn's hand.

'You vandal! No wonder the NHS have problems with their finances if people like you keep destroying their property.'

Brinn smiled, 'You sound more like your old self already.'

The curtain parted and Al walked into the cubicle.

'Al!' Sarah cried. 'Oh, Al, it's so nice to see you, but what about the cafe?'

'Oh, I closed it early for today. It wasn't very busy anyway. How are you, my angel?'

'Tired and sore from all the needles, but it's a good job you've come. I need someone to keep an eye on American here. He nearly landed one on the doctor earlier.'

'It's been a long day,' Brinn offered apologetically.

The doctor appeared at the end of the bed again.

'Excuse me, Mr Peters, can Mr Gregory possibly have a word with you?'

'Yes, of course,' Brinn said, as he stood and followed the doctor out into the corridor.

'Who's Mr Gregory?' Brinn asked as the doctor led Brinn along the passage.

'He's our resident hepatic surgeon,' the doctor replied as he opened the door into an office adjoining the ward, and ushered him inside where Mr Gregory was waiting.

'Please, Mr Peters, take a seat, won't you?' he said as the other doctor left them on their own.

'Thank you, doctor,' Brinn replied.

'Actually, it is Mr Gregory. I am the hepatic surgeon, not a doctor. It is a common mistake, and if it's helpful right now, I am happy for you to call me doctor.'

Brinn nodded his appreciation.

'Now, Mr Peters, we have had the last of the tests back, and I would like to thank you for being so patient with us. I have consulted with my colleagues, and we believe we have found the problem.'

Brinn felt that same anxious nausea rising in his stomach again and he fought hard to suppress it.

'It would appear,' Mr Gregory continued, 'that Miss Miller has had a large dose of Paracetamol, which has resulted in the toxic poisoning that we suspected earlier.'

Brinn exhaled with relief, 'Oh, thank God,' he said. 'She

will be all right then?'

'I'm afraid you don't quite understand, Mr Peters. Paracetamol is a toxic drug.'

'Yes, but it was two days ago, and she is over the worst now, surely?'

'I'm sorry, Mr Peters, there is no easy way to say this. Paracetamol taken in even relatively small amounts under the wrong circumstances can do permanent damage to the liver. The liver, as you may well know, is a vital organ and without it I'm afraid Miss Miller will have little chance of survival.'

Brinn's head was spinning and he thought he was about to pass out, but Mr Gregory continued talking and Brinn tried desperately to concentrate on his words.

'The results of our serial liver function tests show that she must have ingested at least twelve grams of Paracetamol, which is quite a substantial dose indeed.'

Seeing Brinn's obvious distress, Mr Gregory phoned the nurse's station and asked for some tea to be sent in for him.

'Look, I think you need a bit of time on your own. I have some things to see to. I will return in a little while and we can talk some more.'

'Don't tell her,' Brinn said abruptly just as Mr Gregory reached the door.

'Excuse me?'

'I want to tell her myself, okay. Don't say anything to her yet, please.'

'Very well, Mr Peters, as you wish.'

Mr Gregory left, and Brinn continued to sit, staring at a poster on the wall opposite announcing in large letters, DRUGS CAN KILL. He could see the outline of each letter clearly, but his brain could make no sense of their form.

The door opened and the tea came in, carried by Al.

'They are doing a few more tests on Sarah, and the nurse said you could probably use this, so I offered to bring it to you.'

'She is going to die, Al.'

'Yes,' Al replied.

'You knew?'

'I was not sure, but I thought it a possibility.'

'How?'

'Whatever they made her take, it had been in her system too long before you got to her. She had time to absorb it. There was little anyone could do.'

'It was Paracetamol,' Brinn said.

'Yes, that would explain the jaundice.'

'Why did you not tell me, Al.'

'It would have spoiled the last few days for you, I think, American.'

Brinn sat shaking his head.

'What am I going to do, Al? I can't lose her, I can't.'

Al put his rough arm across Brinn's shoulder.

'It is always hard to let go of someone you love, but let go you must. If she sees for one moment you can't, it will be all the harder for her. Sarah is strong, but she can't stay here past her time. So you must try to make it easier for her.'

Al poured them each a cup of tea and handed one to Brinn.

'Was it like this when you lost Carmen?' Brinn asked him.

'Yes,' Al replied, 'and don't trust anyone who says you will forget all about it in time. You never forget it, but the memory does get less painful.'

'Jesus, Al! How could you bear this?'

They sat for a while. Al sipped his tea, but Brinn just rotated the cup in his hands, unable to face it. Mr Gregory stepped into the room again and went to his seat behind the desk. He sighed as he rested his hands on the desktop and reluctantly sat down.

'I'm afraid I have a further piece of distressing news for you. Do you wish this gentleman to remain, Mr Peters?' Gregory said, nodding in Al's direction.

'Yes, he stays,' Brinn replied.

'Very well,' he said shifting awkwardly. 'This is rather difficult. We were concerned about the pain Miss Miller has been suffering. It is not usually associated with this type of liver dysfunction, and after some further tests we have discovered that Miss Miller is pregnant.'

'Pardon me?' Brinn said, staring at the man.

'Miss Miller is expecting a child, the only good news being that the discomfort she is experiencing is only cramp.'

Al put his hand to his mouth, and Brinn started to shake visibly.

'That's ridiculous! You people said she couldn't have children.'

'I'm unaware that we have ever treated Miss Miller before and even the best of us can't get it right all the time, Mr Peters. We are aware of her condition, however, and there was only a very small chance that given the state of her reproductive organs, this might occur.'

Brinn stood up so quickly, he accidentally propelled his chair over onto the floor.

'I have to get out of here! I think I'm going crazy.'

Brinn stormed out through the Accident and Emergency department and out into the fresh air. He looked around frantically for some way to escape the madness. Al touched him on the shoulder and Brinn spun around wildly.

'Easy, American! It is only me.'

'Sarah is pregnant, Al, and it was my fault!'

'So why are you running away?' Al asked.

'How can I face her? I should have been more careful. It was completely irresponsible, and on top of everything else!'

'Running out on her when she most needs you, that makes it all right, then?'

'Of course not, but, Al, listen, please…'

'No, American, you listen,' Al interrupted. 'I can sympathise with what you are going through, but this isn't about you now. If you can't face up to the facts, you might as well go back in there and kill her yourself with your bare hands. But for you, much of this mess might not have happened. I can't say for sure about the Paracetamol, but if you hadn't been around, she certainly wouldn't be pregnant. All you have to know for sure right now is if you love her or not. If you don't, I can make it easy on you, American. Just walk away. I had to pick up the pieces last time, and I could clear up your mess again. If you do love her, well, that's where it gets harder. You just have to go back in there and make it right. Well, American, what's it to be?'

'Al, for God's sake, help me! I'm coming apart at the seams!'

## Chapter Twelve

Brinn paused, and took a deep breath before pulling back the curtain.

'Hi!' he said smiling. 'How's my favourite girl doing?'

'Just exactly how many girls do you have at your beck and call, American?'

'Oh no, you can't get out of it like that. Come on, how do you feel?'

'Why does everyone keep asking me how I feel? I would have thought it was obvious by just looking at me. What did the doctor want?'

'The results are back from the tests they did,' he said, 'and he wanted to run them past me first.'

'Well?'

'It was all down to those tablets the pushers gave you. Apparently Paracetamol is to blame. That is what's screwing up your system.'

'Nothing more than that?'

'No, nothing more.'

'You must be the world's worst liar, American.'

'Okay, there was one other thing, but I was a bit worried about telling you. I thought you might get mad at me.'

'Come on, out with it!'

Brinn leant over and kissed her.

'Don't try to change the subject,' she said, pulling away. 'What is this other thing?'

'We are going to have a baby.'

Sarah looked at him, trying to decide if he was joking or not.

'Could you just run that past me again?' she said.

'You're pregnant, Sarah. You are carrying our child.'

Still staring at him, she shook her head.

'If this is a joke, it's a pretty bad one. It's a mistake, isn't it?' she said wavering.

'No,' he replied, 'it's not a mistake.'

Her eyes filled with tears and the tears rolled down her face and onto the pillow.

'How?' she whispered.

'What? You want me to go through the whole procedure?'

'No, don't fuck with me, American,' she said, her voice uneven.

'Bit late for that, isn't it?' he replied.

Sarah glared at him.

'Sorry. I was never much good at trying to be funny. Apparently, it was a one hundred to one long shot. Even the doc here didn't think it was possible.'

Sarah stretched down with her hand and felt her abdomen as the tears started to flow again.

'It's all right, isn't it? I mean, this problem I've had hasn't harmed it.'

'Everything is just fine,' he said, placing his hand on top of hers.

'Why did you think I would be mad at you?'

'After everything you have been through with your father, it was just very irresponsible of me.'

Sarah slipped her hand out from under his and squeezed it.

'Now, you just rest,' he said. 'I have to go and have another chat with the doctor. I will come straight back.'

'Promise.'

'Promise.'

'You want this baby?' she said, still clinging desperately to his hand.

Brinn made a path through the wires and tubes and,

putting his arms around her, he tried to sound sincere.

'Yes, I want us to have this child. More than anything in this world, I want it.'

He kissed her, and let her rest.

'Ah, come in, Mr Peters,' Mr Gregory said as Brinn opened the door. 'Have you had the opportunity to speak to Miss Miller yet?'

'Yes, just now. I have told her about the baby, but for the time being, I would be grateful if we keep the rest between ourselves.'

'Yes, I agree. No useful purpose can be served by worrying her unduly at the present time, at least not until we have the complete picture. I will instruct the nursing staff as to your wishes.'

'Thank you,' Brinn said. Then, momentarily closing his eyes, he added, 'Where do we go from here? What happens next?'

'As things stand at the moment, we will have to monitor her progress very carefully. The degeneration of the liver tissue may take days, weeks or even months, but the outcome in this case is, I am afraid, inevitable.'

The time factor was one thing Brinn had not given a thought to and, confronted now with the possibility of days, weeks or months, it hit him just as hard as the original bad news.

'Is there any chance she could come home with me?'

'I wouldn't advise or recommend it, but under the circumstances I cannot prevent it, either. She would be required, however, to sign a patient's voluntary discharge form. The whole thing is really up to you. It just depends how much you feel you can cope with. We can provide support, of course, in the form of drugs, steroids to help control inflammation, but how much help they will actually be is uncertain.'

'What about the child?'

Mr Gregory sighed, and with his elbow on the table, put his chin in his hand.

'That's a different problem, of course. The foetus is very premature at this stage. Its survival is by no means assured.'

'But there is a chance?'

'Mr Peters, you are asking me to speculate, and it would be unprofessional of me to make any predictions at this stage.'

'Look, doctor, when I get around to telling her about the other thing, I'll need something to soften the blow. It's the first thing she's going to ask me about and it would mean one hell of a lot to her to know it will be all right. I won't sue if you get it wrong, if that is what's worrying you. If there is even the slightest chance, she would want to know. Can't you just make a guess?'

Mr Gregory thought for a moment and referred to the notes he had on Sarah that lay in front of him.

'Let me see now, Miss Miller is approximately four and a half months pregnant.'

'If you say so, doctor.'

'Well the earliest recorded premature birth was that of a six hundred and twenty-four gram foetus at eighteen weeks' gestation.'

He sighed heavily again.

'I would prefer her to be at least twenty-four weeks to be sure. However if, and I must stress this, Mr Peters, only if, we can get her through the next week, minimum, we may be in with a chance. You must realise that the odds against this happening are phenomenal.'

'Yes, doctor, I hear you. It's a long shot, right? Just like the one where she couldn't get pregnant. Still, it's everything to us right now.'

Brinn made his way back to the phone. There was no one using it this time, and he managed to get straight through to the number.

'Chris, it's Brinn.'

'Oh no, Brinn, not another change to your plans! This really is the limit. You will just have to go on Friday. There is no way New York will sanction another delay.'

'Chris, please listen. It's Sarah.'

Chris was silent as he heard the genuine distress in Brinn's voice.

'She's in hospital, she's... she's not expected to live.'

'Brinn, I am so sorry! What happened?'

'It's a long story, but basically it's her liver. It's failing and there is nothing that can be done.'

'Which hospital, Brinn? I'll come over,' Chris said, feeling a little guilty at his earlier hasty outburst.

'No, it's okay. I'm on top of it now. There is no need.'

'Well, what can I do?'

'This New York thing. I'm really sorry to land you with this right now, but I shall have to pull out altogether. There is no way of telling just how long she has, and, forgive me, but I want to spend every minute with her.'

'Of course, don't give it a second thought, Brinn. I'll take care of it this end. Just keep me updated, yeah, and if I can do anything...'

'Okay, I know. I will ring. Thanks Chris.'

'I'll speak to you later, Brinn, and take care of yourself.'

Brinn was all in. Emotionally and physically, he hadn't an ounce of strength left.

'You look about as good as I feel, American,' Sarah said as he rejoined her.

He smiled and took her hand again, kissing it tenderly.

'Do you think you will be all right here for tonight. I really need to snatch a couple of hours.'

'Sure, I think I can cope. I'm almost used to it now, and besides, I'm not completely on my own,' she replied, running her hand over her lower abdomen. 'Junior will keep me company.'

'You're something special, Sarah, you know that?'

The flat seemed even more empty than it had at any time previously. The words that Al had spoken to him shortly before he left were going round in Brinn's head.

'Make every moment count, American. Don't let her regret anything, and do everything in your power to make her last days happy ones. Then you will find some peace.'

Some of Sarah's things were still strewn on the floor and as he went to pick them up, he found her jacket. Brinn put the other things down and held the jacket close to him for a minute, then laid it carefully on the chair, finding little comfort in it. He lay down on the bed and drew her pillow to him, breathing in the scent of her hair, her body, but still he found no solace.

Still clinging to it he drifted off to sleep.

Something indefinable woke him with a start the next morning. He had slept longer then he had intended, but it had not refreshed him. He was still wearing the same clothes he had had on the day before. The distinctive hospital smell that clung to them reminded him of things he would have rather forgotten, so he stripped off and took a shower. He tried to make some mental notes on how he would cope when he brought Sarah back to the flat. He'd have to tidy the place up a bit and move things round maybe, but it was a pointless exercise. Everything depended on how much time they had and he didn't want to waste any of it on DIY.

He picked up some red roses from the florist's on his way to hospital and a small teddy bear that he noticed in the newsagent's next door. Automatically, he went to the Accident and Emergency department, but when he looked around the curtain into the cubicle, Sarah was not there. His heart sank, and he began to panic.

'Nurse,' he said, 'where is Miss Miller, the woman who

was admitted last night? What have you done with her?'

'Mr Peters, isn't it? Please, calm yourself. She is all right. We have just moved her up to the ward.'

Brinn looked away and shut his eyes. Relief overwhelmed him.

'Sorry nurse, I just…'

'It's quite understandable, Mr Peters,' she interrupted. 'Please don't apologise. If you go along to the lifts and up to the fourth floor, you will find her in Cranleigh ward. The nurse on duty will show you where.'

'Thank you, and again, I'm really sorry.'

Having been uncoupled that morning from all the wires and tubes with the exception of the intravenous drip, Sarah was a little more comfortable. She noticed that the half-drawn curtain at the side of her bed was twitching, and a small furry head appeared from behind it. The head seemed to belong to either a very tall teddy bear, or it was the American messing about.

'Excuse me, Mr Teddy Bear,' she said, 'unless you've seen a tall, blue-eyed, bad-tempered American on your travels, you can piss off. I'm just not in the mood.'

Brinn appeared from behind the curtain,

'You can talk, bad-tempered,' he replied, producing the roses from behind his back.

Sarah's eyes widened.

'Okay, what have you done now?' she said.

'Done? I haven't done anything. I just thought it would be appropriate,' he replied. 'What's up with you anyway? And how's junior today?'

'Fed up,' she said, 'just like his mother. Brinn, I want to get out of here. I've had a terrible night.'

'Hold your horses, Sarah, you're not going anywhere until they give you the okay. There is not just yourself to think about now.'

Sarah sat back. 'But I feel so much better now.'

'That's not the point, and you know it.' Then trying to lighten the mood, he added, 'With all the problems the NHS have, they are hardly likely to keep you hanging around in here if it's not strictly necessary.'

'Okay, don't nag. This is pretty difficult for me, too, you know.'

Mr Gregory entered the ward to do his morning rounds. He checked on, and spoke to, all his other patients first, leaving Sarah until last.

'Good morning, Miss Miller,' he said.

'For goodness sake, doc, call me Sarah. This Miss Miller stuff is just getting on my nerves a bit. I haven't been called Miss Miller in years, and I hope you are going to warm your hands up before you start prodding me about. I nearly fell off the bed yesterday when you gave me a going over.'

'Sorry, doctor,' Brinn interrupted, 'she is always a little feisty first thing in the morning.'

'Yes, I can see that, Mr Peters. Well, young lady, I'm sorry, Sarah. If I warm up my hands are you going to let me do my job?'

'Okay, doc, I'm all yours, as long as you promise to let me out of here soon.'

'We will see. Now if you would lie down, and perhaps, Mr Peters, you would be so kind as to pull the curtains around the bed? Thank you.'

Brinn watched while Gregory pulled back the covers as far as the top of her thighs, and lifted the hospital gown up to her chest.

'That's a whole lot better, doc,' she said as he felt her abdomen.

'Sarah, please,' Brinn urged, embarrassed at her effrontery.

'That's quite all right, Mr Peters. Believe it or not, I have had patients who have hit me for less reason than I have given Sarah here, and besides, I'm quite hardened to this kind of repartee. Well, Sarah, everything seems to be all right there. You are doing very nicely. Now, Mr Peters, about the matter we discussed yesterday. If you still feel you would like Sarah to go home, I think we can arrange something.'

'Oh yes, please!' Sarah burst out. 'He'll do anything, won't you, American.'

Ignoring Sarah's pleadings, Mr Gregory added, 'I just need to speak to you for a few minutes, if you wouldn't mind.'

'Yes, go with him, American. Find out what they have done with my clothes and get someone to take this drip out.'

Brinn followed Mr Gregory out of the ward to the adjoining sister's office, turning as he did so to give Sarah a hard stare.

'Is the baby doing okay, doctor?' Brinn asked, as he sat in the chair.

Perched on the edge of the table, Mr Gregory replied, 'For the moment, at least, but we still have a long way to go yet. I have referred Sarah to a colleague of mine, a very fine paediatric physician. He will be calling in on her later this morning. From what I can see, if our hand is forced, we will have to move quite quickly, and it would be best if he has an opportunity to examine Sarah before that moment arises.'

'I appreciate that, doctor.'

'I have prepared a prescription of drugs for Sarah to take. I'm afraid it is rather a cocktail, but it is all necessary. She will need to take them as directed on the various bottles, until they're finished. You understand me, Mr Peters.'

'Yes, doctor, I understand.'

'If there is any change in her condition, even a slight one, I want her back here immediately. Now, are you still sure you want to go ahead with this?'

'Yes, I want to make these last days special and I can't do that if she is in here. Besides, she would only drive your staff up the wall if I didn't take her home.'

'I think you are probably right, Mr Peters. Now, are there any more questions you would like to ask me?'

'Yes, can she go out? You know, do things, be normal.'

'She will grow increasingly tired as time goes on, and that will help regulate her activities to some degree. There is no need to isolate her, however, and I see no reason, as long as you are careful, why she can't still enjoy herself.'

'Thanks doctor – sorry, I mean, Mr Gregory.'

'I want to see her here for a check-up in two days' time in the outpatients' department. We can use the baby as an excuse. Here, I have made an appointment for you already.'

Brinn stood and extended his hand across the table. Mr Gregory reciprocated and they shook.

'See you on Tuesday, Mr Peters.'

The underwear and T-shirt that Sarah had arrived in were hardly suitable for the return journey in broad daylight, so Brinn picked up a few things from home before returning to her.

'That was a long chat,' she said. 'What were you and the doctor doing, rewriting the Declaration of Independence?'

'Oh, ha ha,' Brinn replied. 'No, I had to go home for some of your things. You might not remember, but you arrived in pants and a T-shirt.'

'Sorry,' she said. 'Can we go now?'

'No, not just yet. There is another doctor coming to see you, about the baby.'

'This is ridiculous. Why do I need to see another one?'

'This one specialises in babies,' Brinn added.

'You mean a paediatrician,' she said frowning. 'So what was the other doctor for, then?'

'Well, he was just on duty last night,' Brinn lied, hoping she wouldn't question it.

Doctor Johnson called in on an increasingly agitated Sarah at about eleven thirty. Brinn was glad to see him. Sarah was becoming almost paranoid about her need to leave.

Fortunately for all concerned, this doctor's hands were already warm and the examination was brief. After writing down Sarah's medical history and an internal examination to which Brinn had to persuade her to submit, the doctor arranged for them to see him again in a week.

'That was dreadful,' Sarah said as the doctor left them. 'I did not like him one bit.'

'You don't have to like him. Just let him do his job,' Brinn replied, handing her the clothes and pulling the curtain closed so she could dress in privacy.

'Ahhhh, that's better!' she said emerging from behind the curtain. 'I'm really glad to be out of that horrible gown.'

Sarah looked almost normal again, apart from the yellow pallor of her skin. A nurse had kindly re-wrapped the roses to make them easier to transport, and she handed them to Sarah, along with Mr Teddy Bear. The voluntary discharge form was produced and Brinn helped Sarah fill it out.

Then, thanking the nurse, and handing over the completed form, Brinn and Sarah walked out of the ward to the lift on the landing. A bell pinged as the empty lift arrived, and together they stepped inside. Brinn punched the ground floor button and the door closed. Then turning to Sarah he said, 'I've been waiting too long to do this.'

The door opened at the ground floor and several visitors watched in amazement, eyebrows rising steadily, as they observed the couple kissing amorously inside the lift. An elderly gentleman cleared his throat, trying to attract their attention.

'Excuse me, young man, may we use this lift?'

Brinn apologised and, dragging a grinning Sarah by the hand, led her out of the hospital and to the car.

They stopped at a chemist on the way back to the flat, to get the prescription for Sarah.

'All these?' she said when they got back into the car. 'Poor little junior will be a junkie before he is even born.'

'No, he will not. I checked with the doctor. Those won't harm him.'

'Him? It might be a her,' she remarked.

'Oh no,' Brinn said. 'One female in the family is quite enough. I'll not get any peace if there are two of you.'

Brinn made Sarah rest on the bed while he tackled a few of the calls he had been putting off. He closed the kitchen door just in case he could be overheard, and called Al, updating him on Sarah's progress and with the itinerary for the next few days.

Then, the long distance call to his mother. Brinn was not sure if he could get through this one quite so easily.

'Hi, mom!'

'Brinn! What is the matter son?'

'Why should there be anything the matter, mom?'

'Come on, Brinn, twice in one week! You never call me twice in a week.'

Brinn was close to breaking point. His mother knew him so well. He could hide little from her.

'Okay, you're right, mom. It's Sarah, the woman I told you about. I'm going to lose her. I found out yesterday she has only a short while to live.'

His mother, a wise woman, did not try to comfort him with old clichés or waste his time with needless reproaches. Simply she said, 'You love her very much, don't you, son?'

Brinn nodded. For some reason, he could not quite manage the words. His mother picked up on his silence.

'It's all right, son, I understand. Take all the time you

need and come on home for a visit when you're ready.'

Brinn rinsed his face in cold water before he went back into the bedroom. Sarah was sleeping, so he lay down on the bed beside her. Sarah stirred as she felt the movement next to her and, opening her eyes, she reached out and cuddled up to him, putting her head on his chest.

'We will have to think of a name for junior,' she said looking up at him.

'How can we pick a name, if we don't know what sex it is?'

'Well, we will just have to pick two, one for a boy and one for a girl.'

'Do you have any ideas?' he asked.

'If it is a boy, I would like it to be something American-sounding.'

'What, like Abraham Lincoln?' he interrupted, teasing her.

'Abraham? We can't call him that. He would be bullied at school.' Then thoughtfully she added, 'What was your father's name?'

'George,' he replied.

'Yes, that's more like it. George, as in George Washington. Perfect! If it is a boy, then, his name will be George Peters.'

Brinn liked the sound of it and he hugged her.

'Now, what about a girl?' she continued.

'Well, it is only fair if the boy's name is American, the girls name should be English. How does Carol sound to you?' he said grinning broadly. Sarah rolled over and knelt astride Brinn's body.

'You want to call our baby after your ex-girlfriend? Un-believable, you slimeball! What are you like?' she said laughing.

Brinn put one hand behind her neck and pulled her

towards him. He kissed her and she responded by sliding down and stretching out on top of him. He held her tightly and kissed her again. Sarah pulled back a little. Her eyes were wide with anticipation and she was breathing hard. Brinn could see her eagerness, but felt uncomfortable with the idea of it. He wanted to make love to her, but was afraid. If voiced, his fears would appear irrational in the cold light of reality. He could say he was afraid he would hurt her, or that it would be harmful for the child. The real reason for his fear, however, was the emotional release he knew making love to her would evoke. Since yesterday, he had felt the need to distance himself from her to lessen the pain of the inevitable parting, so he hid behind the pretence.

'Sarah, I don't think we should do this; I might hurt you.'

'Just be careful, then,' she sighed, kissing him again.

'What about the baby?' he said.

'The baby will be fine. Making love won't harm him.'

'I'm sorry, honey, I just can't do this,' he replied, a little resentful that she did not share his feeling.

He pulled himself free from her, got up from the bed and walked over to the window. Sarah came up behind him and put her arms around his waist.

'I'm sorry, American, it was stupid of me. I just got a bit carried away. Of course, you are right. It would be foolish.'

Brinn was woken by a sound. He looked at the clock. It was only five past midnight. Still drowsy, he waited for his head to clear as he tried to identify the noise. He rolled over onto his back, to discover that Sarah was no longer beside him. Quickly he sat up and switched on the bedside light, and blinking his eyes against the sudden brightness, he called out.

'Sarah, you okay, honey?'

There was no reply. Brinn got up and headed in the direction of the sounds. Sarah was fully dressed and in the hallway shoving things hastily into her backpack.

'Sarah! What are you doing? It's gone twelve,' he said, putting his hand on her shoulder.

'I'm going back where I belong,' she replied, pulling away from him.

'You're crazy. Come on, come back to bed.'

Again he tried to make contact with her, but she shook free of him.

'What is the matter with you? Why are you doing this?'

'I told you, I don't belong here, and I never have.'

Her packing completed, she turned to go, but Brinn went around in front and stood between Sarah and the front door.

'This is ridiculous, Sarah. You can't just go like this.'

'Why is that, American? Go on, tell me.'

Brinn struggled for a reply, discarding the most obvious. He felt cornered, trapped, and she seemed to be goading him deliberately.

'See? No reason. Goodbye, American.'

She pushed past him, but he took hold of her arm firmly.

'Look, Sarah, if this is about what happened earlier…'

Sarah turned towards him. The look of incredulity on her face halted him mid-sentence.

'You think this is about sex? My God, you have an over-inflated opinion of yourself, don't you?'

'Well, what is it about then?'

'I'm tired of being looked after. I was of the mistaken belief that you gave a shit about me, but since we came back this morning, you've done nothing but treat me like I have the plague or something. Frankly, I've had enough.'

Brinn wasn't aware that his feelings had been quite so obvious. He thought he had done a pretty good job of concealing them from her.

'Sarah, please.'

'Please what. Come on, American, what is it? Can't you be honest with me just for once?'

Brinn was still unable to say the words. Sarah turned again and opened the door. She took one step outside and Brinn forced out the words almost inaudibly.

'Mr Gregory told me yesterday that you haven't got long to live.'

Without any hint of emotion Sarah replied, 'What did you say?'

Brinn looked away from her and said again a little louder, the emotion rising in him, 'He said that you are going to die.'

Sarah turned back to him, 'Again, American.'

'You're going to die. Oh God, Sarah, you are going to die!' he cried out.

She stepped forward and put her arms around him. He clung to her, his body shaking, and down his face, ran a few tears of realisation and relief.

'You knew!' he said at last, pulling back.

'Since I came out of hospital. That's why I was so crabby this morning.'

'But how?'

'I couldn't sleep last night. Those wretched wires and tubes. At about two in the morning, the nursing staff changed. I think they were agency nurses. As they did the rounds, checking all the patients, they were constantly talking about some poor woman with liver failure. They joked about how it had been caused by Paracetamol poisoning. A hell of a headache, one of them said, and how sad it was about the baby, that even if it did survive, it would have no mother.'

Brinn held her more tightly, 'Sarah, why didn't you say something?'

'You obviously haven't been paying attention, American. I just did.'

Taking the pack from Sarah's shoulders and putting it on the floor, Brinn picked her up in his arms and carried her to the bedroom. Despite his fears, however real or imaginary, he managed not to hurt either Sarah or the baby that night.

They slept late the following morning, their bodies compensating for the interrupted night. When at last they did surface, she drew the short straw and Brinn pushed the reluctant Sarah out of bed to make the tea, while he had an extra few minutes in bed.

'I guess we won't be going to America now,' she said, sitting on the edge of the bed sipping her tea.

'It doesn't look likely now, honey, but don't worry, I will make it up to you. We will do all the things you would like to do. You will have everything you want. Just say the word.'

'American,' she said, putting the tea down and snuggling up to him, 'I have everything I want here, in you and George. I am happy just to be with you.'

Brinn felt stupid trying to buy her off as though she were Carol.

'Still,' he said, 'I would like to do some things for you.'

'All right, American, what shall we do today, then?'

'First, you must take your medication.'

Sarah pulled a face, indicating her repulsion at the thought. 'But as compensation,' he continued, 'I will take you shopping if you are up to it. You need some new clothes. Those jeans of yours are strained to the limit, what with you and George trying to wear them.'

Anyone on the outside might have wondered why they continued to act as though everything was normal; buying clothes, making plans; all things that couples with years ahead of them do everywhere. They both had now come to terms with the value of the little time left to them, but it did not stop them from wanting more. Living as normal a life as possible, even for this short time, made it seem somehow more permanent, and less transient.

They caught the tube to the city centre and Brinn helped her choose a selection of things from several different shops.

'Now, the last item on our list has to be a bit special,' he said to her. 'I'm taking you out tonight.'

'Where?' she asked excitedly.

'It's a surprise. You will have to wait and see. Perhaps something in black, like the dress you borrowed from Carmen's wardrobe, you remember? You looked incredible in it.'

They tried a few other shops, but could not find anything quite right. Sarah was tiring and looked a little pale.

'Just one more,' Brinn said as they entered an exclusive women's shop in a side street.

The slightly effeminate male assistant came from behind his counter and asked, 'May I help you, sir, madam?'

Sarah smiled broadly.

'Yes,' Brinn replied, 'something in black for madam, not too fancy, sleeveless shift dress perhaps.'

'Why, sir has impeccable taste! I think we can accommodate you. What size is madam?'

'Sarah, what size are you?' Brinn asked her.

'I don't know. I have never bought a dress before.'

'Madam is teasing sir. Never bought a dress before! How *bon mot!*'

'No, seriously, I have never bought a dress before.'

'How quaint,' the assistant replied with a faintly distasteful expression on his face. Then, changing tack completely, he said, 'Well, please don't let it trouble you. I have a tape measure here and we can soon establish madam's size. Would madam please lift her arms for me.'

Brinn nodded to Sarah, who obliged. The assistant put his tape around Sarah's chest, making her laugh a little.

'Please, madam, hold still,' he said seriously, 'I cannot get an accurate measurement unless madam holds still.'

Sarah looked over to Brinn, who was trying hard to conceal his laughter.

'Thirty-five inches, ah, a size ten to twelve. I think we have just the thing for madam. Please wait here a moment while I fetch it for you.'

The assistant disappeared through a door and Brinn, unable to contain it any longer, laughed out loud.

'Shhh!' Sarah said. 'He will hear you.'

'Good God, he's so pretentious,' Brinn replied.

'Oh, I don't know. I think he is rather sweet, and what lovely manners!'

The assistant reappeared carrying a black dress over his arm. It was similar in style to Carmen's, but there was a silver fleck in the material that caught the light as it moved.

'Oh, it is beautiful!' Sarah cried.

'It sure is pretty,' Brinn agreed.

'May I try it on?' she asked the assistant.

'Why, of course, madam. Please follow me; it's this way to the changing room.'

A few minutes later, Sarah emerged; she looked stunning. She had put her hair up the way Brinn liked it, with the help of an elastic band thoughtfully provided by the assistant. As she padded across the floor in her bare feet towards him, Brinn said, 'That's the one!'

'You like it, American?' she replied.

'Sure do. It fits like a glove; come here,' he said, holding out his hand to her.

Sarah walked up to him and, ignoring the startled assistant, Brinn took hold of her and kissed her lavishly. Slightly embarrassed, the assistant fiddled with his tape measure and cleared his throat as he tried to bring their attention back to the matter in hand.

'We'll take it,' Brinn said at last.

'Thank you, sir. Now, if madam would like to change, I will wrap it and make up the bill.'

With the dress in a large shiny carrier bag displaying the shop name proudly on the side, they carried all the booty back to the car and headed for home.

While Sarah showered, Brinn made a couple of calls, one of which was to book a box at the opera. When he rejoined her in the bedroom, she was stretched out on the bed exhausted and wrapped only in a towel.

'It's okay,' he said. 'You rest for a bit. There is no hurry. I'm going to be ages in there. I have to shower and shave.'

Sarah nodded and by the time Brinn had emerged from the bathroom, she had fallen asleep.

'Hey, sleepy head! You going to get dressed?'

A very pale Sarah roused and then sat up slowly.

'Yes, sorry. I just felt so tired.'

Feeling a bit mean, Brinn replied, 'No, it is me who should be sorry, dragging you around the shops mercilessly. Take your time; if we are late it doesn't really matter.'

They dressed together. Brinn wore a white shirt, dark grey suit and the blue tie that Sarah liked so much because it matched his eyes. After Sarah had put on the dress, Brinn stood back to look at her again.

'You look good enough to eat,' he said.

'Thanks,' she replied wearily.

'The car is here,' he said, checking to see if the noise of the vehicle drawing up outside was indeed the car he had ordered.

'Sorry?' she replied a little confused.

'I've booked a car so I don't have to drive tonight. Come on, it's waiting.'

Brinn helped her on with the new coat they had purchased earlier in the day and they went out to the waiting vehicle. Sarah could hardly believe her eyes. It was an enormous stretched limousine, all black and shiny.

She looked at Brinn and said, 'Does it change back into a pumpkin at midnight?'

'Not at these prices it doesn't,' he replied.

Sarah giggled as the chauffeur came round to open the door for them.

'I'm not used to this kind of treatment,' she said to the smartly dressed chauffeur.

'Well, miss,' he replied, 'it's about time you got used to it then.'

Brinn smiled at the young man and patted him on the back, then got into the car after Sarah. As they sat down inside, Brinn leant over to kiss her.

'Why are you doing this?' she said.

'What, kissing you?' he replied.

'No, you know what I mean. All this,' she said, waving her hand at the car.

Brinn sighed and shook his head.

'Haven't you guessed yet?'

'Possibly, but that doesn't mean I don't need to hear it from you.'

Taking her hand, Brinn looked into her eyes and said, 'I love you, Sarah.'

Her eyes brightened and she leaned over and kissed him.

'I know I'm going to wake up in a minute and all this will just have been a dream, but before I do, I just want to say, my dear American, I love you, too.'

The car pulled up outside the opera house. Sarah sat forward to open the door on her side of the car, but Brinn put his hand on hers to prevent it.

'No, you have to wait until the chauffeur comes round.'

She sat back again, and a moment later the young man

opened the door.

'Me first,' Brinn said, stepping out through the opening.

Then, extending his hand to Sarah, he helped her out of the car. She smiled warmly, her face glowing as Brinn tucked her hand under his arm and escorted her up the steps to the foyer. Behind them, the limousine pulled away silently into the night. A doorman dressed in a red and black uniform, tipped his hat as he opened the door for them. Two more steps, and Sarah was inside the building she had longed to see for years. The interior was quite magnificent. The foyer was an extensive room, carpeted entirely with deep red pile. Marble columns rose majestically to meet the ceiling, and at the central point hung a huge chandelier. The staircase, with wide marble treads and an ornate gilt banister, curved around from two sides of the room, meeting at the top. Tall thin porticos holding Romanesque figures were positioned at intervals along the walls. Nestling just beneath the stairs was the cloakroom, where attendants busied themselves with a flood of deposited coats and hats.

Brinn removed his own coat, then helped Sarah off with hers, bringing several admiring glances. Sarah lowered her eyes, a little embarrassed at the attention, as Brinn took the coats over to the cloakroom. On his return, he took her arm again and they headed to collect their tickets.

'Mr Brinndle Peters, box number four, I believe,' he said to the woman in the ticket office.

'Ah, yes, Mr Peters. Here you are. Thank you, sir. Have a nice evening.'

Brinn took the tickets and tucked them into his inside pocket.

'This way, madam,' he said to Sarah.

'Why, thank you, sir,' she replied.

As they ascended the staircase, Sarah looked down over the banister at all the people still filing into the foyer.

'This is unreal,' she said.

A smartly dressed young man, with white gloves on, opened the door to their box. Brinn tipped him and arranged for some refreshments to be brought up during the interval.

'Can't we go down to the bar during the interval,' Sarah called through the open door.

'With all that alcohol on the loose down there, no way. I remember what you're like when you've had a few. I am having some Evian sent up.'

Brinn paid the young man and joined Sarah in the box as she looked over the balcony into the auditorium.

'It's huge,' she said.

Brinn pulled out a seat for her and she sat down, pulling the dress down to cover her knees.

Sitting beside her he said, 'You shouldn't be embarrassed, honey. I think you've got great legs.'

'Possibly, but they don't get an airing very often, and I am a little bit conscious of them. To be honest with you, I feel half naked.'

Brinn smiled and leaned towards her. 'Happy?' he asked her.

'Oh no, American,' she replied with a big grin, 'I'm really quite miserable. Can't you tell?'

Brinn squeezed her hand. Sarah enjoyed the evening immensely. The music was better than she remembered it to be and she was delighted to see the costumes of the performers and the elaborate scenery, something she had only been able to guess at before.

The interval Evian did not go down too well, especially as Brinn had ordered himself a whisky sour and refused to let Sarah have even so much as a sip.

The second half was as wonderful for Sarah as the first half had been, and, as the end came, she began to cry.

'You all right?' he asked her.

'Oh, yes! It is just so beautiful, I do not want it to end.'

The applause filled the auditorium and she joined in enthusiastically. It was a wonderful release after the emotion of the evening.

They were standing outside on the steps of the opera house as the car drew up. Brinn took her arm again and they descended the stairs to the door that was being held open by the chauffeur.

'Did you enjoy it, miss?' he asked her.

'Oh yes! Very much, thank you.'

Brinn climbed in behind Sarah and the young man closed the door.

'Would you like to get something to eat?' Brinn asked her.

'Yes, that would be nice.'

'Driver,' Brinn said, leaning forward.

'Sir?'

'Do you know that little restaurant in—'

'No wait,' Sarah interrupted. 'I don't fancy a restaurant. I have a better idea.'

She leant forward and whispered into the driver's ear. He nodded and pulled out into the traffic.

'Where are you taking me?' Brinn asked.

'You'll see,' she replied. 'This is my surprise.'

It only took a few minutes and the car pulled up along-side the Embankment on the south side of the river. Sarah did not wait for the young man this time, but opened the door herself.

'Please will you give me some money, American?'

A little puzzled, Brinn reached into his wallet and pulled out a ten-pound note.

'This do?' he asked.

'Perfect,' she replied, taking it from his hand, and calling back to the driver she said, 'Would you like one too?'

'Yes please, miss, that would be very nice, thank you,' and then, by way of an afterthought, 'if you don't mind, that is, sir.'

Brinn, still bemused, said, 'No, of course not. By all means, be my guest.'

Sarah returned five minutes later holding three burgers. Handing one to the driver, she dragged Brinn from the car and took him over to the wall by the river.

'Remember,' she said.

'How could I forget?' he replied.

Sarah bit into her burger.

'Mmmmm! These taste so much better than the ones you can get in town,' she said, chewing a mouthful.

'Yeah, I think you're right,' he replied as he held back his tie to prevent the relish from dripping onto it. 'It must be the fresh air. Promise me one thing,' he added between mouthfuls.

'Okay, I can cope with one, as long as it is not too hard.'

'Promise me you will never change. You will always be this crazy.'

'That's not hard,' she replied. 'That just comes naturally.'

Brinn screwed up the wrappings of his meal as he finished his last mouthful.

'You done with yours?' he asked her.

'Yep, all done,' she replied, handing it to him.

Brinn amalgamated the paper with his own and tossed the resulting ball fifteen feet into the nearest rubbish bin.

'Good shot!' Sarah congratulated him.

Brinn smiled with satisfaction and they stood with their arms around each other looking over the wall at the water, the lights and the passing boats.

The limousine pulled up outside the flat and the young man opened the door to let Brinn and Sarah out of the vehicle. Brinn reached for his wallet to give him a tip, but he refused to accept it.

'Please take it,' Brinn urged. 'It would make her very happy.'

The young man looked over to where Sarah was standing and said, 'In that case, sir, I would be glad to accept.'

He tipped his hat again and left.

Sarah was very weary and she leaned up against the wall while Brinn found his keys and unlocked the door. He stepped inside expecting Sarah to follow him, but when she did not, he went outside again.

'You okay?' he asked her.

'I don't think so,' she replied as her knees buckled beneath her.

Brinn caught her and, picking her up, carried her inside.

'What's the matter?' he asked as he laid her down on the bed.

'I don't know. I just feel dizzy and weak.'

'I'm so stupid! It's my fault,' he said smoothing her brow. 'I shouldn't have dragged you everywhere this morning. It was way too much to expect you to do so soon. Come on, into bed with you. Tomorrow, you stay put.'

He helped her off with her things and as she settled, he put the dress on a hanger and put it away in the wardrobe. He was worried, but tried not to register his concern to Sarah. She fell asleep quite quickly and a little later, after he had joined her, Brinn lay watching her, too afraid to close his eyes.

## Chapter Thirteen

Sarah had been dreading the trip to hospital. She felt all right in herself, the drugs had been doing their job, but the trip proved only to remind her of how little time she had left.

'I'll be glad when this is over,' she said to Brinn as they pulled into the car park of the hospital.

'It shouldn't take too long, honey,' he said mainly to reassure her.

They found their way through the labyrinth of corridors to the outpatients' department and Brinn registered Sarah's arrival at the receptionist's desk, while she found a seat in the crowded waiting area. The place was packed and Brinn had to sit quite a way from Sarah until an elderly man opposite her vacated his seat in response to his name being called by the nurse.

As was often the case, everything was running late. Sarah grew more agitated with each passing minute and she began to shift uncomfortably in her chair. Brinn tried to calm her with reassuring glances, but finally she could take it no longer and walked out.

As she stepped into the corridor, the receptionist called her name. Brinn had desperately wanted to run after her, but he halted at the desk and made an apology, explaining that Miss Miller would return in a moment, being temporarily indisposed. Brinn ran down the corridor and caught up with Sarah before she had time to leave the building.

'Sarah, please wait. They are calling for you right now.'

'Sorry, American, I can't wait any longer. I have to get out of here now.'

Brinn put his arms around her, more to stop her fleeing than for affection's sake.

'Look, we can go in straight away, see the doctor and come right out, I promise. Please come back with me. This won't take long now.'

Sarah was breathing hard and her eyes were looking wildly all around her like an animal fearing attack.

'Please, Sarah,' Brinn implored again, 'for the baby's sake.'

Sarah looked at him, and her eyes softened.

'For the baby's sake,' she repeated.

'Yes,' he replied, then, taking her gently by the hand, he led her back to the waiting room.

At the reception desk, Brinn said, 'I must apologise, but we have been a bit detained. Can we go in now?'

'No, I'm sorry, sir,' the receptionist replied. 'I had to let the next gentleman in ahead of you.'

Sarah started to pull back and Brinn just managed to grab her and prevent her from leaving again.

'No, I'm sorry,' Brinn said to the receptionist, 'we are going in.'

The receptionist protested in vain as Brinn pushed past a few patients waiting at the desk, and proceeded towards the consulting rooms, holding firmly onto Sarah. He came to the door marked 'Mr Gregory, Consultant', and went straight in without knocking.

A startled Mr Gregory stood and held up his hand with the intention of ejecting the intruders. When he realised it was Brinn and Sarah who had barged in, he lowered his hand and turned to the equally startled patient before him.

'I'm terribly sorry, Mr Green, but there seems to have been a bit of a mix-up somewhere along the line. I wonder if you would be so kind and go back to the waiting room. I promise to deal with you immediately I have seen this patient.'

Mr Green, who was too surprised by the event to be affronted, dutifully picked up his coat and with profuse apologies left the consulting room.

'Miss Miller, please sit down,' Mr Gregory said, directing her to a chair. She was still clearly agitated as he asked her, 'And how have you been, Sarah?'

She did not answer, and so Brinn substituted for her.

'She's been fine, doc. A bit tired and one time she felt dizzy, but no real problem that we are aware of.'

Mr Gregory tried again to get a response from Sarah.

'If I warm my hands up, will you let me examine you, young lady?'

Sarah smiled weakly and relaxed a little, nodding her head in compliance.

'Good,' Mr Gregory remarked. 'Now, if you wouldn't mind slipping off your jeans and hopping up onto the couch.'

Sarah disappeared behind a screen that also concealed the couch, while Brinn took the opportunity to explain to Mr Gregory that Sarah now knew about her condition, although he didn't go into any detail as to how she had found out.

As he began to examine her, Mr Gregory said, 'Mr Peters tells me you understand about what's happening to you.'

Sarah nodded.

'And how does that make you feel, Sarah?' he added.

Sarah thought for a moment and then said hesitantly, 'At first, I spent the whole night crying. If it hadn't been for George here,' she said patting her abdomen, 'I think I might have finished it there and then.'

'George?' Mr Gregory asked.

'Yes,' she replied, 'that's the name we have decided for the baby.'

Mr Gregory nodded.

'And how do you feel about it now?' he added.

'Well, I know there is nothing I can do to change things, but every moment left with the American is far too precious to waste on regrets. Besides, I want to give George every chance. I know the longer I can hold out, the more of a head start I can give him.' Sarah looked up into Mr Gregory's eyes and added, grasping his arm, 'He must live! Promise me, doctor, don't give up on him.'

Taken aback, Mr Gregory replied, 'I'll certainly do my very best, Sarah.'

While Sarah got dressed again, Mr Gregory took Brinn to one side.

'I have heard from Doctor Johnson this morning, and along with the original tests we made, it looks as though the baby has been largely unharmed by the toxicity.'

Brinn was visibly relieved, and Mr Gregory placed his hand on Brinn's shoulder.

'I must say, Mr Peters, I wish I had a few more patients like Miss Miller. She seems to have adjusted very well to her condition.'

'She still has her moments, doc.'

'By the way, Mr Peters, why, if you don't mind me asking, why does she call you American?'

'It's a long story, doc. My real name is Brinndle, but under the circumstances if it helps, I'm perfectly happy for you to call me Brinn.'

Mr Gregory smiled. They shook hands and Brinn and Sarah left, passing a very sheepish Mr Green going in the other direction towards Mr Gregory's consulting room.

Sarah had begun to prepare them some lunch while Brinn, at Sarah's instigation, tackled the ongoing problem of the untidy bedroom, compounded now by the addition of Sarah's things. Brinn was just trying to shut an already overloaded drawer, when he heard a loud crash from the kitchen.

'Sarah,' he called out. 'You all right?'

'American, come here quickly, please.'

Brinn rushed into the kitchen, to see Sarah had dropped a saucepan on the floor. Her eyes were wide open and she was clutching her abdomen.

'What is it, Sarah? Are you all right?'

'Give me your hand,' she said, reaching out wildly to grasp him by his left. Then placing it on her abdomen she said, 'He's kicking! George is kicking! Can you feel it? There, see?'

Brinn felt the spot where Sarah had put his hand and could just feel a fluttering sensation beneath the surface.

'That's really George?' he asked her.

'Unless there is anyone else in there with him, it's George all right.'

Still keeping contact with the palpitations, Brinn put his other arm around her and drew her close.

'It's wonderful,' he said.

'Wonderful! He had better not start that at night when I'm trying to get to sleep!'

Brinn laughed.

'You can't stop a potential ballplayer from getting some practice in, and besides, he can't tell if it is day or night in there.'

Brinn kissed her, and instead of resuming his bedroom duties, he gave her a hand with the lunch.

'Can we get some things for George this afternoon?' Sarah asked as she finished off the washing up.

'You mean go to one of those baby shops?' Brinn replied unenthusiastically.

'Well, unfortunately, they don't come ready wrapped,' she laughed.

'Okay, but can't I wait in the car? Do I have to come in?'

'Oh, come on! It will not be that bad,' she encouraged

him. 'There will be lots of other fathers in there. You won't be on your own, and besides, if I have to go to hospital, you have to come to Mothercare with me.'

Brinn could not see a way out of this one, so reluctantly, he agreed.

Finding a parking space in the city was always a problem, and Brinn grew a little irritable as his efforts proved futile.

'We should have left the car and come in on the underground,' Sarah observed.

A young man driving a sports car had just robbed Brinn of a parking space. He had slipped in behind, while Brinn was still crunching the gears in an attempt to find reverse.

Brinn slammed his hands down on the steering wheel and let loose with an exasperated, 'Damn this stupid right-hand drive!'

Sarah turned to him and asked, 'Road rage, American?'

The broad smile accompanying her comment did little to quell Brinn's anger and she turned away from his glare, sinking down a little in her seat. He proceeded for a further ten minutes trying to find a space, finally locating one in a side road. He exhaled an enormous sigh as he put on the handbrake and turned off the engine.

It was only five minutes' walk to the large Mothercare store and an excited Sarah pulled Brinn all the way. She had been right. There were a lot of fathers in the store, all of whom looked about as keen to be there as Brinn was. The men exchanged knowing glances amongst themselves, raised eyebrows and shrugged shoulders, a sort of covert sign language that communicated, 'I'm only here because the wife made me.'

Brinn felt doubly awkward as all the men he could see were young, and he could almost have qualified as their father rather than the father of his own child. He was trying to pay attention to Sarah, who was asking him something about a Babygro, but he was distracted by an enormously pregnant woman with her minute husband, who were standing a little farther up the same aisle.

'American, you're not listening! Shall I get the blue or the yellow one?' Sarah said again.

Brinn knew staring was rude, but the sight of this beached whale with her knees slightly bent and her hand at her waist trying to ease her back, was overpoweringly compulsive. He was expecting her to burst at any moment, judging by the expression on her face.

'Sorry, honey,' he said at last, shaking his head. Sarah smiled as she saw the direction of Brinn's gaze.

'It's all right, American, I overheard them talking. She's expecting twins, so put your mind at rest. I don't think I will ever get that big.'

In the absence of a decision from Brinn, Sarah put both Babygros into her basket alongside a packet of disposable nappies, a small yellow plastic duck and a pair of booties. She took Brinn by the hand and led him away from the large woman and to the checkout.

The teenage girl behind the counter processed the items and then turning to Sarah asked, 'Is your father paying for these things, miss?'

For Brinn, the whole expedition had been a total nightmare and this final insult was the last straw.

He turned to the young girl and said, 'That would be a little difficult, miss, as her father is in Basingstoke.'

Then he took hold of Sarah and kissed her full on the mouth. The young girl blushed, and, embarrassed, took the credit card that Brinn held out to her whilst he was still kissing Sarah.

'Father, indeed,' Brinn muttered as they emerged outside the store.

Sarah slipped her arms around him and looking into his eyes said, 'I love it when you get mad, American.'

'Oh, yes?' he said. 'And why is that then? Because it makes me seem so macho?'

'No,' she replied.

'Because it makes me seem so attractive, then?' he pressed her.

'No. Look, even if I tell you, you won't like it.'

'You let me be the judge of that. Now, what about sexy? Does being angry make me look sexy?'

Sarah shook her head.

'Well, tell me why, then,' he urged playfully, grabbing the waistband of her jeans and pulling her closer.

Sarah smiled.

'Because it makes you look so ridiculous. See, I told you you wouldn't like it.'


'American,' Sarah cried, her face buried in the pillow.

Brinn opened his eyes and turned to look at her.

'What's the matter, honey?'

'Pain! Please stop the pain.'

'You sure it's not just cramp, honey?' he said yawning.

'I'm sure! Please, for God's sake, help me, American.'

The urgency in her words roused him from his drowsiness and he replied, 'Hold on, Sarah, I'll phone for an ambulance.'

'No, there's no time! Take me in the car. Now!'

Brinn jumped out of bed and into a pair of jeans and a sweatshirt. He grabbed his car keys and pulled back the covers to lift Sarah out of bed, but hesitated as he saw the sheet stained with blood.

'You sure you wouldn't rather wait for an ambulance?' he said.

'Please, American, take me now,' she urged.

Brinn responded to her pleas and, wrapping her up in the cotton bedcover, picked her up and carried her to the car. It was two in the morning. There was little traffic about, and the trip to hospital took no time at all, but each jolt, each bump, brought an agonised moan from Sarah.

'It's okay, honey. We are here now,' he said, ignoring all the signs to the contrary and parking right outside the casualty department entrance.

Brinn ran round to Sarah and lifted her out of the car. He hurried in through the electronic sliding doors and frantically searched for an empty cubicle. An over-officious male charge nurse, noticing the commotion Brinn was causing, chased after him urging him to wait.

'Excuse me, sir, you can't—'

'She's bleeding,' Brinn interrupted him. 'She is pregnant, and the baby is coming. It's urgent that you get hold of Mr Gregory and Dr Johnson. They have been treating her. Please hurry.'

At the mention of Mr Gregory's name, the charge nurse made space for Sarah by evicting a less than compliant drunk from the end cubicle. Motioning Brinn to place Sarah on the trolley, he went to the reception and made a phone call. A few moments later, he returned and reassured Brinn that both Mr Gregory and Dr Johnson would be there shortly as he had just paged them.

It was another of those occasions when the events around Brinn seemed to be playing in slow motion. It seemed like an age, but was only a short time in reality, that he waited, doing his best to comfort Sarah as she writhed on the trolley, until Mr Gregory arrived.

'Dr Johnson is on his way, Mr Peters,' Mr Gregory said, rushing into the cubicle. 'He won't be long now, and if you wouldn't mind waiting just outside while I assess the situation.'

Brinn was distraught and unwilling to leave Sarah, but with Mr Gregory's gentle coaxing, he finally capitulated. Kissing Sarah on the forehead, Brinn left for the waiting area just along the corridor, from where he could hear a flurry of activity taking place around Sarah's cubicle. Several medical staff rushed in and out, and on each occasion Brinn rose to his feet. He wandered a few steps to one side or the other, craning his neck to get a better view of what was going on, before finally sitting again. He hated the waiting, but more than that, he hated not knowing what was happening. He tried to reason with himself that surely his making love to her earlier could not have resulted in this.

There was an increase in the activity behind the curtain and a moment later the trolley bearing Sarah appeared before immediately being whisked away at a rapid rate in the opposite direction. Brinn could stand it no longer, he stood and began to pursue it down the corridor.

'What's happening? Where are you taking her?' he called out as he caught up with them.

The male nurse halted at the suggestion of Mr Gregory and, placing himself between Brinn and the trolley, bodily prevented him from going any further.

'Please, Mr Peters, we are doing everything we can. Try to be patient. Come back with me and sit down.'

The nurse took hold of Brinn's upper arm firmly, and as an overwrought Brinn looked back over his shoulder, the nurse led him away.

'Where have they taken her?' Brinn asked as they sat down in the waiting area.

'They have taken her to the theatre, and as soon as there is any news, someone will come to see you.'

Brinn did not have to wait long. The male nurse rose to his feet and left as Mr Gregory came out of the theatre and along the corridor to join Brinn.

'Mr Peters, would you come with me, please?'

Brinn immediately stood and followed Mr Gregory into a side room.

'Please sit down, Mr Peters.'

'I want to see her. Is she all right?' Brinn urged.

Mr Gregory was silent for a moment, a moment that was just long enough for Brinn to comprehend.

'No!' Brinn cried with great agitation, shaking his head. 'No, I'm sorry. I don't believe you. I want to see her now.'

'Please, Mr Peters, wait a moment.'

Still standing, Brinn hesitated while Mr Gregory tried to explain in as calming a tone as his professional manner could muster.

'I do appreciate what you are going through, Mr Peters.'

'What do you mean, you appreciate what I'm going through? You have no idea what I'm going through? Oh God, this can't be happening!'

'Please, Mr Peters, try to calm yourself. Surely you must have understood from the very beginning that this was inevitable at some point. I know this must be very difficult for you at the moment, but it was all over quite quickly. Sarah would have felt very little. The baby's premature arrival was unfortunately the causal effect of her problem, and the damaged liver was just unable to produce enough clotting agent. She would have had only a few weeks more at best, even if there had been no child.'

Stunned and still disbelieving, Brinn said slowly, 'You're telling me she bled to death.'

'Yes, I'm afraid that's correct, but we were able to save the child.'

Brinn sat down again, still with a gnawing doubt at the back of his mind.

'Could I have been responsible for this?' he asked, a little embarrassed.

'I'm sorry, Mr Peters, I do not understand.'

Unable to look at Gregory directly, Brinn replied, 'I, well, earlier we...'

'No, Mr Peters,' Mr Gregory interrupted. 'Please put your mind at rest. Intercourse would not have triggered off this event. That was just a coincidence.'

Only partly relieved that he was not the cause of her death, Brinn sat back in the chair.

'Of course, you can see Sarah, Mr Peters. The nursing staff are just tidying her up a little and then you can go in. On a brighter note, your son is doing far better than we had expected. I think he will turn out to be a fighter, just like his mother. For the present, however, we have him in the premature baby unit where we can keep a good eye on him. You can see him now, if you wish.'

Brinn shook his head. He had only one thing on his mind at that moment. Sarah. There was a knock at the door and a nurse came in.

Nodding to Mr Gregory, she bent over Brinn and said quietly, 'If you would like to come with me, Mr Peters.'

Brinn put his hands on the arms of the chair, stood up wearily and followed her out of the room.

A little down the corridor in a room to the left was Sarah, as pale as the sheet she now lay beneath. The nurse closed the door and left Brinn on his own.

For a few minutes, he paced back and forth around the room, his restless hands searching for a resting place on his body. Yesterday – was it only yesterday – they had been doing normal things together. Arguing, laughing, eating, sleeping. Yes, sleeping, and only a few hours ago, she had responded beneath his caress, and he found it inconceivable that she would never do so again. Unable to look at Sarah, he did not think he could ever rid himself of the feeling that he was in some way responsible. Perhaps the precious minutes he had wasted before getting her to hospital? Or was it making love to her? Or the trip to the town?

There was no word of reproach from her, no word of condemnation or resentment, and right now, he would have taken it all gladly just to hear the sound of her voice again. The urge to be near her momentarily silenced his fear, and he approached her.

'Hi, honey,' he said, stroking her cheek with the back of his hand and staring at her, hoping for some sign of response. The pain was gone from her face now, and her expression was one of quiet. Brinn bent forward and kissed her mouth. Her lips were not quite cold yet.

'They tell me George is doing fine. It seems that he was in a mighty hurry to be born. He just couldn't wait another minute. Impatient, just like his mother. Oh Sarah! What will I do without you? I can't do this on my own. I am going to miss you so much. Please help me, honey? Help me!'

Brinn put his arms around her lifeless body as best he could and held on tight. He did not want to let go ever again. Of all the million things he had wanted to say to her, and had fooled himself into thinking he would have enough time to say, of all of them, now he could think of none. He held on for several minutes, trying to will her back to life, but finally realisation caught up with him and he laid her down, smoothing her ruffled hair back into place.

At that moment Mr Gregory came quietly into the room.

'Mr Peters, I have some tea for you, if you would like it.'

'Sure, doctor,' Brinn replied. 'Just give me a minute.'

Brinn bent down one last time.

'Goodbye, honey,' he whispered, kissing her on the cheek. 'Always remember, I love you.'

Brinn retraced his steps to the side room, and tried to drink tea with Mr Gregory.

'I want to thank you, doctor, for all you have tried to do,' Brinn began. 'I know you stuck your neck out for us and I may not have said anything at the time, but we appreciated it.'

'You're very welcome, Mr Peters. I'm only sorry

medical science has failed you and there was little more I could do.'

At that moment Mr Gregory's bleeper sounded.

'I'm sorry, Mr Peters, I must answer this,' he said, pulling it from his pocket and walking to the door. 'Please stay as long as you like. I may be gone for quite some time.'

Brinn was left alone with his thoughts and his unwanted cup of tea. He was more than happy to be in that state; he could find some sort of peace in the quiet numbness where time now no longer had any value.

There was a knock at the door, snapping him back to reality.

'I'm sorry to disturb you, Mr Peters, but we need some information about Miss Miller's next of kin.'

Brinn looked up, unable to believe that anyone could be quite so crass and insensitive.

He gave the male nurse a cursory look and replied, 'Well I'm her…' but then stopped, realising that he wasn't her anything.

He was her lover, companion, the father of their child, but nothing that could be legally termed next of kin. Brinn couldn't believe that the thought of marriage had not crossed his mind sooner. It was not as if he hadn't wanted to. There had just never been time to think about it. He cursed himself now for his stupidity, and wondered if Sarah would have minded.

'Why do you need to know?' he said instead.

'It's hospital procedure. We need to know for any funeral arrangements.'

'Look, she would not have wanted them to be involved. I'm the father of the child. Won't I do?'

'I fully appreciate your situation,' the nurse continued, a note of arrogance in his voice, 'and I'm truly sorry, Mr Peters, but it is the Health Authority's practice. We have to notify the next of kin or a nominated representative. Now, you were not actually married to Miss Miller, were you? Or perhaps she left written instructions nominating you as her representative.'

Luckily for the nurse, Brinn was unable to respond to the anger brewing inside him, as exhausted from the emotional haemorrhage, he found it impossible to argue any more. Dejected, he gave the charge nurse Sarah's parents' name and address, every word making his heart heavier. The task completed, Brinn got up to leave the room and the nurse, who had busied himself with the completion of the forms. In the corridor he bumped into Mr Gregory.

'Hello again, Mr Peters, I'm so glad to have caught you before you left. How are you bearing up?'

'Not too well. Do you think you could spare me a few minutes?'

'Certainly. Shall we go back in here?' he said indicating the side room.

'No, not in there, if you don't mind. Your charge nurse is in there and I could not guarantee to be responsible for my actions.'

'Yes, I quite understand, Mr Peters, and I'm sorry. He does have a rather overbearing quality. Let's go along here a bit and we can sit down. You look as though you need to.'

Farther along the corridor was a recess, quiet and secluded and with a few chairs in it, but no people. They sat down side by side and Brinn related the problem to Mr Gregory while he listened attentively.

'Can you help me?' Brinn asked finally.

'This is a very difficult situation, but I can see it means a lot to you, Mr Peters. I certainly can promise you that as the father of the child, there is no way that Sarah's parents can have any claim on him. A simple DNA test would be all that is needed there. As to the other matter, I am unsure if I can help, but if you will leave it with me, I will see if there is anything I can do.'

Brinn walked out of the casualty department through the same door he had entered, still numb and still expecting her to run out after him at any moment and say it was all a mistake. He stood for a moment watching the next arrival being unloaded from the rear of an ambulance, and though he did not wish it, he wondered if the fate of this man would be the same as Sarah's. He looked around, unsure what to do next, an overwhelming emptiness his only stimulus. His car, which in his haste to get Sarah into the hospital he had not locked, had been rolled backwards out of the way of the entrance. Brinn did not trust himself to drive, and besides, there was nowhere he wanted to go, so he began to walk.

The night enveloped him, comforting and anonymous as he walked around the city streets. Old familiar pathways awakened ghosts from the past, faces, conversations, experiences, all the more potent now because of Sarah's absence. Brinn stopped at the wall by the Embankment, the sight of courting couples making him suddenly feel the loneliness more keenly. He hailed a passing cab and, leaving the memories behind, he headed for home.

The taxi pulled up outside the flat and Brinn leaned forward to pay the driver, but as he looked across to the doorway, he changed his mind. There was to be no easy rest for him tonight.

'Sorry driver, could you take me to Darwin Road?'

The cab pulled up for the second time, outside Al's cafe. Brinn paid the driver and walked up to the door. He had to knock several times before the window above the cafe opened and Al looked out to see who was there. He didn't say a word. He didn't have to. Al came down the stairs in his nightshirt, and opened the door of the cafe.

'Couldn't bear to be in the flat on my own, Al. Mind if I crash out here tonight?'

Al shook his head and with his hand on Brinn's back, guided him in through the door and closed it behind him.

Brinn couldn't really face it, but the next morning he had to go back to the flat for a shower and change of clothes. The bedroom was the hardest room to confront, frozen in time the moment he had left for the hospital with Sarah. The stain on the sheet, the hastily discarded bed covers, and the most difficult thing, the black dress, still hanging in the wardrobe. It hung there waiting, as though she might enter the room at any moment and put it on.

The phone began to ring in the kitchen, and Brinn, glad of the distraction, went to answer it.

'Hello, Brinndle Peters,' he said.

There was a pause, and then a female voice, so broken with emotion that he was barely able to recognise it, answered.

'Mr Peters, it is Mrs Miller here. Sarah's mother, you remember.'

Brinn slumped against the worktop; the charge nurse had wasted little time, and it was too late for Mr Gregory to intervene now. Brinn barely managed to disguise the anxiety in his reply.

'Hello, Mrs Miller. How did you get this number?'

'After the nurse at the hospital contacted me, I rang Al. He was kind enough to furnish me with the number.'

'So you have heard already.'

'Yes, this morning. The whole thing has come as rather a shock. I understand that Sarah was expecting.'

Brinn did not think he was in any state to cope with an outraged mother right now, and as he spoke, he searched for a rapid termination to the conversation.

'Yes,' he said wearily. 'She gave birth to a baby boy

shortly before…'

'It's quite all right, Mr Peters, you need not go on. If my husband finds out that I have phoned you this morning, it will cause a great deal of trouble for me, but after meeting you recently, it seemed only right that you should know. My husband has decided to arrange the funeral for Sarah and he has asked a local funeral director to collect her body.'

Brinn put the receiver down on the worktop. He felt helpless and could not believe that this was happening so fast. The anxious, nauseous feeling swept over him again, caught up as he was in something he was powerless to stop.

'Mr Peters? Mr Peters? Are you still there?' the distant voice called from the worktop.

Brinn picked up the receiver again.

'I'm sorry, Mrs Miller, it's hard for me to think right now. I had hoped to make these arrangements myself. Is it not possible for us to come to some sort of an agreement?'

It was Mrs Miller's turn to remain silent.

Finally she said, 'I'm also very sorry, Mr Peters, but I don't think there is any way, given the circumstances of our last meeting, that my husband would be likely to change his mind. He is, as you know, not a very reasonable man, and I'm sorry to say I think he is doing this purely out of spite.'

Brinn sighed heavily, and already knowing the answer asked, 'What is the chance of me being able to attend the funeral?'

Again Mrs Miller was silent for a moment.

'I have to be honest, Mr Peters, I don't think there is any chance of that happening either. I fear there would be a terrible scene and…'

Brinn replaced the receiver, cutting her off.

He had hardly collected his thoughts when there was a knock at the door. He was in two minds whether to answer it, but the persistent rapping demanded his attention. He opened the door.

'Al!' he said. 'Oh, God, I'm really glad to see you.'

'I wasn't sure whether to come, but I thought you might be needing a hand to sort things out.'

'Thanks, Al. It's much appreciated. I'd hoped things might get a bit better, but I've just had Mrs Miller on the phone, and I don't see how they could get much worse.'

Brinn showed Al into the kitchen and went over the highlights of the phone call for his benefit.

'I'm sorry, American, but I had to give her your number or you wouldn't have known anything about it until it was all over. You knew this was a possibility already, I think, American, after what happened at Pete's funeral.'

'Yes, I suppose so, but I thought it might be different in Sarah's case, because of how things were between us. This just doesn't seem fair.'

'There is nothing fair in this life. Sarah's death is not fair. Your being left alone is not fair, and the little life who will never know his mother, it's not fair for him either. Have you been to see him yet?'

Brinn, embarrassed, walked over to the sink, and with his back to Al, and for no reason at all, filled the kettle.

'Not yet.'

'When you going?'

'I'm not sure. Later today, perhaps. I've too much on my mind right now.'

'Okay,' Al said, 'but remember, American, he needs you right now just as much as you ever needed Sarah.'

Brinn, to make the filling of the kettle seem a legitimate activity, offered Al a cup of tea. There was no sensible reason why Brinn did not want to see his son. Well, not one that he was prepared to admit to at this moment. Logic told him the child was not responsible for Sarah's death, but logic had no root in his emotional state. Brinn, still looking for someone to blame, had intended to defer his visit indefinitely.

He could not face the bedroom again, so Al took over the job of sorting it out, stripping the bed and putting the sheets into the washing machine. He carefully packed Sarah's clothes into a suitcase that Brinn had given him, but as he was about to remove the black dress from the wardrobe, Brinn called from the hallway.

'Not that one, Al. It's stupid, I know, but I would rather leave it hanging there for a while.'

Al complied and, closing the case, slid it under the bed, leaving it for Brinn to deal with later.

Then, sitting on the bed Al said, 'You want me to arrange a funeral? You know, like the one we had for Pete.'

Brinn thought for a moment. 'You think it would help?'

'That's for you to say.'

Brinn thought again, then said, 'I guess it would be a way to mark her going and I think she would have liked that. Okay, Al, if you wouldn't mind.'

In hospital, Brinn had brought Sarah flowers and although she had been crabby at the time, he knew she had liked them because when she returned home, she had pressed one of the rose buds in an old book between blotting paper. Now, as he drove his car along the M3 towards the small village church near Basingstoke, he carried a bunch of the red roses like the ones that she had liked so much. Attached to them was a small white card bearing a brief note in Brinn's own hand.

Sarah's grave was easy enough to find. Though it had no headstone, it was the only one with freshly turned earth. The solitary wreath lying on it had begun to wilt, and Brinn discarded it, laying the roses in its place. The unusually warm spring morning that would normally have lightened his spirits had the reverse effect today. He had come intending to make her promises about the child, but his resolve faded, his own need for her paramount.

The churchyard was peaceful and the air was filled with birdsong. Brinn stood until the aching and longing became too much, forcing him to turn and leave. The card attached to the flowers fluttered in the gentle breeze, turning it over to reveal the message.

Each dawn that brings the early light
To chase away the dreary night,
Cries your name to me;
That calls the birds to flight and sing
On thermals high and outstretched wing,
Fills my thoughts with you.
Just as the dawn before each day,
I'd happ'ly suffer night's decay,
To hear your voice again.
To hold you in my arms once more,
I'd gladly weep at heaven's door,
To have you back with me.

For ever together,
American

Al had been busy since Brinn had seen him last over a week before and there must have been thirty to forty people there as Brinn came up the hill to the monument. The fire had been lit and already people were exchanging experiences and the stories that they knew about Sarah.

As Brinn looked around at the group, some acknowledged him with a wave, others with a nod or a word of greeting. Not only were there the expected faces – Al, Harry, College, and Chris, who was there at Brinn's instigation – but some unexpected ones as well. Mr Gregory was there, much to Brinn's amazement, and in deep conversation with College; the young man from the car-hire firm that had provided the limousine on the evening of the opera; the tramp that had offered Brinn the mis-labelled Volvic, as well as several others whose faces he was familiar with, but with whose names he was not.

Al came alongside and rested a hand on Brinn's shoulder.

'How you holding up, American?' he asked.

'Not so bad, Al. A little shaky, but I'll get by.'

Al nodded and patting his shoulder moved over to talk to Harry. Brinn circulated, listening, as Sarah was brought back to life again through the telling of colourful stories, some of which he had never heard before. This woman that he loved, and yet knew so little about, still had the ability to make him smile.

Behind College stood a young man whom Brinn supposed was his son. With his hands crossed in front of him, he stood motionless, perhaps even a little embarrassed. He looked on with a serious face, fully supportive of his father, nodding occasionally to lend weight to his narrative. College had many stories of when Sarah first came onto the streets. How her care and patience through the many long cold nights when he was, well, indisposed, warranted much eloquent praise. Finally, unable to hold back the tears with words any longer, College broke down as he related how she had helped in the search for his son. The young man took hold of his father's arm and College, half sobbing, half mumbling, struggled through the story.

'The Salvation Army had arranged a meeting between us, but my nerves had just let me down at the last minute, and I had spent the previous night seeking solitude in the bottom of a bottle. I was in a pretty bad way by the morning, unwashed and shabby. I was in no fit state to meet you the next day, my boy, so Sarah offered to go on my behalf, you remember. If it had not been for her, we would never have met again. She made sure I was all right the next time. She slipped me a couple of sleeping tablets that she had acquired from the doctor, to keep me out of trouble. Slept like a baby that night and she smartened me up the next day and brought me to meet you. It seems so long ago now.' The young man nodded and put his arm around his frail, weeping father.

Al told of how Sarah had been invaluable when Carmen was so ill, sitting up late with her when the drugs failed to keep the pain under control. She would get Carmen to talk about her childhood in Italy, about her family and friends in the old country. The warm memories had soothed Carmen and gave Al a chance to catch up on some much-needed sleep. Both he and Carmen looked on Sarah as the child they had never been able to have, and he hoped Sarah had looked on them as substitute parents.

'She was a good kid. Always found a good word to say about everybody, even those that hurt her.'

Even Chris joined in, retelling Sarah's exploits at his birthday party. How surprised he had been at the change from the frumpy thing he had seen in the underpass, to the lovely glowing woman who had turned up at the party.

'Best part of all was when she was a little the worse for the champagne, and wound Carol up, much to most people's delight. Wretched woman, Carol; I doubt if anyone would have minded if Sarah had punched her on the nose.' Then, raising his voice a little to attract Brinn's attention, he called, 'Damn shame you had to take her home so early that night, Brinn.'

Brinn acknowledged Chris with a nod, too overwhelmed to do more. It was hard, very hard. Sarah was well loved and his aching heart just ached the more.

Brinn paused a few minutes to speak to Mr Gregory.

'Nice to see you, doc, if a little unexpected,' he said, holding out his hand. The doctor shook it warmly.

'You have your friend to thank for that,' he said pointing to Al, 'but I'm glad I came. I had been meaning to contact you anyway. I wanted to tell you about the time I spent with Sarah early in the morning the first occasion she was admitted to hospital.'

Brinn was a little surprised; Sarah had not mentioned it to him.

'I had to come back that night to another emergency admission, and before I left, I went up to see her, just to check on how she was doing. It was about 2 a.m., and she seemed a little down, so I sat on the edge of the bed and she began to tell me how you two had met and how much you meant to her.'

Brinn took a deep breath and fought to control his emotion as he exhaled slowly, quietly. The doctor continued.

'It was not so much in what she said, but in how she said it, but I got the distinct impression she was already aware of her condition, even before you told me about the incident. As we had agreed, I had instructed the staff to say nothing for the time being, but somehow she had found out, and I must say her courage impressed me. Her determination that the child should live even against the insurmountable odds, was quite remarkable.' He shook his head slowly and thought for a moment, then added, 'By the way, how is that son of yours doing, Mr Peters?'

'Pretty well, I think. It is still early days yet, but they say they are optimistic.'

'That is good, Mr Peters. I know the consultant in Paediatrics personally, and your son could not be in better hands.'

The only inebriated mourner finally staggered to Brinn's side.

Tugging on his sleeve he said, 'I knew her very well,' he slurred, swaying as he did so. 'She was a great kid, always a few bob spare if I was a bit skint. I remember the day she had an odd American bloke in tow. Weird he was, couldn't hold his liquor. It's all the same with these foreigners. One mouthful, one mind you, of vodka and meths turned him as green as my jacket here,' he said awkwardly, wiping an open flat hand down one lapel. Then, staring at it intently, he added, 'Oh no, not as green as my jacket, 'cause my jacket's brown, isn't it? Well, as green as the grass, then. Yeah, and that's pretty green, isn't it?'

Brinn grabbed the man as he began to slither down, lowering him gently onto the grass.

'You have had a skinful, old-timer,' Brinn said gently to him.

'Yeah, but I can hold mine. This American bloke puked it up all over his shoes and couldn't talk proper afterwards. What a waste of perfectly good liquor.'

Brinn closed his eyes and frowned heavily as he remembered the incident, but his face relaxed into a smile as he heard Sarah's gentle laughter in his mind. Not mocking, more sympathising, reassuring. Brinn reached into his inside jacket pocket, and discreetly withdrew his wallet. Pulling a ten-pound note out, he folded it and tucked it into the tramp's top pocket.

'You must try to take better care of yourself now, old-timer. She's not here to look after either of us any more.'

The fire died down and one by one the mourners wandered away, till only Brinn and Al were left.

'I heard you talking to the doctor, American. When are you going to see your boy? You can't put it off for ever. Sarah wouldn't be happy.'

'I know, Al, I have been meaning to go, but...'

'No buts,' Al interrupted. 'Sarah told me once you didn't know your own father because he had died when you were young. That right?'

Brinn nodded.

'Well, it seems to me that if you keep this up, the poor little mite will have no one either. It's about time you got your act together.'

The tiny body with thin fragile limbs that made involuntary jerking movements in the air hardly seemed human to Brinn. Cocooned within an incubator, the child was lying on a soft fleecy sheet and wearing a disposable nappy that was the smallest of its kind, but was still too large for him. The infant's eyes were closed tightly and he was sucking comfortingly on his clenched left fist. The tubes and wires that helped sustain this tiny life seemed invasive after his already traumatic beginnings.

Brinn had never had much contact with children and none with babies. What had always discouraged him in the past was their total helplessness and dependency, but despite the child's appearance, Brinn began to feel a warmth, a kinship with this, his own offspring.

'May I hold him?' he asked the young nurse.

'Yes, of course you can, Mr Peters,' she replied, lifting the cover of the incubator. 'Now, don't let all these tubes and things worry you. It's really quite normal in a case like this.'

Then, raising the infant, she covered him loosely in a small blanket. After a little confusion over which way round Brinn felt most comfortable, she put the tiny bundle in his arms. At first, Brinn was a little awkward, but he soon relaxed and the contact created an uneasy affinity with the child.

'Hi, little man,' he said in a hushed nervous tone, as he ran his thumb over the infant's brow. 'I'm your daddy.'

Almost as though the child was responding to Brinn, he jerked his hand upwards in a reflex action and grasped Brinn's thumb.

'Well, that's a mighty fine grip you have there, son. I can see I will have to keep a pretty close eye on you. Now, I want you to listen up real good, and no interrupting mind, 'cause I don't want you to miss any of this. I'm going to tell you all about your wonderful mom.'